Unobtrusive

Breanna Engelhardt

Paperback ISBN: 979-8-9908235-0-1

E-Book ISBN: 979-8-9908235-1-8

Book Cover Design by AuthorsHQ.com

Prologue

She knew this Hunter wanted nothing more than to kill her.

She sat on the already-bloodied floor, staring into what seemed like nothing. She was badly injured and so, so tired. She hadn't been able to do it before. What made her think she could do it now?

He had already taken the person she loved most. What did she have left to live for?

None of her training mattered because she couldn't fight. She was scared to death of him, and her fear froze her in place. He had just ripped a life away like it was nothing.

She was next.

She was going to lose.

She took an unsteady breath. He was back, cutting into her thoughts once more.

She looked up and met her Hunter's eyes. They bore straight into her soul, seeing her for everything she was—a Guardian who couldn't fight—and everything she wasn't—brave enough to get up again.

Just like in her nightmare.

He focused on her like a cat gazing at a wounded bird. His arms were crossed over his chest, holding in the Motora, his power, until just the right moment. The air was thick with tension.

Traumatized and tearful, her gaze faltered.

He crossed the distance so fast she missed it. He grabbed her, his supernatural electricity traveling along her arteries and veins like a spark on a power line.

Once, Justin had saved her before it was too late.

But there was no one to save her tonight.

Behind the Hunter was the person she loved most. His body was still, never to breathe again.

He had sacrificed his life to save hers.

She forced herself to look at the Hunter again.

His dark eyes said it all: *I'm going to kill you, and I'm going to enjoy it.*

Chapter One

"Rianne, wait up!" Alex called as she rushed through the classroom door.

Rianne rolled her eyes as she put her phone in her back pocket. "It's not like I was going to leave you, Alex."

They made their way to the first floor of the school, weaving around other students and keeping with the flow of traffic.

"Well, you've left me before, so I had to be sure." She held up a thick stapled packet with the number 96 written and circled in pink pen. "What'd you make?"

"Umm . . ." Rianne reached into her bag and retrieved her own graded test. "Eighty-four. Better than the last one, so I'm satisfied." They both knew that math was not her forte, and anything better than 70 percent was an achievement.

"Looks like my studying technique worked, huh?" Alex nudged Rianne's arm as she tucked some of her long brown hair behind her ear.

She rolled her eyes again and smiled. "Whatever, Alex . . ."

"You're just upset that I was right . . . again."

Alexandria Story had an annoying tendency of being correct

most of the time. The two had been friends since freshman orientation.

"Why are there doodles?" Alex asked, taking the paper from Rianne's hand. "On . . . every . . . page?" She flipped through each stapled one.

Rianne grinned. "I finished and passed, didn't I? Plus, look, Ms. Richardson left a note on the last page."

Alex flipped to the last page of the test, reading the teacher's words out loud. "Nice work as always, Rianne! Good job on your improved grade as well." Alex passed the test back. "I can't wait for you to become an accomplished artist."

"Neither can I," Rianne said as they stopped by the doors that led to the quad. "We just have to finish this year and senior year, then we're off to college to follow the dream." They gave each other high-fives. She had taken up art when she was young. It was one of the few things that relaxed her. She wasn't good at a lot of things, but art was where she excelled.

"What are you about to do? Wanna come to the quad to hang out with me and Chris?" All three of them had seventh period off and used that time to either finish homework for the day or socialize —with the latter usually winning out.

Alex put on the customary grin that always appeared whenever Chris, Rianne's other best friend, entered the conversation. Alex still had feelings for him, even though they had broken up three years prior. She was convinced that they would end up back together eventually. "As much as I'd love to, I'm going to the gym to work on a new routine with Courtney."

Rianne pretended to gag.

"Oh, stop it!" Alex said, pushing her shoulder as she laughed.

"I hate that girl so much," she said through her giggles.

"It's okay; she hates you too."

"For no reason whatsoever." Rianne felt her phone vibrate in her pocket. She pulled it out and smiled at the name on the screen, sweeping her bangs out of her eyes.

Unobtrusive

Alex rolled her eyes. "Yeah, no reason whatsoever. Is that *him*?"

"Maybe." She met Alex's knowing stare. "We're just friends!"

"Uh-huh."

Logan Richards. Rianne's friendship with the quarterback of Felix High's football team, had begun in the fifth grade. The two had lost touch over the years, but every now and then, they would say hey and talk in the hallways. That was about it. It wasn't until about a month ago, when they were having one of these rare interactions, that he asked for her number. They'd been talking almost nonstop since.

This caused Courtney Taylor, co-cheer captain, to take an immediate dislike to Rianne. Logan and Courtney had been dating since sophomore year, and she didn't like the fact that Rianne and Logan were friends. Alex told her that Courtney saw her as a threat. The girl was constantly tormenting her, and it bothered her that Rianne didn't react most of the time. Sometimes.

It didn't help that they shared a lot of the same classes either.

Rianne's crush on him wasn't new though; she'd liked him for years. His messy brown hair, the way his eyes twinkled when he smiled. And that smirk he would show whenever he *thought* he was right.

He sent her a text:

> We both know that it's hard for you to handle most things. Like intelligence.

> Hold on, let me go back over your part in our English project . . . what'd you make again?

Rianne looked up from her screen. "Okay," she said to Alex, "are you about to head to the gym?"

"Yep!" They hugged. "See you later! Tell me what Logan says."

"Hush."

Rianne opened the door, breathing in the cool fall air. She

headed to her and Chris's usual spot in the quad, a stone bench under a tree.

She sent Chris a quick text to tell him where she was, then another text from Logan came in:

Wow . . . low blow. You didn't do much better!

Better than you, though ;)

There are a few things I'm better than you in . . .

Like?

Rianne bristled as she ran into someone. She winced, finally looking up from her phone. "Oh, my gosh, I'm so—"

The world shifted. Her vision blurred, and her peripherals went hazy.

This again.

This wasn't the first time. It had occurred a few times in the past year or so, always at the most random times. She told her father about it. He said it was probably due to stress or fatigue. "I've been telling you to stop staying up so late working on your paintings," he said. If she felt worse at any time, though, he would take her to get checked out. She felt better within seconds after each spell, so she didn't feel the need.

The boy she ran into held her by her arms for a moment. He had brown hair, but her blurred vision made it impossible to make out any more than that. Her stomach turned, but her core felt warm. Like something was stirring within her.

Probably about to puke.

"My apologies," he said. It sounded like he was talking under-water. She couldn't make out his actual voice, just his tone.

He released her and continued toward the school building before she could say anything.

Her vision suddenly cleared, and the sick feeling left her. The only thing left behind was that warm, stirring feeling that she couldn't understand.

The interaction had lasted about five seconds.

It's probably just stress, she thought as she cleared her mind with a deep breath. She looked behind her, but there were already many people in the quad. None who looked like the boy from her blurry memory.

She made it to their bench, pulling out her sketchbook before checking her phone again. Chris and Logan had texted her back. Chris was on his way—he had to talk to one of his teachers about his project—and Logan was still trying to prove he was better than she was.

She smiled. *Game on, quarterback.*

Chapter Two

"I am so tired of that girl and her—ugh, I just want to commit murder sometimes!" Rianne mumbled as she stomped into her room, tossing her car keys on the dresser and throwing her bag on the floor.

Rianne plopped down hard on her bed, taking her phone out in an attempt to distract herself.

"What's the matter with you?" her father asked as he entered the room, leaning against the door handle with one hand. Matt was a well-built man in his mid-thirties with short brown hair and bright brown eyes. He had a small piercing in one of his ears, obtained in his teenage years, as well as a black tribal tattoo on his right arm. "You rushed in without even a hello to your old man—"

"Emphasis on 'old,'" Rianne said.

"Watch it. So, against my better judgment, I decided to check on you."

Rianne gave a humorless chuckle, looking up from her phone. "I'll give you three guesses, Dad."

"Courtney Taylor. Of course, it's about Courtney Taylor." He sat down next to her, elbows on his knees. He knew so much about his daughter's drama with that girl that he could probably write an entire novel about it. "What did the evil witch do this time?"

"Dad, you know she's evil; don't make it seem like I'm crazy!" Rianne snapped. "So, I was leaving school when Logan found me and asked if I was coming to the next football game, since he knows that I never go—the NCAA and NFL are all I care about. We're *finally* talking again! It's been like this for the past few weeks! I'm starting to think that—" She saw his faux bored look appearing on his face, and she took that as a cue to move on.

"Anyway, then Courtney shows up and has the *nerve* to pretend like I'm not even there and then pull him away. How rude is that? Logan tried to apologize, but—nope! Granted, he *did* have practice, but still! I just want to pull all her hair out of—"

"You know, there's so many other things that we could talk about. Global warming, the economy, football . . . I'd really like to talk about some football."

"Come on, Daddy!" Rianne begged, pushing his arm. "I need real, genuine advice!"

Matt groaned and flopped back onto the bed. "I'm a guy; I don't know what advice to give a teenage girl about a witchy cheerleader and some dumb football player she likes."

Rianne raised an eyebrow at him. "And you don't think sixteen years of practice has helped any?"

He snorted. "No."

"Dad! I need your advice!" She pushed on his side with each word for emphasis. "What should I do about Courtney and Logan? You gave me great advice before!"

"Apparently, it was advice that wasn't heeded. Okay, sweetie." He sat back up and patted her back heavily, making her wince. "I would say not to get too worked up about it. The girl knows that anything she does is gonna make you mad, so of course she's gonna keep doing it. You have to act like it doesn't bother you. When she sees you're not reacting, she'll back off. Wait, why do I sound like a broken record? I could have sworn I've told you something like this before."

"Yeah, but it wasn't for a Courtney situation."

"You do realize that the thing I just told you is called a life lesson? Hence, it can be applied to different things in, you know, life?"

Rianne pretended to contemplate his words as she messed with her phone. "Eh, you have a point."

"Only one?"

"Yeah, only one. I'm not going to give you too much credit; it'll go straight to your head."

He smiled at her regardless of her words. "Wow. Remind me to never give you advice again. You don't appreciate it."

Rianne sat back down next to her father. "Oops, you're sounding like a broken record again, Daddy."

Matt pushed her hard enough to make her fall onto her side. She tried to do the same but could barely budge him. "No fair!"

"Work out more, and maybe you'll be able to faze me one day. Handshake."

Rianne smiled as the two exchanged the intricate handshake they created when she was only five years old.

"Well, Dad, I'm gonna head to work," Rianne said as she stood and grabbed her phone and car keys from her dresser.

Matt looked at his watch. "It's only five-forty. Doesn't your shift start around seven today?"

"Yeah, but if I get there early, maybe I can get some extra overtime or tips or something."

"Just be careful out there. And come home as soon as your shift ends."

"Always. You've drilled that into me since I was born."

He stood and made his way out of her bedroom, and she followed him down the stairs. "Didn't you see the news from a few days ago?"

"Do I look like I pay attention to the news, Daddy?"

"Well, you definitely should. You're getting older, and you have to be informed about what's going on in the state, the country, and around—"

Rianne tilted her head back, rolling her eyes as though the speech was killing her.

"Knock that off. There was a girl murdered up in New York. Everyone's been keeping their eye on it."

They continued to the first floor. "Not to sound insensitive, but doesn't that happen often in New York?"

"It does," her father said, "but this girl's death was bizarre."

"How?"

"It looks like she was electrocuted from the inside out. Her body looked completely fine, but the medical examiner found that her insides had been fried."

Rianne recoiled. "What the . . . Well, did they catch the person who did it?"

"Still investigating. Her ex-boyfriend is one of the top suspects, though. Also, our neighborhood watch—"

"The one with sweet ol' Mr. Kempner as the head?"

"The very one. They've told me about a couple of break-ins that happened a few weeks ago. Just a few houses down too. I really need you to be careful out there. Our patrol is always around, but I can't protect you 24/7."

"I know, I know. Stop worrying so much. I can take care of myself just fine. I was taught hand-to-hand combat by my old police officer dad." She turned to head to the front door.

"I mean it, young lady. We haven't sparred in a while. You could be a little rougher than you usually are."

"Sure, Dad," she said as she continued on.

Matt furrowed his brow. "Wait, what do you mean, 'old?'"

She laughed as she opened the front door. "You know what it means!"

Chapter Three

Rianne walked out of Felix's Good Texas Cookin' restaurant and into the chilly night air at around 11:00. She pulled out her phone as she waited for the car to warm up. She had a few texts from Alex, Chris, and Logan, but she would respond to those later. She thought about the way that girl died, *electrocuted from the inside.*

Though she was anxious to get home, Rianne slowed the car as she passed her high school. She parked on the curb on the other side of the street, grabbed the sketchbook she always had with her, and made her way into the massive quad, needing to clear her head.

Rianne sat on her stone bench and looked around at the school in its nightly glow before opening her book to an earlier piece, adding more detail to it.

There was the main school building, in front of which was the quad, sprinkled with various benches. The inside had lockers, classrooms, staircases, and the other essentials of a high school, including two elevators located on either side of the school for injured and handicapped students. The auditorium was its own separate building to the right of the school. In front was the parking lot for the faculty. The student lot was in the back.

Her phone vibrated again. She looked at the screen and saw that Logan had sent a follow-up text, telling her to get home safely from work.

Aww, that's so sweet, Rianne thought, smiling to herself as she typed a reply.

> Hey, thanks for checking up on me! I'm actually at the

She stopped texting as a buzzing went off in her head, and she felt the reverberation in her hands. She felt nauseated. She dropped her phone, and it slipped down her legs, clattering on the ground. *Oh, great, not this stupid stuff again.*

It felt different this time, though. Worse. Ten times worse. Rianne groaned as she pushed the heels of her hands into her temples. She dropped her pencil as her vision blurred again.

Through it all, she felt warm, her heart and hands felt especially so.

"Oh, my gosh, what's going on?" she asked, her eyes watering. She tried to stand, but her legs forced her back down. *I'm not going anywhere right now.* She would have to wait for the spell to end—if it would.

She heard footsteps coming from her right. Breathing hard, she turned to look, but the whole world spun like she was intoxicated. It was still impossible to see through her blurry eyes; everything ran together.

When her vision cleared, she saw a teenager wearing a long black coat. *Didn't I see him earlier today?* It seemed to make sense, but at the same time, it didn't.

The person sat on the bench next to her. The pressure in her head was even more intense now that he was closer. He was definitely familiar.

He tilted his head at her. Inquisitive? She still couldn't make out any facial features.

"Don't worry," he said. Like before, his voice was muffled. "You're all right. Your body is just getting reoriented."

Rianne stood up, then she fell to the ground, groaning. "Get away from me!" She felt that she was shouting, but her vocal cords told her that her speech was normal.

"Whoa there, love. Be careful." He picked her up by her forearms, placing her back on the bench. He was strong . . . really strong.

Rianne swayed on the bench, leaning on its back as she attempted to get a hold of herself. What did he want? Was he going to kill her?

She came out of her thoughts as he said something else, but she missed it.

"What are you doing to me?"

She thought she saw him shrug. "I can't explain it. It's just something that always happens."

Rianne's breathing got deeper, more frantic. She couldn't move; the world was spinning too much, and she didn't feel like traveling to the ground again. She tried to focus by squinting, but nothing changed.

I can't believe this is the last thing I'm going to remember before I die, she thought. There was no way she would make it through the night. Or if she did, her world would never be the same.

"Please . . ." Rianne mumbled, "please, don't hurt me."

The boy chuckled. "That's the last thing I want to do."

"Then . . . then what do you want with me?"

"It's not what I want, my dear."

She looked at him again and saw him leaning toward her. She mustered up enough strength to put a hand on his forearm to stop him, but he just chuckled again.

"It's time for you to awaken."

Unobtrusive

He placed two fingers on her forehead, and everything stopped. The world no longer spun. It went black instead.

Chapter Four

Rianne's eyelids fluttered open.

Where am I? she wondered, her mind groggy.

She sat up and examined her surroundings. Plastered on her walls and ceiling were posters of her favorite bands, paintings from her favorite artists, and her own creations. Her closet door was ajar.

Rubbing her head, she grabbed her phone from her nightstand. It was 7:03 a.m.

She was in her bedroom. Sunlight shone through her white curtains.

Morning.

What happened last night?

A feeling nagged at her mind. Closing her eyes, she concentrated, blocking out everything.

Then it came back to her in flashes—the intensified pain in her head, the dizziness, the boy who—

The boy . . . the boy!

Rianne swung her legs off her bed and stared at the carpet. She tried to control her breathing. She thought she had seen him earlier, and had shown up last night. He was very mysterious and . . . helpful? But she thought she was going to die. Everything he said didn't make sense. It was too cryptic.

But hadn't hurt her, right?

Rianne sighed, running a hand through her thick hair. She didn't feel any different. She checked her arms and legs. *Nope, no bruises or anything. I don't think he touched me. But I still don't know how I got home.*

Rianne chuckled to herself, then stood up. *It was a dream. It had to be a dream. When something doesn't make sense, it means it was a dream.* She repeated this to herself for another minute until she convinced herself it was true.

Maybe the stress of school was getting to her. Midterms were creeping up, and she was focused on her academics and art. Maybe she just needed a break.

Yeah, just a one-day break to get a hold of myself again. That's all I need. She headed downstairs to ask her father.

He was at the kitchen table, reading the morning newspaper. He was dressed in his black police uniform. The aroma of coffee filled Rianne's nose as she entered the room.

"Hi, Daddy," she said as brightly as she could, trying to fight the anxiousness she felt from her bizarre dream.

"Mornin', honey," he answered, not looking up from his newspaper as he sipped his coffee.

She decided to start off with casual morning conversation as she pulled her cereal from the pantry and milk from the refrigerator. "Anything interesting today?"

Matt shook his head. "Is anything ever interesting in a newspaper? I don't know why I keep reading this thing. I feel like your grandfather." He closed the paper and placed it on the table, grabbing his phone instead.

"It's because you're getting old," she replied as she joined him at the table.

"Still young enough to take you down. Now hurry and eat, or you'll be late."

Rianne rolled her eyes. "You don't have to baby me, Dad. Besides, I was hoping not to go to school today."

"Why not?" Matt asked, standing up and putting on his belt. "Was it canceled?"

"No. I just don't feel like going. I'm feeling a little weird."

"Rianne . . ."

"Dad, c'mon! This is, like, the first time all semester I'm going to miss a day. And I've been doing well in my classes, remember? Please?" She looked at him through her eyelashes. He usually fell for it.

After a few moments, Matt gave in. "Okay. Just this once. But please don't let yourself fall behind."

Rianne nodded, staring at her cereal.

A silent minute passed. "I came home all right last night, right, Dad?"

Matt looked at her, a confused expression on his face. "Umm . . . yeah? You threw your keys on the living room table, said good-night, then went upstairs to your room."

"And what time did I come home?" Rianne asked. She might've left the school at around 11:30. She should've made it home about fifteen minutes later.

"Eleven forty-fiveish. Maybe eleven-fifty?"

She nodded, tapping her spoon against her bowl. *Okay, that's good. That means it must have been a dream.*

"You okay, Crayon?" her father asked. The nickname had stuck to her since she was two because of her love of coloring.

Rianne looked up at her dad. Should she tell him? It was just a dream. "Okay, this is going to sound crazy, but you know those weird headaches I've been getting? Well, I had this weird dream that I was at the school after work, and I got one of those headaches again, but it hurt really bad. Like, *super* bad. And then there was this guy who talked really weird, and he pressed two

18

fingers to my forehead, and then I passed out, but I don't really remember—"

Matt laughed. "Sounds like someone was exhausted last night. You know that dreams can be weirder when you're tired. Are you sure you don't want me to call Dr. Aberdam and set up an appointment for those headaches?"

Rianne shrugged one shoulder, taking another bite of her cereal. "I should be fine. I'm dealing with it." *Hopefully, for the last time.*

"Okay, if you're sure." He walked down the hallway to the front door. "I'm off to work. Don't burn the house down if you make food, and lock the door behind me." He took his car keys off the hook on the wall and opened the door. Cool air blew in.

"Don't forget your cane!" she shouted after him.

"I won't forget to smack you in the head with it!" he countered before shutting the door behind him.

After cleaning up the kitchen, Rianne went back to her room. Her cell phone was ringing on her desk, the screen bright. Hurrying over, she didn't even have to look at the caller ID.

"Hey, friend!" she sang.

"Don't sing. Where the hell are you?" Chris asked.

"Good morning to you too, Sunshine," Rianne said, taken aback. "Who ate your rainbow, thundercloud?"

"Don't divert the question. Where are you? You're always here before I am. Did you die or something?"

"Chris, if I died, I wouldn't be talking to you right now, would I?"

He hesitated for a moment. "I don't see your point. Now answer the question."

"God, I swear you act like my dad sometimes. I'm skipping school today, Christopher." Rianne played with her painted fingernails as she waited for Chris to reply.

"Your dad actually let you? Wow, color me surprised. Wait a second, did you just call me 'Christopher?'"

"I don't seem to recall that," Rianne said in a joking voice.

"Oh, you're—" She heard a faint ringing over the line. "Well, that's the bell. Don't forget to fantasize about me."

"I'll make sure to add that to my list." Rianne sighed as she hung up and laid her phone down. She had known her best friend since seventh grade. However, she had recently found out through another friend that Chris was harboring a secret crush on her. He had been giving off a few signs and making obvious comments, and it made him hard to be around sometimes, especially when they both knew that Alex liked him. It was a weird love triangle that she definitely didn't want to be a part of.

Rianne took her sketchpad out of her bag—after trying to remember when she put it back in there—and turned to a blank page. Her pencil had only begun the first few faint marks when she heard the front door open downstairs.

Chapter Five

What's Dad doing back? she wondered. *Maybe he forgot something. Well, he is getting old. Better go help him out.*

She went out and walked down the stairs. Right before she entered the living room, she heard someone grunt before setting something on the floor.

"Dad, what are you—?" She froze as she entered the living room. A man straightened up, the home television at his feet. He was dressed in black with a hood pulled over his blond hair. He looked to be in his mid-thirties, maybe older. His eyes narrowed at her, and his teeth gritted in anger. The break-ins. Her father had told her about them. The man probably figured everyone was out.

Everyone but her.

Rianne's heart dropped for a moment, then her legs regained their strength and forced her to move back. Though her mind was numb with fear, one thought echoed clearly: *hide.*

She bolted up the stairs, two at a time.

"Get back here!" the man shouted, close behind her. Rianne resisted the urge to scream or turn around. When she reached the second-floor landing, she bolted toward the first open door, the guest bathroom. She slammed the door and locked it. The man slammed into the door, a second too late, then pounded on it.

"Open this door, you little—" The door's handle jiggled a couple of times before the punching and kicking continued.

With nowhere to hide, Rianne realized she needed to call someone.

But my phone's in my room. Rianne bit the inside of her cheek. *Why didn't I go to my room?*

The man threw his body into the door, causing the side of it to crack. Rianne screamed. Looking around for a solution, she opened the cabinet under the sink and climbed inside, ignoring all of the supplies inside. It was only slightly quieter under there, but at least she could hear herself think.

What was she going to do once he *did* get in? She had nothing to defend herself with, and she was trapped—the window was too small for her to fit through and too high to reach.

Why hadn't she locked the door like her father told her?

Her thoughts were cut off when the door burst open.

Everything went quiet. Rianne tried to stop her breathing, holding her hands to her mouth and nose as footsteps went around the perimeter of the small bathroom. The shower curtains rustled as he shoved them aside to expose the empty shower. She heard him mumbling, accompanied by his deep, raspy breathing.

Then silence returned.

Did he leave? Did he give up?

The cabinet door opened, and Rianne screamed as the man grabbed her arm and yanked her out. She winced as her back scraped against the top.

The man pulled Rianne out of the bathroom and slammed her against the wall in the hallway, pushing his forearm against her throat. "I'm not going back to prison over you, you little—"

"Get out of my house!" she yelled. "And I'm not a little girl. Get off me!"

Unobtrusive

He pushed harder, and she gasped. The man chuckled. "No one's home," he said. His eyes traveled up and down her body. A shiver ran up her spine, and her heart raced. She tried shaking the man's hands off, but he held her tight. "Hmm . . . You could be a lot of fun."

He jerked her off the wall and forced her down the hall to the guest bedroom. Holding her wrists behind her with one hand, he grabbed her hair with the other, forcing her head back in a painful position to keep her from fighting.

Once in the room, he slammed the door behind him. Then he studied her as he took off his jacket and gloves. His gaze made her feel violated. Dirty.

The window is big enough. She could climb onto the roof and make her way down and get help.

Rianne bolted toward the window and tried to unlatch it. She screamed when one of the man's arms wrapped around her waist, yanking her away.

"Let me go! Let me go!" she screamed, but he easily forced her onto the bed. "Get off me!" She struggled to escape his grip, tugging at his hand. "No! Stop! No! I said get off—"

"Shut the hell up." His lips replaced his hand on her neck, and she felt his hands on her hips as his body pinned her down. She grabbed at his hair, trying to pull him off. "Just let me enjoy this."

"Like hell I will!" She grabbed at his face, trying to push him away with everything she had. "I said, get *off*!"

A warm, almost hot feeling grew in her palms, and she squinted at the bright light that engulfed the room. Then something she did forced the man into the wall before he crashed to the floor, taking the bedside table lamp down with him.

Rianne's heart pounded, and she almost couldn't breathe. She looked down at her shaking hands. *What the hell was that?* It looked like a force field, but it also seemed to be energy. It was bright and the color of amber.

This must be another dream. This isn't real. This isn't real. She felt powerful though. She felt . . . strong.

The man stirred in the corner. She had time, and she wasn't going to waste any more of it.

She ran out the room and into her own. She slammed the door and tried to lock it with fumbling hands. If she could stall him long enough to reach her phone and call for help—

But she was too slow. He twisted the handle and forced his way through, coming toward her. His lip was bleeding, and parts of the flesh on his face looked like it was suffering from a terrible sunburn. Had she done that?

"I don't know what the hell you are," he said as he pulled a pocket knife out of the back of his jeans and came toward her.

Confidence flowed through her, but she still backed away. "Get back! Get away from me!" She aimed one hand out at him, though she didn't know if she could do it again. Whatever *it* was.

He drew closer now. *How can I make it come back?* she wondered, trying to think as her mind fumbled over itself. Closing her eyes, she pushed her hand in front of her in a fluid motion. The man cried out as he was pushed out of the room by the same amber energy. His back hit the rafter that overlooked the downstairs hallway with such force that he flipped over it. His scream was cut short as he landed with a *thud*.

Everything went quiet again, but the energy in the house was different. Her body shaking, Rianne sank to her knees. He had just fallen from the second story onto the floor below, and it was all her fault. It didn't sound like he was moving, but she was too scared to check.

Oh, my God. What if he hit his head too hard?

"Relax. He's just unconscious."

Rianne screamed, then turned to face the voice that had spoken behind her. The force field thing appeared out of her hand once again, but this time it was deflected, and the energy smashed against the wall, leaving a black mark.

Unobtrusive

Rianne tried to breathe through short, frantic gasps. "What . . . what's going on? What?" She backed away on her hands and knees until she ran into the wall. Then she made eye contact with the new intruder.

It was him, the boy she had run into the day before at school. The one from her . . . dream? But this time she could see clearly and make out his features.

He was tall and looked to be about eighteen or nineteen, with wavy dark brown hair. His chin had groomed stubble, and his eyes were a deep brown. He wore black jeans and a loose red shirt. If she hadn't been so petrified, she would have noticed how attractive he was.

Rianne saw her phone on the floor between them. There was no way she was going to try to dive for it. She could run out of the house and get some help, but who knew if the burglar was still unconscious or not?

She decided for the latter, running out of her room and back onto the landing. The stairs were so close.

Then the boy was in front of her, holding his hands up, palms out. "My dear, I need you to take a moment to breathe."

Rianne felt like fainting as she swayed on her feet, but she pushed through and ran back into her room. Her phone was still on the floor. *Good, he didn't take it.* She grabbed it, then heard her room door close as he walked back in.

"Who are you? What do you want? How did you get in here? Are you with *him*? I should warn you that my dad's a cop!" She started to dial 911.

He held his hands up, indicating he meant no harm. "Listen, I'm going to need you to calm down."

"Calm down? You expect me to *calm down?*"

He sighed. "I know. You've been through quite an ordeal. But I'm not a complete stranger to you."

Rianne allowed her breathing to slow a little. She didn't know what the hell was going on, but he didn't seem to want to hurt her.

He certainly wasn't violent like the other man. "I've seen you before . . . yesterday at school. And you might have been in my dream. What the hell do you want from me?"

"Rianne, that wasn't a dream," he said, taking a step toward her. She didn't notice, though. Now that she wasn't as frantic, she realized he had an English accent.

"How do you know my name? And what do you mean that wasn't a dream?"

"I promise to explain everything. Just give me a chance to do so." He motioned for her to sit on her bed.

She narrowed her eyes at him. "I still don't know what's going on or why I'm going through with this, but if you try anything, 911 is at the ready."

"Understood."

Rianne sat on the edge of the bed, her muscles taut. The boy sat in her desk chair, facing her. "I go first," Rianne said. He nodded. "So, you were with me last night? For real?"

"Yes. I'm the reason you've been getting those headaches and dizzy spells lately. Whenever I was near you, my Affera was interacting with your Fuora, awakening it."

Rianne stared at her phone—the only normal thing she could hold onto at the moment. Affera? Fuora? "It's time for you to awaken," she whispered, remembering the feeling of his fingers on her forehead.

"Oh, good," he said, smiling. "You remember what I said last night."

Rianne rolled her eyes. He was annoying, but something about him put her at ease. "Speaking of last night, did you . . . I mean, were you the one—"

"Who brought you home after you passed out? Yes."

"So, I really passed out?"

"Yes. Your body was overwhelmed to the point of exhaustion. You should be completely fine now, though."

Yeah, fine. "And you . . . you didn't . . . do anything?" She stopped, her heart racing again. "Oh, my God. Did you . . ."

He frowned, offended. "What kind of person do you take me for? I'm a gentleman."

"If you're such a gentleman, why didn't you help me with the psychopath downstairs? You seem to know a whole lot, and you sure seem to know about him, since you said I didn't kill him!"

"Oh, speaking of." He snapped his fingers. "There we go; that'll take care of that. You don't have to worry about that man any longer —he's in custody. And to answer your question, I wanted to see what you could do now that your Fuora has surfaced, so I didn't interfere."

There was that word again. *Fuora. Maybe that's what that weird, warm energy is called.* "How . . . how did you do that?"

The boy furrowed his brow. "What do you mean? I just put my fingers together like so and . . ." He snapped again. "Don't you know how to snap?"

Rianne glared at him. "You know what I mean." She pointed to the black mark on her wall. "How did you do *that*? How did *I* do that?" Nothing made sense, and it seemed as though he had some of the answers. "What's going on?"

"Of course, please forgive me. Let me clarify. I, Miss Rianne Jarrett, am your Protector. It's my duty to keep you safe before the upcoming Great Battle. I possess many different powers, which we call Affera, including the two you were born with. This makes me an Advancer, appointed by the Wise Ones, our rulers and superiors. There are also Sterlings—magical beings with only one power.

"You, my dear Guardian, are the most recent in your long line. A Guardian surpasses all Sterlings and Advancers—and even the Wise Ones—on a higher magical scale. This makes you the most powerful being in the Estona—the magical realm.

"From what I've found, you have two magical powers, as normal humans, or Standards, would call them. However, your powers have their own special name—Fuora. Your first is one we call Blade, a form of energy. It can be used as an offensive or defensive mechanism, which you just used as the wave. Once it's mastered, the color of that energy changes to match its user. The second, from what I felt last night from being near you, is the ability to heal. Your Fuora is already very strong. Impressive power that still waits to be unleashed to its full potential."

Rianne blinked, then shook her head, laughing as she ran her hands through her hair, attempting to put it in a ponytail. "Nope, this isn't real. This is still a dream. A super-weird dream. These headaches must've really gotten to me. I'm just gonna sit here, close my eyes, and wait to wake up." She closed her eyes and took a deep breath.

Time to wake up . . . just . . . wake up.

A minute passed before he spoke again. "So, how's the hypothesis working out for you over there, love?"

Rianne didn't open her eyes. "Shhh, dream apparition. I'm trying to wake up. This super long dream has gone on long enough." She continued to take deep breaths.

"I know it's a lot to take in. Trust me, it was hard for others too."

"I'm not gonna ask what that means, but I said, shhh . . ."

Zen . . . quiet . . . peace . . . wake up . . . wake up . . . wake up . . .

"What if I can prove this isn't a dream?" He sounded closer.

She opened her eyes. "I'd like to see you try, whatever your fake name is."

"My name is very real, as am I." He stood up and took her hand, making her blush. "My name, dear Guardian, is Braedon, at your service." He bent down and brushed his lips against her knuckles.

He looked back up at her, and they stared into each other's eyes for several moments until Rianne pulled away. She cleared her throat, trying to calm her warm cheeks. "What are you from, the 1800s?"

"Very accurate guess, Miss Jarrett." He straightened as he winked at her.

Unobtrusive

Rianne crossed her arms over her chest. "You still haven't proven to me that this isn't a dream."

Braedon chuckled. "Okay, I'll give you two bouts of proof. Number one." He reached over and pinched her.

"Ow!" Rianne shouted, jumping back and grabbing her stinging arm. "What the hell?"

Braedon brought the desk chair close to her and sat down. "I don't believe that dreams can pinch you like that. And if they could, you would have woken up." Before she could speak again, he held a hand up and cocked his head to the side, his eyes searching her face. "Let's see here . . . you're still freaking out, but I'm flattered that you find me attractive. Yes, my accent is real. And yes, I can hear your thoughts. I'm able to do so because I'm an Advancer, and one of my powers is mind reading."

Rianne blinked, her mouth opening and closing. Braedon had explained a lot and proved a lot, but it still didn't make sense. *If this isn't a dream, what's happening?*

Braedon laughed at the expression on her face. "Let me give you more concrete proof." He stood up and held his hands out in front of him. The amber-colored energy appeared, glowing, shimmering, and controlled. Then it turned into a light shade of red.

Rianne jumped back. It didn't have a definite shape, but it stayed within the confines of Braedon's hands. Streams of light danced within the energy, some of it reflecting off Braedon and the walls. It was beautiful. She could have been imagining it, but Rianne swore she saw the energy going in and out of Braedon's hands and arms. She felt heat radiating from it, and it scared and exhilarated her. "This is the same power you were using today. Do you think you can do it again?" he asked.

Her heart racing, Rianne's eyes jumped from Braedon's face to the Blade thing. Her entire body was tingling. Something inside her wanted to get closer and allow it to take over. It felt familiar, like it was already inside her. Like it *was* her.

"It won't bite; I promise," Braedon joked. "Come on. Don't be afraid of it. Try to embrace it."

Rianne snorted. "Yeah, embrace it. Embrace some weird sci-fi force field power thing created by some random British guy in my bedroom?"

Braedon shrugged. "Hey, I'll take that over other weird situations I've been in."

"How many situations like this *have* you been in?"

"More than I care to admit. Want to try it again? Want to feel that sense of power?"

Rianne came closer to him, holding her hands out to mirror his. *What am I getting myself into?* she wondered. For all she knew, Braedon would attack her this time. Everything was still unsure.

"I don't know," she replied. "I'm not sure if I felt powerful. That might have just been adrenaline."

"Adrenaline can help, but I know you can do it without it."

Rianne exhaled, staring at Braedon's hands. The red light reflected off her face, and the heat was more intense but not uncomfortable. "So, how am I supposed to do this? I mean, when it showed up before, I was angry—and scared. I'm not either of those things now." She glanced at Braedon's face. He had one eyebrow raised. She reciprocated. "At least I don't think I am. Can I do it while I'm feeling neutral? Or freaked out? Whichever one I am?"

"Try. Focus your energy on something that makes you happy. Anything at all."

An image of her father popped into her mind. She nodded.

"Now, close your eyes, and focus on that thing. Relax, and feel the warmth inside, coursing through you. Imagine it showing itself, and it'll come on its own."

She shut her eyes and focused on her father's face, the way he snorted when he laughed too hard, how secure his hugs felt. She felt something in her core getting stronger and warmer, her hands tingling with excitement.

"You're doing it," Braedon said, sounding awed again.

"I am?" Rianne's eyes snapped open. She had conjured a small amount of power that matched Braedon's. It was beautiful, even brighter than his. The ball of amber energy left her hands and flew at Braedon, hitting him in the chest. He grunted as another bright light filled the room, and he was slammed back into the wall. He fell to the floor, landing on his side.

She rushed over to him, kneeling and covering her mouth with her hands. "Oh, my gosh, I'm so sorry! I didn't mean to do that! I don't know what happened! I just got excited! I'm so sorry! Are you okay?"

To her surprise, Braedon laughed and then looked up at her. "I'm okay. Just shocked me, is all." He rubbed his back and winced. "Your Fuora is *very* strong. I was foolish to underestimate it, even so early on. But you're definitely going to need some practice." His eyes shone as he pushed himself up to a seated position. "And I know just the guy who can help."

Rianne looked at her hands in shock. "I can't believe I just did that," she mumbled.

"It's pretty amazing, isn't it?" Braedon said, holding his hand out to her.

Rianne shook her head. "Just because I'm starting to believe in this 'magical powers' thing doesn't mean that I'm going to hold your hand."

"Technically, it's called Affera—"

"That information isn't going to make me hold your hand."

"Just take my hand. I'm going to show you another power."

Rianne sat down on the floor in front of him.

"Well, aren't you a special one?" she said..

"Just one of many." He motioned with his hand again.

Rianne held up one finger. "Just a second." She reached over and pinched her arm as hard as she could. Braedon was still there, and nothing had changed. "Okay, just needed to verify things again."

"Ready?" Braedon asked.

Nodding, Rianne took his hand. As soon as they made contact, Rianne's vision blurred, and she felt sick. *I thought he said this phase was over!* she thought. Her body felt light, like it was made of air. Her hair blew around her, and her mind buzzed. Then the sensations stopped as suddenly as they had started.

They were in a different house now. It looked like they were in the living room, complete with a fireplace and plush couches. Evening light streamed through the windows, giving the room a homey feeling. She spotted a staircase behind her.

"Braedon, what was that?" Rianne asked. "Where are we?"

Braedon smiled. "That, Rianne, was teleportation."

"So, that's a real thing too?"

"It is. You'll learn all about the other Affera soon. And we're now in Estona, a part of the magical realm."

Rianne looked around the room. "Doesn't seem too magical to me."

Braedon chuckled. "Estona is just like the Standard world, the only difference being that its residents have extraordinary abilities."

"So, are we on another planet or something?"

"No, but that part gets a little weird to pinpoint. Let's just say we're in an in-between of sorts."

"In between what?"

"The ordinary and the extraordinary." Braedon looked around. "I could've sworn he'd be here. Justin, are you here?" He took a couple of steps out of the living room. Rianne followed. "Mr. Allan? Hello? I need help with something very important!"

Rianne heard a chuckle come from behind her. They turned around to find a man materializing out of the air as he walked down the stairs. He was like a human chameleon, blending in with the shades behind him until he became his own again. Rianne shook her head to clear it.

Come on, girl. Wake up.

"Braedon," the man said. "Welcome back! And I told you before to stop calling me 'Mr. Allan.'" He clasped a hand on Braedon's shoulder. "You're one of the most powerful Advancers in Estona! I should be using *your* title, not the other way around! Just call me Abraham, 'kay? And sorry about the blending. I heard someone in my house, and I went on the defensive. I'm sure you understand."

Braedon nodded. "Yes, sir, I do."

Abraham turned to Rianne, his eyes twinkling. "And who might this young lady be? Your new girlfriend?"

Rianne's eyes widened, and she looked at Braedon. He mouthed "No" with a smile and then turned back to Abraham. "No, Mr. Al—Abraham."

"Then why are you two holding hands?"

Rianne and Braedon looked down at their hands, which were still locked together. They both let go at the same time and looked away from each other. Braedon cleared his throat, as embarrassed as she was.

"Oh, don't be shy, Braedon! Why don't you give it some thought?" Abraham asked, a smile on his face and his eyes twinkling even brighter. "She's very pretty. How's her Affera? You remember the last one you had? Very sketchy, I must say, very, very sketchy with her Affera. Oh, and let's not forget the college freshman before her—"

"Abraham!" Braedon said before he could go on any further. Rianne covered her mouth to hide her grin. "We're getting off topic. Is Justin here?"

"Not right now. He's in Felix."

"But I thought he'd be back in Estona on this rotation."

"He was supposed to be, but the Wise Ones switched him for this quarter. Why do you need him?"

Braedon glanced at Rianne. "She's our new Guardian."

Abraham's jaw fell open. He looked at Rianne and then back at Braedon. "Is she really?"

Braedon nodded.

Abraham took her hands in his, squeezing them. "Bless you,

young Guardian. Bless you and your mother." Leaving her even more perplexed than ever, he turned back to Braedon.

As the two men spoke, Rianne tried to sort things through in her mind. *Bless you and your mother?* What did that mean? She didn't have anything to connect that to with the limited knowledge she had been given in the past hour. Did Abraham know her mother? Did Braedon? Did either of them know where she was? Her mother wasn't a big topic of conversation in her family; her father always avoided it. "She left us when you were young, and that's all there is to it," he would tell her. Her grandparents would confirm it. She learned to stop bringing it up and accepted the fact that her mother didn't want her. Even so, Rianne wondered about her—what she was doing, where she was, if she ever thought about the daughter she left behind.

Growing up without a mother had been hard. Her dad was amazing, but she missed having a maternal figure in her life. Everyone around her had a mom, but she wasn't given that option. And now, amidst all this magical power stuff, she might actually get the chance to find her! Maybe there was an upside to this after all.

Her attention returned to the men as they wrapped up their conversation.

"Would it be best for me to wait until he's back here?" Braedon asked.

Abraham shrugged. "It's up to you. You know best."

"So," Rianne interjected, "this other magical person goes to my school too?"

Abraham laughed. "'Magical person.' You haven't filled her in on much, have you?"

Braedon made a faux-insulted face. "I gave her the short version. I was going to get to it in time."

"Well, don't wait too long. I'm surprised she even believes all of this with a 'shortened version.'"

Rianne smiled at Braedon. "I'm still fifty-fifty at this point."

Abraham grinned. "And funny too. You got a good one on your hands, Advancer."

Braedon gave her a side eye. "I'm still fifty-fifty on that too. Well, we'd better get going. We'll find Justin at a later time. Thank you, Abraham."

Then, taking care not to grab her hand again, Braedon touched Rianne's shoulder. The next second, the two were back in Rianne's room. The light, airy feeling didn't feel any more natural than it had the first time.

"I'll have to go back when he gets home," Braedon muttered, making a mental note to himself, "and tell him the situation."

"So, what's going to happen from here?" Rianne asked.

Braedon sighed. "Don't worry about it. I'll take care of everything."

"And are you going to let me know what that is?"

"Eventually. Once I figure it out for myself."

Rianne went over to her window perch and sat down. "Man, my head hurts. I still don't understand any of what's going on. I was assaulted, I have magical powers, someone else with powers goes to my school—"

She just wanted answers. Her mind was a confused blob of information, and Braedon was the only one with the ability to clear it. "Braedon?"

"Hm?" He was sitting in her desk chair again.

"I need a lot of questions answered. I mean, you just showed up and told me I have these powers and that I'm the Guardian or whatever. What does that even mean? Why me? And how is my mom involved? Where is she in all of this? And why—"

"Whoa, slow down, my dear." Braedon stood and made his way across the room to her. "There's nothing to be confused about." He took her hand again, and Rianne felt her cheeks heat up. He smiled a crooked smile that made her heart rate increase. "I promise that all of your questions will be answered, and all of this will make sense. Unfortunately, I have to dash and take care of a few things. But I'll come back and explain everything to you."

"When?"

"I don't know. But soon."

She smiled. "You promise?"

He wrapped his pinky finger around hers and squeezed. "I promise."

Then he became transparent and disappeared. If nothing else solidified the fact that magical powers existed, that certainly sealed it.

She stared at her hand, recalling the feeling of his pinkie intertwined with hers. There was something about him that she couldn't figure out, but it was something she liked.

She cleared her throat. She had just met him, and now he was supposed to be her "Protector," whatever that was.

Rianne leaned her head back against the wall and sighed as she looked up at the ceiling. "I'm the Guardian with magical powers, but what in the world does that mean?"

Chapter Six

"Now, who can tell me the symbolism behind Holden's red hunting hat in The Catcher in the Rye? Anyone? Go ahead, Miss Ramos."

Rianne was in her fifth-period English III class. She should have been listening to Mrs. Carter discuss their current class novel, *The Catcher in the Rye,* but she opted to busy herself by drawing in her notebook until class was over. She had already spent enough time exhausting her mind thinking about the previous day's events.

After Braedon left, Rianne tried to get back to her plans of drawing and watching television, but her mind was too preoccupied.

She had magical powers, and she had seen them with her own two eyes.

It wasn't the most normal of days—not by a long shot—but at least it wasn't a boring one.

As expected, her father came home with a wild story of a man who appeared in the police station, going on and on about the houses he had broken into and a girl he had attempted to assault. Rianne pretended to be surprised as she listened to her father recount the odd occurrence. Little did he know she had been more involved in that story than she should have been.

She felt a tap on her shoulder. Turning around, she saw Logan smiling at her. "What?" she whispered.

"What are you drawing?" he asked, poking her arm with his pencil's eraser.

"None of your business. Shouldn't you be paying attention?" She motioned to their teacher.

"Shouldn't you?"

Giggling, Rianne rolled her eyes and faced forward, focusing on her sketchbook. Mrs. Carter was still talking about symbolism.

"Will you draw me something?" Logan whispered.

"Maybe."

"Can it be a drawing of me?"

"No. Pay attention."

"Just make sure it captures how handsome I am."

Rianne turned back around to look at him and shook her head. He raised an eyebrow, which earned him another eye roll. She rotated back and saw a folded sheet on notebook paper hanging off the left edge of her desk. She looked in that direction to find Courtney smirking at her from across the empty desk that separated them. She nodded at the paper. Against her better judgment, Rianne opened it.

Wish you weren't here today. The fact that your face wasn't here yesterday was the highlight of the class.

Just do what Dad said, Rianne told herself as she looked back at her notebook and clenched her teeth. *Just don't let her know it bothers you.* Did Courtney really find enjoyment in annoying her? Did they both like Logan? Yes, but Courtney was already with him. What purpose did she have in constantly poking at her?

Stupid, jealous girl who thinks she's in control of everything acts like she can say whatever she wants to me. One of these days I'm gonna rip all of her hair out—

Rianne felt another nudge on her shoulder. "What did Courtney just give you?" Logan whispered.

She waved her hand in dismissal. "It's nothing, don't worry about—"

"Lemme see." He held his hand out.

Rianne passed him the note, making sure Mrs. Carter wasn't watching. As Logan read the paper, his expression went from nonchalance to surprise. Courtney had been watching him, and when he looked at her, she waved and smiled innocently. Her face fell, though, when Logan shook his head at her in disapproval. "Not okay," he mouthed. Rianne's lip twitched, but she maintained her composure. It was about time Courtney was put in her place.

Logan wrote on the paper, then gave it back to Rianne with a heart-stopping smile. She read it.

Where were you yesterday, anyway? You weren't answering my texts.

Old-school texting to keep us out of trouble. Nice. And I was sick. Too sick to come to school. I'm feeling better today, though.

He wrote back and then flicked the note onto her desk with the accuracy acquired from football.

Well, I'm glad. So, since you didn't see my texts yesterday, are you planning to go to the Homecoming game and dance?

Rianne wrote the next message without much enthusiasm. She had done her best to ignore all of the Homecoming festivities. The pep rally and game were on October 30, with the dance the following Saturday night. Only two weeks away. She didn't like dances, and she hadn't planned on going to the first big one of junior year either.

No, I wasn't planning to. It's not really my thing. Just gonna stay home and binge Netflix. Why do you ask? Need help figuring out how to tie a tie?

Logan frowned in discouragement, then he smiled as he wrote a reply.

Ha ha, you're SO hilarious. Do you have a date?

If I wasn't planning on going, why would I have a date, genius? lol

But how would you feel about going with me?

Rianne almost dropped her pencil. Logan Richards—the school's quarterback—wanted to take her to the Homecoming dance? Her? Was this some kind of prank? It had to be.

She was having a harder time believing she might be going to Homecoming with him than that she possessed magical powers.

Rianne turned around in her seat. "What?" she mouthed.

Logan shrugged and winked at her, motioning her to continue writing.

You're not serious

I'm dead serious.

You're not funny, you know.

I'm hilarious, thank you very much. But this isn't a joke.

Unobtrusive

You literally have a girlfriend.

I'm not going to the dance with Courtney. I'm taking care of that today. I missed you, okay? Why do you think I've been texting you nonstop? Now would you just say yes? I'm not used to waiting for an answer from a pretty girl.

Rianne was practically shaking with excitement, but she contained it. She turned around to tell Logan her reply when the bell rang.

"All right, class," Mrs. Carter said, trying to fit in their homework assignment before they rushed out of the room. "Read your syllabus! Don't forget to write me a three-page paper on the symbolism in the novel over the weekend. I *will* be counting it as a quiz grade."

The class groaned as they gathered their things and put them into their school bags.

Rianne looked back at Logan, who was waiting for her answer, then shrugged. She didn't control the bell system.

"Wait, Rianne," he said. "What's your—"

Courtney grabbed his hand, pulling him toward her, and gave him a kiss. "I couldn't wait till we got in the hallway," she said.

Rianne rolled her eyes and left the classroom, but not before Courtney gave her a triumphant look, a smug smile on her face.

Chapter Seven

Rianne opened her locker and put her books inside.
Suddenly, her locker door slammed of its own voli-
tion. Her fingers would have been crushed if she had
been a second too late. It was a good thing she had quick reflexes.

"What do you think you're doing, flirting with *my* boyfriend?"
Courtney demanded, crossing her arms.

"I wasn't flirting with him, Courtney," Rianne said. "We were
just talking."

Courtney rolled her eyes. "Yeah, right! I know that you've been
texting him. I'm not an idiot."

Rianne snorted. "Okay, keep telling yourself that, Courtney."
She turned to open her locker again, but Courtney slammed it
shut. "You should know that the only reason he talks to you is
because he feels sorry for you. No one ever gives you any attention.
I mean, look at what you're wearing—purple, black, black, black,
black. You even have a choker. Does anyone even wear those
anymore?"

Rianne gave her a snarky smile. "So, you admit that Logan is
giving me his attention? Are you jealous it isn't turned to you

twenty-four-seven? Maybe he likes all my black. There's an air of mystery about it, unlike you, who's as deep as a puddle."

Courtney's jaw tightened. "I'm only going to say this once, Rianne. Drop this *stupid* little crush, and stay away from—oh, hi, Logan, baby!"

Rianne turned around and found Logan standing behind her, holding his backpack by one strap over his shoulder. There was a scowl on his handsome face, and it was directed toward his girl-friend. "Hey, Court. Hope I wasn't interrupting."

"No, you weren't, baby!" she said in that fake voice Rianne loathed. "It wasn't anything important. I was just letting Rianne know she shouldn't test Mrs. Carter. She could really get herself into trouble." As she said those words, she looked straight at Rianne. Then she gave Logan a peck on the cheek. "Well, I gotta go find Alexandria and discuss some routines before practice today. See you afterward, babe! Bye, Rianne!" She left without another look in their direction.

Rianne had one of her hands balled into a fist. The nerve of that girl. She opened her locker and grabbed her French textbook and Algebra II book for homework, putting them both in her bag. "Did you hear what she just said?"

Logan sighed. "I caught the gist of it. Rianne, I'm really sorry about that. You know everything she said isn't true, right?"

She nodded, though she didn't look like she meant it.

"You don't believe me, do you?"

"What am I supposed to believe, Logan? Yeah, we've been reconnecting, I guess, but that doesn't mean the things you said today are true. And with what Courtney just said, how do I know this isn't just some prank?"

He grabbed her shoulders in both of his strong hands and looked her straight in the eye. "Rianne, I told you that I wanted to take *you* to Homecoming. I want to be with you because I like *you*. I'm done with Courtney. I know I'll be happier with you.

"Look, why don't you come over to my place next Friday? We

can hang out like we used to—and maybe do a little more than we used to." She opened her mouth to ask a question, but he continued. "I'll text you my new address and time and all that. You don't need to bring anything. I'll take care of the movies and food. Just bring your cute self. It'll be fun. Just like old times."

He released her shoulders, then leaned down and kissed her cheek. With a final smile and a wink, he continued down the emptying hallway.

Rianne touched her fingertips to her cheek. *Oh . . . my . . . gosh. He* actually *likes me, and he wants to hang out next weekend.*

Then the full realization of her situation hit her. "He wants to date me," she whispered. "I need to ask Chris to cover for me!"

She pulled out her phone as she rushed to her math class.

Chapter Eight

"Like I said on the phone, you've got to be kidding me," Chris said.

He and Rianne were sitting in the quad on one of the benches positioned farther from the school building. It was still a bit chilly, so they kept their jackets on, though others had taken theirs off. Their backpacks sat on the ground next to them. "You're really going over to his house to *hang out*? Are you insane?"

"Wow, thanks for your enthusiasm, Chris!" Rianne said. "I'm so happy you're as excited as I am!"

He groaned. Rianne had told him the bare minimum over text, then gave him the full synopsis when they got to their spot. He couldn't be more aggravated. Logan Richards? Of all people.

"Sorry. This is just so . . . so stupid!"

"What's stupid about it?" Rianne crossed her arms over her chest. "You know I've liked Logan for a long time, and we've made a whole bunch of progress! And he wants to take me to Homecoming! Can't you at least *pretend* to be happy for me?"

Chris sighed.

Rianne laughed, snapping Chris from his thoughts. "What's so funny?"

"You're jealous, aren't you?"

"No," Chris mirrored her, folding his arms. "I have no reason to be jealous of that dude."

"You are jealous."

"Am not." He looked away.

"Are too. Look, you even have that cute puppy-dog face you put on when you're pouting."

Chris's frown deepened. "I don't have any look on any face."

"Okay, then I guess you won't be upset when I tell you what I want to wear over to his place."

Chris rolled his eyes. He wasn't going to give in. Not yet anyway. "Nope. Shoot."

"Something casual but still super cute. Who knows? We might end up making out—which would be fantastic. So, I'm going to wear that cropped blouse I got a while ago. You know, the one I never wear, the one that shows a lot of my back, with the pair of wedges that make my butt look great."

Chris growled.

"Told you that you were—"

Chris flinched as something slammed into his neck. "Ow! What the . . .?" He winced as he rubbed the stinging area.

"Chris, are you all right?" Rianne asked. She put a hand on his. Butterflies fluttered in his stomach at her touch.

"Yeah, I'm fine." He reached under the bench and picked up what had hit him—a football. *How ironic,* he thought as he turned toward where the ball had come from.

Two guys raised their arms. "Hey!" one called. "Sorry 'bout that, bud! Pass it back, man?"

"Sure thing." Chris threw a perfect spiral, and the ball landed in its owner's hands.

"Thanks!"

"Anieyo," Chris answered. Rianne smiled at him as he turned back to her. "It's not funny."

Rianne shrugged. "I just think it's hilarious that we're talking about a football player, and a football almost took you out."

"It didn't almost take me out."

"I think I saw the light leave your eyes," Rianne teased. "Ooh, I'll sketch it out!" Rianne reached for her sketchbook, but Chris grabbed her wrist.

"Don't you dare," he said, a smile teasing his lips.

Rianne laughed. "So, two things to ask you. Actually, one thing to ask and then a comment."

Chris rolled his eyes again but smiled as he played with his phone and leaned back against the bench, one arm resting along the back. "Shoot."

"First, when are you going to teach me more Korean? I know you just said 'you're welcome,' but I only know that because you say it to your mom all the time."

"Never," he replied. "It's a lot more fun to say anything I want about you that you can't understand."

"Fine. I'll just ask your mom, since you know she loves me."

Chris smirked. "I'd love to see you try."

Rianne raised an eyebrow. "I'm going to. And my comment was about that throw you just made."

Chris shrugged. "What about it?"

"I still think you should have tried out for the team this year. I know you play for fun, but you have a really good arm! You would have been a great asset to the team!"

He groaned. "You've said that before. You know I'm not one for team sports—or being a total tool. And you would only use me as an excuse to see Logan more."

"I would not," Rianne protested, then stopped herself. "Actually, that's a pretty good idea."

"Glad to see my friendship means so much to you."

"Also, they're *not* tools."

Chris gave her a look.

"Okay, not *all* of them are tools. Besides, don't you want girls falling all over themselves for you? You love girls!"

"Thanks for the clarification. I almost forgot."

Rianne's phone dinged. She looked down at the screen. "Alex is on her way." She looked over Chris's shoulder and pointed. "There she is."

Chris turned and saw Alex as she exited the school. Her long brown hair was pulled over one of her shoulders, and she looked nice in her white blouse. She had a huge smile on her face, and she waved excitedly when she made eye contact with him, like an enemy ship locking a missile on its target.

Chris groaned. "I don't feel like dealing with this today," he mumbled, rubbing his eyes. He stood up and grabbed his bag.

"Where do you think you're going?" Rianne asked.

"Away from her and her hints."

"Hints? You mean that she still likes you? She's not that obvious."

Chris gave her another look.

"Oh, Chris, stop being such a baby and sit down," Rianne scolded, grabbing his shirt and forcing him back onto the bench. "It's only Alex. I thought you liked her."

"Correction, Rianne. I like her as a *friend*. That's what we are, *friends*. But she doesn't want to believe that."

"Well, don't date her next time!"

Chris opened his mouth to reply but he was interrupted.

"Hi, Chris! Hi, Rianne!" Alex hugged Chris hard around the neck. He gave her a halfhearted hug in return.

"Hey, Alex," Rianne said as Alex sat down between her and Chris. "I gotta make this draft for English really quick, so you two talk. Alex, convince Chris to try out for football next year."

Alex looked at Chris, her eyes widening with excitement. "Chris, you *totally* should! I've seen you play, and I think you'd fit right in."

Chris shook his head. "No, I really don't think so. I prefer to stay in the background. Besides, you guys know I have dance. Football wouldn't fit into that."

"I guess that's true," Alex replied, "but think about if you *did* try out and made it! We would get to see each other for all the pep rallies, games, *away games!* Especially if we go to State! You know, we could really spend quality time together again—without Rianne!"

"Wow, thanks!" Rianne said, laughing.

"Oh, stop it. You know I love you."

Chris faked a chuckle, rubbing his eyes again. *And there's the not-so-subtle hint.* "Well, I already told Rianne that it's *never* going to happen. Now, if you'll excuse me." He stood up and grabbed his backpack. "I gotta go see Mrs. Rivera about that assignment for the thing."

"What thing?" Rianne asked, a faux confused look on her face. "We didn't get any history homework today."

Chris gave her a look that said, *"Shut up, you're not helping,"* but Rianne just smiled and shrugged. "Ugh, I'm going to see Mrs. Rivera," he said. "I'll see y'all later." He hurried toward the school, ignoring the girls' laughter behind him.

Chapter Nine

Alex watched as her beloved Chris left her, then she sighed and looked at Rianne.

"Chris is so dumb," Rianne said.

"Agreed," Alex replied. She looked back at the school as Chris opened the door and went inside, then turned back to Rianne. "We need to talk."

"About?"

"Chris!"

Rianne blew air out of her cheeks. "Is this going to be the same conversation we always have?"

"You're one of my best friends. You're *supposed* to have these merry-go-round conversations with me."

Rianne rolled her eyes but smiled. She leaned her head against the palm of her hand, resting her arm on the back of the bench. "Okay, go ahead."

Alex made herself comfortable, tucking one leg under the other. "So, you know I've been dropping these subtle hints around Chris about wanting to get back together, right?"

"Subtle, Alex?" Rianne raised an eyebrow.

"What? They're subtle!"

Rianne shook her head. "Okay, you've been dropping these *subtle* hints."

"And Chris isn't picking up on them! Or if he is, he's ignoring them, and I don't know why!"

Rianne sucked in air through her teeth. "Alex, I hate to be the one to break it to you, but maybe he's not looking for a relationship right now."

Alex scoffed. "I've thought about that, and I'm fine with just being his friend—I've been his friend for so long—but I want more. How can he *not* want more? I'm the full package!"

Rianne laughed.

"Rianne, it's not funny, I'm serious!"

"I know you're serious," Rianne said, her laughter subsiding. "Okay, how about this: I'll talk to him about it. *Subtly*. I'll bring it up to him every now and again just to get him thinking about it. Maybe that'll help?"

Alex shrugged. "Maybe. Thanks, Rianne."

"No, problem. Now, let me tell you what Logan did—he kissed my cheek!"

Alex's jaw dropped. "He did *what?* Wait, what's the full story?"

Chapter Ten

Courtney tapped her fingers on the hood of Logan's car. It was 6:30 p.m., and their practices had ended thirty-five minutes earlier. She checked the time on her phone again. *Oh, my God, Logan, let's go!* She was about to call him again when she saw him entering the parking lot.

"Logan, come *on!* How long does it take to shower? You could've done that at your house, but of *course* you didn't think of that! Hurry *up!*"

"Oh, my God, I'm coming!" Logan called as he reached the car. "I *would* have showered at home, but you complain every time I don't shower after practice. And you really shouldn't rush me, you know. *I'm* giving *you* a ride because you didn't feel like driving."

Courtney rolled her eyes as she opened the door and got into the passenger seat. "Whatever. Let's just get to your house before I change my mind about coming over."

She heard him mutter something as he threw his bag into the backseat, but she ignored it. She was tired of his attitude. *He'd better fix it by the time we get to his place.*

Courtney played on her phone until she felt the car come to a stop. Looking out the window, she realized they were outside her house. Her small red car was sitting in the driveway. "Logan, does this look like your house to you?"

Logan leaned back in his seat and looked at her. "No, it looks like your house, Courtney."

"Then why are we here?"

"Courtney, we need to talk."

"Get on with it," Courtney said, rolling her eyes and unlocking her phone again.

"Fine, if that's what you want. We're done."

Courtney giggled. "Very funny, Logan. Your little attempt at hilarity. Now, let's go."

Logan smiled at her, even though the situation called for anything but. "Courtney, I don't know why you think I'd be playing some game with you right now. I'm breaking up with you. I don't want to date you anymore. What part of that aren't you getting? I'm done with you. Now get out of my car, so I can go home."

Courtney finally looked at him. "You've got to be joking. Is this about Rianne?"

Logan snorted. "No."

"Do you think I'm *stupid*? I *know* you've been talking to her!"

"So? I talk to a lot of girls. And it's none of your business who I talk to."

"But it's my business if you like her!"

Logan leaned over to her, touching the back of her neck the way she liked, placing his lips near her ear. "Look at it like this: I like you, but I also like girls who will give," he kissed a section of her skin, "me some," he kissed another part of her neck, "variety." He kissed her jaw. "Besides . . ." He looked her in the eye, their faces close. "I'm just bored with you."

Courtney was dumbfounded. Logan was leaving her for Rianne. *Rianne?* Everyone thought she was being paranoid, but she had a reason to be threatened by that girl. She had succeeded in breaking them up.

"You can't just break up with me!" Courtney said in a quiet, volatile voice. "Who do you think you are?"

Logan smiled. "Don't worry, baby. I'll take you back eventually. Like I said, I just wanna have a little fun."

Anger coursed through her. "Fine," she hissed, forcing his hands off her. But I'm not coming back to you. I'm going to wait for you to *crawl* back to me and then drop your ass like the loser you are." She took her bag and opened the door, slamming it behind her.

Logan rolled down his tinted window. "I'm looking forward to it." He winked before rolling up the window, blocking his handsome profile from view.

She crossed the front of the car and stormed into her house, fuming as Logan sped away.

Chapter Eleven

Rianne stood outside of Logan's front door that Friday night. He'd texted her his address earlier in the day. Her father thought she was at Chris's house studying and would be back home at around eleven. He really was a good friend for covering for her, even if he had doubts about the whole thing.

She wrung out her hands, exhaling. "Okay, girl, you can do this. It's just hanging out. Like we used to do. Just be normal. Don't be weird." She did another once-over of her outfit. She was wearing the blouse shirt under her jacket, light-colored jeans, and black wedge boots. It felt like a little much for just watching movies, but technically, it was her first date with Logan, and she wanted to look nice.

Can this even be called a date? she wondered as her phone buzzed in her pocket. It was Chris.

> Please be careful, and don't do anything stupid.

Rianne chuckled as she replied.

Stop worrying! I'll tell you everything
tomorrow ;)

She rang the doorbell and waited, reminding herself to breathe.
A few moments later, Logan opened the door with a wide smile on
his face.

"Hey, Rianne! You made it!" he said, pulling her into a hug
before welcoming her inside. He wore black joggers and a white tee
with a black design. His cologne had a woodsy scent. Not her
favorite, but it smelled nice regardless. "You look really good."

Rianne blushed. "T-thank you. So do you. Whoa," she said as
she looked around the first floor. There was a large flat screen in the
living room, a leather couch, and a coffee table made entirely of
glass. Three white pillars divided the dining room and large
kitchen from the foyer. Both rooms were lit by chandeliers, which
were on dim. There was also a side hallway.

Logan touched the small of her back, leading her toward a wide
staircase on the left. "I'm going to take your wide-eyed wonder as a
thank you about the house," he said with a chuckle.

"Oh! My bad. Where are my manners?" They started up the
stairs to the second floor. "Your home is gorgeous."

Logan shrugged. "Thanks. Perks of having lawyers for parents."

The second floor had another flat screen had an Xbox system
connected to it, resting in a slot under the television stand. A few
other gaming consoles sat in a different corner. A bookshelf held an
assortment of games. Rianne didn't care for video games, but she
liked watching others play. Down the hallway were several closed
doors—probably guest rooms and bathrooms.

"You know, it must be nice being wealthy," Rianne said.

"Ah, there's that sarcasm," Logan said. "I was wondering why
you were being shy. Nervous?" He raised an eyebrow.

Rianne rolled her eyes, trying to save face. "Please."

They now walked up another staircase to the third floor,
which was similar in layout to the second. They continued chat-

ting until Logan stopped in front of one of the doors and opened it.

Her ears were filled with the sounds of Escape the Fate's song, "There's No Sympathy for the Dead." Always curious, she paused to take in the décor. His room had two counters on either side, providing lots of space to put things and to help with organization. He didn't seem to be taking advantage of it, though. A backpack had been thrown into a corner of one counter, school books and papers scattered across it. On the walls were posters of various professional football players. On one wall was a flat-screen television.

"Ooh, I *love* this song!" Rianne said, jumping in excitement.

Logan rolled his eyes as he closed the door behind him. "I still don't know how you can listen to that twenty-four-seven," he said, turning it down with a remote from his dresser. "I sat here for, like, fifteen minutes, listening to this song and some other bands you told me you liked, and I swear I felt myself losing my mind. I've been telling you for years to listen to better music."

"You know for a fact that a lot of the music of today doesn't make a lot of sense. May I sit on your bed?" she asked.

"Go for it." He crossed to the other side of the bed and got comfortable as Rianne pulled her shoes off. "And *not* true. "If we're going to go to Homecoming together, you need to know the songs I'm going to request."

The two exchanged music artists and song for a while, chatting and eating the candy that Logan had pulled out of his bedside table drawer. Rianne missed times like these with Logan—just hanging out and messing with each other.

The only difference was that now Rianne wanted him to be more than a friend.

"Okay, let's watch something," Rianne said. "Do you want to watch a show or a movie?" She started to reach for the remote between them.

"You."

Rianne stopped and looked at him, her heart beginning to race. She was surprised he couldn't hear it—or feel it, since they were sitting so close to each other. "What?"

He ran his fingers through her long black hair. "Just you being here is enough, Rianne."

She swallowed, trying to dispel her nervousness. Her mouth went dry, and words wouldn't form in her mind.

"I really missed you, Rianne. I hated that we kind of . . . fell off. We never got to hang out and be together like we used to. And then Courtney came along, which didn't help anything. She tried to keep me away from you. And I'm sorry I let her do that. But I've tried to make things better. Get back to what we used to have. It's you I really want." He looked into her eyes, still playing with her hair, and bit his lip.

After a moment, Rianne wriggled out of his appealing grasp and stood up. "I'll be right back."

"What? Where are you going?" Logan asked.

"I just need to get some water."

"Are you okay?"

"Oh, yeah, I'm fine." She sounded less than convincing. She wouldn't have believed herself if she were in Logan's place. She quickly pulled her shoes back on. "I'll be right back."

She hurried down the two flights of stairs and made her way into the kitchen. She ran her hands through her hair, remembering the feeling of Logan's fingers in it. *Why am I being so stupid?* she chided herself.

She knew that Logan wanted to kiss her. He was definitely about to before she had her mini heart attack. She opened a couple of cabinets before finding the glasses. Knowing that glass wouldn't be wise with how much she was shaking, she opted for a plastic cup.

She had never been kissed before. What was she supposed to do? What if she was a terrible kisser?

Oh, my gosh, she thought as she filled her glass from the

dispenser in the refrigerator door. *What if I'm not a good kisser? That will destroy whatever Logan and I might have going here.*

Rianne nearly jumped out of her skin as a pair of hands grabbed her waist. She dropped her cup, and the water splashed onto the floor. Turning her head, she met Logan's amused face. "Oh, my God, you scared me!" Then she looked at the floor. "Oh, I am so sorry!"

"It's fine, Rianne, don't worry about it." He opened a drawer and grabbed a rag from it, bending down to clean up the mess. He wrung the excess water into the sink before wiping any errant droplets that escaped.

"God, I am so clumsy. I am so, so sorry," she said again as she picked the cup off the floor.

Logan shrugged. "I'm telling you, it's fine." The humor didn't leave his voice. "Besides, seeing you be so clumsy is kind of cute." He came toward her, backing her up until she was against the kitchen's island. He blocked her in, his hands on the island on either side of her body.

Her heart jumped into her throat, and then traveled back to its home where it beat like a piledriver.

Logan's eyes studied her for a moment. "You look like you're nervous again," he said. He took her chin between his thumb and forefinger, tilting her face up to him.

"N-n-no."

"That didn't sound very convincing, Rianne," he said.

Rianne's brain restarted before going into hyperdrive. "Um, uh, did you still want to watch TV?" she asked.

He chuckled. "We can do a little more than watch TV." He took one hand and started to unzip her jacket; the other snaked up her thigh before his fingers hooked around one of her belt loops, tugging.

Rianne jumped. "Logan, what are you doing?"

"Something I know you're going to like." He lowered his lips to her neck, his breath hot against her skin.

Rianne didn't like it at all. There was no doubt in her mind what Logan wanted, and she wasn't going to give it to him.

"Logan, no. Stop. Get off!" She struggled to get him off her, but he held on.

"Oh, come on, Rianne, baby," he cooed in his smooth voice. "Don't be like that. I know you want this as much as I do. Why else would you come over?"

"Logan, get *off*!"

She screamed as he grabbed her waist and lifted her up with ease, carrying her into the living room. "Logan! Let go of me! Let me go! Let me go!" She screamed again, kicking and hitting him, but he wasn't fazed.

"Babe, *shut up*!" He threw her onto the leather couch, causing her to grunt due to the impact. Rianne pushed on his chest with her forearm, trying to keep him at bay as she grabbed her phone from her back pocket. *I have to call Chris or Dad or Alex.* Someone. Anyone to help her.

"Nope," Logan said, grabbing her wrists and forcing her back down. He had her pinned with his body, prohibiting her from escaping. Rianne tried fighting back, but he was too strong. "You won't need this." He tossed her phone onto the floor. "Now, I'm going to need you to calm down, babe."

Rianne continued to struggle. "Logan, why are you doing this to me? I thought . . ." They had been reconnecting over the past few weeks. He said he cared about her. He made her laugh. Made her feel wanted. Now she realized it was all a lie.

Logan smiled at her, the expression full of malice and deceit. His brown eyes no longer twinkled. Now they were hard and determined. Ready to attack. "Hey, I'm going to need you to calm down. Everything's better when you're not all tense, babe." She struggled again, but he held her down. "Hey, hey, hey, quit! Stop! You knew what you were coming over for."

"No, I didn't!" she shouted. "I thought that—"

"Shut up." His voice was commanding, harder. "None of that

matters now." He stroked her hair. "You're here now, and you're going to relax for me."

Rianne's throat tightened. "No," she whispered. "No, no, please—"

"Your outfit's really nice, but I don't want to see it on you." He took one of his hands off her wrists and started to remove her jacket.

"No. No, no, no, Logan!" Rianne struggled again, tears spilling down her cheeks. She wasn't going to let him do this to her. She had to get away from him.

"Help!" she shouted. She screamed, her vocal cords feeling raw. "Help! Someone help me! Someone please, please help me! Help!"

Logan's free hand covered her mouth, muffling her screams. "Shut up. Shhh. Shhh, shhh, shhh . . . . Stop trying to fight. It's no use anyway, baby. Nobody can hear you. My parents are working late—like they always do—and our house is practically soundproof. You get to be all mine tonight." He threw her jacket on the floor and began working on her shirt. He kissed her neck again.

She kept trying to break away, to get him off her. She struggled and struggled, desperate to keep him at bay. He had pinned her arms, but she tried to aim her hands toward him, willing the power she had used before to come back and save her again.

But nothing happened.

She felt nothing. No warmth. No strength.

Nothing.

After several more minutes of fighting her, Logan seemed to have had enough. "I really wanted you awake during our time together," he growled, squeezing her wrists, "but since you're being difficult . . ." He grabbed one of the pillows that she had knocked over and pressed it over her face.

The pillow smothered her. It was impossible to breathe. Rianne fought to give herself air, but dizziness took over, consciousness faded, and her arms fell away, limp.

Chapter Twelve

Braedon closed his eyes as he pressed his fingers to his temples, resting his thumbs on his face. He leaned forward and rested his elbows on his desk. The warmth of the study as late-morning sunlight poured through the curtains helped him slow his breathing. He exhaled through his mouth.

Concentration was the key to making this work, and he couldn't have any distractions. He had been so close last time.

It was silent other than the ticking of the clock on the study wall.

Just think back to that time, Braedon told himself. *You were in her room. It's small. You saw her mouth moving.*

After months of practice, Braedon had grown accustomed to meditation. It took him no time at all to get in the correct headspace. Seeing back that far was like watching his life through a blurry spyglass. He could make out surroundings and people, but details were impossible.

What was she saying? Come on, what were you saying?

"B-B-Brae-Braedon . . ."

Unobtrusive

There it was.

Finally, he thought, but he kept his mind focused. *She said my name! She said my name!*

He had only gotten the breath of a name, a silent whisper, for weeks. But there it was. She had said his name. Ada had said his name. He couldn't remember much from his past life, but now he could remember a room and see a person. It had to be his younger sister. Only her mouth moved at first. No sound, like watching a video on silent. Now it was like her words were moving through molasses.

Now that he had conquered that feat, he had to see if she said anything else to him. He could barely remember what happened between them, but if he could get some part of the conversation, he would be able to piece the memory together.

He took a large breath through his mouth before letting it out, allowing his mind to relax more. *Come on, Ada. Give me something else.*

"Brae . . . don . . . I . . . I—"

One of the study doors burst open, and Ellis rushed in. "Braedon, guess what just happened!"

With his focus shattered, the memory jolted away like a wind had torn it apart.

Not opening his eyes but still holding his temples, he sighed in exasperation, and then snarled. "Ellis, shut up. And get out."

Ellis stopped, holding his hands up in a defensive position. "Oh, I'm *so* sorry." His tone was sarcastic, as it often was. "What were you doing that was so important that I have the honor of receiving attitude from you this early in the morning?"

Braedon didn't move from his position. "Ellis, could you just leave?"

"Oh, God, Braedon! Are you really doing this again?" No response. "Ugh, this whole adventure of yours is so stupid. I need you to just accept that the Wise Ones wipe our memories, and there's no way to get them back. You would think that two hundred years would've taught you that."

Braedon sighed in a rougher tone. "Oh, my goodness, would you please shut it for one moment?" He finally broke out of his stance. "Ellis, you are *beyond* irritating, you do know that? The only reason it hasn't worked for *you*, Ellis, is because you have the attention span of a newborn kitten. And for your information, I did get something. I heard Ada say my name. That's more than anyone has ever gotten. Now, I ask again, please shut it, I'm trying to—"

Before he could finish his sentence, his vision shifted, and he was back in the room. Ada was standing before him, her hands balled into fists. Her face was angry, and there were tears in her eyes.

"I hate you, Braedon!" Ada said, her voice cracking. "I hate you, I hate you, I hate you! You ruin everything for me! I wish you would just leave forever, so I can do what I please!"

"Is that the way you feel? Well, then I wish I was gone, Ada, so I would be rid of you and all your foolishness!"

Ada gave him a furious, unforgiving look, then pushed past him and left the room.

His vision was suddenly sucked back to the present.

"Whoa!" Braedon shouted as he fell out of his chair, the room spinning around him.

Ellis hurried to his side. "Braedon, what the hell just happened?"

"What happened?" Braedon repeated, disoriented.

"You just froze for about thirty seconds, staring into space. Then you fell out of your chair like someone pushed you or something."

Braedon was breathing heavily, his heart racing and his head pounding. He had seen it. He had actually seen a memory from his past life. A full memory. Made Advancers weren't supposed to remember *anything* before being chosen. It was impossible.

"I . . . I . . . I saw her," he said between breaths.

"Her? Be more specific."

"Ada."

Ellis's eyebrows shot up. "Ada?"

Braedon nodded.

"Well, what happened? What exactly did you see? What does she look like?"

Braedon put his elbows on his knees as he sat on the floor, running his hands through his hair. *I saw into my past. And if I can do it and no other Advancer has or can, what does that mean? A new power? Something that makes me stand apart from everyone else?*

But why did it have to be *that* memory? He could recall it so clearly now. The fight he had with his younger sister over . . . he didn't know yet, but it must've been something important for them to speak so harshly to each other.

He felt deep down that those were the last things they said to each other before he was taken away. Ada was the only person from his past he could remember. But every time he thought of her, he was filled with pain.

"Hello. Braedon. I need you to focus. Focus, little brother."

"Sorry. She, um, had a nice round face and long brown hair and these *beautiful* hazel eyes. That's all I got."

"Well, out with it then." Ellis sat down next to him. "What did you remember?"

"We were fighting. We said horrible things to each other about wishing we weren't in each other's lives. And I'm pretty sure those were the last things we said to each other before we were chosen."

Ellis patted his back. "I'm sorry, mate. Just remember, though, that we all had to have loved each other. We were siblings, after all. No fight could ever break that apart."

Braedon smiled at Ellis . Though he could be the most insufferable person on the planet at times, he had his moments.

"Dude, I just had the greatest idea!" Ellis said.

Braedon's smile disappeared. "Here we go . . ."

"No, no, this time I'm pretty sure it's the greatest idea I've ever had."

"Why is it that every time you say something like that, it usually ends up with me getting in trouble?" It was true. Master Nathaniel had sentenced them both to twenty laps as a result.

"It doesn't."

Braedon gave him a look.

"Just listen. You're going to thank me for this later."

"Which brings us right back to my point."

"Braedon, shut up and listen. You just demonstrated a new ability—something Advancers have never done. Think about it: if we tell the Wise Ones, they'll have tons of questions! Hell, they might even ask you to be a Wise One, for all we know! You won't have to be the Protector anymore, and *I* may move up to your duty! You have the sweetest gig!"

I really wouldn't be able to be the Protector anymore? Braedon thought. Granted, it wasn't *guaranteed* that the Wise Ones would ask him to move up, but the risk remained. Being the Protector was all he ever knew. Rianne popped into his head, a smile on her face and trust in her eyes. Could he run the risk of not seeing her anymore? She still knew close to nothing, and . . . no, he couldn't leave this Guardian. He'd never done it before, and he never would. They had to keep this secret. From everyone.

"I would be a pretty good Protector, don't you think?" he heard Ellis say as he tuned back in to the conversation. "I kinda wish the Wise Ones had given me your job when we were first assigned. I'm liking this idea more and more as I think about it. Come on, we're going to tell the Wise Ones." He pulled Braedon up off the floor.

Braedon was being pushed toward the door when his senses returned. "No!" he said, planting his feet on the floor. "Don't tell *anyone* about this. Don't tell the other Advancers, and *certainly* don't tell the Wise Ones. *We* are not telling them about this, and *you* are not telling them about this. Please, brother, swear to me you won't."

Ellis rolled his eyes. "Fine," he said after a reluctant silence. Then he took Braedon's hand, exchanging their centuries-old hand-shake. "But remaining in silence is only keeping you from—"

"Ellis . . ." Braedon warned.

Suddenly, a slight pressure filled his head, though different from his memory-retrieval process. It felt like something was wrong. He winced, closing his eyes and squatting. His vision shifted behind his eyelids. He saw Rianne lying on a couch, a boy who appeared to be around the same age pressing a pillow to her face. She was screaming, struggling. The scene changed to reveal a green street sign reading "Alexander Street."

She was in trouble.

"Braedon, Braedon! Are you remembering something else?"

Ellis reached for him, and Braedon grabbed his arm, pulling himself up. "No. Something's happening right now. I need to get her."

"What? Who?"

Braedon rushed out of the study, heading to the front door. He and Ellis lived in an incredible home with more than ten bedrooms and half as many bathrooms distributed throughout its five stories, not including the attic, where Braedon's items from the last two centuries were stored for safekeeping. The parlors were equipped with the best entertainment technology, and the downstairs kitchen was the size of five average kitchens combined. The Wise Ones gave only the best to their Advancers, since there weren't many of them.

He focused on Rianne's hometown, Felix, Texas. He couldn't pinpoint the house she was in, but he knew she was on Alexander Street. He just had to focus on that location.

Braedon threw the door open and ran through it, finding himself on the dark Alexander Street. Over a dozen houses lined the street on either side. He breathed out through his nose. Had to start somewhere.

He ran to the first house, 5605, and peered through its window, taking care to stay hidden. A couple sat on the couch, their children lying on the floor in front of them, watching television. Not in there. He checked the next house, going down the row. Number 5607 contained an older couple, talking and cleaning up their home.

Where in the realm is she?

Braedon looked through the window of house 5611. Thick curtains were drawn. He squinted until his eyes focused through them. He saw a guy take off Rianne's shirt and throw it on the floor.

I'm going to kill him. Braedon ran to the front door and banged on it with a tight fist.

"Go away!" a voice said from inside.

Gritting his teeth, Braedon pushed his elbows behind him and then brought his hands forward in a quick, aggressive movement. With a flash, his Blade knocked the door off its hinges. It crashed to the floor, and Braedon stood in the doorway, his shoulders heaving.

Logan cried out in shock, jumping off the couch, but he recovered quickly. "Get out of here!" he shouted. "My girl and I were just getting started!" Then he saw the door. "What the—"

Behind him, Rianne was barely stirring. Her eyes fluttered open a couple of times and then shut again.

Logan rushed Braedon.

They met in the middle.

Logan threw a punch, but Braedon slipped it and punched Logan in the gut. Logan doubled over. Braedon grabbed Logan by the shoulder and bicep, kneed him in the gut, then hurled him against the wall. He followed it up with a solid punch in the face, causing blood to gush.

Logan dropped and lay on the floor, catching his breath. "Do you know who my parents are?" he said, gasping. He held a palm to his nose as blood drenched him. "You're going to prison."

Braedon grabbed Logan's shirt, lifted him in the air, and hurled him into the glass coffee table, shattering it. Logan didn't move after that.

Good.

Braedon turned and saw Rianne pushing herself to her feet. "Whoa, whoa, hold on, Rianne," he said, catching her in his arms before she fell. Braedon grabbed a throw blanket from the recliner and wrapped it around her.

"Thank you," she said, her body shaking. "I thought he was—" She nestled closer to him and sniffled.

He pulled her into a hug. "I'm here now. I'm here. It's okay."

Braedon held her like that for a minute as both of them settled down. "To take you home, I'm going to have to carry you. Is that okay?"

Rianne nodded.

He picked her up, cradling her in his arms, then closed his eyes, concentrating on Rianne's home. The world shifted for a moment, and when he opened his eyes, he was standing on her doormat. Braedon tried the doorknob. Locked. He concentrated on it until he heard it click. Then he twisted it and entered the house.

He made no move to put Rianne down, and Rianne seemed content to stay in his arms.

In the living room, Matt was asleep on the couch, facing away from the television. *He still looks the same after all this time,* Braedon thought. He remembered Chelsea gushing about him when she and Matt began dating and how happy Matt made her.

The staircase was in front of him to his right, but to get to it, he would have to cross in front of the television, blocking the light for a moment.

As he did, Matt moved, turning toward the television. Braedon nearly froze.

Just as long as he doesn't open his eyes.

Matt remained asleep. Braedon made his way to the staircase and climbed the steps, letting out the breath he hadn't realized he was holding.

At the top of the stairs, Braedon turned into Rianne's bedroom, then closed the door behind him with his foot. It had been a week and a half since he was last in there. He liked how Rianne had hung up some of her artwork in the meantime.

Rianne was asleep, so he pulled her bed covers back and set Rianne down as if she were a piece of glass. As the Guardian, she practically was. If anything happened to her, half of the realm would be massacred, and it would be his fault. And he couldn't let that happen yet again.

Braedon took off her shoes and pulled the covers over her. Then he focused his mind on Estona . . . but stopped. He really looked at her. One of her arms was draped over her stomach, and her head was turned toward him. Braedon couldn't help but smile. She looked so pretty as she slept. Breathtaking, even.

I can stay for an extra moment. Just to make sure she's all right.

He knelt and placed a hand on hers. "You're going to be okay, Rianne," he whispered. "I promise to keep you safe." He leaned down to kiss her forehead. As he pulled away, Rianne's eyes opened. She started to sit up, tears running down her face.

"Shhh. You're back home. You're safe."

"What happened to—"

"Don't worry about him. I took care of it."

She put her hands over her face and sobbed, her shoulders heaving. "He wasn't supposed to . . . I didn't go over there to do—"

"I know," he said. "I know. And he paid for that. He's lucky I didn't kill him."

"Is my dad okay?"

"He's fine. He's asleep downstairs."

She was quiet for a moment. "Braedon, can you stay with me a while? Please? I'm still a little . . . oh, God." She began crying again.

Braedon nodded as he leaned over to hug her. "As you wish. I won't go anywhere." She squeezed him, pushing her wet face into his neck.

He sat on the floor next to the bed, leaning his back against the frame. Rianne turned and laid on her side.

Braedon stared into the darkness, strangely at peace. Something about the situation felt right. Out of all the Guardians he'd protected, Rianne was the first to have this effect on him. It was his duty, of course, but protecting her from *anything* that could hurt her was all that he wanted to do.

As he closed his eyes, he felt Rianne's hand come to rest on his shoulder. Butterflies swirling in his stomach, he reached up and intertwined his fingers with hers.

Chapter Thirteen

Rianne sighed as she blinked her eyes open. The sun was bright. Too bright, it seemed.

She groaned as she thought about the night before, then pushed her head down into her pillow, pulling her comforter up to her chin to wrap herself in a cocoon.

Logan.

It came back in flashes.

Worst of all, the warmth was gone. The strength.

She had been powerless.

How could he do that to me? she wondered. *How could he lie to me like that? What did I do so wrong to make him want to . . . to—*

Rianne couldn't even finish. It hurt to think about. She didn't want to relive it.

She sat up and pushed the covers away from her face. Her misery dissipated when she saw Braedon, still seated on the floor next to her bed. He was asleep, his chest rising and falling. His head was lying back against the mattress, his lips slightly parted. One hand rested on his side, and the other lay across his lap. He looked as peaceful as the sunlight entering through her curtains.

Unobtrusive

A smile tugged at the corner of her mouth.

She swung her legs over the side of the bed, then dropped to her knees beside him. She almost didn't want to wake him. *I feel like I could watch him sleep forever and be okay with it. He looks so nice when he sleeps.* Her heart did the tiniest of leaps.

Rianne nudged his arm. "Braedon," she whispered. "Braedon." She nudged a little harder.

Braedon let out a long breath as he opened his eyes. He grunted as he moved his neck around, then stretched his arms behind his head. She cleared her throat as she noticed the outline of his muscles underneath his sweater. Then he looked at her and smiled. "Good morning, Rianne."

"Hey," she said, pulling her knees up to her chest. "Thanks for staying. And for everything you did last night."

Braedon shrugged. "I would do it again. I'm your Protector."

My Protector, right, Rianne thought. "You didn't have to sleep on the floor, you know. I could've made you something to sleep on. Or you could've just . . . just, um—" She cleared her throat again. "Laid next to me, or whatever. Not too close, but you know, that's better than the floor, and . . ." She felt the blush creeping into her cheeks the more she spoke, and she stopped herself before allowing more stupidity to flow out.

Braedon chuckled. "It's quite all right, Rianne. I was fine. And I wouldn't intrude on you like that. Like I said before, I'm a gentleman."

Rianne rolled her eyes. "Something a British man would say."

His face turned serious, his eyes searching hers. "How are you feeling?"

Rianne shrugged. "I'm fine. Just trying not to think about it."

"Then I hate to say it, but the same thing has happened to you twice, Rianne. That can be pretty traumatic. I think you should talk to someone."

"I'm telling you, I'm fine." She pushed herself to her feet, then walked to her dresser and grabbed a pair of loose shorts and a shirt. "I'm gonna take a shower."

She didn't look at him, didn't want him to see the lie in her eyes.

She closed her bathroom door behind her, then leaned against it for a moment before starting her routine. After she brushed her teeth, she climbed into the shower, letting the warm water flow over her and fighting to control her memories of the night before.

Logan, no. Stop. Get off!

I'm going to need you to calm down, babe. Shhh, calm down.

Fifteen minutes later, she dried herself off, then looked at her reflection in the foggy mirror. Everything appeared normal, other than the bruises on her wrists and stomach.

Today would be a normal day. She would paint, listen to music, and draw.

Normal.

When Rianne returned to her room, Braedon was still there, looking at a realistic sketch of a small blue house overlooking a golden field. He was wearing different clothes—tan pants and a white long-sleeved shirt—and there was a hint of cologne. When did he have time to freshen up?

"You're still here," she said, drying her hair with a towel.

He turned to look at her. "Still here," he confirmed, grinning. "You didn't think I would leave without saying goodbye, did you?"

She smiled. "No."

She walked over to her easel and grabbed her palette. "When did you have time to change and everything?" she asked, picking a brush out of the water cup.

"While you were showering."

Rianne made a face; he was so annoying sometimes.

He shrugged. "Affera is a pretty handy thing."

"Hm." She looked at her current abstract piece. She had been strategic in where she wanted each stroke, each color, but every person who looked at it would have their own interpretation. She thought for a moment. Then she made a large stroke of red go across the middle. Was she angry or mostly sad? Upset? Maybe a little angry.

"Rianne, are you all right?" Braedon asked.

She didn't look at him as she continued to work. "I already told you."

"And I'm really good at reading into things."

"Well, you're reading into this too hard. It happened, you saved me, and it's over." Why was he pushing her so hard?

She went to make another mark on the canvas, but Braedon took the brush and palette from her hands, putting them down on the side table.

"Braedon, what the hell—"

He took her forearm above her blackening wrists. Although his movements were harsh, his touch was gentle. He looked at her wrists and then back at her face. "You can't possibly look at what that excuse for a human did to you and tell me you're all right."

"Well, what do you want me to say?" she asked a little too loudly. She lowered her voice. "That I'm hurt? That he tricked me? Lied to me for so long? That I'm sad? Angry? Because I'm all of that!"

His face softened, then he ran his thumbs over her tender skin, causing her to wince. "Yeah, they still hurt."

"Then heal them."

"And how do I do that?"

"You can heal yourself without using your hands. When you use the Fuora to heal others, you need to make physical contact with them. We trigger it the same way we did with the Blade. Focus on the content, warm, happy feeling within yourself. Pinpoint a moment in your life when you were healthiest. It can be any time, as long as you weren't ill or injured."

So, before last night, she thought, closing her eyes. Pushing everything out of her mind, she thought back to a few months ago— before she got back in touch with Logan. She, Alex, and Chris went to the zoo together. The sun was warm, the animals were cute, and she ate so many pretzels.

Warmth began to wrap around her wrists as well as her stomach and back. She opened her eyes and saw a white glow around her arms. Content. Easy. Light.

"This is still so weird but also really cool."

"I think you should tell someone what Logan did."

She exhaled through her nose. "Do you want me to lose my happy feeling? I don't want to tell anyone about it."

"I understand, but what if he tries something like this to another girl?"

Despite the topic, she smiled a little. "After the beating you gave him? I highly doubt it."

"As true as that may be, you can't sit on these emotions forever."

She stayed quiet for a moment. He was right. Holding everything in would only cause her to explode—or implode—eventually. But who could she tell? Her father? Alex? Chris? All of them seemed to be viable options, but what would come out of it?

"Can I talk to my Protector about it?"

Braedon smiled. "It would be my honor." He was still holding her forearms, but she didn't mention it. She liked it. Trusted it. Trusted him.

"Well, first things first. I'm afraid to go to school on Monday. I'll see him there, in my fifth period. What if he tries something?"

Braedon squeezed her arms. "I assure you that he won't. I'll be there with you."

Rianne furrowed her brow. "And how will you manage that?"

Chapter Fourteen

"So, remind me how this works," Rianne said as she climbed into her car. Braedon was already in the passenger seat. She had had breakfast with her father and found Braedon waiting in her room afterward. He was wearing gray jeans and blue flannel.

"I stick with you the entire day, but I remain invisible. Quite simple, really."

The weekend had been nice—leagues better than she imagined it being after her ordeal with Logan. Braedon stayed all of Saturday, allowing her to talk and work some things out within herself. They even practiced her Fuora for a bit—both the Blade and her healing. Affera and Fuora were all about tapping into emotions—relaxed, happy ones. She used her art, her friends, her father and—unsurprising to her—Braedon.

Braedon left for Estona on Sunday to finalize some of his plans and check in with the "Wise Ones," whoever they were. She spent that day with her father, watching football and sitcoms. It was nice to get her mind off everything that happened.

Chris and Alex texted her over the weekend as well, demanding (especially Chris) to know how the date with Logan went. She dodged the questions, constantly changing the subject. The time for excuses had run out, though. She would have to tell them something.

Rianne pulled out of the driveway and headed toward school.

"And no one will be able to see you?"

"No."

"Or hear you?"

"No."

"Are you sure?"

"Rianne," Braedon laughed as he looked over at her, "this isn't my first time using Affera in such a situation. The only person who will hear or see me is you. Others will be able to do the same only if I allow them. So, please relax."

"It's kind of hard to relax with your invisible Protector following you around all day," she replied as they pulled into the student parking lot overlooking the quad at Felix High.

As they walked toward the quad, she looked at Braedon and then at the other students socializing and studying before the first bell. A couple of people she knew waved, and she waved back. Did they see Braedon? He looked completely normal to her, but what would she say if someone questioned his presence?

Her phone dinged. It was Alex, telling her they were at the bench.

"How much time before your first class?" Braedon asked.

"About twenty minutes. We're meeting up with my friends first, Alex and Chris."

Braedon smiled. "I'm excited to meet them."

"No, you won't say a word," Rianne replied as Alex and Chris came into view.

"They wouldn't be able to hear me if I did."

"Rianne! Rianne! Rianne! Tell me *everything*!" Alex gushed, running up to her. "What did y'all do? What did he say? What did *you* say? Were there even *words*?" She gave Rianne a suggestive look.

Chris rolled his eyes. "Alex, give her a moment to breathe." He nudged her.

Rianne swallowed. *Here they come. The questions. No avoiding it forever.*

"Are you going to tell them?" Braedon asked.

"Not planning to."

"Not planning to what?" Chris asked, confused.

Braedon laughed, and Rianne resisted the urge to hit him. To Alex and Chris, it would look like she was swatting at air. "Uh, nothing. Pretend that didn't happen."

"So, how was your weekend?"

"Yeah, you *refused* to answer my texts!" Alex said, bumping her shoulder.

Rianne shrugged, trying to appear nonchalant. "We watched a movie, but nothing really happened. I wasn't feeling it."

"You weren't *feeling* it?" Alex asked. "You've been in love with him literally forever!"

"I was definitely *not* in love with him."

"So, he didn't try anything?" Chris asked.

"If he tries anything again, I'll do his face in," Braedon mumbled.

Rianne almost responded to him, then remembered his invisibility. "I mean, he *tried* to kiss me, but I didn't let him."

"You *didn't*?" Alex and Chris asked, the former surprised and the latter relieved.

Rianne smiled. "Nope. I mean, we talked and stuff like we normally do, but there was no . . . no spark, or whatever. I guess too much time had passed."

"Or real life wasn't as grand as you imagined?" Chris suggested.

Rianne nodded. "Yep. Exactly."

The school bell chimed, telling them that they had ten minutes to get to class. Other students started toward the building, continuing their conversations.

"Hey, I'll see y'all in class," Rianne said. "I'll be there in a sec." They nodded, then Alex intertwined her arm in Chris's as they continued their conversation, which was undoubtedly about her. Rianne blew out a breath and then turned to Braedon. He lifted his eyebrows in question. "That was so hard," she said, nodding for him to follow her.

"What was?" he asked, sticking his hands in his jacket pockets.

"Pretending you weren't there."

"Oh, you did fine." He held the door open for her; she hoped no one noticed. "So, you're not going to tell them?"

Rianne shook her head. "No. They don't need to know. I just hope they drop it."

"I hope so too, for your sake. So, where are we off to?" he asked as they maneuvered the crowds. "Good Lord, Estona doesn't have this many people in one school, let alone the schools I grew up in."

"Well, Braedon, there are definitely more people in the world now than there were two hundred years ago."

"Was that an age joke?" Braedon asked. "I'll have you know I'm only nineteen years old."

"So, two hundred and nineteen. Cool."

Braedon laughed.

"And to answer your other question, my first class is chemistry."

"Splendid. I love chemistry. May I provide assistance?"

Rianne smiled at him. "Why would I need your help?" She turned into a room with long tan tables with beakers, tubes, and textbooks on them.

"I'm your Protector. It's my job to know about your life, including how bad you are in chemistry and mathematics."

"You're this close to being locked out."

Braedon grinned. "You know that you'd rather have me around."

Unobtrusive

Rianne sat down in her seat, then gave him a snarky look. "That's still a fifty-fifty chance at this point."

Rianne hesitated outside the door of her fifth-period English class, gripping the strap of her bag so hard that her knuckles turned white. This was the moment she'd been dreading the entire day. He was in there, waiting to give her a haughty look. Unapologetic. Would he smirk at her? Would he try touching her during class? He only sat one seat behind her. All he would have to do was reach forward and—

Oh, come on, Rianne, baby . . . Don't be like that. I know you want this as much as I do. Why else would you come over?

Braedon touched the small of her back, making her jump. "Relax, Rianne. Breathe." His eyes were concerned, but his smile reassured her. "You can do this."

"I really don't know if I can, Braedon." Realizing she was holding her breath, she let it out.

He took her shoulders and turned her toward him. He had to lean down a bit, so they were eye level. Had he always been so tall?

"I'm telling you that you can do this. And remember, I'm with you. Right here. He won't hurt you again."

She nodded, running a hand over her wrist, which was no longer bruised. She had healed it herself. She could do this.

As she entered the classroom, the bell rang. Rianne made her way to her seat, staring at the floor. Braedon followed her.

Come on, girl. At least look at him. Let him know he doesn't have any power over you. She looked at his seat, and her jaw almost hit the floor.

It looked like Logan had been in a fight with twenty guys—and he was definitely the loser. His nose was bandaged, and both of his eyes were black. His bottom lip was split, and random bruises were scattered across his face. He wore a long-sleeve shirt, but she saw some cuts peeking out. He held a pencil in his hand, making marks in his notebook. His other hand rested on his temple. Other students were asking him what happened, but he brushed them off, telling them to leave him alone.

"What did you *do* to him?" Rianne whispered through the side of her mouth.

"Nothing he didn't deserve."

Logan looked up as Rianne neared, and his face went as white as the paper in front of him. He dropped his pencil, looked around in fear, then returned his gaze to his notebook. His body was shaking. He looked so feeble and worthless now. Was this the boy she had had a crush on for so long?

Why did he just give me a look of terror and refuse to make eye contact? she wondered.

Braedon leaned against one of the supply counters to the right of her and crossed his arms. "Oh, no, dear, he's giving that look to *me*."

Rianne's eyes widened. *He can* see *you?*

Braedon glared at Logan so hard that she was sure Logan would burst into flames. Braedon could probably make it happen with his Affera. "Yep. Just so he remembers not to mess with you again."

Logan glanced at Braedon, saw him glaring, then turned back to his desk.

Courtney entered the classroom. When she saw Logan, she rushed over to him, touching his shoulder. He jumped in response.

"Logan, what *happened* to you?"

"N-nothing," Logan stammered, glancing at her before grabbing his pencil.

Braedon didn't let up on his hateful look.

Three minutes passed, then Logan's hand shot into the air. "Mrs. Carter," he said, not waiting for her to call on him, "I need to go to the nurse. My nose is acting up again."

Everyone turned to look at him.

"Okay, Logan, let me just write—"

Unobtrusive

He didn't wait for her to finish before gathering his things and rushing out of the room.

Everyone looked at one another in confusion. Had *the* Logan Richards just rushed out of the room in what looked like fear?

Rianne looked at Braedon, who shrugged, a grin on his face as subtly touched a copy of *Catch-22* resting on the counter. It disappeared—without anyone noticing—and he began reading.

Chapter Fifteen

"What did you do to him?" Courtney asked as she met Rianne at her locker after school. Thankfully, she didn't slam her locker door again. Braedon had left Rianne for the first time all day to use the "loo," as he called it.

Rianne groaned and looked at the ceiling. "Why do you always feel the need to bother me when I'm at my locker? Is this where you feel most powerful?"

Courtney clenched her jaw. "What did you *do?* He breaks up with me, goes after you, and the next thing I know, he has a broken nose!"

Rianne rolled her eyes. Courtney was the last thing she wanted to deal with. "Look, Courtney, I didn't make him do anything, and I didn't do anything *to* him. And you can have Logan; I want nothing to do with him." She placed a couple of textbooks in her bag.

"I don't believe you."

"You don't have to believe me. Just take him. You two deserve each other, seeing as you're both terrible human beings." She closed her locker.

Unobtrusive

Courtney stepped closer to her, glaring. "You are so insignificant, and I've just about *had* it with you and your *stupid* attitude."

"Love, we're going to be late," Braedon said as he swooped in. He took Rianne's hand in his, pulling her close. "Oh, who's this?"

Rianne looked at him, at a loss for words. Had he made himself visible again? And had he just called her *love?* She looked at Courtney, who was just as surprised at Braedon's appearance. "Oh, um, this is Courtney."

Braedon nodded at Courtney. "Charmed," he said, then he looked back at Rianne. "Do you have all your things?"

Rianne nodded.

"Splendid. Let's go, then." He smiled at Courtney, and then walked toward the doors leading out to the quad, Rianne in tow.

"I didn't need your help, you know," Rianne mumbled as she tried not to bump into the people.

"I am aware that you're fully capable of fending for yourself," he said, "but this Courtney girl seemed to have an issue with you and the waste of human space known as Logan, so I wanted to show her that she truly has nothing to worry about."

"By making it seem like I'm with you?"

"It worked, didn't it?"

Rianne turned around to see Courtney off in the distance, still standing next to her locker. Courtney's face was red from anger, and she was mumbling something to herself as she took her phone out and began typing.

"What is she thinking?" Rianne asked.

Braedon stopped and glanced back. Then he began moving again, opening the door to the quad. "She doesn't think it's fair that you have a guy with an accent."

Rianne raised an eyebrow as they walked out into the cool air. The sun was still shining, giving the day a nice autumn feel. *I guess there was a lot of good that came out of Braedon being with me today.* The boy who assaulted her was terrified of her and her "bodyguard," and Courtney had been bested. It might earn Rianne more scorn, but she could handle anything Courtney dished out. But most of all, she wasn't scared, hurt, or confused. She felt . . . normal. Safe.

She sighed as they walked to the bench that she and her friends always occupied during seventh period. Her heart still pounded whenever she talked to Braedon, but it was feeling more like talking to another friend.

"Braedon, thanks for being here with me today. You made it a lot easier to take on what seemed to be the hardest day of my life." She looked at him. "Thank you, really."

Braedon smiled. "It was my pleasure, and honor, my Guardian," he said as they sat down facing each other; Rianne was cross-legged, and Braedon had his upper body turned toward her, one ankle resting on the opposite knee. He draped his arm across the back of the bench. "Anything to fulfill my duty to you."

"I think we both know that wasn't the only reason you decided to take another day to hang out with me."

Braedon shrugged. "I will neither confirm nor deny."

Rianne's phone dinged. She opened the new message in her group chat with Alex and Chris.

Chris

I'm on my way; had to pick up my assignment from Calculus.

Alex

I'll be in the gym. See y'all after school though!

"Chris is on his way," Rianne said.

Braedon nodded. "You have really great friends, Rianne. You

don't have to tell them everything you told me, but cherish them. People like them don't come along every day."

Rianne smiled. "I love them to death."

"Well," Braedon uncrossed his legs, putting his hands on his lap. "I should be heading back to Estona. I think we both need to return to our normal routines."

Though Rianne wanted him to stay, she understood. "No problem. But, Braedon, before you go . . ." She paused, and he gave her an expectant look. "I want to feel powerful. I never want to feel helpless again. I . . . I'm ready to learn more about my . . . Fuora. I want to know exactly what I am, so I can control it. I'm ready."

Braedon smiled. "You *are* powerful. And I promise that you'll feel that way and believe it yourself. I'll be back by the end of the week. I must finalize some things in Estona, then I'll explain everything in its entirety."

"Everything?"

"Everything." He held out his pinky to her, and she wrapped hers around his. "I'll see you later."

"Later." He glanced around, making sure no one was looking in their direction, and then disappeared.

Rianne played on her phone until Chris showed up a few minutes later.

"Hey, you," he said as he took off his bag and sat down.

Rianne looked up from her phone and smiled. "Hey, friend. Did you embarrass yourself in the rest of your classes?"

"Ha, ha," Chris said. She was referring to how he had caused a chemical to overflow onto his counter and then onto the floor earlier that day in chemistry, much to their teacher's chagrin. "You read *one* ingredient wrong, and no one lets you live it down."

"Well, be smarter next time!"

"'*Be smarter next time*,'" Chris said, imitating her in a mocking tone. "So . . ."

"So what?"

"So, you're not gonna tell us what *really* happened on Friday?"

Rianne knew they would be able to see through her lie, and she had expected them to call her out on it. There was obviously more to the story, but there was no way she was going to let them know. It would be too messy to fabricate how she had gotten out, what she had done for the rest of the weekend, and who she had or hadn't told. She didn't want to deal with it.

"There's nothing to tell, really." She shrugged. "There wasn't anything there like I thought there would be. It happens all the time."

Chris nodded. "Yeah, makes sense. Sometimes it just works out that way."

Rianne looked at him, then her breath caught in her throat. *Oh, no. He's not going to, is he?*

"Rianne, can I tell you something? It's going to sound like a confession, but I figured that now is just as good a time as any now that you aren't tied to Logan." He turned to fully face her. "Look, I like you, okay? And not just as a friend—even though I love having you as my friend—but I've had a crush on you for a while now. I know it might get weird with Alex liking me and all, and I don't want to ruin any of our friendships, but I had to get that off my chest. And if you're up for it, I wouldn't mind taking you on a date sometime." He said most of his speech in one breath, then he let out another, as though a huge burden had been lifted off of him.

And here I am in the position I never wanted to be in. How was she going to let Chris down gently? She didn't want to hurt him, and she still wanted to stay good friends.

Rianne smiled, then placed her hand on his forearm. "Chris, that is so immensely sweet, and I'm really glad you told me. But listen, things didn't end well with Logan—at all—and I'm really not ready for anything right now. It's just too soon, you know?"

Chris nodded. His seemed deflated, but he wasn't looking at her with hatred in his eyes, which was a good sign. "Yeah, I get that."

"Thanks. And I still want to be friends, if you're up for it. *Best* friends."

Chris smiled. "You didn't think I would stop being friends with you just because you *rejected* me, did you?"

Rianne opened her mouth in faux shock. "Why did you have to use the word *reject* like that? And kinda, yeah! I didn't know how you would react!"

Chris gave her a playful shove. "I'm a big boy, Rianne. I've been rejected before. I'll be fine. I'm just glad I got it off my mind and said it to you, you know? Would it have been nice if you said yes? Of course. But I understand where you're coming from, and I respect your decision. And thank you for being honest with me. I'd rather stay your best friend than for you to jump into a relationship you weren't all the way into."

"Wow, Chris, you're more mature than I thought!" She laughed as he made an insulted face. "But if you're looking for a relationship . . ."

Chris rolled his eyes. "Alex?"

Rianne held up her hands. "What? You know how great she is!"

"And how obsessed she is with me."

"And why is that a bad thing, buddy?" She dug into her bag to get her sketchbook. "All I'm saying is, give her another shot. It's been a long time since y'all last dated. Maybe something will be different now."

She glanced at him as she started to draw. He had a contemplative look on his face as he pulled out his phone. She smirked and then looked back down.

The day had gone much better than she expected.

Chapter Sixteen

On Saturday morning, Rianne sat at her easel. It was raining outside, the drops running down her window and creating the perfect atmosphere to work, but it was still bright enough for her to work without turning on the lights. She was wearing headphones. She believed the music she listened to made her art strong. She and her music were reflected in her work. She was more into the graffiti style than anything else, but she loved and appreciated all types of art. She drew and painted whatever came to mind—people, scenes, her emotions. It was the perfect day for inspiration to hit. Her father already left for work, saying he wouldn't be back until late that night.

As she started outlining her new modern piece, she reflected on her week. Life had continued, as it always did. She spent time with her friends and her father. Her dad had no idea what happened, and she planned to keep it that way. As each day passed, she became more and more herself. Spending all that time with Braedon had helped. It was nice to think that she had a guardian angel.

Thankfully, Alex and Chris didn't bring up Logan again, which helped keep her mind off everything that happened the week before. Logan kept his distance from her during English class. He had even asked to be moved to the back of the room, which she didn't mind in the slightest.

Good riddance.

Alex relayed to Rianne that Chris seemed to be acting differently around her—different than normal, anyway. A little flirty. Rianne was glad he was taking her advice to heart. She would be happy if her two best friends got together. They really did make a cute couple.

About an hour had passed when Rianne heard a voice behind her. "I'll never understand how you do that."

She jumped, hitting her knee on the bottom of her easel. She pulled her headphones to her shoulders and turned around to see Braedon—looking as good as ever. He was dressed in a pair of gray jeans and a dark green shirt. Around his neck was a golden cross, and he was wearing white shoes.

"Hell, Braedon, give me a heart attack while you're at it!" she said, rubbing her throbbing knee. "Ow..."

Braedon laughed as he sat in her desk chair. "I apologize. I thought you heard me."

"You mean when you teleported in here? How can I hear you through these?" She pointed to her headphones. "You're lucky I didn't blast you like I did last time!"

"Do you remember what it's called? The thing you blasted me with?"

Rianne thought for a second, then smiled and pointed at him. "Blade! It's called Blade! And my powers are called Fuora!"

Braedon nodded, impressed. "Good. I thought you would've forgotten."

Rianne rolled her eyes as she made her way to her bed and plopped down on the edge. "Okay, I'm ready for whatever you have to tell me."

"And you'll actually believe me?" Braedon asked, rolling the chair closer, so that they were sitting in front of each other.

"I think I've gotten past the 'this can't be real' stage, Braedon."

"All right." He leaned back in the chair and crossed his ankles. "The Great Battle began in 1763. In those times, Estona was a peaceful place, much more so than today. Everyone was carefree and happy. There was one young woman, though, who felt torn and overpowered by her abilities."

"Who was she?"

"Your great-great-great-great-grandmother. Her name was Elizabeth Crenshaw, and she was extremely powerful. She might have been even more powerful than the Wise Ones, in fact. She had the ability to control the natural elements, telekinesis, and she could even control other people's thoughts and movements. She could do it all. She was an anomaly. Everyone to this day—other than the Advancers and the Wise Ones—have only one Affera. No one knows if she was born that way or if her Affera manifested itself into what it was as she aged.

"I've been told that Elizabeth was exhausted with all of the turmoil within her. I can only imagine the toll that took on her. As a Sterling, keeping one power controlled and contained is a feat of its own, but she had as many powers as the Wise Ones themselves—and no idea how to deal with them.

"At age nineteen, she went to see the Wise Ones about her troubles, hoping they would be able to separate her from her Affera so she was only left with one or to find another solution."

"Who are the Wise Ones?" Rianne asked. "You've mentioned them a few times."

"The Wise Ones—forever the ages of twenty-nine to thirty-five —are the most powerful beings in Estona. Think of them as kings, a sort of monarchy. They've had their Affera since the second century, and some believe the four of them created Estona for others like them—since they were considered witches in their time and couldn't live in the Standard world without being persecuted and killed.

"So, after the Wise Ones heard her plight, they invited her to become one of them. They didn't know how or why Elizabeth had the power she did, but they wanted to be sure that her talents and intelligence were put to good use—primarily, alongside them. To be offered the title and position of Wise One is an immense offer. Anyone would be foolish to turn it down."

"So?" Rianne urged, glued to his words. "Did she take the offer?"

Braedon shook his head. "She didn't. She wanted her powers gone, but they refused to oblige her. They would've taught her to control her Affera, but she was so fed up and tired at that point. She felt betrayed.

"Elizabeth ran away from her home, friends, and family. Working off of a rumor, Elizabeth somehow managed to find her way to the Standard world—this world. It wasn't surprising that she figured it out, given her skill set. Going to the Standard world as a Sterling is *highly* forbidden. Back then, this offense was punishable by either the abolition of one's Affera or death."

"Death?" Rianne repeated, mortified. "They . . . the Wise Ones were that serious? They wanted to kill Elizabeth?"

"Not necessarily, but they had the law to uphold. They couldn't have magic revealed again to the Standard world under any circumstances. It's just the way they are. They've calmed down about the rule now—they won't put anyone to death—but there's still a stiff punishment for it.

"The Wise Ones found out that Elizabeth was gone six months later. After deciding how to handle the situation, they sent Wise One Hakim to the Standard world to find her and bring her home."

"How many are there? Wise Ones, I mean?"

Braedon smiled, and she felt her cheeks heat up. Why did her body insist on working against her? "I love how curious you are."

Rianne almost choked on her own spit. "Well, I want to know more about Estona and its magical people."

He chuckled. "They're called *Sterlings*, dear."

"Sure. So there are Sterlings, Advancers, and Wise Ones." She listed them off on her fingers.

"Correct." Braedon swiveled back and forth in the chair. "And the Guardian, which is you. There are four Wise Ones, and each has a certain area they excel in, but keep in mind that they have every power imaginable. Wise One Alaric, who is the head of the four, dominates in telekinesis and compulsion. He's able to make others do what he wants and more, which is a great advantage in battle.

"Wise One Hakim—Wise One Alaric's right-hand man and who would become leader if anything should happen—specializes in taking over the abilities of different species of animals, i.e., the speed of a cheetah or the strength of a bear. Wise One Emil and Wise One Piers both surpass in the elements department, seeing as they're twins. They can control fire, water, earth, air, electricity, thunder, and any other element of nature you can think of."

Rianne nodded. "Okay, I see. And I'm assuming you're saying 'Wise One' each time as . . . ?"

"A sign of respect for their position in Estona. Like I said, they're pretty much royalty. Think of it the same as saying 'Queen Elizabeth.'"

"Right. Will I ever meet them?"

"I really hope you do."

"Hm. And why do you keep calling this world the Standard world again?"

"It's just what we Sterlings call the world of humans without Affera. It keeps the two places separated."

Rianne nodded, then motioned for him to continue.

"So, Wise One Hakim came to the Standard world to retrieve Elizabeth, which was extremely dangerous for someone like him back in 1763. Some people in the colonies, where she was residing, still believed in the whole witchcraft business. Fortunately, he discovered her unmarried and safe, living in a small house on the outskirts of Boston.

"Wise One Hakim demanded that she return home, but she refused. Imagine talking back to a Wise One back then. Their row got more intense until—"

"'Row,'" Rianne whispered. "You're so British."

Braedon stood and moved to sit next to her on the edge of the bed. "Are you making fun of me again?"

She nodded. "What else would I be doing?"

He rolled his eyes, grinning, then continued. "So, legend has it that their argument got so heated that they, well, began kissing each other. Apparently, they'd been attracted to each other ever since some chance meetings when she ultimately came to them, but no one really knows all the details about that. But when this happened —because of their vast magical energies—it caused a catastrophic boom so large that it created another person: the Hunter."

"And who is the Hunter?"

Braedon's expression turned hard. "The Hunter is the evil equivalent of the Guardian, created out of the torment of Affera going on inside of Elizabeth's body and released through the kiss that she and Wise One Hakim shared. Because she had run away, the Hunter immediately resolved to destroy Estona. He was dark and twisted and loved nothing more than causing pain and despair. Because he was Elizabeth's equal, he obtained half of her Affera upon his release. But like him, the Affera darkened. Where the Guardian's powers are called Fuora, the Hunter's power was called Motora.

"He attacked Wise One Hakim and Elizabeth. Wise One Hakim wasn't killed, but his heart stopped beating several times before he was retrieved. Elizabeth was able to escape back to Estona, but the Hunter was right on her trail.

"Elizabeth had just made it to the other Wise Ones and told them what had happened when the Hunter found her. Trying to protect Elizabeth, the Wise Ones told her to flee, then they began fighting. Elizabeth, however, stayed to fight with the power she had left at her disposal. But even with their combined powers, they were no match for the Hunter's strength. After hours of fighting, they met the same fate as Wise One Hakim, and Elizabeth had no one to protect her."

Rianne's heart was pounding. "What happened after that?"

"The two didn't fight one on one, at least not then—he was weakened by his battle with the Wise Ones. But the Hunter left her with these words: 'Don't think you're safe. I'm going to come back, and when I do, it will not matter how much you try to protect this place. I will destroy Estona and its people if it's the last thing I do.'

"He left to the Standard world after that, and Elizabeth followed suit after caring for the Wise Ones. Wise One Hakim actually gave her, her first child—a baby girl and the next Guardian in line. But, unfortunately, after several years of hiding under the Wise Ones' instruction and protection, Elizabeth was found by her Hunter, now named Peter, and killed.

"With her murder, he regained her Fuora, making him invincible. He returned to Estona and began killing, as he had promised. More than eight hundred people were murdered that day.

"The Wise Ones, knowing that the Guardian and Hunter bloodlines would continue, gathered the most powerful beings in Estona and created the Advancers. The Advancers were split into groups to train the Sterlings for the next Great Battle. One Advancer was always chosen to protect the Guardian, to make sure no harm came to her until it was her time to defend Estona against the Hunter.

"However, there were so few of the magically adept Sterlings that the Wise Ones began selecting Standards and giving them powers to help replenish the Advancers' ranks. That's how Ellis and I were made."

Rianne felt sorry for him. That must've been hard. "If you were made into an Advancer, did you . . ." She paused, trying to pick her words carefully so as not to offend him. "Did you ever see your family again?"

He seemed dejected—his face and his voice. "No. I . . . I don't even remember who they are . . . their names, what they looked like . . . nothing. Everything about my life before becoming an Advancer was wiped away. When I try to think back, all I get is a blank. There's only one person I can think of, and that's my younger sister, Ada. Whenever I think of her, though, I'm filled with so much pain that it makes me not want to remember her."

Rianne placed a hand on his arm. "I'm sorry, Braedon."

He smiled at her. "Thank you. But it was for a good cause. The night Ellis and I—Ellis is my older brother by a year—were taken away, we were both in his room, talking about these powers we had. I had the Blade, and Ellis could levitate objects. When an Advancer is chosen, he is given his main power a few months prior to being taken away—sort of as a way to get the body acquainted with Affera. That was when an Advancer appeared in the room with us. We tried to fight him off, calling our father for help, but he knocked us unconscious.

"Next thing we knew, we were waking up in Estona. We were scared and confused, and we didn't know what was happening to us or why. The Wise Ones explained everything I just told you in more or less detail and then gave us the rest of our amazing powers and our assignments. I was to protect the Guardian from then on—at the time, your great-great-great-grandmother was the Guardian—and Ellis was assigned to the high school to teach the teenagers how to defend themselves just in case they came face to face with the Hunter."

He sighed again. "I protected the Guardians to the best of my ability for two hundred and five years. The Guardians' Mentors taught them to use their powers to defeat their Hunters. But, so far, every single Guardian has been killed. Each time, Estona was attacked, leaving hundreds or thousands dead."

He hesitated before continuing. "Rianne, this is what happened to your mother, Chelsea. She was the past Guardian, and her Hunter found her and killed her when you were two years old. I know that you never knew her or what happened to her, but . . ."

Rianne stayed silent, staring at her carpeted floor. Now she knew. After so many years of wishing she had a mother like everyone else, believing the lies her father told her—that her mother left them when she was young—now she knew the truth.

She was dead. Murdered in an ancient battle.

Her father never gave her any concrete facts about her mother —he didn't like to talk about her. All she had was a framed photo of her that she kept on her desk. They looked similar with their black hair and round faces. Even their smiles matched. Now that she knew the truth about what happened to her, in some ways, she wished she didn't.

Braedon remained silent, allowing her to process everything for as long as she needed. Then he took her hand, comforting, apologizing. She appreciated it. It was easier to go through this with him. She was even glad he was the one to tell her.

After several minutes, Rianne trusted her voice enough to speak, though her throat still felt tight. "Since you're the Guardian, you knew my mom?"

He nodded. "Yes, I did."

"Can you tell me some things about her?" She fought to keep the tears out of her eyes. "My dad doesn't like to talk about her."

"It's not because he doesn't want to, Rianne. Chelsea told me a lot about him. She loved him very much. It probably just hurts him to talk about her seeing as she left so suddenly. But your mother was beautiful." He traced circles on her hand with his thumb. "She was ambitious and smart and was able to put a smile on anyone's face. She was a lot like you—headstrong, funny, sensitive, amazing willpower. She wanted to become a guidance counselor for at-risk teenagers. Like I said, she loved your father, and she loved you more than anything. You were the light of her life, Rianne."

Rianne smiled as tears fell from her eyes. She wished she could have known her mother in person. She sounded amazing. "What was her power?"

"She had power over the air."

Rianne nodded. If her mother were still alive, maybe she could have shown her the things she could do with her magic. "Thank you, Braedon."

Braedon reached over and wiped away some of her tears. "You're welcome, Rianne. And I'm sorry."

"It's all right." She took a deep breath, steadying her emotions. "Um, so, after my mom was gone, did her Hunter come to Estona too?"

Braedon's eyes glazed over as he recalled those days. "Yes. And he did with full force, no mercy. We can always feel when the Guardian dies in the Great Battle. It's like you turn cold for a moment. Your Affera inside seems to lose its radiance. If you happen to be using them the moment she's gone, they falter, and you feel yourself go weak. It's unsettling to feel something like that and then know what has happened and what will be coming.

"The Wise Ones always send a couple of Advancers to confront the Hunter, to at least try and slow him down as the Sterlings get to safety. After the death of your mother, the Wise Ones sent Ellis and me, and we were terrified.

"We found him at the high school. Everybody was in safety regiments, ready to fight in case we failed. He said, 'Get out of my way, or I'll kill you with the rest of them,' but we held our ground. I armed myself with my Blade, but I was shaking. He was terrifying. He had these pitch-black eyes that seemed to take control of me, suck me in. I could feel his energy and power radiating off him. It hit me like a force. It made me ill. Made me feel weak.

"The Hunter made the first attack. Just the speed and power with which he moved was staggering. But I still took a risk.

Between Ellis and me, I'm more skilled at hand-to-hand combat, so I teleported to the Hunter and landed a hit. He was surprised at first but recovered quickly. We fought, stopping each other's attacks mid-swing. His blows felt like getting hit by a truck. Ellis helped me with his gravity manipulation to throw the Hunter off balance, which is the only reason I was able to stay in the fight for as long as I did.

"But then . . ." He closed his eyes, kicking himself mentally. "Then I messed up. I left myself open during one of my hits. He saw the opportunity, grabbed my neck, and lifted me off the ground as though I weighed nothing. I heard Ellis scream my name, but there was nothing he could do. I struggled and kicked, but it did nothing.

"The Hunter threw me across the quad, and I smashed through the school's brick wall and landed on the floor inside atop of the rubble. I got this splitting pain that started from my head and spread throughout my body. Then I blacked out.

"When I came to in the hospital several hours later, everything was in shambles. I was bedridden for weeks, even with healing Affera. All Advancers received damage statistics from the towns—number of burned houses and land, shattered buildings. It seemed like I could hear screaming and crying from every direction. The death count was one of the highest we'd even seen—three thousand and forty-two people. The majority of those dead were between the ages of seven and fifteen. The Hunter had no mercy. It was the worst massacre I'd ever experienced."

Rianne closed her eyes to keep from imagining it, but in her mind were the people, their lives ruthlessly taken from them, some not even having the chance to live it at all. "What happened to your brother, Ellis?" she asked. "Did he make it?"

Braedon nodded. "Yeah, thankfully. He was beaten as well, but he survived with only some broken bones and a herniated disk."

"What did the Hunter do to him after you were gone?" She didn't really want to know what kind of horrible torture his brother was put through, but if it was part of the mystery of this whole Guardian and Hunter business, she had to know. "What happened to him?"

Braedon's smile reappeared. "That part of the story isn't mine to tell. You'll have to ask him yourself."

Rianne gave him a look. "What do you mean?"

"Remember when I left to Estona to finalize things? Well, things have been finalized. We have a meeting with my brother and his student, Justin Allan, who will be your Mentor."

"Right now?" Rianne asked.

"Right now."

"And this kid I'm meeting will be training me for the Great Battle?" Though the name of the centuries-old war struck fear into her heart, she was ready to start this new part of her life. Ready to take on the duty that her mother had carried out before her.

"That is correct." He held out his hand for her to take. "Ready?"

"Always."

"Right. But be warned: try your best to land on your feet. This one will be a little rocky."

She took his hand and closed her eyes, ready for the shift in reality to take place.

Chapter Seventeen

Rianne landed hard on her back. She groaned, feeling a muscle twitch as a rock pressed into her side.

"Didn't I tell you to land on your feet?" Braedon asked. She opened her eyes and saw his face, and a shiver ran up her spine. She took his waiting hand, and he helped her up.

"And, what? Have the same pain plaguing my knees that's now killing my back? How dumb do you think I am?" He opened his mouth to reply, but she beat him to it. "Answer that negatively, and you'll regret it."

He chuckled.

Rianne looked at her new surroundings. The sun was setting in the distance, casting the land in a bluish haze. They were standing on a hill that sloped down to a nearby school. It was large enough to be a high school but didn't look nearly as big as Felix High. The building looked to be made of white marble, shining as the last bits of sunlight hit it.

The hill was a luscious, calming green, the sight of which soothed the annoying pain in her back—but that could've been her healing power for all she knew. Behind her, the hill stretched into land that was covered in flowers and a few trees.

"Where exactly are we?"

"Estona."

Rianne looked at him in exasperation. "Thank you, Sherlock. I mean *where* in Estona are we?"

Braedon crossed his arms. "We're at the high school where the older teenagers learn more about their various Affera and how to use them. Estona is much smaller than the Standard world. There are a few towns with about a thousand people each, but there are two elementary schools, two middle schools, and one high school. There's also a collegiate level, but that's farther in that direction." He waved his hand toward the south. "I thought meeting here would be appropriate for you and Justin, seeing as you're both still in high school, but you'll be at the training center for your daily sessions."

Rianne gave him a look. "Daily? What do you mean *daily?*"

"Come on, Rianne. You're a smart girl." He nudged her arm, lingering there for a moment longer than necessary. "Do I have to break it down for you, dear?"

Rianne smiled, nudging him back. "You know, I detect sass, and I did not ask for that. I don't want to give up my free time to come here and train all the time!"

"You'll still be able to do your art."

"When, Braedon?"

"Like I said, you're a smart girl; you'll figure it out." Rianne tried giving a witty comeback, but Braedon talked over her. "And I would like you to be on your best behavior when in training."

"I'm not a kid," Rianne said, rolling her eyes.

"You are a kid; you're sixteen."

She turned to face him. "Then what are you, Mr. I'm-Really-Nineteen?"

"A legal adult."

Rianne laughed. "You are so annoying." He chuckled with her. "And isn't Justin supposed to be the same age as me? Why would I need to *behave?*"

"Because he'll be your Mentor and in charge of you."

"What about you?" She raised her eyebrows. "Aren't you going to be there supervising or something since you're the 'legal adult'?"

Braedon shook his head. "No. You're going to be training in the afternoons after your schooling is over. During that time, I teach classes here."

"Of course, you teach high school classes. Protecting me isn't enough for you."

Braedon shrugged, then stepped closer to her, leaning down and lowering his voice. "Trust me, you make it difficult," he said, then gave her a gentle smile.

His close proximity and soft yet intense gaze set Rianne's heart racing, causing her to blush.

After fifteen minutes of waiting, Braedon checked his watch. He seemed agitated. "Where in the world are they?" he muttered.

Rianne looked around and saw two tall figures approaching. "Is that them?"

"Yes. Finally."

The one on the left looked a lot like Braedon. He was just as handsome, but he was clean shaven, with short, straight hair. She assumed he was Ellis. He wore gray jeans like his brother and as a black shirt, black shoes, and a gray beanie.

The other boy had dirty blond hair and a pierced eyebrow. His jaw was clenched, and he looked unhappy. His hands were jammed in the pockets of his red hoodie.

"Is this not important to you?" Braedon asked, his arms crossed.

Ellis rolled his eyes. "Ooh, so I'm a few minutes late." He lacked the accent his brother had.

"Try fifteen!"

"Well, sorry." His tone gave away that he wasn't. "Justin and I were just—"

"If you're going to 'apologize,' it would be nice if you actually meant it," Braedon said.

Ellis put on a fake, sorrowful face. "Dear brother, I am *so* sorry we were late. In the future, I will be sure to inform you of my tardiness."

Braedon narrowed his eyes at his brother. "You know, I don't appreciate your tone."

Ellis's eyes widened in faux surprise. "Whoa, so we're going to speak to me like a child, are we?"

"You pretty much act like one, even though it's been, what, two hundred and five years since we were chosen? This is serious business, and when I give you a time, I expect you to be here at that time, if not earlier. Especially for anything related to the Guardian."

Ellis rolled his eyes again. "Come off it. You may be the Protector, but you're still a lowly Advancer like the rest of us."

The other boy sighed. "This is so stupid," he mumbled.

Braedon's jaw clenched in irritation. "If I'm such a lowly Advancer, how come I excel so much more than you? Let's think back to that one time . . . oh, wait! Pardon me, I forgot that *you* can't!"

"Back off, Braedon."

"Oh, yes, that's right! Your attention span is so short, you can't concentrate long enough to remember anything, can you?"

"Braedon, you really don't want to go there."

"Guys, I may not know what you two are fighting about, but is it really that serious?" Rianne asked. "Can we go back to completing this meeting please?"

They ignored her.

"Or what, Ellis? Or what?"

Above them, thunder rumbled, and lightning crackled across the darkening sky. Rianne assumed it was Ellis's doing, the result of his anger. Rain began to fall.

"I mean it, Braedon. Don't go there," Ellis growled.

Braedon gave him a cocky smile, continuing despite his brother's warning. "I'm starting to remember things from our past life. Admit it: I'm stronger than you, and you hate it. Don't you?"

The crackling of lightning became more frequent, and the rainfall grew heavier. Ellis rubbed his nose, then punched Braedon in the face.

"Whoa! You guys knock it off!"

Braedon hit him back, and it wasn't long before they both tumbled down the hill, shouting profanities at each other.

"Braedon!" Rianne called, watching them roll down the hill.

"Just let them fight," her Mentor said. "They do this kind of thing all the time."

Rianne turned and looked at him. "Well, just because they're being stupid doesn't mean we can't get to know each other." She smiled. "After all, we're going to have to see each other every day after this, right? I'm Rianne."

"Please tell me why I would care what your name is?" he snapped as the rain dripped off his long hair.

Rianne was taken aback, wondering if she had said something wrong. "Excuse me?"

"Ugh, I wish I was anywhere but here right now," he mumbled. "Look, you don't want to be here, and I *definitely* don't want to be here. You don't care that I'm Justin, and I don't care that you're Rianne, so why don't we both just pretend like the other doesn't exist, all right?"

Rianne stepped closer to him. "Listen, Justin, you're *not* going to talk to me any way you feel like—"

"And what are you going to do about it?" he asked "You couldn't even save yourself when you were pinned down a couple of weeks ago."

Something in her snapped. *He's dead.*

Rianne tackled him to the ground, straddling him in the mud and wet grass, punching him in the face with her Blade. She didn't know how she made it appear in her anger, but she didn't care.

Unobtrusive

Though caught by surprise, Justin blocked some of her hits with his own blue-colored Blade. "Stop! Stop it! Stop it! Get off! Stop hitting me! Knock it off!"

But she couldn't. How dare he? He wasn't going to remind her that she was weak. She refused to be that way anymore.

Chapter Eighteen

Braedon got another hit in with his Blade when he heard shouting coming from the top of the hill. The rain Ellis produced had soaked through his clothes and caused his wavy hair to hang loosely around his face, making it difficult for him to see. Thunder rumbled.

"Rianne?" he said, pausing. One of his fists was wrapped around the collar of Ellis's shirt, and the other was about to smash into his brother's face.

While Braedon was distracted, Ellis punched him in the jaw. Braedon's world shook for a moment, and he let go of Ellis and fell off of him, landing on his back. Another shout rang out.

Blinking his world back into focus, Braedon regained his bearings as the throbbing in his jaw settled. Ellis brought his fist down to hit him again, but Braedon grabbed it before it could make contact. "Hold it a second, Ellis!" Braedon said. "Didn't you just hear that?"

There was another scream. "Stop! Stop! Please! Knock it off!"

"That's Justin," Ellis said. "What's going on up there?" The rain slackened, and the lightning flashes became less frequent, the thunder quieter.

Braedon teleported out from under Ellis to the top of the hill. He was just in time to see Rianne punch Justin in the face with her Blade. He was trying to defend himself with his own Blade, but Justin was losing with no chance of redemption.

"Take it back!" Rianne shouted as she punched him again. "Take it back!"

A second later, Ellis was standing next to Braedon. "What the hell?"

Braedon smiled. "I guess your star pupil isn't much of a star, is he?"

Ellis closed his eyes, squeezed the bridge of his nose between his thumb and forefinger, and groaned. "This is so embarrassing." Ellis had been bragging about how well Justin was getting along with Ellis as his Mentor. It was a constant stream of ego with no apparent end in sight after every training session.

"Ha, payback's a bitch, isn't it?" Braedon said, looking at his brother.

"Shut the hell up, Braedon, before I punch you again."

"Do you want me to break them up?" Braedon asked in a voice that would have been appropriate for a two-year-old. "We wouldn't want your ego bruised any more today, would we?"

Though Ellis glared at him, he nodded. "Please."

The next second, Braedon pulled Rianne off, and Ellis helped Justin to his feet. They were both breathing heavily.

Rianne tried lunging at Justin, her Blade still armed, but Braedon held her back. "Whoa, there, girl. Calm down. Calm down. Sheath your Blade. There you go. Now, what happened? What's the problem?"

"Him," she growled through her teeth, narrowing her eyes at Justin. "*He's* the problem. You should've heard the crap he said to me while you guys were gone."

Braedon looked at Justin. One of his eyes was turning black, and blood was flowing from his cut lip. His nose was bleeding as well. "Is that true, Justin?"

He didn't say anything, just reciprocated Rianne's glare.

"Well, that's as good an answer as any. Now, Rianne." He let her go and locked eyes with her. "I know you might not want to hear this, but you really caused Justin some damage, and you need to heal him."

Rianne scoffed. "Why the hell would I help him?"

"Because it's what the Guardian does. The Guardian is kind-hearted, and she not only protects Sterlings and Estona, she also helps them when they're in need. No matter who they are or what they've done. What do you think Elizabeth would have done?"

Rianne thought about it. Then she rolled her eyes. "Fine."

"Good. We'll give you two some time to yourselves." He looked at Ellis, who nodded. They both seemed to have forgotten about their fight from earlier; the elements of the thunderstorm have blown over. They gave the other two some space, though they continued listening and watching.

"Come here," Rianne said, motioning Justin over, but he was reluctant. "I'm not going to hit you again—unless you say something stupid. Now come here. We need to get those injuries fixed up before they set in."

He walked over to her. She took his bruised and slightly bloody face in her hands and closed her eyes. She let out a slow breath and concentrated on her father. She felt a warmth in her core, and it transferred to her hands, making them tingle. Her hands glowed with a dim white light, and Justin's bruises began to disappear.

He sighed, the pain easing away. "Rianne, I'm sorry. About earlier, I mean."

"Oh, so you *were* listening when I introduced myself," she said, her eyes still closed.

"Yeah, I was."

"So, is there any specific reason you were being such an ass? Hand."

Unobtrusive

He gave her his right hand to heal next. It was much more bruised than the rest of his body. He had used that hand to defend himself. "Actually, I had a pretty terrible day."

"Sorry to hear that. Wanna elaborate?"

He hesitated but decided to trust her since she was healing his wounds—and it didn't hurt that he was going to be her Mentor. "It was my girlfriend. Well, *ex*-girlfriend, I should say. She broke up with me today, and I haven't been taking it very well."

"Here at this school or at Felix?"

"Felix," he said. "She—wait, how do you know what school I go to in the Standard world?"

"Because I go to the same school. Braedon mentioned it the first time I met him. Who's the girl?"

"Samantha. Samantha Carbone."

"I know her. She's in my history class."

"Yeah, everyone knows her. I've been pretty pissed off. She broke up with me over text. *Text*. She couldn't even tell me in person. Something about 'we don't have anything in common.' Over *text*. I bet you she's probably with someone else. I swear if I find out who it is—"

As he told his story, his Blade glowed blue around his hand.

"Whoa, whoa, whoa, calm down, Justin," Rianne said, putting a hand on his chest. "I don't want to stop healing you right now since I'm in the middle of it, and I seriously don't think mixing your Blade with my healing is a good idea."

"I can't calm down," Justin said through clenched teeth. He seemed as if he wanted to settle down, but he was too wrapped up in his own head.

"If there was one thing, *one thing*, you could do in Estona or in the Standard world, what would it be?"

Justin furrowed his brow at her. "What?"

"You heard me. What would it be?"

"I guess . . . I guess it would be to make something of myself. And using that, to make things better for others."

"So, sort of what you're doing now?"

"What do you mean?"

"You're my Mentor. You're going to train me to make sure I'm ready for the Great Battle. And if—no, *when*—I win, that'll make things better for everyone here. Don't you agree? Don't let some girl throw you off from what you want to do."

Justin smiled. His Blade receded, and Rianne was able to continue healing.

"You know, Rianne," he said as she released his hand, "I think we're going to be good friends. Being a Mentor isn't going to be as bad as I thought."

"Good to hear you were dreading your new assignment." Rianne laughed. "And yeah, I think we're going to be great friends."

Braedon let out a sigh of relief. One hurdle down.

"You know," Ellis said, "all the Guardians have been really cute, but this one's especially so. You said she's about to turn seventeen, right?"

Braedon gave him a wary look. "Yes. Why?"

Ellis shrugged. "No reason."

"Don't even think about it."

"What?" Ellis looked at him. "You want her for yourself?"

Braedon was taken aback. "What? No. I'm just not going to let you pull the same stupid tricks on her that you pull on everyone else. She needs to focus on her training."

Ellis rolled his eyes. "Yeah, I bet that's the reason. Don't worry. I won't touch your little girlfriend."

Braedon headed toward Rianne and Justin. "Not my girlfriend," he mumbled.

"Sure. Whatever." Ellis followed him, his hands in his front pockets. "She's pretty powerful. I can feel her energy from here. I can't remember a Guardian as strong as her this early. And she hasn't even started training yet."

Braedon nodded in agreement. Rianne had a lot of potential. Her Hunter was going to have an extremely tough time with her.

Unobtrusive

Maybe she would be the Guardian to save them all.

Chapter Nineteen

"And switch to the opposite leg . . . try to pull your nose to your knee," Justin said, demonstrating the stretch. Rianne followed his instruction, trying to remember to breathe. The hamstring stretch felt amazing to her sore yet strengthened muscles. She was drenched in sweat, but she had cooled down halfway through their standard stretching moves.

It was the end of the sixty-first day of her training with Justin. Every day, Braedon would already be in her room when she got home from school, ready to take her to Estona, where it was early morning, for two hours of training. Ellis was responsible for Justin's transport. Their sessions began only a couple of days after their first meeting, and Justin had made them hit the ground running—by literally making her run a mile before subjecting her to jumping jacks, pushups, and planks. She hadn't done that much physical activity since sparring with her father ages ago.

After a few days of getting her back into some sort of shape, Justin started her on different exercises and routines, including bodyweight, strength training, core conditioning, and high-intensity cardio. Her Fuora training was integrated soon after, and she was starting to get the hang of proper defense and punching, as well as some other techniques that Justin had shown her. They were about to move to full-on sparring, which she was looking forward to.

She had a leg up thanks to her father—who was surprised yet pleased when she brought up sparring with him recently—but the extra practice with someone as skilled as Justin made her feel more confident. The great thing about having Justin for a Mentor was that he did all of the exercises with her. That way she didn't feel so alone after being thrown into an entirely new dimension.

The two had become fast friends in the short time they'd known each other. It just so happened that he had two classes with her—health and homeroom—which allowed them to interact all the more. She integrated him into her small friend group as well, and they would hang out whenever possible.

The two were in the training center after their Standard-world schooling, the massive retractable sunroof letting in the cool morning air. They were finishing up on the track before people began trickling in. Though the center was open twenty-four hours, certain areas of the center would be closed to give the Guardian and her Mentor privacy.

The training center was located in Estona's version of a downtown area, attached to the college campus. The 240,000-square-foot building was made of white brick and pure marble to complement the look of the major buildings in Estona. The multiple indoor areas included a free-weight room and a circuit-training room, two cardiovascular equipment areas with an attached speed-bag room, two aerobic and dance studios, four basketball courts, an elevated one-mile jogging track, a rock-climbing wall, an indoor swimming pool, and locker rooms with showers and saunas. Housed on the upper levels were offices, including Master Nathaniel's main office.

Master Nathaniel was Estona's most respected and skilled trainer. He worked with all of the Advancers at all points of their development. His fighting skills were unmatched except for the

Wise Ones themselves, having honed his craft for over three hundred years along with his fire Affera. Sterlings could study under him during their high school and/or collegiate years to become trainers like him and other select Advancers, but it was a highly selective and grueling process.

"I'm determined to be one of the ones to make it through the program though," Justin said with a wink when he first began training Rianne, which included a rundown on how Estona operated.

Justin's ambition meant a lot to him, which Rianne could see whenever Master Nathaniel left his main office to check on them. Justin's jargon would change to sound more professional and knowledgeable, and his easy-going nature would disappear. Master Nathaniel must've picked up on it as well, so he usually left them alone. Justin trained with Ellis every day and with Master Nathaniel once or twice per week. Rianne had underestimated how grueling a Mentor's job could be. It made her want to perform that much better.

The pair were seated on the track with their hands in prayer position, breathing deeply. Rianne focused on a spot on the ground in front of her. Justin had his eyes closed. She had tried that, but she'd found over the past several months that she preferred to be aware of her surroundings.

"And . . . ten," Justin said, letting out a final breath through his mouth. He opened his eyes. "And we're done!" He planted his hands on his knees. "Great job today, Rianne."

Rianne fell onto her back and groaned. "I've never been more tired in my life!"

Justin rolled his eyes. a smile on his face. "You say that literally every day, you big baby."

"Because I keep getting more and more exhausted dealing with you every day!"

Justin leaned over and pressed a finger into her bicep. She leaped up in pain.

"Ow! Justin! You know my arms are sore!" She smacked his shoulder.

He continued to poke her, laughing. "Aw, is the big baby Guardian gonna whine some more? 'Wah, wah, wah, my name's Rianne, and I had to do heavy curls wahhhh!'"

Rianne smacked him again but couldn't maintain the annoyed expression on her face. "What time is it?"

Justin checked his watch. "It's 9:43 Estona time, 5:26 Standard. How long do you have until your 'shift' ends?"

"I don't like your tone, Justin," she mumbled. She didn't like taking off work so frequently as of late—or lying to her father about it—but she'd gotten accustomed to the "duty calls" trope. "A couple of hours, give or take. Making some money would be nice right about now, though."

Justin looked into the air, as though he was gazing at something far out of reach. "Imagine getting paid to do your job. That sounds *so* nice."

She rolled her eyes. "You're so dramatic."

"Pot, meet kettle!" He leaned over to the faux grass that the rubber track encompassed and grabbed his phone and a key ring. "Master Nathaniel is at the palace right now, so he needs me to open everything. Want to come with?"

"Sure!" Rianne grabbed her water bottle and jumped to her feet. She didn't mention it, but she was eager to have the opportunity to meet a Sterling or another Advancer. She and Justin isolated themselves during training sessions, so there weren't any distractions, but she wanted to get to meet some of the people she was supposed to be protecting. The people her mother had tried to protect.

They made their way down the metal railways to the ground level. "Hey, Justin?"

"Yeah?"

"Speaking of jobs and things, this is 'technically' your job, but you *don't* get paid or anything for it. Did you volunteer to be my Mentor? Or were you chosen or something?"

"Good question," he said. "Surprised we haven't talked about it sooner." They made it to the cardio area they'd used for the majority of the day's session and unlocked the glass door. No one was in the area yet, but it would fill up soon. He started toward one of the lounge areas, and she followed. "I did make a comment once to Braedon and Ellis that it would be a good opportunity for me to train you for the Battle, once I found out that your Fuora was Blade. Since you know I want to be a trainer here under Master Nathaniel and everything."

She nodded. "How did you end up training with Ellis anyway?"

"My dad signed me up for fighting and Affera lessons when I hit the fourth grade. I was placed with Ellis at random."

"Estona has training lessons? But I thought you said that was what the high school was for."

"It is," Justin said, "but parents can sign their kids up for extra lessons if they want. A lot of people opt to do that, actually. The Hunter's last attack has everyone pretty terrified."

Rianne noted how he spoke about the fear in the present instead of the past.

Once they arrived at the lounge, they plopped down on the couches.

"My dad was a part of the huge group of adults who wanted their kids protected at all costs," Justin continued. "Braedon already told you how bad the last Hunter was, right?"

Rianne nodded.

Justin's eyes turned downcast. "My mom was one of the ones who didn't make it."

"I'm sorry, Justin."

"Do you remember much about your mom?" He looked at her. "Sorry if you don't wanna talk about it. I've just always kind of wondered."

"It's all right." She sighed. "Well, I was only two when she died. I guess we both were. I honestly don't remember a whole lot—nothing, really. My dad doesn't talk about her. He always told me that she walked out on us. I only ever saw her in pictures."

Justin nodded. "Yeah, we saw pictures of her in our history books growing up. You look just like her."

"Spitting image." She played with her black hair, which was tied in a ponytail, fiddling with the ends. "I didn't know anything about her until I found out that I was the Guardian. Then Braedon told me more about her. Like how her Affera was air and how she wanted to be a counselor, which is so cool. I wish I could have known her." She now looked over at her friend. "What about you? Do you remember your mom?"

"Sorta kinda. Just like you, not a whole lot. Wish I could, though. My dad told me stuff about her all the time growing up. I don't think he wanted her to fade from my mind—which she never could. I do remember a glimpse from the Great Massacre, though. I think I might have seen her die. My dad tried to keep me from seeing it, but . . ." He sighed, leaning back on his hands.

Rianne pulled her knees to her chest. "You don't have to talk about it if you don't want to."

He shrugged. "Nah, it's fine. It's kind of therapeutic, you know?" He crossed his legs and picked at the couch's plastic upholstery. "I remember the sirens going off. Apparently, your Affera goes cold when the Guardian dies, but mine hadn't manifested yet; I was too young.

"My dad was carrying me, gripping my mom's hand, and we were rushing to the palace. I must've been making a lot of noise, not making their jobs any easier. Dozens of others were fleeing, trying to get to safety. The Wise Ones were already in the shelter, and we only had around fifteen minutes to get inside before it was shut down, and we had to find somewhere else to hide and wait out the attack."

Rianne remembered Braedon telling her something about that.

When the Great Massacre was upon them, the Wise Ones were ushered to a shelter with eight guards for their protection somewhere in the castle. The location changed every time, so the Hunters couldn't pass down knowledge of where to find the leaders of the realm. The people of Estona were given twenty minutes to reach the castle before it was locked down from the inside.

"If we didn't make it in time, it was probably already too late to save ourselves. He told me that all the teleportation stations were backed up—too many people rushing to too few stations all at once. Systems malfunctioned. Dad said that he could feel the Hunter before he saw him when we reached the overpass.

"We had just made it through when the Hunter collapsed the bridge. The stone fell, crushing people. That's the part I sort of remember. The force of the explosion threw us to the ground. My dad lost my mom's hand. She fell, and a big piece of the stone pinned her to the ground. Her upper body was the only thing not crushed. There was a lot of blood.

"My dad screamed for her, tried to cover my eyes, but I had already seen it. He got back up and kept running. I couldn't comprehend anything that just happened other than that we were leaving Mom behind."

Justin sighed, running a hand through his hair. "We made it to the palace just in time."

Rianne took Justin's other hand. "I'm sorry," she whispered. "I'm so sorry."

Justin glanced out one of the windows toward the college campus. "I'm glad I get to be one of the people helping you out so that doesn't happen again. I don't want anyone else to lose their moms or dad, brothers or sisters, or children."

He nudged her, the familiar glow in his eyes reappearing. "And, so, to answer your question, all of that contributed to me being chosen as your Mentor. I was interviewed by the Wise Ones. I swear my soul left my body while talking to them. They can be so damn intimidating. And they watched a couple of sessions between me and Ellis and Master Nathaniel, who both gave me glowing recommendations." He chuckled, taking a drink from his bottle. "When you win the Great Battle, I swear to God I better get a mansion and a parade or something."

Rianne's heart glowed at his confidence in her. He never used the word "if" when it came to the Great Battle. He always used definite terms to describe her victory. She knew Braedon felt the same, but did the other Sterlings have the same amount of faith in her, or do they always expect the worst but pray for the best?

"Would you have a marching band and everything?"

"Hell yeah! Put me up on a throne! I want fireworks and confetti everywhere."

"And where will I be? I mean, I would have won and beat the Hunter and everything! Where's my fanfare?"

He shushed her, closing his eyes. "You're ruining the fantasy of my awesome parade. You're off painting a wall or something."

The air shifted, and Braedon appeared. Rianne couldn't stop the smile from jumping to her face in his presence. *I swear he's too handsome for his own good,* she mused.

"There you are," he said. "I've been looking all over for you two. I thought you'd be finishing at the track today." He took in their appearance. "You still haven't showered? Didn't your session end at least twenty minutes ago?"

Rianne reached over and clasped Justin's shoulder. "We were bonding, Braedon. Like a good Mentor and Guardian should. Aren't you proud of us?"

Justin reciprocated by taking Rianne's shoulder and looking up at Braedon with puppy-dog eyes.

"Oh, please." Braedon glanced at his watch. "You brought your extra pair of clothes, right?"

"Yeah." Rianne pointed to the lockers down the hall. "Why did I have to bring that anyway? Am I not going home?"

"No, not yet," Braedon said, a mischievous smile on his face. "I'm going to take you exploring for a little bit."

"*Ooh,*" Justin said in a sing-song voice. "Sounds fun."

"Are you coming with us?" Rianne asked, looking at him.

"Nah. I'm gonna head home and take a nap and maybe chill with my dad for a bit."

"Make sure you shower first," Rianne muttered, earning her a playful flick on the temple.

"Besides, I wouldn't want to ruin your *date.*"

"It's not a date!"

"It's not like that!"

Justin heard none of it, covering his ears as he stood up and headed to the lockers. "*La la la,* I can't hear you, have fuuunn!"

Once he was down the hall, Braedon glanced at Rianne before averting his eyes. The blush on his face was as deep as hers. "You know this isn't a date, right?"

"Of course I know that!" Rianne replied, trying to hide her embarrassment. "Justin's just an idiot."

Chapter Twenty

"Can you get me a smoothie?"

"Didn't I get you one last week?" Braedon asked as he took her arm and guided her across the busy street.

They had just finished touring the middle and elementary school campuses. Sterlings and Advancers were in classes, and the two dropped in to a few to observe. She was surprised to find that Estona's schools were just like Standard-world ones, albeit with minor differences—mainly involving Affera. Braedon gave her the details during transitions. Schools were year-round with holiday breaks. Advancers served as teachers at all levels. The majority of Advancers had the important duty of training and schooling the younger generations. Elementary school lasted five years, middle school lasted four, and the high school five. At the younger levels, Sterlings learned about the inner workings of Affera along with the history of Estona and general education, with occasional opportunities to begin using their Affera. Once Sterlings reached high school age, they worked on mastering their Affera.

"Students move through the levels at the end of May after their qualifying exams. They also have their core classes and electives such as music, woodshop, languages, journalism . . . just as many as average Standard schools. And, of course, sporting games and school dances give much-needed relief to everyone."

Everyone gazed at her at the schools, just as they were now as they traversed downtown Estona. Rianne even got to meet and talk to some of the Sterlings and Advancers.

"That was last week. This is now," Rianne said. She looked around and spotted a juice bar café nestled between a record shop and a clothing store. She stopped him in his tracks, pulling his arm. "Look! There's one right there. C'mon, let's go!"

Braedon protested but let himself be dragged along. "I need to be getting you something healthier and with more protein after your session, not a beverage spiked with copious amounts of sugar."

"It can be a healthy smoothie! We can ask them to put some spinach and protein powder and whatever healthy thing you want in there! Just as long as it's strawberry banana. Please?" They stopped outside the colorful shop with various fruits decorating it.

Braedon looked at her, contemplating. Rianne gazed back at him, batting her eyelashes. Finally, he sighed. "Fine." He opened the door for her.

"Whoo-hoo!" Rianne cheered, hurrying inside.

"But this is the last time," he said as he followed her.

Sure, Braedon, Rianne thought, smiling.

The two ordered their beverages and then sat at a circular table for two by the front window. Rianne looked around, taking in the décor. The juice bar had a cute rainforest theme, with plastic fruits and decorations hanging on the walls and ceiling. A large chalkboard on the opposite wall had a menu of juices, smoothies, and treats written in multiple colors and fonts. The order counter was like what one would find in a bar, with tall stools lined up along it. The shop was moderately filled with patrons, many of whom were stealing glances at them.

"Braedon," Rianne whispered, "everyone keeps looking at us."

"It's probably because you're sweaty," Braedon remarked,

moving his leg out of the way of her kick as he sipped his drink. "It's because of our energies."

"Our energies?"

"Of course. With me being an Advancer with multiple Affera residing within me, I give off a different aura than an average Sterling. You, on the other hand, as the Guardian, have an effect on Sterlings that's off the meter. Sterlings can sense you before you enter a building. And being the Guardian and the bearer of the positivity and joy that magic brings, your Fuora boosts the Affera of those you're around."

Rianne looked down at her hand, allowing a small ball of her Blade to manifest before reabsorbing it. "Wow. Elizabeth really gave me that much power?"

Braedon nodded, smiling at her. "Now imagine how your world will feel once you take your full power after defeating your Hunter." He nudged his juice toward her. "Want a taste?"

Rianne blushed, and her heartbeat increased. He had said it so casually, and though she knew he meant it in a friendly way, it felt like something he would have said to her on a date. "S-sure," she said, hating herself for stuttering.

The two spent a few more minutes talking. Several people greeted Braedon as they entered or exited the café, and some were bold enough to introduce themselves to Rianne. They approached her, starstruck, asking for pictures and thanking her for working so hard to protect them. She even talked to a gorgeous goth girl, and they gushed about their styles and favorite bands.

Braedon's phone buzzed. He checked it as Rianne said goodbye to Emily, a new friend, then he sighed in exasperation.

"What's wrong?" Rianne asked, taking a long draw from her smoothie.

"Ellis saw you on social media."

Rianne cocked her head. "Estona has social media?"

"We're a magical dimension, Rianne, not a 1900s village."

Rianne resisted the urge to level another kick at him.

"He saw our location and said he's heading here now."

"I thought he would be teaching right now," Rianne said. Ellis's duty was at the high school.

"He's on a lunch break or his conference time," Braedon replied.

I wonder why he looks annoyed, Rianne thought, but she didn't ask. She didn't have a sibling, but from what Alex and Chris had told her, annoyances between siblings occurred all the time.

Ellis appeared about a minute later through teleportation. "Hey, hey, hey!" he said, pulling up a chair. "What's going on?"

"Nothing much," Rianne replied. She nodded toward the bar. "Are you going to get anything?"

"Nah," Ellis said, dismissing the question with a wave. "Just saw that you were here, and I needed an excuse to leave campus for a bit. How's training with Justin going?

"Really good! I'm going to start sparring soon!"

"That's great!" He scooted his chair closer to Rianne, and their arms grazed each other. "If you want, I can help you with anything you want to keep working on whenever Justin or Braedon are busy. I promise to take it easy on ya—if you want me to, I mean." His eyes lingered on her lips before meeting her eyes again.

Is he flirting with me? Rianne wondered. She flicked her eyes over to Braedon, whose jaw was tight as he glared at his brother. He hadn't said anything since Ellis arrived. If she didn't know any better, she would have said that Braedon looked jealous.

She turned back to Ellis and smiled. "Sure, sounds fine. Thanks for offering."

"Of course. Anything for the Guardian."

Braedon glanced at his watch. "Oh, look at the time. It's getting late in the Standard world. Rianne, I need to take you back." She took the hint and stood up with him.

"See you at home, little brother," Ellis called, wiggling his fingers at Braedon as they left the shop.

Chapter Twenty-One

Rianne walked out of the school building after saying goodbye to Alex and Chris at the end of the day. It was a few weeks past her seventeenth birthday, and the warm April air felt nice on her skin. The sun peeked out of the gray clouds. It had just stopped raining. Other students filed out behind her.

Rianne's phone rang as she made her way across the quad to the parking lot. She pulled it out of her back pocket and raised it to her ear without bothering to check the caller ID.

"Hello?"

"Hello, Rianne, how are ya?" a rough voice on the other end asked.

"Oh! Hi, Mr. Newman," Rianne said, confused as to why her boss from Good Texas Cookin' was calling. "What can I help you with, sir?"

"Listen, Rianne, I know it's your day off, but . . ."

Rianne winced as she unlocked her car and climbed in. "Do you need me to come in, sir?"

"I'm so sorry. I know it's your day off, but Stella really needs some help, and three other servers are out today because they're sick or their allergies are acting up. You don't have anything planned for today, do you?"

She thought about her training schedule for this week—mostly endurance and Blade work, with a bit of healing practice if there was time. Justin would be upset if she canceled without any prior notice, but she hadn't been able to pick up many shifts in the past several months due to her packed schedule, and she needed cash desperately. On top of that, her father would become very suspicious if she began asking him for money. He still assumed she was working almost every day after school when, in fact, she was in Estona. She didn't want to think of a new alibi when her job was much more convenient.

"Um, no, I don't, Mr. Newman." She started her car. "I can be there in fifteen minutes."

"Thank you so much! Really appreciate ya!"

"No problem." She ended the call and then sent a quick text to Braedon notifying him of the change.

"He'll understand," she mumbled as she put on her seatbelt. "He always does."

* * *

Two hours later, Rianne leaned against the front counter with a huge, exaggerated sigh. Her friend and co-worker, Stella Cassy, laughed. She was behind the counter, holding the notepad she used to take orders. Stella was a beautiful, dark-skinned senior from Andrew High. When Rianne first got the job, Stella had welcomed her with open arms. The two had decided to give themselves a quick little break before the next rush came in.

The owner of the restaurant was a Felix native. His grandfather opened the restaurant in the early 1960s, and it had remained family owned ever since. It was a favorite hole-in-the-wall place in the city. The restaurant had the look of a log cabin and was decorated with Texas symbols and knickknacks, giving off the feel of a welcoming home. The menu contained Texas- and Mexico-influenced dishes, all of which Rianne loved. She enjoyed working there. The owners and their family and her coworkers were fantastic.

"It's not that bad, Rianne," Stella said, always the more optimistic of the two.

"Really?" Rianne gave her a dumbfounded look.

"No."

"Well, would you still be saying that if you had to come in on your day off?"

Stella tried to find a counterargument but then shook her head in defeat. "No."

"Exactly."

"Well, at least you get to spend an extra day with me!" she said, throwing her arms around Rianne's neck. "Aren't you happy?"

"Happy isn't the word I'd use," Rianne replied, though a smile tried to edge onto her face.

Just then they heard the jingle of the door opening, and a family of two adults and five kids walked in. Rianne and Stella looked at each other and then held their hands out for a rock-paper-scissors duel.

Four hand movements later, Rianne lost. "Damn it," she said as she grabbed her notepad.

"Love you!" Stella whispered. Rianne looked back at her and rolled her eyes.

* * *

"Have a great evening, guys," Rianne said to the customers, her smile hurting her cheeks. As soon as she turned around, it disappeared.

She went behind the counter with Stella. "Did you already check on your other table?"

"Yep. Four times," Stella said. "I think they're getting annoyed with me."

The front jingled again, and they both groaned. Why couldn't they just get one break? The other waiters and waitresses were busy, and their zone was the only one with available seating.

At the door was a man in a black leather overcoat with a high collar. He was also wearing a brown hat and faded blue jeans. He cast a furtive look around the restaurant.

"Your turn," Rianne said, looking down at her notepad.

"I already have that big table!" Stella said.

"So? I had to come in on my day off. You'll survive."

"You can't keep using that as an excuse!"

"Fine," Rianne said. "Rock-paper-scissors. And this time I won't lose!"

Seconds later, she lost yet again. "No!" Rianne hissed. "You rigged that! Best two out of three!"

"No, ma'am. We never do best two out of three!"

"Those who don't adapt, die, Stella!"

"Not gonna change my mind," Stella sang. "I don't have to take it, and I won't."

Rianne groaned and stomped her foot. "I'm getting you back for this."

As Rianne neared, he kept his head down, so she couldn't see his face. "Hello, and welcome to Good Texas Cookin'," she said for what seemed to be the fiftieth time that day. "My name's Rianne, and I'll be your server this evening. May I get you a drink or an appetizer to start?"

The man looked over the menu on the table, pondering the appetizer section, then reached a decision. "Yes, thank you. I'll have the tortilla chips, a water, and my Guardian who didn't show up for training."

Rianne's pen stopped writing as she stared at him. *You got to be kidding me.*

The guy took off his hat, revealing wavy brown hair, and looked up at her, revealing his brown eyes and his dazzling white teeth in a grin.

"Hello, Rianne," Braedon said. "It's good to see that you skipped training to come here and . . ." He looked her up and down, mulling over her black-and-white uniform and red apron. "Work? And through text, no less? A text? Really? You couldn't even bother to call?"

Rianne sighed in exasperation. "Oh, come *on*. You tracked me down?"

Braedon shrugged and smirked. "What else would I have done? We have training today."

"But my boss called me in and—"

"No, no, no, my dear." He stood and placed his fingertips on the table. "We had a deal. We arranged your weekly schedule so you could still work and have some semblance of free time, but training comes first."

Rianne pursed her lips. "I'm in so much trouble, aren't I?"

He shrugged. "That depends. I should give you *some* kind of punishment for skipping, leaving me worried like that."

Rianne couldn't help but smile. He had been worried about her?

"Well, there goes the day off I was going to give you next week."

Rianne's mouth fell open. "I was going to get a day off? Wait! Can't we—"

"Nope. Decision's been made. Now, come on, let's try to salvage what we have left of training today, shall we?" He held out his hand to her.

Rianne looked back toward where she had been talking to Stella, but she wasn't there anymore, probably checking on one of her tables. Rianne couldn't just leave in the middle of her shift. That would get her fired for sure.

"Braedon, two things—"

"It's always 'two things' with you."

"Shut up. One: you can't just teleport in the middle of a public place like this. Are you insane? And two: I can't just leave. Mr. Newman will fire me, and then what'll I do?"

Braedon cocked an eyebrow and gave her an incredulous look. "Do you really think I'm stupid enough to teleport in a public place?" When she nodded, indicating she thought he was, he narrowed his eyes at her. "I'm insulted. This certainly isn't my first time in the Standard world. And you're more worried about a job than the lives of thousands of innocent people, not to mention your own?"

Rianne rubbed her cheek, thinking. "Well, when you put it like that . . ."

He turned toward the front door. "So, what are you waiting for? C'mon." He held out his hand.

Rianne smiled as she took his hand. As soon as they touched, she felt warmer, and her heart raced. Did he feel it too? He didn't move for a moment, just squeezed her hand, holding it tighter. Then he looked into her eyes and smiled.

"Whoa!" Rianne gasped as he pulled her out the front door. She jogged in an attempt to keep up. "Want to slow down a bit?"

"Sorry, my dear," Braedon replied, weaving in and out of cars in the parking lot. "There's much to do."

Chapter Twenty-Two

"**B**raedon, you do realize I could still be at work earning an honest living, right?" Rianne asked, lying on her back in the tall grass of the high school's quad. She had changed into her customary training outfit, which consisted of shorts and a tank top. Instead of the training center, Justin had switched up the scenery and was holding practice in a section of the quad before Sterlings arrived for school.

The only problem was, Justin wasn't here.

Braedon was sitting next to her instead, playing with some of his Affera as they made witty banter with each other. Enough time had passed, though, for them to see the sunrise and the sun to begin its trek across the sky.

"Yes," Braedon replied, his tone indicating he didn't care about her dilemma. He played with some air, making little tendrils appear around his fingers.

"So, aren't you going to take me back *before* I get fired?"

"I believe you mean before you get *yourself* fired." He continued to play with the air tendrils. "You're the one who decided to get a job."

Rianne rolled her eyes in exasperation. "For your information, I had a job before I ever met you."

"And for *your information*, you were the Guardian before you even learned about jobs."

She hated it when he was right, especially when he used her Guardian status.

"I do apologize on Justin's behalf, though. The lad is more than an hour late—which I will talk to him about later. However, we shouldn't waste any more time doing nothing."

"So, what do you propose we do, wise Advancer?" she asked, propping herself up on her elbows.

He gave her a sly look, then stood and brushed his pants and jacket off. "I propose that *I* help you train. We will have plenty of time before I have to cover for Advancer Nikolai."

She looked him up and down. "Do you really expect me to take you seriously? How are you even going to move?"

"Of course I'm not wearing this," he said. He twirled his hand twice, and, starting at his chest, moved it down to his shoes. After his hand passed over a section of clothing, it changed. Now instead of wearing the hideous black cloak, gray sweater, faded pants, and worn-down shoes, he was sporting a pair of loose black pants that tapered at the ankle, a black tank top, and white running shoes. "Is that better?"

Rianne stood too, shamelessly looking him up and down. "*Much.* And maybe you can help me with the problem we've been having."

"Which is?"

He already knew what the problem was; he was just being a smartass. "I still can't summon my Blade when I'm frustrated, like that night when I first met Justin. I can make it appear with the happy feeling but not when my back's against the wall or I'm faced with an abrupt challenge, you know?"

Braedon chuckled. "Well, of course that makes it more difficult. Affera operates off of positive feelings. It doesn't really come to be when one is angry, and when it does, it's more ominous, thus making it harder to summon. To fix this—since it isn't your natural state—you just need to concentrate harder."

Rianne raised an eyebrow. "Isn't that always the all-important answer?"

"Okay, then, let's make you mad," Braedon said, cracking his knuckles. He snapped his fingers, and his form changed. His hair turned stylishly messy, and his eyes turned blue. A smirk crossed his lips. He looked just like Logan.

He *was* Logan.

"Not funny, Braedon," Rianne said as she backed away.

"Who said this was funny?" Braedon asked in Logan's voice. He took a couple of steps toward her. "This is real."

"Braedon, knock it off," she said, her hands beginning to sweat and itch. What made him think this was a good idea? She wasn't scared of Logan—not anymore—but seeing him there in her domain, in Estona, pissed her off.

"Don't be scared, little Guardian," Logan mocked. He pushed Rianne hard on her shoulders. "Get angry. What are you going to do? Nothing? Figures." He pushed her again.

"Quit it!"

"Make me, then!" Logan shouted. "You didn't make me stop before, so what are you going to do to make me stop now?" He grabbed her arms and threw her to the ground with surprising strength, straddling her.

She felt something stirring in her palms. Her heart raced, and her blood boiled. She even felt her anger in her teeth. Amber waves of brilliant, glowing energy swirled around and through her fingers, ready for her command. "Get off me!" she shouted. She bridged her hips, and he fell forward on his palms. She meant to grab one wrist and put him in a joint lock, breaking his shoulder, but an amber glow flowed from her hands, sending him flying several feet away.

He landed on his back, doing a perfect breakfall, then changed his appearance back to Brandon again. *Good,* she thought, not knowing how much longer she could have looked at Logan's face.

"There you go!" he said, his voice his own again too. He summoned his red Blade. "You just summoned your Blade through anger. Mine was through the normal method of calm energy. With our two different Blades, this session should be fun. But before we begin . . ." He grinned as she stood, her Fuora making her arms feel deliciously warm. "Let's make this a bit more interesting."

"How so?"

"The first person to pin the other wins."

"Wins what?" she asked, intrigued.

"You'll see when I win." He winked at her. "Ready?"

Rianne replied with her next attack, officially starting the training session.

Over and over again, attacking, blocking, and sometimes almost blocking. Blocking had been Rianne's weak point over the past couple of weeks, and Braedon's Blade was hitting her with so much power that she could practically feel the bruises forming.

"You've been doing really well with your offensive, Rianne, but when you need to block an attack with your Blade, you have two options. The easiest one is creating a shield." He demonstrated by forming an X with his wrists, and his Blade materialized in front of them. Then he moved his hands apart and spread his arms like they were wings, and the Blade created a shimmering screen in front of him for about four seconds before disintegrating. "Try it," he said as he threw another attack.

Rianne followed Braedon's instructions, making an X, and then made a fluid motion in front of her as the attack came. A shimmering, translucent barrier appeared, hard and steadfast. Braedon's Blade hit the shield, shattering and dissolving into nothing. A moment later, her barrier disappeared.

"Good. Now the second method is to send the attack back to the attacker, but this one takes some concentration, which may be a bit hard for you."

Rianne rolled her eyes. "Just tell me how to do it."

"You make a quick, fluid motion with your hands in front of you, as if you're physically pushing it back to me." He demonstrated. "Try it."

Another shot came, and Rianne stepped forward, placing one leg in front of the other. *Concentrate, concentrate, concen—* Her mind wandered, and the Blade didn't appear the way it should have. The attack hit her in the face, and she stumbled back.

Braedon chuckled. "I told you that you need to maintain your focus! Do you want to try again?"

"No, I don't want to try again!" Rianne said, rubbing her face. "Damn it, that hurt!"

"Shake it off! We have more work to do! Let's go back to the offensive. We'll come back to that move after you've recovered."

They worked on the offensive for a few minutes more until Braedon teleported closer to her, ending with another Blade attack.

"Whoa!" Rianne shouted, jumping out of the way as she dodged the attack. "What the hell was that?"

Braedon laughed at her surprise. "To have a good offense with Affera, you need to have an open range of movement to prevent others from landing an attack on you. Craftiness doesn't hurt either. If you can catch your opponent off guard, your advantage increases tenfold."

The two began fighting again, alternating between using their Affera and hand-to-hand combat. Rianne was getting tired, but regular training had built her stamina and strength. She knew Braedon was taking it easy on her, though. He had been alive for over two hundred years, so his combat skills were impeccable.

Braedon said that anything that catches my opponent off guard will be an advantage, she thought. She redirected one of his hits with her forearm and punched him in the face. What could she possibly use against Braedon that would surprise him? He probably knew every trick in the book.

As she got herself out of a headlock, an idea came to her.

"Hey, Braedon," she said between hits. "I don't think I've told you how nice that shirt looks on you."

Braedon was preparing to throw another punch, his hand covered in Blade, but he stopped and glanced down at his shirt, then back at her. His cheeks turned pink. "Pardon?"

"It really does! It shows off your body really well, you know. I like it. A lot."

He opened his mouth to say something, but nothing came out. He was practically frozen.

Now.

She threw a powerful wave of the Blade into his stomach. He grunted and hunched over. "How much advantage did that little trick give me?" she asked, her chest heaving.

Braedon chuckled, a cocky look still on his face. "Not much, Rianne." In a flash, he was right in front of her. He grabbed her hands, and Rianne winced as their powers created a bright flicker of light.

Their interlocked hands were trembling from the strain of trying to control their raging power levels. Her arm muscles ached, and her fingers burned. Neither of them wanted to be the first to break. She looked down at the ground and closed her eyes, concentrating on her breathing. *It's just like any other workout,* she told herself. *If I keep breathing, the pain will go away.*

Braedon grunted with exertion. "This is getting very difficult," he said. She looked up at him and saw one of his irresistible grins. His hair was wet with sweat, beads of it rolling down his face. "You're making this hard for me, Rianne."

"Well, you're not exactly making it easy for me." *It doesn't actually hurt. It doesn't actually hurt.*

"You know, out of the six Guardians I've helped train, you're definitely the best so far—and the most powerful." He grunted again.

"I am?"

"Yes. Your hand-to-hand combat is coming along extremely

well, and your Blade definitely packs a punch. There's something about you that I can't seem to figure out. I find you very . . . what's the word I'm looking for? Very—"

Suddenly, their hands shook back and forth. On her right was the quad. On her left was the hill that Braedon and Ellis had toppled down on her first visit there.

"Mind telling me what's going on?" she asked as their hands jolted to the side again.

"It's like a magnet. Like I've told you before, we're both very, very, *very*, powerful magical beings—you being the stronger, of course. Your Fuora and my Affera could just be contradicting each other so much that—whoa!"

Before he could finish, they fell and tumbled down the hill.

They winced and shouted as they rolled over each other, unable to control their speed or separate. Rianne's head was pounding, and she felt sick.

"Oof!" she exclaimed as she landed hard on her back. She thought she saw stars, the sun in her eyes taunting her with its harsh rays. Then Braedon's face replaced it. He had her trapped, straddling her, her hands still locked in his.

"I win," he said, a smug look on his face.

Rianne rolled her eyes in annoyance. *Damn it! I forgot. I could've gotten him up there!* "You wouldn't have won if I had remembered the stupid bet. But are you proud of yourself, Advancer?"

Braedon still had the smile on his face, minus the arrogance. "That sounds like an excuse. And yes, I am. I beat the Guardian, so that's always a plus."

She tried to move, but he kept her still.

"You did extraordinarily well for your first try using the Blade while angry. It's difficult to control magic in that state, but you handled it with grace. And like I said when we first met, you have a lot of power that's still waiting to be tapped. I'm very proud of the progress you've made over these five months."

Rianne smiled, feeling nervous again. He still hadn't gotten off of her, and he was just staring with that adorable yet annoying smile on his face.

"You remember The Lion King?"

The question caught her off guard. "Yeah. It's one of my favorite movies. Why?"

"Remember the part when Simba and Nala find each other after all that time, and they're both tumbling down the hill, like we just were?"

"Yeah," Rianne said. "Simba landed on Nala, and that's when . . ."

"They fell in love," Braedon finished in a quiet voice.

Rianne's heart stopped, and a shiver ran down her spine.

Ask him. Just ask him.

"Braedon . . . what do you see when you look at me?"

"I see a beautiful, powerful young woman who is capable of so much. And I see a girl whom I really care about."

A breath hitched in her throat as Braedon stared into her eyes, searching. His eyes . . . there was something about them. They were deep brown and wholesome. Caring.

He glanced at her lips a couple of times. Rianne's heart was racing. Could he feel it? He leaned down toward her—

Someone cleared their throat. "Am I interrupting something?"

Rianne and Braedon turned their heads to see Justin standing there with his arms crossed and a knowing look on his face.

Braedon got up, not looking at her again, and brushed his pants off. "Hello, Justin," he said. "It's about time you got here. Where have you been?"

Justin shrugged. "Sorry. Overslept. Sue me. But I don't think that's the big conversational topic here."

"Nothing happened."

"I think Miss Guardian here would beg to differ."

"What? Oh! I mean, no, I wouldn't, because, like Braedon said, nothing happened." Rianne and Braedon glanced at each other, then looked away.

Justin blew air out through his lips. "Yeah," he said. "Okay."

"Where's your Mentor, Justin?" Braedon asked.

Justin looked toward the school. "He just got here. I think he wants to talk to you, actually."

"Yeah, I figured. Thank you. I'll see you." He glanced over at Rianne one last time. "Uh, I'll see you both later." He left without another word.

Justin walked over and held out his hand, and Rianne allowed him to pull her to her feet.

"What just happened between you and Braedon?"

"I told you, nothing." She averted her eyes. "He was helping me train since you were late."

"I said I'm sorry."

"No you didn't."

"*Anyway*, how did it go? What did y'all work on?"

"Summoning my Blade when angry. Which I can do now!"

Justin gave her a high-five. "No way! We've been working on that for weeks! What did he do to bring it out of you?"

"Do you know Logan Richards?"

Justin shrugged. "Yeah, I guess. Plays football, right?"

"Braedon pretended to be him."

"Oh."

Judging by his response, Rianne knew that Justin had been debriefed.

"Yeah. Don't copy what Braedon did. Let's find another way."

Justin held up his hands. "No problem. We can do that. Well, we still have a bit of time." He checked his watch. "About thirty minutes. Let me think of something that would get you worked up, so we can do some more practice. You go warm back up over there, and I'll meet you shortly."

Chapter Twenty-Three

I *'m so bored,* Matt thought as he cruised downtown in his police vehicle. He was one of the officers assigned to patrol on Wednesdays, and it was one of the things he enjoyed least about his job. Nothing happened on his patrols. He would occasionally run across a public disturbance or a driving violation, but that was about it. He didn't even have his partner, Benjamin, with him—he was filling in for another officer.

Matt turned onto the road that led to the city's technology district. Well-established and up-and-coming businesses had their main headquarters there. The majority of the businesses were technology based, but some didn't fall into that realm.

As he drove through one of the parking lots, moving down the long lines of cars, something caught Matt's eye. In a corner of the lot, away from pedestrian traffic, was a juvenile in his late teens, wearing a black beanie, a long-sleeve black T-shirt, and black jeans even though it was warm out. He was crouched beside the passenger door of a gray Honda, seemingly deep in concentration.

What the hell is he doing? Matt wondered as he stopped his car. The teen didn't seem to hear Matt pull up or open his car door.

Unobtrusive

As Matt drew closer, he heard a sharp, scraping metallic sound and realized the kid was etching an intricate flame design with a key.

"Hey! Hey! Stop!" Matt shouted.

The teen looked up at Matt, then took off running.

"Hey! Hey, come back here!" Matt shouted as he chased him.

The juvenile moved fast; it looked as though he was a quarter of a mile away in a matter of seconds. There was no way Matt could catch him.

Matt keyed his lapel mic and radioed for backup, though he thought there was no way anyone would make it in time.

Moments later, however, as he turned to head under one of the freeway bridges, he heard sirens going off, and police cars zoomed past and above him.

Well, I stand corrected.

When he reached two other police cars and his fellow officers, the teen was on the ground. His hands were behind his back in handcuffs, and the pockets of his sweat jacket were being searched by Nancy Schmidt, an older officer. The juvenile was struggling but not enough to cause a problem.

"How close were y'all?" Matt asked as he approached, breathing heavily from the run. He was conditioned, but it still tired him out.

"Not that far," Nancy replied. She pointed at the freeway above. "We were cruisin' along when we got the call. Just took the exit and headed where you told us the suspect was runnin' to."

"Fantastic. Find anything?"

"Just some matches and some cash." She showed them both to him. "Nothin' else, though. Okay, pal, get up!" She grabbed the teen's arms and forced him to his feet. She smiled at Matt, knowing what he was thinking.

"Okay, Jarrett, here you go. Your find, your capture." She passed the teen to Matt. "I'll remain in the chain of evidence for the matches and put them into evidence."

Matt winced as soon as he touched the teen's hand. A shock went through him, and it hurt a lot more than a normal shock from static electricity would. "Damn it."

"What?" Nancy asked.

"Nothing. I just felt a shock, but damn, that hurt. It was just the handcuffs. Forget it. Anyway, thank you, Schmidt. Y'all planning on heading to the parking lot?"

"Yeah. While you take care of him, Ramirez and I will find the owner and let them know the situation and how best to go forward from here."

"Thanks." He passed her his keys, and all but one of the other officers, Benjamin, got in their vehicles and left.

Benjamin went through the kid's pants pockets until he found his wallet. "William Rogers," he said, looking at the teen's ID. "Oh! Lookie here, you just turned eighteen!"

Matt advised William of his Miranda rights, then he and Benjamin took him back to the station. William didn't say a word the entire time.

Once at the station, Matt brought William into the interrogation room. It had dull gray walls that gave the place a gloomy feel.

He sat William at a metal table, keeping the cuffs on him. Matt sat on the other side of the table. William didn't seem like he cared that he was there. His face was lifeless, and looked bored.

Matt had William fill out his Miranda rights form. For some reason, he decided to waive his rights. Matt tried to make some small talk to get the kid to relax, but William just responded with one-word answers or shrugs.

"So, do you want to tell me why you keyed that person's car?"

"Not really."

"Does it belong to someone you know?"

William looked at him and shrugged. "No. I was just bored." His voice was so dead it made Matt a little disheartened, just listening to him.

"So, this wasn't a personal vendetta?"

"No."

"Okay. Did you hear me telling you to stop?"

"Uh-huh."

"You saw I was a cop, right?"

"And?"

"Do you know how serious it is to run from an officer? Resisting arrest?"

William nodded, followed by a slow blink.

"Do you know what charges you can receive now that you're eighteen?"

William shrugged again. "I'm assuming that you want me to say yes?"

Matt raised an eyebrow. "Do you know that keying a car is a Class C misdemeanor? You can get fined five hundred dollars for that. And if the damage is substantial, it's bumped up to a Class B, and the fine is two thousand dollars and up to one hundred and eighty days in jail."

Another shrug. "My father's life insurance can cover it. And I've been to juvie. Jail can't be that much different."

"A real-life jail makes juvie look like an amusement park. How long were you there?"

"Six months."

"So, you survived six months in juvie." Matt laced his fingers behind his head. "And you think you can take on jail with no problem?"

"I can handle myself just fine," William said. "And if anyone *tries* anything, they'll learn quickly not to."

"What landed you in juvie, son?"

"Fighting. And other things."

"Hm. Well, would you like to go to actual jail this time? Seems to me like juvie didn't teach you much."

William didn't reply.

Matt sighed, running his hand over his face. *What to do with this one?* William's father was no longer in the picture, since he had mentioned life insurance. "Is your mother still around?"

William rolled his eyes. "I live with her."

Matt nodded. "Okay, Mr. Rogers, I'm going to let you go—this one time—but if I get any more trouble out of you, you're not getting any sympathy from me."

He stood up, noting how William had rolled his eyes again, and unlocked the handcuffs. As soon as he was freed, William headed for the door, but Matt grabbed his arm. "Oh, no, sir. I'm gonna take you home myself to make sure you don't do anything else stupid."

William groaned and clenched his fists.

"Oh, stop complaining. You could have it a lot worse."

Chapter Twenty-Four

J essica jumped at the sound of the doorbell as it reverberated through the empty apartment. She had been alone all day since she didn't have work scheduled. The television wasn't even on; he had told her to turn it off before he left, and she wouldn't dare disobey him. She had tried it a few times—even attempted to put the remote exactly where it had been the night before, made sure the show was exactly where he had paused it— but he always knew.

The doorbell chimed again. She got up from the couch and went to the front door. When she opened it, she gasped. A uniformed policeman—not a bad-looking one either, she noted with shame—was standing there with her son!

"Oh, my goodness! William! William—what? Officer, what's going on here?"

"Good evening, ma'am," he said. "Are you this young man's mother?"

"Yes I am. What's going on?"

"I'm Officer Jarrett with the Felix Police Department. Mr.

Rogers here was apprehended for destruction of property and resisting arrest."

Jessica covered her mouth with her hands. "What? Again? William! Sir, I'm so s—"

Matt held up his hand to silence her. "I've let him off with a warning—for now. The next time he's caught doing something like this, though, I'm going to arrest him. Is that understood?"

Jessica nodded. "Yes! Yes! Oh, Officer, this won't happen again. I'm so sorry for the trouble he's caused." She took William's arm as Matt handed him over. "It won't happen again. I promise."

"I hope so. Enjoy the rest of your evening, ma'am."

Jessica watched as Matt walked down the stairs and got into his car. When he looked back and saw her still watching, he smiled and waved at her. She blushed and waved back, then closed the door. Something about him was familiar. His voice or maybe his look? What was his last name again? Jarrett?

William was gone from her side, scouting the fridge for the one thing he always wanted from it—alcohol. He took out a beer and sat at the small kitchen table, not looking at her.

"William Skylar Rogers, what did you think you were doing? Are you crazy?"

"Oh, would you just shut up?" William took a gulp of the beer and started messing with his phone. If she tried to stop him, he wouldn't listen.

She took a deep breath. It was probably time to tell him. It was now or never. She had hoped it would be never, but life wasn't that easy. "Um, William, honey, while you were out today, I, well, I—"

"Just say what you have to say," he growled. "It isn't that hard to talk. Geez."

Jessica gulped, swallowing an ounce of her gallons of fear. "Okay. Um, today while you were out, I went to the local high school and talked with the principal. I just talked with him, I swear. I asked if you would still be able to enroll so you could get back to earning a diploma. He said if you come in on Monday or sometime next week, the process can get started."

William choked on his beer mid-swig. "You did *what*? What the hell were you thinking?" He slammed his drink and phone on the table, then stood up and advanced toward her. He was tall, and he towered over her.

"William, William, please." She put her hand out in front of her and backed up in panic. "I only did it for you. I was only thinking of you. William, you're eighteen and still a junior." She bumped into the back of the couch. "I thought it would be a good idea. Your father would have wanted you to have the opportunities it could get you—"

"Don't even *try* to bring Father's wishes into this," he snarled, grabbing her wrists. She screamed.

"William, please don't hurt me! Please! Think about all the possibilities it'll create for you. You'll be able to figure out what you want to do with your life. You'll make so many new friends, maybe meet a nice girl, or—"

William's grip on her wrists loosened, and he gave her a quizzical look as if remembering something. "You know, you actually might be right for once in your miserable life. Fine, Mother. I'll go to school."

He let go of her and went down the hallway to his bedroom.

Jessica's breathing was heavy and labored. She didn't like it when her son did such things to her. She didn't like the way it felt—the feeling that she was getting shocked . . . the way her chest hurt after the conflicts ended.

But she had gotten William to agree to return to school. At least she'd done that much.

Chapter Twenty-Five

"So, Rianne, when did WWII start?" Alexandria asked, holding her history textbook open in her hands.

"In 1939, when the Nazis invaded Poland." She definitely knew that one.

"Good. And it ended . . ."

Rianne bit her lip. This one should be easy. "Um . . . 19 . . . 40 . . ."

Rianne and Alex were outside the main quad doors on Monday morning, waiting for the first bell to ring. They both had a test in their history class during second period, and they were quizzing each other on important dates. The weather was comfortable, but it would get warmer as the day went on. Springtime in Texas tended to be off kilter. Many other students were also in the quad, either studying or talking.

"Come on, Rianne! You got this one! Remember the song I made?"

Rianne rolled her eyes. "Please don't—"

"The war started in 1939, but it would end in six years' time!" Alexandria looked so proud of her little tune.

Unobtrusive

"And you did." Rianne sighed. "Forty-five. The war ended in 1945. Do you have to make songs for everything?"

Alex held up her hands in apology. "Songs help me remember things better! And they're fun!"

"If you say so, friend." Rianne took the book and flipped through some pages. "Okay, um . . . when did Pearl Harbor happen?" Alex was about to answer, but Rianne cut her off. "And no singing!"

"How else am I going to remember it if I don't sing it?"

"Well, you sure can't sing during the test!"

"I can in my head!"

"Ugh, fine. Just answer."

"This attack was one of the most pivotal ones, and it happened on December 7, 19—"

Suddenly, a loud, piercing roar ripped through the quiet air. Some kids nearest to the teachers' lot began to make their way over.

"What was that?"

Rianne rolled her eyes. It was about time for her sarcastic remark of the day. "Hold on. Let me use my mind powers to figure it out."

Alex glared at her. "Rianne, you have one more time to be sassy with me."

Rianne chuckled and was about to make another sarcastic statement just to spite her when Alex shook her arm. "Oh, my God, Rianne. Look at *him!*"

A small paparazzi of teenagers had moved to reveal the source of the roar. It was a motorcycle—and a beautiful one at that. It was painted black with dark red tints mixed into it. But Rianne's eyes didn't linger on the artwork for long as its owner pocketed his keys, stepped off the bike, and made his way toward the school.

The teen had straight dark brown hair and small gauges in his ears. He was wearing black jeans, a gray shirt, and a striped belt. Over the shirt he wore a thin black jacket with the sleeves pushed up to his elbows, revealing several tattoos on his forearms. Around his neck was a chain, and on his face was a pair of sunglasses. He had earbuds in his ears. He ignored the people around him as he carried some notebooks in one hand and twirled a pen with the other.

A few girls looked him up and down as he made his way through the quad, whispering amongst themselves and giggling. The guy didn't turn to look at anyone as he walked up the sidewalk. He transferred his pen to his other hand and did something on his phone.

As he made it to the doors, though, he glanced at Rianne and Alex. Rianne felt her heart jump. He pulled his sunglasses off his face and tucked them into the collar of his shirt, revealing piercing blue eyes. He smiled—a dazzling white smile that could have melted an ice cap. Rianne felt one of her knees go weak.

What the heck is wrong with you? Be normal!

He winked at them, then grabbed the door handle and went inside.

"Wow," Alex said. "I never thought a guy could be that insanely cute."

"What about Chris?" Rianne asked as she returned her attention to her history textbook. Alex and Chris had been dating for several months by that point.

"Don't get me wrong," Alex said in a hurried voice, "I love Chris with all my heart, but that new kid . . . wow. And did you see how he looked at you?"

Rianne hit Alex's arm. "Oh, stop it! He was checking *you* out."

"No, ma'am. His eyes were locked on you. It's a good thing you wore your skirt today." She winked and nudged Rianne.

Rianne shook her head and smiled. "Stop it! Let's get back to reviewing. I'd like to pass."

"Whatever you say, Ms. 'I Have A Crush.'"

Even as Rianne continued to quiz Alex, though, Rianne felt the blush in her cheeks. Not a lot of guys had that effect on her—other than Braedon, but she wasn't getting anywhere with him. He had been avoiding her since their training session together, and she could see why. He was her Protector. He couldn't be involved with the Guardian in an intimate way.

Maybe the new kid could help distract her.

* * *

Fifth period rolled around, and Rianne was planted in English III, listening to Mrs. Carter drone on and on about *Romeo and Juliet*. She resorted to doodling in her notebook, only half paying attention. Mrs. Carter was in the midst of explaining the horrible tragedy's true meaning when the classroom door opened. Rianne dropped her pen and heard it clatter to the floor as the new kid walked in. The room was so silent that she could hear her heart beating.

You've got to be kidding me.

"I'm sorry I'm late," he said in the most perfect voice Rianne had ever heard. It was so smooth, with a hint of mystery. "Couldn't find the room. This school's pretty large."

Closing the door behind him, he passed Mrs. Carter a note.

"That's quite all right, Mr. . . . ." She looked down at the note, searching for his name, "Rogers. Welcome to Felix High. You can take a seat next to . . . ." She looked around the room, and her eyes stopped on the empty seat between Rianne and Courtney. "Miss Jarrett in the back. Rianne, raise your hand, please."

Nope. Not real life. I need to tell Alex.

Rianne raised her hand, and the new kid made his way through the rows of desks to the empty seat next to her. The other kids stared at him, some turning around to get a better look at him.

Mrs. Carter turned back to the board, resuming her lesson.

Before the new kid sat down, he bent down and picked up the pen that Rianne had dropped in her daze. "I assume this is yours?"

Rianne swallowed. She was shaking—from shock?—but she

found her voice. "Yeah, it's mine. I must've dropped it. Thanks." When he handed it back to her, their fingers brushed.

Keep your cool, she told herself. *Don't act like an idiot.*

He sat down. "I know she didn't really introduce me to the class, but my name's William," he whispered, leaning over to her.

William. That's a really nice name, she thought, smiling. "I'm Rianne. Rianne Jarrett." They shook hands, and Rianne felt an electric bolt shoot through her. She didn't know if he felt it too, but they held each other's hand a little longer than necessary.

After listening to Mrs. Carter explain that they were about to transition to group discussions, William rolled his eyes and looked at Rianne. "This is boring."

"Extremely."

"Like, mind-numbingly boring."

"Welcome to my world." She continued doodling in her notebook as papers were passed from the front down the rows.

"And you do this every day?"

Rianne smiled, feeling in her element again. "That's kind of what school is. Sounds like someone hasn't been in the education system for a while." She took a stack of papers from the girl in front of her, placed one in front of herself and William, then gave the rest to the student behind her.

"You're not incorrect." William pulled his sunglasses out of his shirt collar and put them on, then leaned his head back. She knew his eyes were closed the moment they were on his face.

"Don't come crying to me when you get in trouble," she whispered.

William blew air out through his lips. "Please. I don't cry."

"But you do get in trouble?" Rianne asked as she read over the worksheet. The first question wanted them to discuss the play's themes and why Shakespeare might have chosen them.

She saw him glance at her behind his sunglasses, a smirk on his face. "Ah, a curious little girl, aren't we?"

"I'm *not* a little girl."

"Don't worry; I can see that."

Rianne hated herself for blushing. He chuckled, closing his eyes. She had to restart the conversation or risk dying of embarrassment. "So, where did you move from?"

"New York."

"Ooh, the Big Apple. And what made you come to the Lone Star State?"

"Speaking of which, this state really loves itself," he said, his eyes still closed. "The only thing I think Texas loves more than Texas is telling outsiders how great Texas is."

Rianne shrugged. "Can you blame us? Texas is pretty great. I could give you a list—"

"Don't you dare start."

Rianne stifled a laugh.

"Anyway, my mom moved us back down here after . . . just for some job stuff. She's from here, so she's happy to be back, I guess."

"And how are you taking the move?"

He shrugged. "I'm fine. It doesn't bother me much. This city's keeping me out of trouble at least. And things have been looking up. Today I met this really pretty girl."

Rianne inhaled, willing her blushing cheeks to behave themselves. She wanted to ask about the trouble he referred to, but her mind was stuck on the "pretty girl" comment.

"Is that so? What does she look like? I can introduce y'all."

William chuckled. "'Y'all.' I've heard that word today more than I've ever wanted to hear it in my lifetime. But it sounds cute coming from your mouth."

"Take off your sunglasses, Mr. Rogers!" Mrs. Carter called.

"Told you," Rianne sang from the side of her mouth.

"Shut up," William replied in the same manner. He took the sunglasses off and rested them on his head before looking at Mrs. Carter. She opened her mouth to scold him again, but the bell cut her off.

"How does it feel to be shouted at by Mrs. Carter for the first time?" Rianne asked as she gathered her things.

William pretended to think for a moment. "I feel like I accomplished something great."

She laughed. "What's your next class?"

He pulled out his schedule, his eyes skimming the page. "Um . . . chemistry with Dorton. Room 602. Oh, God." He looked up at her. "There's a room 602? Where is that? How big *is* this school?"

"Huge. My next class is close to yours. I can take you there. I mean, I don't want you getting lost again and making an even bigger fool of yourself."

"My own personal escort. I love it." He smiled that brilliant white smile again, leaving her speechless.

Mrs. Carter stopped Rianne and William before they could walk out the door. "Come here, you two."

They exchanged puzzled looks but obeyed.

"Yes, Mrs. Carter?" Rianne said.

"I want you to tutor your new classmate to help him catch up with what we've been studying thus far this semester."

Rianne's mind went straight to Braedon and Justin—training. She didn't have any free time left to tutor William seeing as she was in training almost daily. She was having a hard enough time keeping up with all of her responsibilities, including having to make up alibis since being let go from her job after leaving during her shift. This would just be another spoke in the frantic wheel that had become her life.

"Um, Mrs. Carter, I appreciate you considering me, but I really can't do that. I already have so much to do and worry about. Why don't you get Britnie to do it? I'm sure she'd love—"

"I'm a little offended that you're so adamant about not helping me after we bonded so well," William said, pretending to be hurt.

Rianne ignored him as Mrs. Carter spoke. "I want you to take this task, Rianne. Use it as an extra-credit opportunity. You've been asking me what you could do, and this would be great for you. And, according to William, you two are already getting along nicely." The tardy bell sang. "I'll send an email to your teachers to let them know you were with me. Bye, now!" She sat down at her desk, already beginning to type.

Rianne stomped out of the room ahead of William and into the empty hallway. She had to calm down, or she would accidentally show her Blade. She squeezed her fists to keep the energy in. *Calm down. Knock it off.*

"Well, don't we have a little anger-management problem," William said, walking next to her.

"Oh, don't you even try to joke your way out of this," she said, turning on him. "I should . . . I—ugh! I don't have *time* to be doing all of this. And I really don't *want* to do it anyway."

He smiled. "Aw, you make spending time with me sound like a bad thing."

"It's not. It's just—" He raised an eyebrow at her insinuation. "Shut up. I'm going to have to figure something out. You know . . . since I have to do this for you, I want you to do something for me."

"I'll gladly do anything you want me to do to you."

"Oh, my gosh, it's nothing like that!" Rianne giggled, hitting his arm. "Since I'm doing this for you, I want you to tell me about something you mentioned in there."

"Which was?"

"Whatever this trouble is that you've gotten into."

He cursed under his breath. "I didn't mean to let that slip. I didn't want anyone knowing about that, but you seem cool enough not to freak out." He sighed, running his hand through his hair. "Back at my old school—schools, I should say—I used to fight. A lot. I used to be weak, targeted, bullied, I guess you could say. It's all been worked out now—I don't have issues with it anymore—but I didn't handle situations in the best way. If someone said something about me or my family, I responded with my fists. If someone pushed me, I hit them back.

"It got to the point that I beat this one kid up so bad that he ended up in the hospital. Internal bleeding. Was in a coma for a few weeks. I was arrested. Went through a trial and everything. They also presented evidence of other stuff that I've done—graffiti, damaging vehicles, stealing—and I was sent to juvie for six months.

"The kid woke up, and last I heard he was doing okay. When I got out, I didn't go back to school. It wasn't until we moved back here that my mom decided it was time for me to finish." He didn't look at her the entire time he told his story, just stared at the tile floor.

Rianne took a moment to process everything he had just told her. He used to fight, but it seemed to be out of self-defense. *But he hurt that one kid so bad. Does he not have any self-control?*

"I scared you, didn't I?"

Rianne looked up and found him looking at her. She shook her head. "No, William. You don't scare me."

"You don't have to lie."

She stepped closer to him. "I'm not. The way I see it, you were bullied and trying to protect yourself. And in one instance, you took it too far. You did some stupid stuff, but I hope you learned from it. You don't come off as the violent kid you just described."

William smiled. "So, you're gonna stick with me then?"

"Yep! You didn't lose the first friend you made here."

He cocked an eyebrow. "Maybe my new friend will become a friend with—"

"I will still gladly punch you. Give me your phone." He complied, and she put her number in it. She started down the hall, heading to her next class, and he walked beside her. "This tutoring thing is stupid, but I could use that extra credit. I can't be available this week or next week after school because of those responsibilities I mentioned before, but I'll try to make myself free next Saturday." She passed him his phone. "Send me a text, so I have your number." She turned right and climbed a staircase to the second floor.

Unobtrusive

"Why didn't you just do it when you had my phone in your hands?" William asked.

"Because I'm leading you to class, and you're not doing anything."

"That doesn't make sense, but whatever." He smiled as he sent her a text. "Read it," he said.

She took her phone out of her pocket as it vibrated and opened the text.

> I've known you for a total of thirty-five minutes, and you've already given me your number.

> Are you sure you're not wanting to take advantage of me?

Though Rianne secretly did, she rolled her eyes and shoved him. "Shut up, William. You should be *honored*."

Chapter Twenty-Six

Justin received Rianne's excited group text about some new kid named William Rogers. As he and Alexandria walked toward her, she was practically buzzing with energy as she ushered them to walk faster.

"Oh, my God, Rianne, we got your text!" Alex squealed as she sat down. The two girls locked hands as though they were attempting to keep each other contained. "Tell me everything!"

As Rianne went into detail about her interaction, Justin pulled out the notes app on his phone. They had training after school that day, and he hadn't planned for it as he normally did. *Okay, light stretch for a warm-up, then straight to weight training. Let's do legs today. Then we'll work on Muay Thai techniques, then Blade work.*

Justin tuned back in when Rianne said his name. "Justin, stop acting like Chris and pay attention!"

"Hey!" Alex said, laughing. "Chris pays attention!"

Rianne and Justin gave her a knowing look. "He's popping and locking half the time," Justin said.

"That's just what happens when you're such a great dancer in one of the best studios in Felix," Alex said in a dreamy voice.

Unobtrusive

"Y'all, there he is!" Rianne said in a hushed voice as she pointed to another bench about eighty feet away.

"No need to whisper," Justin said, grinning. "Don't think he can hear you." Rianne swatted at him but missed as she glanced at William.

Justin looked over to where Rianne had been pointing and saw William and a few other boys standing together in a group, talking. All of them had an alternative style, but William stood out, especially with the tattoos. Once Justin identified which one was William, a chill rippled down his spine. He couldn't explain why, but something about the boy made Justin uneasy.

As though he could sense them looking at him, William glanced over at the trio. When he saw Rianne, he smiled, looked her up and down, then gave her a "what's up" nod. Rianne turned bright red and smiled back before looking away and giggling with Alex.

Then William made eye contact with Justin. Justin's breath became shallow and frantic at the same time. A ringing sounded in his ears, deafening him. Once again, he couldn't explain why he felt that way, but he hated it. William gave him a split-second glare before returning to his conversation.

Justin felt like his body had just been taken and then given back to him. No one seemed to notice his momentary lapse. He looked at Rianne with worried eyes. Something about William was off, and he didn't want his best friend to get hurt again. She had already gone through so much. Even though he wasn't her Protector, he sure as hell wasn't going to allow her to go through such pain again. She had told him that she didn't want to be weak anymore, and as her Mentor, he would ensure that.

Chapter Twenty-Seven

Rianne sidestepped out of the way as Justin sent a fast slice of his Blade toward her. Then she locked her arms straight out in front of her, ramming them into his chest.

Justin tumbled through the grass in one of the center's outdoor fields but regained his footing seconds later. He sent a kick at her face, making contact.

"Pay attention, Rianne!" he shouted for the fifth time since they'd started. Normally, she would have blocked that easily.

A minute later, he sent a Blade-covered hook above her head. As she ducked, he brought his knee into her chin. "Damn it, Rianne, block!"

His phone alarm beeped, signaling the end of their session. He walked over to where it was resting on their bags and turned off the alarm. Then he placed his hands on his waist as he caught his breath, watching her as she crouched onto her knees.

"Straighten up, and put your hands behind your head. Breathe." As she followed his advice, he shook his head. "What's wrong with you?"

Rianne scowled at him. "What do you mean?"

Unobtrusive

"I mean where the hell is your head at? This is the poorest I've seen you perform in a long while."

Rianne shrugged. "I don't know. Maybe I'm just tired."

"You know how to push through that." He knew her well enough to know when she wasn't being forthcoming. "Besides, you had a rest day yesterday. Did you take your protein?" She nodded. "Then I don't see an excuse."

She looked away, her mind somewhere else.

Or *on* someone else.

"William is already distracting you," he said, crossing his arms.

Rianne gave a humorless chuckle. "You sound like a dad. Jealous because he hasn't noticed you yet?"

Justin would usually have a snarky comeback, but he wasn't in the mood. "I'm serious, Rianne. You just met the dude, and you're already slacking."

"Oh, my gosh, you're being overdramatic. So, I had one off day. Doesn't mean that all our work up to this point is null and void."

"Something's off with William," he said, coming clean.

Rianne scrunched her eyebrows at him, taken aback. "What are you talking about?"

"You know today when we saw him in the quad? I just . . . I got this feeling. This cold feeling. He glared at me. Something about him rubs me the wrong way. He isn't a good guy."

"Have you even talked to him yet?"

Justin hesitated before replying.

"All right, then," she said. "So I don't think you get to tell me what to do or who I can or can't talk to."

"Rianne, don't be dumb. Just listen to me for once."

Her eyes flashed with anger. "I know you didn't just call me dumb."

He sighed. "I didn't mean it like that. Just don't be so naïve."

"Yeah, Justin, that word makes it so much better."

At that moment, Braedon arrived. She grabbed her things and stomped past both of them.

As Justin watched her leave, his blood was boiling. Why did she have to be so stubborn?

Braedon frowned in confusion. "What's wrong with her? What happened?"

Justin shook his head in disappointment. "She's just off. She knows how to fix it, but she won't."

Braedon grunted. "I'll talk to her and keep you updated."

"Please do."

Chapter Twenty-Eight

Braedon sat at the desk in his study that afternoon, scrolling through his gallery on his phone. Pictures of Rianne flitted by in different scenarios—training, hanging out with Justin at the mansion, looking at her phone, petting a cat that had come across their path downtown, balancing a pen on her upper lip, smiling at him, her Blade surrounding her in glorious amber, causing her long hair to float around her.

There were also photos of them together. He couldn't help but smile as he stopped at one where they were both laughing up at the camera. Rianne had barreled into him in a rushed hug, wrapping her arms around his waist. He had reacted by reaching his arm around her and pulling her close. If one didn't know any better, they looked like a happy couple. Although he didn't want to admit it, he wished they were.

Braedon sighed as he went to his messages app. He needed to talk to her, just to make sure she was okay after whatever had happened between her and Justin.

Hey, is everything all right?

> Yeah, I'm fine. Why? What's up?

> Nothing . . . I was just concerned. You looked upset after training.

> Did Justin put you up to this?

> No. I'm just worried about you.

Braedon's phone didn't receive a message for over thirty seconds. Had she walked away from her phone, or was she purposefully not answering? He sent a follow-up.

Want to talk about it?

> Don't be offended, but not with you.

Braedon found himself making a sound that he couldn't describe. *I know she said not to be offended, but that hurt.* She talked to him about everything.

> Okay, I get it. But you usually talk to me about things that are bothering you.

> Well, it's hard to do that when you've hardly been around.

Braedon swallowed as his breath hitched in his throat. He had been keeping his distance lately, trying to keep their relationship strictly professional. They had been flirting and getting closer for months, which was dangerous. There couldn't be another Wise One Hakim and Guardian Elizabeth catastrophe. The photo of them together crossed his mind, and he swallowed.

> What do you mean?

Unobtrusive

> You know what I mean, Braedon. Don't act like what happened between us didn't happen.

What he sent next seemed like the right thing to do—the honorable thing to do—but he hated himself for it. Why did she have to be the Guardian, and why did he have to be her Protector? Why couldn't they just do what they wanted?

> You know why, Braedon. You know exactly why.

> Rianne, I'm sorry. I got carried away. I think we both did. You need to focus on your goal, and I have to remember that my job is to protect you. We shouldn't try to push it.

He could feel the anger and hurt behind Rianne's next message. She always tried to be strong, but he saw right through it.

> Of course you don't know what you want. One day it seems like you want me, and the next you spew this stuff about "duty."

> I'm sorry. I'll give you a couple of days off training. I'll give you some space.

> You've gotten good at that lately, so it shouldn't be too hard.

Braedon slammed his phone down, putting his face in his hands. *It had to be done. It had to be done,* he kept telling himself. But it felt wrong. Had he made the wrong decision? What was he supposed to do? He couldn't even talk to anyone about it. No one would understand. His throat tightened.

Had he lost her?

Braedon's head snapped up, his eyes glowing white. He felt

ethereal, as though his mind were floating. His lips parted on their own, and his breathing slowed as he inhaled and exhaled through his mouth. "Yes, Wise Ones?" he asked.

"Advancer Braedon," the Wise Ones replied in unison, "report to the palace immediately. We have pressing issues to speak of."

"Yes, sires. I'll be there momentarily."

Moments later, his eyes shifted back to normal, his body became his own, and his mind cleared. When the Wise Ones needed to speak with one of their Advancers, they informed them telepathically.

Braedon bit his lip as he stood, anxiety pulsing through him. Maybe they just needed another report on Rianne's progress.

Or maybe they already knew too much.

Chapter Twenty-Nine

"I've been summoned by the Wise Ones," Braedon told the two men guarding the entrance to the Wise Ones' palace. They were dressed in military attire, which was customary of all Wise One guards.

The one to his left nodded. "We have been notified of your arrival, Advancer Braedon." They both aimed a hand at the large doors behind them and then moved their arms forward. The doors responded by opening.

"Thank you, sirs," Braedon said. The guards nodded and then closed the doors once he was inside the palace.

As he walked down the red-carpeted floors and through the glorious golden halls filled with archaic, hand-painted portraits of the Wise Ones, Braedon tried to calm himself. He ran through all the options in his mind, having a gut feeling that he had done something seriously wrong. Was it his memory work into his past? Was it his "relationship" with Rianne? Could it be both? Or was it another matter altogether?

Braedon came to another set of guards outside a set of golden doors. Once the guards let him in, the doors closed behind him with a bang, mimicking the pounding of his heart as he approached the thrones.

The red carpet continued past the doors until it branched into the four different directions of each of the Wise Ones' thrones, set in a wide semi-circle—Wise One Alaric, Wise One Hakim, Wise One Emil, and Wise One Piers. They were wearing gray suits—the four preferred to look uniform. Braedon lowered himself to his right knee, bowing his head. "You asked to speak with me, sires?"

"Good evening, Advancer Braedon," Alaric said. "We assume that all is well with your protection duties of the new young Guardian?"

"Yes. Although she has gotten herself in numerous predicaments, I am doing my best to keep her safe before the Great Battle."

"And her training with Justin Allan?"

"From what Justin has reported to me, her training is coming along. Every day she grows in strength and skill."

"Very good. Now, please, Advancer. Stand."

Braedon obeyed, placing his hands behind his back, the standard etiquette when granted an audience with the Wise Ones.

"Just a few hours ago, we were told some interesting information about you," Wise One Piers said.

Braedon tried to keep his expression neutral. "Is that so, sire?"

"It is rumored that you have seen your past," Piers continued, "the past that *should* have been erased." He stole a furtive glance at his twin, who gave him a look right back. "But apparently, that was not so in your case."

"We are very interested in how you made that happen," Alaric said. "We do not make mistakes, and you are the first Advancer—to our knowledge—to rediscover old memories. So," he leaned forward on his throne, "how did you do it?"

Braedon tried to think of some lie to tell but couldn't come up with anything. All he could focus on was the fact that Ellis must have told them. Why would he do that? *Lord, what else did he tell them?*

"I don't know exactly how it happened, sires. It just . . . happened."

"Hmm . . ." Alaric said, leaning back.

Braedon knew his answer was inadequate, but he couldn't say that he'd been sitting in his study for months, concentrating on getting it back.

"What have you seen?"

Braedon took a deep breath. He didn't want to share that information with anyone but Ellis.

"Advancer?" Alaric probed.

Braedon sighed. "The last one I saw was of my younger sister and me. We, well, had gotten into an argument."

"About what?" Hakim asked. His head was resting in his thumb and index finger, a ruby ring glinting in the light.

"I . . . I don't know."

"Yet," Hakim tacked on. Braedon averted his eyes. "Anything else we should know about, Advancer?"

They already knew. They were just testing him to see what he would say. Braedon decided not to reply.

"Have you been having inappropriate relations with our recent Guardian, Advancer Braedon?" Hakim asked.

Braedon dug his nails into his hands behind his back. Ellis had told them. Ellis had told them everything. "No, sires."

"No feelings have developed since awakening the Guardian's Fuora?" Wise One Emil asked.

"I apologize, sires, but I'm afraid I don't know what you speak of. My duty is to serve as the Guardian's Protector. Nothing more."

Alaric chuckled. "Oh, how you lie, Advancer. It's understandable. You are not the first Protector to fall for a Guardian's charms."

"Do not speak ill of Guardian Elizabeth," Hakim said with an edge in his voice.

"I wouldn't dare," Alaric said, waving his hand. He turned back to Braedon. "We have reached a decision about you, Advancer Braedon. We're going to look past your indiscretion with the

Guardian due to your new ability and willpower to be able to reach back into your memories, which we made sure to erase from your subconscious, to remember some of your past life. No other Advancer has ever been able to accomplish such a feat, though we are sure many made-Advancers have tried.

"You have now become even more of an asset to us, Advancer. You have shown us that your mind surpasses those of your fellow Advancers, telling us that you are stronger than we ever could have imagined. Your drive to protect those you love, as well as protecting the Guardians for all these years, showed us that you will do the same—if not better—in a higher position. We can train you to expand your Affera and make you more powerful than you ever thought possible. In conclusion, we would be pleased to make you one of us, Braedon."

Braedon's mouth fell open. "Sires, I . . . I'm honored that I would even be considered for such a high status, but how can I possibly accept? Who would see to the Guardian? She trusts me."

Or at least she used to.

"Do not let that be a reason to refuse. There are plenty of other qualified Advancers who will be able to continue the legacy you have created as the Guardian's Protector. Perhaps your own brother would be a sound candidate."

Braedon deciphered the hidden meaning behind Alaric's words: *We will be keeping an eye on you, and this is the most convenient way.*

Braedon felt himself shaking from a number of different emotions. There was no turning away from this. He couldn't outright refuse like Elizabeth had done. They wouldn't let another powerful being escape their grasp. They would have him one way or another—even by force, if necessary.

Rianne, please forgive me.

Getting down on his right knee again, Braedon bowed his head. "It would be an honor to serve beside you as a Wise One."

Chapter Thirty

The day of the double ceremony had come. All of Estona was in attendance to witness Advancer Ellis's promotion to the Protector, followed by Advancer Braedon's ascension to Wise One.

It wasn't long after Braedon had accepted the responsibility of Wise One that the news was announced across the realm. There was speculation at every turn about what Braedon had done to receive such an honor. The only other person to be asked to serve as a Wise One was Elizabeth, the original Guardian, and that was well over 300 years ago. Braedon had received a copious number of congratulations—and questions—from his colleagues and students before having to report to the palace.

Once there, Braedon spent his days learning about the responsibilities, etiquette, and powers of a Wise One as well as reviewing Estona's written laws and policies. Every night he went to bed exhausted. He missed his home in the mansion, but when his head hit the pillow on his elegant new bed in the largest room he had ever seen, he could think of little else but sleep.

He was expected to help rule over the entire realm, and that terrified him.

Palace guards and Advancers surrounded the perimeter, keeping the Sterlings at an appropriate distance and maintaining order. The guards were dressed in their formal black uniforms, complete with a round black hat, white belt, and gloves. Some were equipped with sabers, but they were mainly for show. The Advancers—including Ellis—wore similar attire, with the exception of gold cords to proclaim their status.

The Wise Ones' apparel, and Braedon's, was the most gallant by far. They all wore black suit pants with a red jacket adorned with gold tapestries and buttons, white gloves, and a black hat with a solid gold plate across the middle. The Wise Ones' jackets included a dark blue sash that went across their chests from the left shoulder; Braedon would be presented with his sash during the ceremony.

Braedon stood before the Wise Ones on an elevated white stage. He smiled at the crowd, trying to keep his emotions under control. He was filled with apprehension. He hadn't seen Rianne in over four months. From what Ellis and Justin had reported to him, she hadn't been attending training. He was worried about her. He wished he could go to the Standard world and see her, but he knew he was being monitored.

Alaric began the ceremony by welcoming the guests and congratulating the brothers on their jobs well done as Advancers. Ellis was the first to be acknowledged, and Braedon had been chosen to perform his promotion. Braedon approached him with a thin gold-and-red sash, trying to keep the hard look off his face.

"Oh, don't look like that, brother," Ellis whispered through a smile. "This is a happy day!"

Braedon grunted. "Of course you would think so, Ellis. Status is all you seem to care about."

"Hey, you're gaining something as well! You're becoming one of the most powerful beings in Estona. I'm doing you a favor."

"I asked you not to tell, Ellis," Braedon whispered. "And you betrayed me. I *told* you time and time again that nothing was going on with Rianne and me."

"Braedon, you can lie to me and everyone else, but you can't deny that you felt something other than duty for our Guardian."

The smile on Braedon's face didn't reach his eyes. As much as he wanted to punch Ellis, he couldn't with the whole realm watching.

"Protect her, Ellis. Don't let anything happen to her. I mean it."

"No harm will come to your girlfriend, sire."

Again, the thought of punching his brother crossed his mind.

Then Braedon spoke in a loud voice that rang across the area. "Do you, Advancer Ellis, take this honor and privilege of Protector and vow to perform your role to the best of your abilities for the good of Estona?"

"I do."

"Do you, Advancer Ellis, vow to protect the Guardian to the best of your abilities, even if it means giving up your own life in the process?"

Ellis took a deep breath. "I do."

"Then I willingly pass my duties as Protector onto you. It is now up to you to keep our beloved Guardian safe until her day of destiny comes. Do us proud."

Ellis knelt before Braedon, and he placed the sash around Ellis's body. The crowd cheered, but Braedon heard none of it.

The crowd was hushed as Alaric addressed them once more. "This is a momentous day," he said. "A man we've seen grow from a Standard and come to our world and surpass what we expected him to be as an Advancer is being honored with the greatest reward.

"Advancer Braedon has shown us that not only can he handle any duty given to him, he will do so with grace and humility. Only one other has ever been given this honor, our adored Guardian Elizabeth, may her sacrifice be honored.

"He is ready to lead and serve you and my fellow Wise Ones, and I have no doubt that he will do just that. Today, you gain a new leader." He paused as the people cheered. "Today, you gain a new hope to look to in times of need." The shouting grew louder. "Today, we all gain a fellow Wise One!" Everyone lifted their voices, and Braedon couldn't help but smile when he saw some Sterlings with light-manipulation Affera shooting sparks into the air.

Braedon took his stance in front of the Wise Ones and bowed his head, which they all reciprocated.

"Do you, Advancer Braedon," Wise One Piers said, "vow to accept any consequences that may befall you as seen fit by your fellow Wise Ones and the people of Estona if you fail to carry out your duties in your new position?"

"I do," Braedon replied, struggling to keep his voice steady.

"Do you, Advancer Braedon," Wise One Emil continued, "vow to be of clear mind and judgment at all times in all matters involving Estona and her people?"

"I do."

"Do you, Advancer Braedon," Hakim asked, "vow to serve Estona to the best of your ability and put the needs of her and her people above all else, even yourself?"

"I do."

"Do you, Advancer Braedon," Alaric concluded, "take this honor and privilege of the title of Wise One and vow to perform all duties and responsibilities of a Wise One, even if it means sacrificing your own life?"

"I do."

Alaric nodded. "Then I, with my fellow Wise Ones and all of Estona as my witness, bestow you with the title of Wise One, with all the honor, responsibility, and Affera that comes with it."

The four of them each placed a hand on Braedon, closing their eyes. Braedon followed suit. His body felt warm as it began to glow. The Affera already inside of him welcomed the addition of the others that only the Wise Ones could possess, and his body became light.

A minute later, they all opened their eyes. Braedon's senses seemed heightened. He could hear individual excited whispers in the crowd and feel their Affera. He could even pinpoint who had what specific power.

Two guards approached the Wise Ones, one with a blue sash and the other with a solid gold ring. Wise Ones Hakim and Alaric took them, respectively. Braedon bowed his head as Hakim put the sash on him. After taking off his right glove, he held out his hand to allow Alaric to slide the ring onto his ring finger. The objects proclaimed him as a new ruler of Estona.

He turned around to face the crowd, holding his left wrist in his right hand, displaying the ring.

"Estona, I present to you, your new ruler, Wise One Braedon!" The cheers and shouts tunneled into Braedon's ears, and he closed his eyes and took a deep breath.

This was his life now, and he would lead it honorably.

But what would he do without Rianne in it?

Chapter Thirty-One

Courtney sighed as she made her way up the public library steps on a Saturday morning. Squinting in the sunlight, she stared at the instructions of the English project Mrs. Carter had assigned the previous week. Her laptop had just died, and her father couldn't get her a new one in time, so her only option was to use a computer at the public library—if that was still possible.

This is so stupid. Why couldn't this at least be a group project?

Not much had changed over the past few months. Logan had tried to weasel his way back to her after he'd healed up, but there was no way she was taking him back. He seemed so pathetic to her now.

Rianne still sat close to her in English, which was unfortunate, but at least they were separated by the hot new kid.

Even if he does spend all of his time drooling over stupid Rianne. What did guys see in her anyway? And why would William go for Rianne when Courtney was sitting right next to him?

Unobtrusive

As she was about to enter the library, she heard an ear-splitting roar behind her. She covered her ears and turned around. It was a motorcycle. The rider cut the engine and took off his helmet.

It was William. She didn't care why he was there, but he was. She looked up toward the sky and mouthed a silent prayer. "Thank you."

As she looked into his eyes, the bluest eyes she had ever seen, she realized it was time to turn on her charm.

"Hey, you're William, right? Aren't you in my English class?" She flicked her brunette hair over one shoulder.

William looked her up and down, and Courtney mentally congratulated herself for wearing her shorts. "Probably," he replied in a placid voice.

He climbed the steps and reached for the door. She followed. "Then how come you don't talk to me?"

"Probably because I didn't want to."

Courtney poked out her bottom lip. He was rude, but his looks made up for it. Maybe he was the misunderstood type. "Well, I'm Courtney Taylor. Are you here to work on Mrs. Carter's project?" She held up the assignment.

William sighed, realizing she wasn't going to be put off easily. "No, I have to catch up on the plot of the play and all that before she gives me the project."

"Oh! I can help you!" Courtney stepped closer to him. "We can—"

"Actually," William said, "I'm already set to study with someone. Right now, in fact."

Courtney's mood deflated. "Oh. Who, if you don't mind me asking?"

"Rianne Jarrett. She's in class with us. Know her?"

Courtney rolled her eyes so hard that it actually hurt.

"I'll take that as a yes. Don't like her?"

"To put it nicely."

William chuckled. "Well, I can't say the same."

"Wait, are you actually *into* her?" Courtney asked, dumbfounded.

William shrugged as he went through the door. "Maybe I am." He winked at her, sending a shiver of anticipation up her spine. "See you in class, Courtney."

Chapter Thirty-Two

Rianne parked her car in front of the public library at around 3:00, the time William had assigned for them to meet. They decided it was a good place to study. He didn't want anyone at his house, and Rianne didn't feel like being interrogated by her father if she brought a boy home.

Reaching into the backseat, she grabbed her backpack, which contained paper, pens, and two copies of *Romeo and Juliet,* and headed inside. William had insisted she hold onto his copy. "You're way more responsible than me," he said when she asked why she had become his personal pack mule. "Do you really want to explain to Mrs. Carter why one of her copies is missing?"

She tried to fight him on it, but he won the debate. He did that a lot.

They had only been friends for a couple of weeks, but Rianne loved being around him. He was funny and smart, even though he tried to act like he wasn't. He always found her when they weren't together, and over time she had learned quite a bit about him. He was still mysterious, though, and he never let her learn too much about his past, just bits and pieces here and there.

Alex and Chris told her that rumors were circulating that the two were hooking up or even dating already, but Rianne blew it off. Dating William *did* seem like a nice fantasy, but they were only friends. Even though he joked about it, if he wanted them to be more, he would have done something about it already.

Justin still had nothing to say about it. Training had become awkward. No more friendly banter, it was strictly professional. She hated it, but she couldn't stand that he was being so judgmental about William when he still had made no effort to get to know him.

Braedon had fulfilled his promise. He made it a point to stay away from her. He didn't even bring her to training anymore. Ellis had taken on that job. When she asked about it, Ellis said that Braedon had been assigned to a new position, though he claimed he wasn't allowed to give specifics.

After a few days, she told Ellis that she was taking an extended break from training due to her new responsibilities at school. The two had argued about it for over an hour, but Ellis soon found that the Guardian was persistent, and who was he to disagree?

Although the outside of the library was archaic, with white ivory pillars and worn-down brown steps, the books and magazines on the inside couldn't have been more modern. It was divided into two sections. On the left were books used mainly for research. On the right was the fiction section. She wasn't the reading type. She preferred art.

The library was practically empty. After greeting the librarian, she searched for William. He wasn't in the main study area, where numerous tables and chairs were set up. She wondered if he was in the lounge in the back of the library.

He was. Although there were tons of bean bag chairs that he could have chosen, William was at the only table, leaning on its small, round surface. He had his head in his folded arms. He didn't hear her approach, so she slammed the books onto the table.

He jumped and rubbed his head as if he had been hurt in the

impact. "Damn, girl, you could've just told me you were here." He was wearing his sunglasses. Weird. Who wore sunglasses indoors?

"But that wouldn't have been as fun," Rianne replied. She didn't care if she was studying with a cute boy; he was still wasting her precious Saturday. She could have been sketching out new ideas or working on her unfinished watercolor painting. "Here." She passed him his copy of *Romeo and Juliet*. "And you said you read the play, right?" She opened her notebook.

"Unfortunately," William replied, his head in his hand and his voice sounding drowsy and bored. She couldn't blame him.

"Okay, that'll save some time. We can just skip to the questions I've prepared."

He groaned.

"Oh, stop. Now, what's iambic pentameter? Shakespeare uses it a lot in his sonnets and in this play."

William sighed and put his head back in his arms. If she didn't know any better, she would've sworn he was asleep.

"Your answer would be well appreciated before the end of the century," Rianne whispered, poking the top of his head. His hair was extremely soft, like a cloud.

After another groan, his reply came out muffled. "This is stupid."

"You know, William, I think this whole thing is dumb too, but at least give me a decent answer, so we can hurry up and leave."

"Okay, okay. Um, that honestly sounds like machinery to me."

Rianne shook her head. "William, how can you be a junior and not know what this is?"

He groaned again. "I really don't care." She didn't see the point of explaining what iambic pentameter was to him; he either wouldn't listen, or he'd just forget by the time their study session was over.

"Okay, then . . . let's try an easier question. Hopefully, you can figure this one out." She skimmed the questions. "What's the main plot of the play?"

"Betrayal," he replied, though he still didn't look at her, keeping his head in his arms.

"Oh, my God." She groaned under her breath, looking up at the ceiling. "That's a *theme* in Julius Caesar, not Romeo and Juliet. William, I don't want to be here, either, you know. This isn't any—"

"I know, I know, I know. Sorry. Just . . . just give me another question, but make it easy. *Very* easy."

"Okay. This is the easiest question anyone can come up with: what are the last names of the two main characters?"

Silence. William didn't move.

"William? Answer, please." She pushed on his arm, but it was flaccid.

He's asleep. He's sound asleep.

"William, wake up!" Rianne hissed, pushing him even harder.

He jolted up. "What? What?"

She shook her head at him. How inconsiderate could he be? "William, you're being so unfair right now! I could be at home or doing something, *anything* else, but I have to be here to catch you up! And you can't even stay awake! Were you up all night or something?"

William rested his head in his hand again. "You could say that."

"Well, what were you doing?"

"Nothing, Rianne."

Rianne raised an eyebrow. "Really? You're gonna tell me that you weren't doing anything last night?"

William shrugged. "Yep."

"Then let me see these." She had an idea of what was going on, but she wanted to be sure. She snatched his sunglasses off his face before he could retaliate.

Just as she suspected, his eyes were bloodshot, and it was hard for him to focus on her. He squinted and winced as the florescent lights attacked him.

"Ha! I knew it! You were drinking last night! You were drinking even though you *knew* we had to meet up today!"

Now he looked angry. "It's none of your business, Rianne."

She crossed her arms. "It *is* my business since *I'm* the one who's wasting my time with you. Where are you even getting alcohol from, anyway? You're not even close to being legal."

William snatched his sunglasses back. "You know what? Maybe we should do this another time." He grabbed his backpack and stood up to leave.

"Oh, no, we're going to talk about this."

"We're *not* talking about this, Rianne," he said as he made his way to the front entrance.

"William? William, get back here!" She gathered her things and followed him out.

He didn't slow down as he walked out into the bright sunlight. "Would you just leave it alone?"

"Nope." She grabbed his arm and stopped him on the steps. "You know how stubborn I can be." She poked him in the chest. "Apparently, this is more than a one-time thing. What's going on with you?"

"I told you I don't feel like talking about it. And stop doing that!" He grabbed her wrist to keep her from poking him again.

A tingle went down her spine from his touch, but she ignored it. "William, I just want to help. I want to make sure you're okay. Is it the move? Just tell me why—"

"Do you have any idea how *annoying* it is for you to be this persistent? Why is it so important for you to know? Huh?"

Rianne bit her lip before answering. She knew she was getting on his nerves, but she didn't want anything to happen to him. Just driving his motorcycle there hungover was risky. He could have hurt himself or someone else. She had gotten to know him in the past couple of weeks, and it would kill her to see him get hurt.

"William, you know my dad's a cop. He's had to respond to calls where people were in car accidents because of drunk driving. He's had to go to people's houses and see that they've overdosed on alcohol. People's lives spiral out of control because of this stuff.

There are even kids at school who dropped out because they couldn't get it together. I don't want that to happen to you too."

William rolled his eyes as he took off his sunglasses. He didn't squint as hard as he had inside, and the whites of his eyes seemed to have lightened up. "Right now I'm not even that bad. I just had a bit last night and then went to sleep. I woke up when it was time to meet you, but I didn't feel like coming here today. I don't need anyone's help, Rianne. I've been managing fine on my own so far. I don't need you worrying about me, so leave me alone."

Rianne scowled at him. "Fine. If you don't care, I won't bother you anymore."

She pulled her wrist out of his grip, then went down the remainder of the steps and walked toward her car.

After a moment, William followed her. "Rianne, Rianne, wait. That came out wrong. Let me explain."

Rianne looked at him before unlocking her door and getting in. "No. You missed your chance to explain." She slammed her door.

He laughed. "You're not driving out of here when I'm trying to talk to you." Standing next to her door, he placed his hand on the hood, trying to see past the tinted glass.

"Don't tell me what to do!" she shouted, locking herself in just in case he tried opening the door. She refused to make eye contact with him. He was such an idiot. All she wanted to do was help, but he was such a jerk about it.

After throwing her stuff in the passenger seat, she turned the key in the ignition, but the engine just sputtered and refused to turn over. Rianne twisted the key over and over again, but each time it was the same. She punched her steering wheel in frustration. The car had gas; she had filled it the day before. None of the indicator lights had been flashing lately. What could the problem be?

William crossed his arms and leaned against the car. Then he knocked on her window, a knowing look on his face. Rolling her eyes, she opened the door slightly.

"There we go with that same anger-management problem."

"Shut up."

"You know, I can help with your little car issue. I'm really good with mechanical stuff."

"I bet you are. And what would I have to do in return?" she asked, finally looking at him.

"Let me take you home and allow me to answer your previous questions."

"You want me to get on your bike with you even though you're hungover?"

"I'm not as hungover as you think. Just a little tired. When I answer your questions, that'll prove it."

She sat there, contemplating. It seemed to be her only option at the moment. She didn't want to call her father while he was working. Calling a tow truck would cost money, and she couldn't just sit there all day. And he said he would tell her why he drank so heavily. Maybe things would make a little more sense with him. She might even be able to help.

"Fine."

She got out of her car and locked it. William was already on his bike. He gave her his helmet, the only one he had. "Don't worry," he said. "I'm practically a professional at this thing. I can drive a couple of minutes without a helmet on."

"You sure?"

"Yes. Now get on, and make sure you hold on tight."

Rianne got on and raised an eyebrow at him. "You just want me to hold your waist."

William chuckled. "That's just a fortunate bonus."

She slipped on the helmet—taking note of the way it smelled of aftershave—and wrapped her arms around his waist as he started the motorcycle.

"You ready?"

"Not really. I've never been on a motorcycle before."

"You'll be fine," he said, patting her thigh. "Just lean into the turns with me." She gripped him tighter as they started to move.

Rianne kept her head against his back. When they rounded a corner, she took his advice and leaned with him, but that didn't ease her fear of falling off. She was practically squeezing the life out of him. William hadn't lied, though—he was really good when it came to his bike.

The rumbling beneath her stopped when they made it to her home on Ortiz Drive. She let out a sigh of relief, glad the ride was over.

"You're such a baby," William said as she took off the helmet and shook out her hair.

"That's not very nice," Rianne said in a mock hurt voice. "That was my first time. Now, tell me what's going on with this whole drinking thing."

William sighed and turned around on the bike to face her, their legs touching. "You don't waste any time, do you?"

"Call it a talent."

He took a deep breath and exhaled. "Fine. Look, I don't drink a whole lot. But when I do, sometimes I overdo it. And I don't get hungover a lot. I just get really tired, and it shows in my eyes. I can still function and do normal things."

She gave him a look.

"*Without* hurting anyone."

"Well, why do you drink in the first place?"

He was quiet for a few moments, and he spoke, his voice was hushed. "A couple of years ago, when I was sixteen, my dad died. In a car accident."

"Oh, my God, William. I'm so sorry." She put a hand on his arm. "Someone hit his car?"

He shook his head. "No. He was hit by one. The driver didn't even stop to see if he was okay. The paramedics tried to revive him, but it wasn't enough. It was really hard for my mom and me. I used to fight and do stuff before then, but after he died, it got worse and turned into what I told you about. That's when I picked up drinking—to get my mind off of it. My mom moved us to Felix a few months ago, hoping the change in scenery would help. Sometimes I just want to forget about him for a little while. It hurts less."

"William, I'm so sorry. My mom died too. When I was two." She was about to tell him how, but she stopped herself. "It must've been really hard for you, and I'm sorry for that. But look." She took his hand. "Drinking isn't going to help. I know that your dad wouldn't want you to do that to yourself. I don't think he would want you to forget him. You have to remember him and try to make him proud. He's still alive in you if you do that."

William searched her eyes, then chuckled. "You really are something else, aren't you?"

Rianne tried to hide her blush by looking down. "I just try to help whenever I can." She got off the bike, returning his helmet and giving up her car keys. "So, you can fix my car, right?"

"Yeah. I'll have a look at it and bring it back here tomorrow. I'll put the keys under the doormat and text you. But until then, how does tonight at nine thirty sound?"

She put a hand on her hip. "What are you talking about? You just said you'd have my car ready tomorrow."

"No, you loser. I was talking about a date. Tonight. Does nine thirty sound all right to you?"

"Are you serious?" She looked behind her at the house, as if paranoid that her father was inside, listening in on their conversation.

"Yeah. I really wanna go on a date with you. You're a really cool chick, although you may be a little over the edge sometimes. And you just proved that you can handle me. I want to get to know you better." He cocked his head at her and flashed a dazzling white smile that sent shivers up her spine.

He *was* cute—very cute—and she would like to get to know him more as well. Maybe her secret wish of being more than friends was about to become a reality.

"Okay, William. I'll take you up on it. My dad will be at work tonight, so I'm free. Just don't be late."

He looked her up and down before answering. "I definitely won't be."

Chapter Thirty-Three

Rianne climbed onto William's motorcycle at nine forty that night. "You're late," he said.

"Shut up."

He started down the street at high speed, having her wear his helmet again. She was wearing black boots and a pair of jeans with a crop top. She kept her hair down. William had changed to a pair of black jeans and a nice gray shirt that showed some of his tattoos. He hadn't given her any details of the date, but she hadn't asked—yet.

As they stopped at a red light and William put his foot down to steady it, Rianne finally worked up the nerve. "So, where's our date?"

"And why should I tell you?" William asked, looking at her with a mischievous smile.

"Because you're not going on this date by yourself. So tell me—"

"Oops, light turned green!" William shouted over the roar of the bike as he took off again.

"William!" When they stopped again, he was going to hear a word or two from her.

The next time they did stop, though, they must've reached their destination because William turned the motorcycle off and pocketed his keys. They were in front of a run-down building somewhere in downtown Felix. From the outside, pulsating music could be heard, muffled by the stone walls.

"Voila," William said, extending his arm with a flourish.

"William," Rianne said, "where did you bring me?" The building looked uninhabitable. She recoiled.

He got off and walked to the line of people waiting to get in. She followed, though hesitantly.

"Calm down," he said. "It's just a club. A new buddy of mine is the manager here."

"And what makes you think I'll like this place?" Rianne asked as the line moved.

"Because I know you and what you like."

She rolled her eyes. "Oh, please. You don't know anything about me."

"I know more about you than you think, sweetheart."

She nudged him playfully, and he did the same. "So, we're going to get in through your buddy's connections?"

"Of course. The club's only for eighteen and up, and what are you, sixteen?" He reached into his pocket and pulled out his ID. By then they were close to the front.

Rianne pushed him again. "Wow, I'm offended! I turned seventeen on March twelfth, thank you very much!"

William raised an eyebrow. "March twelfth, huh? Looks like we have more in common than just our taste in music and love of Shakespeare."

Rianne smiled. "Wait, is that your birthday too?"

"Yep, March twelfth. I'm exactly a year older than you." He showed her the ID, and she raised her eyebrows in surprise.

"Don't think that gives you any power over me," Rianne said. "I'm obviously the more intelligent one."

"And what makes you think that?"

"Please tell me what iambic pentameter is again."

"Shut up," William said, snaking his arm around her waist as they made it to the front. Rianne shivered in response to his touch. Whatever effect he had on her, she loved it.

The bouncer—who sported tattoos and a piercing in his nose and lip—eyed her warily but smiled at William. "Hey, Morgan," William said as he gave him his ID.

Morgan barely glanced at it before handing it back. William had obviously been there plenty of times if the bouncer didn't even give it a second thought. "And who's this?"

William held Rianne closer. "My date."

"Oh, so William was actually able to snag a date? What a surprise."

William made a face that implied he wanted him to stop talking.

"What? Am I embarrassing you?"

"Morgan, please, man."

The bouncer chuckled. "Fine, fine, go on in." He nodded to Rianne. "Let me know if he gives you any trouble."

Rianne smiled. "Trust me, I will."

As they entered the building, William held her hand and led her down a dimly lit hallway. Rianne could hear the music better, but the cement walls still muffled it. She gripped his hand tighter.

"He didn't even ask for my ID."

"When you're friends with the manager, you become friends with everyone. Just don't bring it up, and you'll be fine."

They made a left, and a few steps later found themselves at a metal door. He turned to her. "Ready?" When she nodded, William opened the creaky handle and led her inside.

A band was playing against the back wall on a slightly elevated stage, in the midst of an energized acoustic cover of a Linkin Park song. A few people were gathered around with their drinks, singing along and socializing.

The main room, like the hallway, was also dimly lit, creating a mellow vibe. It was bigger than the outside of the building appeared. It wasn't a dance club like she had thought but more of a lounge. Tall tables, benches, couches, and booths were scattered across the floor and against the walls. Several people were occupying these areas, laughing and talking over the music. A brightly lit bar was to their left, complete with stools.

"William, this is amazing," she said as he led her toward the bar.

"I told you I knew what you liked." He pulled out a stool for her, then took the one to her left.

The bartender came and greeted William, then asked for their order. William asked for a whiskey and got Rianne a soda. The bartender checked William's ID before getting their orders.

Rianne stared at William for a moment before he noticed.

"What?" he asked.

"You know that the legal drinking age is twenty-one, right?"

William shrugged. "Not in Europe."

"We're not *in* Europe! Besides, what about your little problem that we talked about earlier today?"

William laughed and placed a hand on her thigh. "Girl, calm down. It's fine. It's only one drink. And like I said, I'm buddies with everyone. Stuff like that doesn't matter to me. You gotta relax." He gave her leg a squeeze.

The bartender brought their drinks, and they both smiled and nodded. William nodded to one of the empty booths. "Now, let's get this date officially started, so I can get to know more about you than I already do."

Rianne smiled as she walked next to him, messing with the straw in her drink. The band launched into a cover by Avenged Sevenfold, and a few people cheered.

The date was definitely going to be an interesting one.

Chapter Thirty-Four

T he sounds of a piano and guitar filled the club.

William looked toward the band, disdain written all over his face. "Is this country? Where's Tre? I'm going to kill him."

Rianne chuckled, amused by his frustration. Over the past couple of hours, they had been deep in conversation. It was nice learning new things about William. He loved cars and motorcycles —he was even thinking of going to a trade school to become a mechanic. He also worked out, which didn't surprise her. From the first day she saw him, she was captivated by his toned physique. He liked art too. He showed her some of his sketches on his phone, and she was impressed. He became more amazing as the night went on.

A few people had come over to socialize with William—mostly pretty girls who smiled when they spotted him. They practically fawned over him.

The guys would acknowledge and exchange words with Rianne, but the girls pretended she didn't exist. Why was William there with her when so many pretty, older girls knew him? Whenever one tried to start a long conversation, William would say, "I'm actually on a date right now, so if you don't mind?", and they would leave. That always filled her with renewed confidence. He only wanted her.

"Hey, country isn't that bad," she said.

"Says the one born in the South."

"It's not! I think they're playing Brad Paisley. He's one of my favorites. He has a nice crooning voice and a super handsome face."

William rolled his eyes. "Am I getting jealous of a famous country singer you're never going to meet?"

Rianne leaned forward. "I don't know. Are you?"

"Well, maybe I can do something that'll put me above him." He stood and reached his hand out to her. "Would you believe me if I told you I can dance?"

"I'll have to see it to believe it."

"Challenge accepted." He took her hand and led her to the dance floor where other couples were dancing slowly in time to Paisley's smooth voice. He took her left hand in his right and wrapped his other arm around her waist. She put her free arm around his neck.

The lyrics were about the singer telling a girl she was his whole world.

William was looking at her, but she tried to avoid eye contact, staring at his chest instead. Even after getting to know him these past few weeks and during their date, William still made her nervous. Being so close to him in such an intimate setting wasn't helping. What if he wanted to kiss her? She had yet to experience her first kiss. What she was supposed to do was still a mystery to her, not to mention her traumatizing past with men wanting to take advantage of her.

"Rianne?" She knew he was trying to get her to look at him, but she held her ground. His voice dropped to a whisper as he leaned in closer. "Rianne, look at me. That's what people do when they slow dance together. It's kind of a rule to make eye contact."

She pressed her lips together, then tilted her head up to look at him. There were his beautiful blue eyes again, always sending those glorious shivers up her spine. But now he was looking at her differently.

She was about to give a witty remark, but he spoke first. "I know it's only been a couple of weeks since I met you, but I just want you to know that I like you. Really like you, I mean...there's something about you that just draws me to you. I really, *really* like you."

Her eyes widened. Had he just said that?

She took a deep breath. "I know what you mean. I feel drawn to you too." She wanted to say more, but her mind was a jumble of thoughts that caused her to forget what speech was.

A minute later, William said her name again. When she turned back, he gently took her face in his hand, then leaned in close and put his lips on hers.

Rianne didn't know what to think. It was her first kiss. Her first kiss was with William. William Rogers. It was amazing. He was amazing.

But then the intrusive thoughts came.

You get to be all mine tonight.

Her blood ran cold, and she pulled away.

"Rianne, what—"

"I'm sorry, William. I have to go."

She made her way to the front door. Other people were trying to get in, but she pushed past them until she was outside.

"Rianne! Rianne, wait! Come back!" He was coming after her, but she couldn't stop. She couldn't look at him again. But as she made it to the sidewalk, his fingers caught her arm. "Rianne, what are you doing? What's going on with you? I thought—"

"William, I'm sorry." She shook his hand loose. "I have to go. I —my dad must be home by now." She bit her lip.

William slammed his arms to his sides. "That's the lamest excuse I've ever heard! You told me he would be out late tonight. What's wrong? Is it because I—"

"I'm sorry. I just . . . I have to go."

"At least let me get you home safely."

"I can take care of myself. Please don't follow me." She looked into his hurt eyes one last time before she started down the street, her own eyes welling up with tears as she pulled out her phone to call for a ride.

He didn't follow.

Chapter Thirty-Five

"Rianne, Rianne, hold on. Stop. Come on, Rianne, please wait. Rianne. Rianne! Stop walking away from me!"

Rianne stopped in the hallway on her way to her first class on Monday morning. William had been trying to contact her all weekend, but she ignored his texts and calls.

"What?" she asked, turning around.

William was wearing black jeans with a dark gray shirt layered with a thin olive jacket. On his wrist was a black leather wristband, and around his neck was his chain. He looked as gorgeous as ever, and it took every ounce of restraint she had not to ask him to hold her. She looked away, staring at a locker.

He took her arm in his hand and made her look at him. "Why have you been ignoring me? You know we're going to have to talk about what happened sooner or later."

"Can it be later?" Rianne asked. "I'm going to be late because of you."

William cocked an eyebrow. "And *I'm* going to be late because of *you*."

"Don't play smart with me, William."

"Then don't play dumb with me."

Wow, she thought. *He's playing this game well.*

"Why did you run away from me after I . . . after I kissed you? Just tell me. Please. When I told you how I felt about you, did you get scared? You can't say you don't feel the same way." He put his free hand on her other arm and looked deep into her eyes, searching for answers.

The flashbacks that had been plaguing her all weekend came back.

"Oh, come on, Rianne, baby. Don't be like that. I know you want this as much as I do. Why else would you come over?"

Bruises littered her body that weren't there anymore, but the mental scars still remained.

"Logan, why are you doing this to me?"

Screaming. She was screaming for help.

She felt herself trapped under the sink in her bathroom again. She could hear the man's voice rasp in her ear, *"Let me enjoy this."*

Rianne wanted to give him those answers. She wanted to so badly. But she was scared. Too many men had hurt her up to that point, and now she was hurting William. She couldn't keep doing this to him.

Gritting her teeth, she replied in the most callous voice she could muster. "William. Let me go. Right now."

He stared at her for a moment and then released her arm as if he had been burned.

"The date was a mistake. Everything was a mistake. We've only known each other for a few weeks and . . . and there's no way you feel as strongly as you say you do. I can't do this right now. I'll ask Mrs. Carter to get you a new tutor or something, but I . . . just forget about me, William. It'll be better for both of us."

She spun back around as the first bell rang, clearing her throat as it tried to tighten on her.

* * *

Unobtrusive

Counting sheep wasn't working.

It had been forty-five minutes, and Rianne was still stuck staring at the ceiling as though it would give her answers. Or knock her out so she could finally sleep. Too many thoughts crowded her mind to allow that to happen.

Rianne played with the frayed edge of her pillowcase. Even though she was still furious with Braedon for leaving her, she missed him. A lot. It hurt to be so close to someone for months and then have him suddenly severed from her world. She found herself scrolling through photos of the two of them together. She couldn't bring herself to delete them. What if she never saw him again? Those photos and her memories were all she had left of him. Even going to Estona would be a constant reminder for her.

I know that I'm the Guardian, but I don't know if I can ever go back there because of him.

I have to stop thinking about Braedon. Think of something else. William.

Great.

She couldn't get him out of her mind either. Every time she tried to forget about him, he would push his way through again and remain there, refusing to move. Wanting her to remember. Replaying that moment on loop, over and over.

What had happened Saturday night was both incredible and terrifying. Their date was amazing and so much fun. And then their kiss on the dance floor. That kiss sent a fire through her. He was so gentle and sincere, but the way she had treated him afterward. Ignoring his calls, lying to him in the hallway, leaving him to stand there, his face filled with pain as he watched her walk away.

And for what? Because she was scared? Scared of getting attacked again? That was a valid reason, wasn't it? Why was she so afraid to take another chance? William had probably taken her advice and forgotten about her, and that hurt more than saying those things in the first place.

Three quiet knocks came from her door. Rianne groaned. "Go

away, Dad," she said. It was quiet once more. At least for a few seconds. The knocks became more numerous and louder. "Daddy, I'm trying to sleep!" she shouted, sitting up in bed and glaring at the closed door. Only when she heard more knocks did she realize they weren't coming from her door.

They were coming from behind her.

She turned on her lamp and twisted around. There, right outside her window, was William, his brown hair swirling in the wind, gripping the edge of the sill. He had that crooked smile on his face that she couldn't resist.

"Open up!" he called, his voice muffled by the pane.

"Oh my God," she whispered as she hurried to the window and opened it, greeted by a gust of warm wind. "William, what are you doing here? What do you want?" She paused. "How the hell did you even get up here? And why are you stalking me?"

"I'm here to see you, duh. And I'm not stalking you!"

"So you say," Rianne replied, standing in front of him with her arms crossed. "You don't know when to quit, do you?"

"It's one of my most redeeming qualities, sweetheart. I didn't want to wait until tomorrow to try and force you to talk to me again."

"You still didn't answer my last question."

"And I don't intend to. Let's just add that to the romantic mystery." He looked at her with his piercing eyes and smiled. "'But soft, what light through yonder window breaks? It is the east, and Rianne is the sun.' Iambic pentameter found in that monologue by Romeo in act two, scene two, There. Now you don't have to ask Carter to find me a new tutor. You're doing just fine motivating me. Now move over. My arms are getting tired."

Rianne backed away from the window so he could climb in. What was wrong with her? Why was she letting him in? She was supposed to be creating distance between them.

He hoisted himself inside and then smirked at her. "You know, you don't have to look at me like that. I know I'm handsome, but damn." He closed the window behind him and then walked to the center of the room, looking around with a small smile on his face as he took in all of her posters and artwork.

"Sick room," he said, sounding bored. "I like how you decorated it. Okay, that might have sounded sarcastic, but now I'm being serious. All this that I'm seeing is absolutely amazing." He went over to her easel. She had been working on a new project involving the colors of her Fuora and an indefinite shape. There was no way she could recreate the actual colors of her powers with just paint, but she was close. "Wow, this is beautiful. How long have you been working on this one?"

"I appreciate the compliment, but can you please tell me why you're here?" Rianne asked, nearly nose to nose with him.

"I'm pretty sure I already—"

"No, I mean, *why* you're *here*. Do you know how much trouble I could—no, *will* be in if my dad decides to check on me and you're in here? Do you have any idea what he'll think?"

"Well, I can think of one pretty obvious word."

She made a move to punch him, but he grabbed Rianne's wrist. "Let me stop you right there," he said, using the opportunity to pull her close to him.

For a few moments, Rianne and William just looked at each other. Rianne felt her cheeks heat up. Then she pulled away, out of his grasp. "Ugh, you are so irritating." She turned her back to him and crossed her arms. This was crazy! *He* was crazy. This was irresponsible! This was—

He chuckled behind her. "That's what you say, but do you really mean it?"

She didn't answer. She had to keep him at bay. She didn't want him in her life anymore . . . did she?

"William, you have to go. You're going to get me in trouble. I mean it. I don't want to see y—" She stiffened as he wrapped his arms around her.

"Do you really think I would get you in trouble with your old man?" he said into her neck. "I'm not going to get caught—trust me —which means you won't get into trouble." He turned her around to face her. "Now, are you going to tell me what's really going on, or are we going to keep playing this game, because you should know that I only play to win."

Then Rianne's phone went off.

Chapter Thirty-Six

Justin sat on his bed, spinning his phone in his hands. He had been in Estona for the past few weeks. Being in the Standard world was too hard at the moment. Between avoiding his best friend and keeping an eye on William Rogers, it was all becoming too much. He was only one person; he didn't know how Braedon had done it for so long.

Rianne hadn't been to training in over two weeks, and he was worried about her. Ellis had told him that she had refused to come with him. Justin knew their relationship had become strained since their argument, but he hadn't expected her to abandon her training.

He felt like a failure. He hadn't known what to say to Master Nathaniel when he asked where the Guardian was. He prayed the Wise Ones wouldn't summon him to report on the Guardian's training. Failing the Wise Ones was something he did not want to experience.

Justin sighed and then, swallowing his pride, opened his phone and swiped on Rianne's number.

"Justin?" Rianne answered in a soft voice. He figured she probably didn't want her father to hear that she was still awake. It was well past 10:00 p.m., and her dad was a stickler about his daughter staying up late on school nights.

"Hey, Rianne. Sorry to call you so late, but I wanted to check in on you."

Her silence made it seem like she was struggling inwardly. "Where have you been?"

"In Estona."

"Estona? You mean you've just been staying there? Why haven't you come back?"

"Why haven't you come back for training?" When she didn't answer, a pit formed in his stomach. "Have you still been hanging out with William?"

"Are you still on that about him?" she grumbled.

"Rianne, please listen to me. I'm trying to trust my intuition about this. I just feel like—" He stopped when he heard mumbling on the other end. "Hello?" he said, glancing at the phone screen before putting it back to his ear.

"Quit it," Rianne hissed.

Though it was hard to make out, Justin heard a male voice speaking. "I just want to know why he doesn't trust me," the voice said.

"Will you shut up? I'm trying to—"

"Hell no. Now I *really* want to know. Tell me."

Rianne yelped. Then she giggled. "Stop it!" She giggled again. "I'm talking to someone."

"Well, obviously. I hope you aren't just talking to yourself. Ask whoever it is why he doesn't trust me."

"He's going to figure out that you're here!"

"Oh. Excuse me while I find some cares to give."

Justin leaped out of bed, pacing. "Rianne, what is William doing in your room? Does your dad know he's there?" All he heard was Rianne giggling and her scolding William again. "Rianne!" he shouted, trying to regain her attention.

"Calm down, Justin!" Rianne said. "It's not a big deal."

Unobtrusive

Justin felt his blood boiling. He couldn't stop the next words from flying from his mouth. "Rianne, how fucking stupid can you be? Do you want another Logan situation?"

Rianne was shocked into silence. Then she replied in the darkest voice he'd ever heard from her. "*How dare you?*"

"Give me the phone," William said in the background, followed by a shuffling sound. "William speaking," he said in a hospitable voice. "And I'm going to presume this is Justin Allan?"

Justin's breath caught in his throat. That feeling overtook him again. "How do you know my last name?" he asked, his voice trembling.

"I'm going to make this quick. What I'm doing here is between Rianne and me. And maybe you shouldn't be so worried about me hurting her. You seem to be doing a phenomenal job at that anyway."

The call ended, and Justin pulled the phone away from his ear, unable to do anything but stare into space.

Chapter Thirty-Seven

With an air of finality, William tossed her phone onto Rianne's bed.

She wrapped her arms around herself, trying to keep her eyes from welling with tears. How could Justin say that to her?

William put his arms around her waist again, pulling her close. She wrapped her arms around his neck, holding onto him like a lifeline. "I'm so sorry he said that to you, Rianne."

Rianne didn't answer. She just focused on him.

"I'm not going to let anyone hurt you again," he said. "I promise."

"How can you promise that?" she asked, finally able to speak. "Too many people have hurt me already in the past year alone. There's no way you can promise that."

William pulled away, so he could see her face. "Then I promise to try. I promise to be there for you when you need me. I'm not going anywhere. I know it's a lot to ask, but trust me."

Rianne rested her forehead on his chest, finally allowing some tears to fall. "A man broke in here once and tried to rape me. A boy from school tried to do the same thing. Too many people I thought I could trust either lied to me or abandoned me. What if you're just another repeat? I feel like I'm broken. Surely, you wouldn't want to deal with all of that."

"Oh, Rianne." He pulled her close. "I'm so sorry."

She sniffled.

"And you're wrong," he continued, "very wrong, in fact."

"What are you talking about?" she asked, her voice muffled.

"You're not broken. If anything, I'm the broken one. I'm willing to be here for you if you want me. You don't have to trust me right away, but know that I'm ready to deal with whatever you throw at me, because I'm not going anywhere."

They hugged each other harder. *Maybe it'll be worth it to trust him,* she thought.

William placed his forehead on hers, then put his hand on her heart. "Let me take care of this for you."

She reciprocated his touch. "As long as you let me take care of yours too."

His lips finally made contact with hers again.

Second by second, the kiss became more passionate, more intense. William moved his hands from her heart and placed them around her face. Rianne followed his lead, running her hands through his hair. Now *this* was what a first kiss was supposed to feel like. She wanted it to go on forever.

"Rianne?" Her father's voice was accompanied by his shadow under her bedroom door as the hallway light turned on.

"Oh, God. William!" she whispered, untangling herself. "You have to hide!"

She pushed him toward her closet, but he was fighting her, being his usual stubborn self. Why in the world was he fighting her? Did he *want* to get killed?

The door opened, and her father entered. Rianne let go of William and turned toward the door, ready to meet her father's fury.

"Rianne, you're still up?" He did a massive yawn and scratched the back of his head.

Rianne looked to her left where William should have been, but he was gone. Despite her confusion, she tried to play off her astonishment when she spoke. "Yep. Still awake."

"Well, it's eleven thirty, young lady. Get to bed."

Rianne rolled her eyes. "Okay, Dad." He still treated her like a child even though she was literally training to save an entire realm. She walked over to her nightstand and turned off her lamp.

"Goodnight," her dad said, then he turned and walked out, shutting the door behind him.

Alone in the dark, Rianne exhaled in relief. That had been too close for comfort.

"William," she whispered, her eyes scanning the darkness. She grabbed her phone off her nightstand and turned on its flashlight. "William, where are you?"

Suddenly Rianne's ankle gave out from under her, and she fell flat on her back onto the carpeted floor. She heard a faint noise from under her bed, then a pair of hands and legs pinned her limbs to her sides.

"Scared ya!"

"Did not!"

"Did too."

"Did not."

"Did too."

"Okay, you did!" she admitted. She knew that if she didn't give up soon, they were going to be back and forth all night.

"I knew you were going to give up eventually."

Rianne rolled her eyes. "How did you get under there so fast?"

"Why would I tell you my secret?"

"Because you really like me?"

"That's not enough."

"Why don't you ever—"

"Shhh. You ask way too many questions." He leaned down and kissed her again.

After that breathtaking kiss, Rianne pulled back and caressed his cheek. "William, I think it's time for you to go now. For real this time."

He smiled, his teeth glistening in the darkness. "What if I just spend the night here?"

Rianne giggled. "Don't be stupid."

William chuckled. "I'm sort of kidding and sort of not. Sure you wouldn't want to spend the night with my arms around you?"

Rianne tried—and failed—to keep her heartbeat under control. "As much as I would love that, I don't want to push it."

William helped her off the floor. "Ugh, fine, but I've been told I'm an amazing cuddler."

Rianne rolled her eyes. "We'll test that theory later, but not tonight."

He gave her a peck on the cheek. "Don't avoid me tomorrow."

She returned his kiss. "Wouldn't dream of it. 'Parting is such sweet sorrow.'"

"'That I shall say goodnight till it be morrow.'" He kissed her one last time—leaving her dizzy yet again—before leaving out the window. She stood there for a minute longer, a smile on her face as his bike roared to life and then faded into the night.

Chapter Thirty-Eight

William loved the sense of control he felt when driving his motorcycle.

He was in control of everything.

Everything was going his way.

He turned left off Rianne's street and drove several blocks down. *I finally have her trust,* he thought. Now he had to wait just a bit longer. His father had said that sometimes it was just about patience. Playing the long game. Making sure he had the upper hand at all times.

He turned onto Fritz Parkway. Speeding down to the end of this street, he turned into the apartment complex and parked his motorcycle in one of the empty spaces closest to his unit. He pulled out his phone as he crossed the walkway and went up the stairs to the second story, heading to his apartment door. His mother had to be back from work. She worked two jobs now, so she was out of the apartment a lot. Now that he had school to worry about, he saw her less and less, which he didn't mind. He hated the woman almost as much as he hated Rianne.

"William! There you are!" his mother exclaimed from the

kitchen as he entered. She hurried over to him. "I was getting worried."

William didn't look up from his phone. "I'm fine. When did you get home?"

She glanced at her watch. "Around nine-ish. You weren't here."

"Obviously," William mumbled.

"I know it's late . . ." she said. William flicked his eyes at her for a second before returning to his phone as he started toward his bedroom. "But I thought we could, I don't know, spend some time together."

"And why would I want to do that?"

Her breath hitched in her throat. "Well, we don't really get to see each other much, and I want to know how everything's been going at school."

"It's going fine."

"William, will you please just stop and talk to me?" She grabbed his arm but screamed and jumped back as an intense shock went through her body.

His eyes had turned black, but he settled them as he spun on her. "Don't touch me," William hissed, causing the color to drain from her face. "I've told you before *never* to touch me. *Ever*. I mean it, Mother."

"William, I—"

The rest of her sentence was cut off as he slammed the door to his room.

As he started to undress, she knocked. "William?" she said, her voice quavering with tears. "William, please. Just come out and talk to me. I'm sorry. Please."

William rolled his eyes as he laid down on his bed. "Leave me alone, Mother!"

"William, please. I feel like I'm losing you. I know you miss your father, but *please*, just talk to me!"

William aimed his palm at his light switch. A dark blue spark emitted from it and hit the switch, causing it to go dark in the room.

Then, the electricity came back to him, hitting his side and absorbing into his body. He heard his mother sniffle some more, then her shadow left. Finally, she had taken the hint.

It had been two years since his father was killed. He was a hopeless alcoholic—William hadn't even gotten as drunk as his father used to get—and that dulled his ability to use his Motora. New York City was dangerous, and he didn't even see the oncoming cab as he crossed the street to get to work. He couldn't move out of the way like he should have.

William sighed and gritted his teeth. He didn't believe that the paramedics did their best to save him. If they had, he'd still be alive.

The man he had inherited so much from was gone forever. William had always wanted his father to be there when he found the Guardian. He had been excited to tell him his plans on how to fulfill his part in the Great Battle, to spar and practice with him to ensure that he was ready because failure was not an option.

William's mother hadn't taken his father's death well. She had been quiet before but became even more so after he passed. It was like she was stuck, not knowing what to do with her newfound freedom. He had abused her for years, hitting her whenever she did something he didn't approve of or when she spoke when not spoken to. He also beat her when she tried to make a stand for herself or shout or fight back. William had a deep respect for his old man, who could have killed his son in a heartbeat. Hell, he almost did once. Now his mother feared him as much as she had feared his father.

William smiled. His desire to hurt and kill had been passed down for generations. All of that raw aggression to be used to demolish Estona. It was a part of him, just like his father was. He admired the man deeply. And he missed him.

He looked up at the ceiling. "Don't worry, Father," he said. "I'll kill the Guardian if it's the last thing I do."

Chapter Thirty-Nine

Six months had passed, and the chilly season of October had settled into Felix. Rianne was outside during free period, drawing in her sketchpad and listening to music. She was sitting on a bench under the shade of a tree.

Though it was only the second month of the new school year, being a senior was looking great. Her classes weren't too challenging. Two of them were art classes as well. Her art teacher, Ms. Rosario, was helping her create a portfolio to submit to colleges. Rianne was excited to start a new chapter in her life as well as study what she loved every day.

Her current sketch depicted what was going on in her mind. She was drawing a side portrait of a girl who looked vaguely like her. The girl had long, flowing hair and a troubled look on her face. Looking at her profile, one could get a clear look into her head where a war between light and dark was raging. On one side was flowing light and graceful patterns, similar to what the Blade looked like. On the other was rigid darkness, trying to overcome the other. Her Fuora and the Hunter's Motora. Of course, she didn't know what her Hunter's powers looked like, but she could only assume it would be dark, the opposite of hers.

Rianne sighed and tapped her pencil against the side of her sketchbook. She couldn't help but feel guilty. Her Guardian training was pretty much nonexistent. Almost seven months had passed since she had had proper training with her powers.

Justin had yet to return to Felix. Their phone argument was the last time they'd talked. She trained on her own, but without her Mentor, she didn't know how to expand her knowledge of her Fuora and what else she could do with it—or what else it could do for her. The Blade was more like a convenient magic trick for her now. She missed training with her best friend. She missed feeling powerful.

Her eyes turned downcast. She missed Estona, but going back felt too painful, and she didn't want to face that. Ellis checked in on her about once or twice a week, but that was her only connection to the magical realm. Guilt filled her. Maybe it was time to let everything go and start tending to her duties.

Wanting to get her mind off the subject, Rianne flipped to a new page and began to outline a tree with elaborate branches. Focusing on the real world would get her to stop thinking of the magical one.

Suddenly everything went dark, and Guns 'n' Roses stopped playing in her headphones.

"Why am I not surprised to find you here, drawing?" a deep, husky voice whispered in her ear.

"Six months with me and you're still surprised to find me drawing every free moment I get?"

"Free moment? I've told you time and time again that we can do a lot more in our free moments."

She felt a hand slide up her thigh.

"William!" Rianne jolted, grabbing William's hands and throwing them away from her. She turned around on the bench and was met by his usual smug look. As always, Rianne's heart thumped harder than normal as she took in how nice his long-sleeve shirt looked on him, accompanied by his chain necklace and beanie.

Rianne and William had officially been dating for six months now, and their relationship was great. Of course, they had fights and disagreements here and there, but that was to be expected with their two personalities. She loved being around him—which she had gotten to do a lot over summer break. Whenever they could, they would get together to create art, laugh, listen to music . . . and a few other things. Rianne was glad she had taken a chance on him. He had kept his promise. He hadn't hurt her, and he cared for her.

"You can't even give it a break in public, can you?"

William shrugged. "Hey, you're all mine. I like to touch what's mine." He pushed the back of her head as he circled around to sit next to her on the bench. "Whatcha working on now?"

"Just starting a new tree. No big deal. However," she raised an eyebrow at him, "there's a better question to be asked."

He grabbed her water bottle, which was sitting near her back-pack, and drank from it. "Which is?"

"Where have *you* been all day?"

"You mean aside from avoiding you on the regular?"

She glared at him but kept a smile on her face. "Just answer the question."

"Well, I woke up late, so I decided to take the day off."

Rianne raised her eyebrows. "A day off? Shouldn't you be keeping your grades up? I mean, you're planning to go to college, right?"

"Trade school."

"Even still, you have to keep your grades up."

He took another drink of water. "It's not like there's anything else for me here, anyway."

Rianne chuckled. "Oh, really, William? Nothing?"

"Nope."

"Not even your girlfriend?"

"Not really."

"Wow!" She put her earphones back on and refocused on her sketch. The tree wasn't going to draw itself.

"Oh, come on, Rianne," William said. "Don't be like that. You're gonna have to talk to me at some point."

Rianne was drawing the tree's base when her sketchbook was snatched out of her hands. "Hey!" She tore her headphones off.

"Oh, now you wanna talk to me?" William replied, wiggling the book in front of her, teasing.

"Give it back!" Rianne shouted, getting up from the bench. "Give it back, you jerk!"

He raised the book above his head even though he was already five-foot eleven to her five-foot four. "Funny, last time I checked, I was your boyfriend. But I'll give it back under one condition."

"You're being a bully!"

"That sounds more like insulting than compromising."

"Well, that's what you hear when someone doesn't want to compromise!" She jumped for it, to no avail.

"You really don't want to draw for the rest of the day, huh?" William said, holding it higher still.

"Fine," she said, relenting. "What do you propose, sir?"

William lowered the book, then wrapped that arm around her waist, pulling her close.

"William," Rianne whispered.

"What are you complaining about now?" he murmured, leaning his head forward and caressing her face with his free hand.

"Nothing. It's just that—"

"We're in public?" He snorted. "So? Besides, I need to give you my terms and conditions."

Rianne's heart was racing, but she tried to keep her breath steady as he placed his forehead against hers. Even after so long, he had the same effect on her as he had when they first met. "And what are these terms?"

"Just kiss me. As simple as that."

Unobtrusive

It didn't seem like a bad deal at all. But on the quad? Granted, there weren't hundreds of other students and teachers around, but still, couldn't they keep their intimate moments to themselves?

"William, I'd love to, but—"

He pressed his lips to hers, cutting her off. He put his free hand on her neck, pulling her in. Rianne became lightheaded, as she always did, forgetting how to breathe for the hundredth time. But too soon, he pulled away. She hated it when he did that.

"See? That wasn't so bad, was it?" he asked, pressing his forehead to hers.

"No, it wasn't, actually. But now . . ." She reached behind her back and took his hand.

"What are you doing?" he asked, frowning.

"Nothing. I just—" She snatched the sketchbook out of his hand, then held it up. It was her turn to mock now. "Want my book back."

William laughed. "Ooh, I bet you feel so accomplished."

"One could say that."

"Which is why I love you. You always have that feeling of accomplishment, even when it isn't deserved."

Rianne froze. "What did you just say?"

"That you always have that feeling—"

Rianne thumped his shoulder. "No! Not that! You know what I—"

"I love you, Rianne," William said. "I'm crazy about you."

Rianne broke into a smile, and she felt her heart swelling. He had never said those words to her before. He loved her. He was in love with her.

"Ah, and she is left speechless," he whispered, kissing her again. "So, I do have a question for you." She raised her eyebrows expectantly, still too shocked to speak. "What are you doing tonight?"

"On a Tuesday?" she said. "Um, nothing, I guess. Why?"

William began rocking back and forth with her in his arms. "I just want to spend some extra time with you."

Rianne giggled. "And that couldn't wait until the weekend when we don't have school?"

William shook his head. "That's what happens when you're in love. You want to spend every moment of every day with the object of your affection."

"Rianne! William! Hey!"

William turned his head toward Alex's voice. She and Chris were coming across the quad, hand in hand, to meet them. William looked backed at Rianne and gave her a wink before shifting to hold her waist with one arm. Rianne's friends were a bit annoying, but he dealt with it. They were all friends by that point, as much as he hated being around them.

"You two are so *adorable!*" Alex squealed when they made it to the couple, her voice piercing William's ears.

William hid his grimace with a smile. "Why, thank you, m'lady."

Rianne leaned in closer to Alex. "Alex, I gotta tell you what just happened."

"Wait, what happened?" Alex asked, failing to mimic Rianne's soft volume.

Chris leaned in. "Oh, come on, you can't just tell Alex. You have to tell your other best friend too!" He straightened up. "Unless it's a lady thing. Then I definitely *do not* want to know."

Alex giggled. "Like you haven't heard us talk about that kind of stuff before."

Chris looked at the sky. "After knowing y'all for so long, there are many conversations I wish I could forget."

William stifled a yawn.

Rianne looked at him, asking his permission with her eyes.

William smiled at her, a look of adoration on his face. "Go ahead, babe. I don't mind them knowing."

Rianne turned back to her best friends, beaming. "It happened! William said that he loves me!"

Alex screamed, jumping up and down. Others looked over at

them before continuing with what they were doing. "Oh my gosh, oh my gosh, oh my *gosh*! Congratulations, babe!" She threw her arms around Rianne's neck.

William chuckled. "Well, on that note, I'm gonna go see what I missed today before school's over."

"Yeah, since you've only spent a grand total of twenty minutes at school today," Rianne remarked, sitting back down on the bench.

"Shut up. And I'll see you later." He leaned down and pressed his lips to her cheek, lingering by her ear for a moment. "I'll text you where to meet me," he whispered. "I have something really special planned. Just make sure you're ready by midnight. Bye."

"Bye."

William bid farewell to Alex and Chris as well, then headed toward the school. As soon as he was gone, Rianne patted the seat next to her, beckoning Alex to join her.

Inside the school, a couple of teachers were heading toward the teachers' lounge. A few students were also in the hall. The principal was ushering them to either head outside or to their tutorials. None of them paid any attention to William as he passed. Though he had told Rianne, Alex, and Chris that he was going to get makeup work, he just wandered the building instead. He couldn't care less about education. The only thing that mattered to him was the Great Massacre.

He headed up one of the staircases, pulling out his phone to text Chris. One of her best friends would have the honor of helping him achieve his goal.

What are you doing tonight?

It took a minute for Chris to respond.

Homework probably. Why?

221

I have a surprise for Rianne, and I need some help since you know her just as well as I do. Can you meet me in the quad at 11?

At night?

No, genius, in the afternoon. Yes, tonight.

Whatever. I'll see what I can do

William didn't worry. Chris would show up to anything involving Rianne. Everything was falling into place, and it was time to make his move. Rianne believed he was actually in love with her, which meant when he broke her heart that night, she wouldn't fight back. As he predicted from taking so many months to figure her out, she would be too wrapped up in her emotions to fight the man she thought loved her. She would be killed easily.

And with Chris's help, she would have no choice but to surrender.

He was about to finally achieve the full power of the Fuora and the Motora. The Great Massacre was going to happen.

Tonight.

Chapter Forty

"I'm going to bed, Dad," Rianne said to her father that night after glancing at her phone—it was 11:00. She stood up from the couch and made her way toward the staircase. They had been sitting in the living room watching an NFL game. The team she was rooting for was down by three.

"Oh, you big baby," Matt kidded, pausing the game. "You're leaving before halftime."

"Daddy, have you seen the time?"

Matt checked his phone. "What's your point?"

Rianne laughed. "I'm sorry, but aren't you the one who tells me to go to bed when it's late? I told you we should have waited for you to have a day when you get off early to watch the game!"

"You just know your team's gonna lose." Whenever the two watched sports, they would bet on the victor. Whoever lost had kitchen duty for a week.

"You're only up by *three* points!" Rianne countered. "And the first half isn't even over. Plenty of time for a turnaround."

Matt chuckled and then turned back to the TV, resuming the game. "We'll see. Night, Crayon. Love you."

Rianne smiled as she shook her head. "Love you, too, Dad." She skipped up the stairs.

As soon as her bedroom door was closed, Rianne went straight to her closet and changed into a denim skirt with leggings, a green shirt, a gray beanie, and black boots. She knew how much William loved it when she wore a skirt. After fixing her hair and reapplying her makeup, she deemed herself ready.

She walked over to the window and opened it. She looked at the tree next to her window.

If William can do it, so can I. It shouldn't be that tricky.

Rianne put one foot on her windowsill and climbed out, reaching for one of the thick branches. It took a couple of tries to grasp the wood, but she eventually caught hold and inched her way toward the ground.

Rianne was doing all right until she lost her grip and fell the rest of the way.

"Ouch!" she yelled as the side of her body made contact with the hard earth. Then she fell silent and glanced at the front door. When her father didn't come out, she relaxed, then got up.

Chapter Forty-One

William got off of his motorcycle and made his way to the quad at around 11:10. Several of the school's outdoor lights illuminated the darkness.

Chris was already there, toward the center of the quad. He was pacing around, swinging his arms back and forth. He looked restless.

Like he didn't suspect anything.

An arrogant smile crossed William's face as he made his way to Chris. Thinking about life—specifically Rianne's—and death—especially the Guardian's—always made him smile. There was nothing more exhilarating than being the reason air stopped moving through someone's body. He loved the feeling of being Maria Garcia's killer, and he couldn't wait to do the same to hundreds more. He could only imagine what it would be like to kill the almighty Guardian of Estona.

"Chris," he said as he neared.

Chris stopped pacing and let out a breath, putting his hands in his jacket pockets. "Hey, William," he said, sounding wary. "So, you have something for Rianne? Something that involves me for some reason?"

William stopped in front of him. "Yeah. I kind of wanted to keep it a surprise. I have this whole plan laid out. It's gonna be huge."

Chris smiled. "So, what is it, lovebird?"

Now.

"Oh, Christopher, I'm not in love with that girl." He sighed as he ran a hand through his hair.

Chris froze. "Excuse me?"

"Hell, she's nothing to me," he continued. "She could die tomorrow for all I care."

Chris gaped.

"Six long months with her. Six months of pretending. And to think, I almost got her to sleep with me a few times. That would only make her heartbreak worse tonight."

Chris clenched his jaw, his chest heaving with anger. "You bastard. You've been playing with her feelings this entire time? Did you call me down here just to tell me that? Is your big surprise that you're going to break up with her? What the *hell* is wrong with you?"

"It was a lot of fun too."

Chris yelled and threw a fist at William's face, but William parried the blow and followed up with a body shot, then a liver shot.

Chris dropped to the ground in agony.

When he finally stood up, William teleported behind Chris, then whistled to make his new presence known.

Chris whirled around, his eyes full of confusion. "How the hell?"

William cracked his knuckles. "Just stay calm, and this won't hurt as bad."

He teleported again and grabbed Chris by the front of his shirt. Then he punched him four times in the face. Chris didn't have time to retaliate before William threw him to the ground, grinding his nose into the concrete and slamming his face into it a couple of times. Blood flowed freely, and William felt bones cracking.

He laughed as the smell of iron filled his nostrils. What a nice warm-up to the actual event. Chris tried to pick himself back up, but William wouldn't allow him that bit of dignity.

"Oh, I'm not done with you yet," he said. He grabbed Chris by the hair and yanked him to his feet. Chris was nothing more than a ragdoll by that point. He weighed practically nothing. He *was* nothing.

At least to William.

William placed his free hand over Chris's neck, still holding him by his hair in the other. Chris tried to speak, but with what looked to be a broken nose and jaw, it wasn't working.

William spoke for him. "Like I said, just stay calm." He took a deep breath and let his Motora free from his hand. His eyes clouded over, then turned black. He felt dark blue sparks crawling through every limb of his body and into Chris's.

Chris screamed in pain, struggling to escape William's grasp. He was like a helpless little fly caught in William's deadly web. His screams echoed across the quad.

As William saw the life leaving Chris's tired eyes, he felt more of the exhilaration he craved. The sparks flashed with thousands of volts, trying to claim Chris's life. William could use all of his energy and kill this stupid kid now.

No. I have to be smart. I can't waste energy on this idiot.

He released him from his lethal grasp. Chris fell in a crumpled heap on the ground, his chest barely moving and his slack jaw unable to close. The heat from the electricity caused some of the blood on his face to cake over and dry. A few sparks still jolted through his body.

William chuckled again as he reached into his back pocket for his phone. "Hostage acquired. Now to tell my girlfriend where to find us."

Chapter Forty-Two

Sitting up, Rianne held her left wrist, which was throbbing with pain. She sucked in air through her teeth. It was probably sprained. How had William been able to climb up to her without hurting himself?

"At least it's not my drawing hand," she mumbled. *Nothing a little Fuora can't fix.* She focused on the pain in her wrist, then thought of William's smiling face and how happy she was when with him. A moment later, she felt warmth filling her body, and she pictured the gentle white glow enfolding itself around her injury. Her pain melted away, replaced by warmth.

It took maybe two minutes, but once Rianne opened her eyes, she was able to move her wrist without feeling any pain. It was practically as good as new—maybe better.

"Man, I love being the Guardian," Rianne said to herself, as she stood and headed to her car. A pang of guilt hit her again, but she brushed it off.

She drove a safe distance away before parking, turning on some music. By then it was almost 11:45.

She received a text five minutes later.

Unobtrusive

> I have something big planned for you. Meet me at the theater I told you about. The one I go to when I need to think.

> Come in through the side doors and go to the main stage when you get here.

> Call me if you forgot which one I'm talking about.

> Love you, babe.

She remembered him telling her about that downtown theater during the summer. He found it when he first moved to Texas, and though it was off limits to the public, he would sneak inside when he needed to get away and be alone. When she asked him when he would take her there, he said, "When the time is right."

She put her car in drive and headed downtown. Whatever he had planned had to be big if he was finally taking her to his place of solace.

She couldn't wait.

* * *

Rianne pushed open the side door to the aged theater. *I wonder how William managed to get these open,* she thought. The doors had to be locked and bolted if the area was barred to civilians. *Then again, it's William.* She walked through the hallways, finding her way to the main stage.

The Felix Theatre Auditorium had been closed down for several years due to some construction mishaps. One too many beams and heavy curtains fell, posing a danger to patrons. At the time it wasn't worth the money to repair its infrastructure, and the theater closed shortly after. That happened years before she was born, though, so being inside of it for the first time gave her a bit of a thrill. It was dangerous, but William probably knew the place like the back of his hand. She and her boyfriend were about to have a romantic night—she could feel it! Maybe William had decorated the place. Maybe he was planning to have a romantic movie night in there.

After trying a few doors, all of them locked, she opened another door that led to the main performance area. The stage and the theater lights were on. There was dust on the seven-foot-high rotting wood stage and the hundreds of red seats. The walkway's blue fabric was torn and frayed from years of neglect.

She coughed a couple of times as the movement from the door created a billow of dust around her. *Okay, I take back the romantic evening part.*

"Very romantic, William," she mumbled, hoping he'd hear her. The doors on the other side of the theater were also locked and chained.

As she looked around, her eyes locked on a motionless body at the bottom of one of the staircases, facing away from her. Her knees buckled, and her heart jumped in her throat.

"Oh, my God!" Her hands scrambled for her phone, but when she unlocked it, she had no signal.

Of course.

Maybe the person was still alive? Maybe they needed help. *Heal them. I can heal them if they're still alive!* she thought as she dashed toward the body on legs that felt like rubber.

"Hey, are you okay? Can you hear me?" she asked. As she got closer, she saw that he was slim with brown hair. His face was badly bruised and bloodied, but in a flash, she recognized it.

"Chris?" she whispered. What was he doing there? She thought back to her previous worries. *Oh, no, Chris, please don't be—*

Chris winced in pain, clawing at the carpet. He looked like he wanted to scream but couldn't.

"Take one more step, and I kill him."

She knew that voice. Deep and chilling.

Rianne looked up toward the top of the stairs and saw William standing there, his eyes narrowed at her and his arms crossed. Under the stage lights, his dark brown hair gave him an ominous glow. It scared her.

"William? What's going on? What is Chris doing here?"

"I told you that I found this place quite a bit ago," he said, making his way down the stairs. "I thought it would be the perfect place for us tonight. You and I, alone in this abandoned building, where no one can hear you beg for mercy."

Rianne furrowed her brow, her heart racing. "William, what in the world are you talking about?"

She flinched at his deep chuckle. "You know, my father always told me the Guardians were pretty clueless."

He was halfway to her now. Had he just said "Guardians"?

"Ever since Elizabeth, the line of protectors hasn't been the brightest. You're no exception. Congratulations."

Rianne's breath caught in her throat. No. There was no way he knew what that was. She hadn't heard that right. "William, I— What are you talking about?"

"Don't play dumb with me, Guardian. Drop the charade."

"What charade? What are you—"

"I said don't play dumb with me!"

Suddenly right in front of her, he punched her in the stomach. When she doubled over in pain, gasping for air, he hoisted her over his shoulder as if she weighed nothing, then threw her into one of the theater seats. She winced in pain, unable to process what was happening.

He leaned down so they were eye to eye, his hands on the armrests to block her in. "So, here's my Guardian," he purred. "Tell me, how does it feel to meet your Hunter for the first time?"

Rianne's eyes widened as she caught her breath. This couldn't be real. This couldn't be . . .

She shook her head, her voice trembling when she spoke. "No. No, William. You can't . . . you can't . . . I thought . . . I thought . . ." She felt her heart breaking. "You said you would never hurt me.

You told me I could trust you. You promised! William," she whispered, "you said you loved me."

William rolled his eyes. "Well, Rianne, Hunters never tell the truth. I never, *ever,* loved you. As a matter of fact, I *hate* you more than anything else in this world." It was like he had just stabbed her with a knife. "I just needed you to reveal your weaknesses to me—which are your family and friends. Typical. My method might have been unorthodox, but it worked."

He has to be making all of this up, Rianne thought. *He must've heard all of this from someone. This can't really be William. But he's already hurt me—physically and mentally. Only a Hunter would . . .*

"E-Even if you are my Hunter, how do you know I'm the Guardian?"

"Another little secret about Hunters, babe: we can see the aura of Guardians and other magical beings." He began playing with her hair, but she recoiled from his touch—something she never thought she would do. "When I saw you in the quad on my first day, I knew you were the one. And your friend Justin Allan—a Sterling. Must be either your Mentor or your Protector. Every time I look at you, all I can see is that taunting little aura. It's surrounding you right now, telling me you're the one I have to kill."

He yanked her hair, but she didn't make a sound. No way was she giving him that satisfaction.

"Plus, another dead giveaway—March twelfth. Our birthdays. The Guardian and the Hunter always share the same birthdate, even if the year is off. Your Mentors must be dumber than I assumed. I'm surprised you don't know all of this. Aren't you supposed to be able to feel energies too?"

When she remained silent, he continued to taunt her. "Aww, it might be because you're not that strong. Good. That makes my job easier. But I didn't expect it to be *this* easy! You believed *everything* I told you! Being hungover at the library that day was a lie to get you to make me open up. Being bullied and weak? Obviously a lie. And I don't drink to forget my dad; I drink in *honor* of him. I mean, he was the man who murdered your *mother*. What an inspiration. Oh, and your car was fine. I just sapped the electricity from it when I touched it. All of that to make you go on a date with me. Our whole relationship was a lie, and you were dumb enough to believe all of it. Maybe Estona would be better off not having you around. How are you going to protect it when you can't even protect yourself?"

Rianne swallowed, taking in his words. Was this really his true nature? He was so sadistic, so casual about the evil in him. How could she have fallen for him?

"What power do you have?"

"Pow*ers*," he corrected her.

"Don't get too full of yourself," Rianne said. "I have more than one power too."

He squeezed her upper arm, hurting her. "Don't interrupt me—ever. Understand?" She nodded, and he loosened his hold.

"I inherited two powers from my father, the third one being my own. The first is teleporting. That's how I got to the second story of your house and how I got under your bed so quickly. My second is strength. And my third is electricity."

He straightened up and held his hands out in front of him. He made a twisting motion with both, and bright blue sparks engulfed them. Rianne's eyes widened even more, the audacity draining out of her.

"Isn't it beautiful?" he asked. "With it in my control, I can electrocute anyone or anything from the inside out." He played with the bolts, making them transfer from one hand to the other like a twisted game of catch.

"Oh, my God," Rianne whispered, remembering the news about Maria Garcia. She had died in New York, where he was from. "Did you kill Maria Garcia?"

"Ding! ding! ding! That was me. Can call her a warm-up to the big game. I just wanted a bit of practice with people, you know? I had killed small animals before to see the effects of what I could do,

233

but practice makes perfect, they say. Didn't expect it to make national news, though. Oh, and Chris over there?" William pointed to where he was lying on his side, motionless. "He probably doesn't have a lot of time left."

"What did you do?" Rianne shouted. She tried to stand up, but William pushed her back down. "What did you do to him?"

"Calm down, babe," William said. "I just needed someone you cared about with us on this most special of nights. I needed you to see that anyone close to you is one of my targets. Anyone you care about is on my radar because of you. So, if anything happens to them, it's *all your fault.*"

William aimed a hand at Chris, his palm out, then he closed his fingers, centimeter by centimeter.

In time with William's movements, Chris began to shift. Then he winced and screamed in pain, tears spilling from under his eyelids. His body shook and spasmed, threatening to break itself in two. Blood flowed from his mouth, choking him.

"Stop! Stop it! William, stop!" Rianne yelled. She grabbed his arm, trying to point it away from Chris's body, but he was too strong. "Stop it! Your fight is with me, not him!" She pounded on his chest, but he grabbed Rianne's arm and held her at arm's length. "Please!" she cried. "I'll do anything, *anything.* Please, just stop!"

William looked at her and then cut the connection between himself and Chris. Chris gasped for air and coughed, blood gurgling onto the carpet.

"Anything?" William said. "You would do *anything* for this pathetic piece of trash?"

She glared at him. "You will *not* hurt him again," she said through gritted teeth. "And you're not going to hurt anyone else I love either. Your fight is with me, no one else. So, what do you want?"

William eyed her. "Hmm . . . looks like we have a little deal to make. How about this." He pulled her toward him, face to face.

"Let me kill you. Don't fight back. If you do that, I'll let him go. Reverse all the damage I've done."

"You can do that?" Rianne asked. How powerful was he?

"Motora is capable of a lot of things. But yes, I can do that. Or you can *both* die tonight. I don't care either way. It's your choice, Guardian."

Rianne debated with herself as her eyes darted from William's face to Chris's barely living body. She didn't want to do it; she didn't want everything she had worked for over the last several months to be wasted in a few short minutes. But she had no choice. Not only was her life on the line, so was Chris's.

"Okay," Rianne said, her voice cracking. "You can kill me."

Chapter Forty-Three

Matt sat on the living room couch, waiting for Rianne to come back from wherever she was. He had already sent ten furious texts and left around twenty voicemails.

He had gone upstairs about thirty minutes earlier to tell her the final score—his team had won, of course—and saw her window ajar and her car missing from the driveway.

Where could she be? he thought, his arms crossed in anger as he chewed on the inside of his cheek. *How dare she sneak out of this house? How did she even get out without me noticing?*

He never thought *his* daughter would do something like that. Sneaking out of the house? He never did something that dumb in high school. Okay, he *had*, but at least he didn't get caught.

"This was just sloppy," he said, talking to himself. "She left the window open and everything! Everyone knows you close it after you go out. And you're supposed to have an alibi to back yourself up." Matt shook his head. If Rianne snuck had snuck out that night without him noticing, how many other times had she done it?

When I get my hands on her, I'm gonna—

Unobtrusive

The doorbell rang, breaking him from his thoughts. When he answered the door, he froze. The mother of that William boy was standing on his doorstep, looking anxious—and gorgeous. Her long blonde hair framed her heart-shaped face, and she wore a simple black shirt and jeans. He felt self-conscious in his T-shirt and baggy sweatpants. Like before, something seemed familiar about her, but he couldn't pinpoint what it was.

"Oh, um, hi. You're William's mother, right?"

She didn't look him in the eyes, settling for her hands, but she tried to smile. "Yes. I'm sorry to show up here unannounced, but I couldn't think of anyone else to turn to. I hope that's okay and I'm not too out of line."

"Oh, sure. Come in."

"Thank you." He moved to the side to allow her into the foyer.

"So, what can I help ya with?" Matt asked, attempting to flatten his unruly hair.

She nodded. "Right. Well, I can't find William. He left the house earlier, but he hasn't come back, and he won't pick up his phone. I'm really worried. Again, I'm so sorry to call on you like this, but since you've dealt with William before, and I'm still getting used to Felix again, I thought that maybe you could help me. Please, I'm really worried about him." She made eye contact with him for a second and then looked away again.

It was an ironic twist, but he'd take it. "Of course, I'll help you out. My daughter actually snuck out too. They're probably at the same party or something." He gritted his teeth but relaxed a second later. "We can take my car and look together. Good thing you showed up here, eh?"

"Yes, I'm really lucky. Thank you so much, Officer."

Matt grabbed his keys from the hook near the door, then followed her outside. *Hopefully, they're not doing something completely stupid.*

"I didn't know you had a daughter," she said as he led her to his truck.

237

"Yeah. She's seventeen. She and William actually share the same birthday."

"Wow. That's interesting. Are you, um, a single parent?" She caught herself. "I'm so sorry. I don't mean to be nosy."

"It's fine. I am. Rianne's mother passed away several years ago."

"Oh, I'm sorry. My husband passed away too."

Matt flinched as he unlocked the doors of his Ford. It looked like they were in the same boat.

"By the way," he said as they got in, "my name's Matt. Don't know how I didn't mention it until now."

The woman gasped as he started the truck, then smiled as a look of awareness came over her. "Oh, my goodness, I knew you seemed so familiar! Matt Jarrett? It's me, Jessica! Jessica Stowe! From high school! You probably didn't recognize me because of the hair color and everything, and my name changed, but it's me! Do you remember?"

Matt smiled, the realization finally coming over him as he recognized his old friend from so long ago. "Jessica!" he exclaimed. "Oh, my God! I can't believe it's actually you! This whole time—"

"We've been right in front of each other—"

"And we didn't notice!"

"It looks like we're still—"

"Finishing each other's sentences."

Matt smiled.

Chapter Forty-Four

Braedon sighed as he sat in his throne beside the other Wise Ones. He put his face in his hands, rubbing his eyes. They had just finished another meeting and had another lined up in thirty minutes. His mind was tired. The others were meditating now that they had some off time, but Braedon couldn't focus. He didn't want to.

Day in and day out, all they did was sit in their fancy thrones in their fancy suits, sign paperwork, and have the most boring meetings with palace personnel. Occasionally, they got some outside interaction when a Sterling or an Advancer came for an issue that couldn't be solved without their help and when training with Master Nathaniel, but other than that, life was monotonous.

Braedon sighed again. He missed being an Advancer. He missed teaching the students at the high school. He missed being with his friends. But most of all, he missed Rianne. The ache in his chest taunted him daily. He knew that she probably hated him. He had disappeared from her life just as quickly as he had arrived. He thought back fondly of her sense of humor—which had been directed at him countless times, but he loved it. He loved her witty, idiosyncratic sarcasm. She was so beautiful, inside and out. God, how he adored her. Her smile. Her wonderful, beautiful smile—

A sharp pain entered Braedon's side, tightening and imploding. He gripped it, and though he tried to keep quiet, he cried out. As the pang hit again, he fell out of the throne and tumbled down the stairs to the red-carpeted floor below. He was dizzy, the world was spinning around him.

He had felt such pains before when something wasn't right, but this was different. It caused him extreme physical pain.

It was Rianne. She was in serious danger. Lethal danger. Maybe even danger that included . . . her Hunter.

His vision blurred, then everything came to him in flashes.

There was a . . . a . . . a large . . . theater.

He then saw Rianne. She was scared out of her mind.

A boy was squeezing her arm.

Another boy was lying a few feet away from them on the floor, bleeding.

The boy in front of her was speaking. He had the same energy level as Rianne, but it was more ominous. Darker. But what was he saying?

Braedon cried out in pain again as the vision became clearer.

"*Hmm . . . looks like we have a deal to make,*" the boy holding her said. "*How about this—*"

Braedon's eyes snapped open. Palace guards were bearing down on him, reaching for him, asking if he was all right. The other Wise Ones were standing in front of their thrones, their eyes full of questions. Braedon waved the guards away, and they gave him breathing room.

"Braedon, what's wrong?" Alaric asked, his face the definition of calm.

Braedon was still breathing heavily, but he tried his best to speak as he sat up, holding his side. "It's . . . it's Ria—I mean the Guardian. She's in serious trouble. I think . . . I think she's with her Hunter."

Unobtrusive

The air in the room went tense. Everyone froze, their minds all thinking the same thing: the Great Battle had arrived.

Would it end in death yet again?

"Should we do anything?" Hakim asked.

After a moment of thinking, Alaric shook his head. "No."

"'No?'" Braedon said. "What do you mean? We have to do something. She's only a teenager. She hasn't had a chance to have another Guardian. If she's with her Hunter . . . She hasn't been to training in months; you know that! I don't know what's been going on with her, but she isn't in tune with her Fuora. She might lose."

Alaric made his way down his steps. "I realize that. It's a large risk, but it's one we're willing to take."

The guards exchanged uncomfortable glances as Braedon staggered to his feet. "*We* or you?" Braedon asked. "She doesn't stand a chance! There must be something we can do! To delay it! You're willing to risk the lives of the Sterlings and Advancers like this?" He couldn't believe his ears.

"Yes. We are prepared to take this to heart," Alaric said. "But if what you say is true—that she hasn't produced another Guardian—there is the possibility that the current Hunter hasn't either. If the Guardian is defeated and the Hunter comes, it would be the last Great Battle. The last Great Massacre."

Braedon shook with anger. Alaric. The head Wise One. He was going to let the Hunter kill Rianne without a second thought. He was going to sacrifice the lives of everyone in Estona. And it didn't look like the other Wise Ones were going to say anything about it. They were either behind their leader 100 percent, or they didn't have the audacity to go against his word. What happened to the oaths they made to protect Estona and her people at all costs?

"No."

Alaric's brow furrowed. "Excuse me?"

"I said, no. There's no way I'm going to let her die like this."

"Are you really trying to defy me, Braedon?"

Alaric's patience was wearing thin, but Braedon's was too.

Braedon turned and walked away, only for his body to be slammed into the gold wall behind him. His eyes closed, and his teeth gritted from the impact. He slid to the floor, groaning and coughing. When he got the strength to reopen his eyes, he saw Alaric's hand still aimed at him. The guards did nothing—what could they do? The other Wise Ones just looked on, their faces blank, unreadable.

Wait—

"If you won't obey my commands willingly, I'll be more than happy to make you." Alaric's eyes went misty, and the other Wise Ones motioned for the guards to leave the room. Braedon felt his eyes cloud over too.

"Wise One Braedon?" Alaric asked.

He had to fight the compulsion, but . . .

"Yes?" Braedon replied against his will.

"You will do nothing to stop the Great Battle and its named course of events. You will let everything proceed as necessary. Understand?"

You have to fight it! Braedon urged himself. *You can't let him control you! You can't let him tell you what to do! Come on! Fight!*

He began to sweat, and he coughed a couple of times. Was his throat closing on itself? Was Alaric doing that?

"Braedon, I'm waiting for your answer," Alaric said. "Answer me. Now."

"I . . . I . . . I . . ."

Don't let him do it! Don't let him tell you what to do!

Braedon was fighting a losing battle, the easy feeling taking over his mind. The calm telling him to abide by Alaric's rules. It would be so much easier if he just did what he . . .

Rianne will die tonight if you don't do something. You made an oath to Estona. You made an oath to her.

"Braedon," Alaric said. It had never taken this long for someone to succumb to his powerful telepathy.

Lie.

"I . . . I understand."

Alaric was back at ease now. Back in control. "I want to hear you say it. Agree with the terms I have laid before you."

Braedon saw the fog thinning. He was breaking through. He was almost there. He was fighting Alaric, and he was winning. He was so close. So close.

Lie again.

"Yes, Alaric. I understand. We will allow the Great Battle to run its course and then wait for the Massacre to blow over."

"And you will do nothing to stop it, correct?"

"I will do nothing to stop it,"

"Thank you, Braedon. I do not want to be forced to do that again." He lowered his hand. "Now come, all of you. We have to prepare. Braedon will follow suit after his mind clears. Guards, lead him to his chambers." Alaric headed to the main door. The others, after looking at Braedon for a moment, followed him to the meeting room. "Hakim, call the advisors."

After catching his breath, Braedon stood and headed in an opposite direction to his bedchambers. Three guards flanked him on the sides and behind him.

He blocked his mind from everyone in the palace. They had just underestimated how strong he was.

Chapter Forty-Five

Justin hit the training dummy with a roundhouse kick, followed by a burst of his Blade, causing it to fall backward. When it hit the floor, its head popped off. Again.

"Damn it." He looked around to make sure no one had seen it happen, especially Master Nathaniel.

As he walked over to pick it up and perform emergency surgery, his body went cold before returning to its normal temperature and going cold again. He made a small ball of his Blade appear in his hand. It flickered, trying to keep itself alive.

Rianne was trying to keep herself alive.

He sucked in a breath. "Rianne. Oh, God, no."

Justin's head snapped back as a warm, light feeling overtook him. His eyes glowed white, and his breathing slowed.

"Justin, Rianne is in trouble," Braedon said.

Chapter Forty-Six

"Great," William said in response to Rianne's decision. He snapped his fingers, and Chris disappeared in a flash of green light. "As promised, he will wake up at the school once his body settles, all trauma reversed." Rianne wondered why he was trying to give her peace of mind before killing her.

He punched her in the face, then grabbed her upper arms and slammed her back against the stage. Her heart raced, and she felt sick. Her breathing became ragged.

He put a hand under her jaw, and Rianne's eyes widened as he closed his eyes and then reopened them. The whites of his eyes were gone, replaced by pure black.

Suddenly, her jaw and neck felt staticky and pained, as if she had pulled a bare wire out of an electrical outlet with her teeth. Rianne whimpered, trying to hold back the tears as she grabbed his wrist.

"Oh, oh, no. Shhh . . . . Don't cry, sweetheart. It's only going to hurt for a while." He chuckled. "I am so looking forward to watching your last breath leave your body," he whispered, his breath on her lips. The static feeling increased.

When William opened his free hand to attack, Rianne sent her elbow into his throat. As he leaned forward, struggling to breathe, she drove her knee into his face and heard something pop. He reeled back, holding his nose. Then she sent a wave of Blade at him, striking his chest and knocking him to the floor. She kicked him several times before bolting toward the exit.

"That wasn't part of the deal!" he shouted.

She turned around, her hands in front of her to send more Blade attacks at him, but he teleported to her left, and before she knew it, he was upon her, scarlet blood running from his nose.

In her muddled state of mind, she tried to remember what Justin had taught her so long ago and sent a jab toward his jaw, but he grabbed her fist and squeezed, shattering it. She screamed and fell to her knees.

"And to think that I was going to kill you quickly," he snarled.

Tears of agony streamed down her face. She tried to send her healing power to her broken hand, but her mind was too overwhelmed with pain.

"Look how helpless you've become," William said. "That's the kind of stuff that gets me going!" He aimed his right hand at her, and a long stream of hot blue electricity shot out of his palm, twisting and curving. It hit Rianne in the chest and blasted her into the stage. She crumpled to the floor.

Trying not to scream again, she leaped to her feet, cradling her hand while trying to focus on healing it before she blacked out.

He teleported toward her, and she kicked him in the groin. He doubled over, and she kneed him in the face again. He dropped to the floor, stunned, and rolled onto his back. Before she could do anything else, his hand snaked out and grabbed her leg. She kicked his hand, forcing him to let go. Rianne was about to kick him in the groin again, but he teleported to her, grabbing her around the waist, and hoisted her into the air.

Unobtrusive

She dropped her weight and his grip loosened slightly. She pounded him in the face with her fists, twisting her hips to make the blows hit harder, feeling his nose crack.

He threw her into one of the aisles, and she blasted through several armrests before hitting the floor.

He stormed toward her, ripping out the chairs in his way. He laughed. "You're making this kind of fun, but I'm about to fuck you up good."

I have to do something to stop him. I have to get him away from me.

Standing over her, he reached down for her stomach, but she raised her right hand, and the amber-colored force of the Blade hit him, knocking him back several feet. But otherwise, he was unscathed.

No. It did nothing.

She looked at her hand. Her Fuora had weakened. It was faint.

He chuckled. "Aw, what happened? Don't have any more fight left in you?" Then he was on top of her, squeezing her neck, choking her, making it impossible for her to move.

She knew he wanted nothing more than to kill her.

She bridged her hips, and he fell forward, landing on his palms. She grabbed one of his wrists, then reached up and wrapped her arm around his forearm and grabbed her wrist above it with her other hand, swinging around, but he flipped to his side and kicked her away.

"You're just making this more difficult for yourself," he said, his black eyes getting darker by the moment. "Why can't you just accept defeat and let me kill you?"

Suddenly back on top of her again, he unleashed his Motora. Her heart was pricked by thousands of volts, and she felt her blood boiling from the heat. Blood shot out of her mouth and ran back down her throat, choking her. She couldn't breathe or speak, only gurgle.

Everything was blurry and obscured. Her head throbbed, and

each pound caused her world to shake. She could see two Williams now, both of them grinning.

"Let's count how many seconds it takes for your heart to stop beating," he said, his voice sounding far away. Was he even there anymore?

"One . . . two . . . three . . . four . . . five . . . six . . . seven . . ."

As the light in her eyes dimmed, she looked into the eyes of the boy she once knew. The sweet, caring, blue eyes that used to be filled with so much love and kindness had been replaced by deep black pits of oblivion, full of deceit and hatred.

"Nineteen . . . twenty . . . twenty-one . . ."

She heard the sound of metal bending and splitting apart. Rianne felt William's hands leave her, and she coughed a few times as her heart attempted to search for its natural rhythm.

The last blurry thing she saw was William tossed over some of the chairs and another figure looking down at her, lifting her head.

Could she breathe?

"It's all right. You're going to be fine."

Then the world stopped.

Chapter Forty-Seven

C hris opened his eyes, feeling the cool autumn air on his face. It was still early in the morning; the sun hadn't made its appearance, but the sky was turning a bluish hue.

Startled, he jumped to his feet and looked at his surroundings. He was in the school quad near one of the benches, and he was alone.

What in the world happened?

He couldn't remember anything. William had asked him to meet there, something about a surprise for Rianne, but anything beyond that was . . . gone. His neck, face, and jaw were a little sore, though. He opened his mouth wide a few times, trying to work out the stiffness.

His phone vibrated. He looked at it: a text from Alex. Nothing from Rianne yet. And nothing more from William.

Chris ran a hand over his face. "I need to get back home," he mumbled, then headed to his car. It hurt his head to try to make sense of anything.

Chapter Forty-Eight

Rianne groaned as her phone alarm rang at 7:35 a.m. She didn't want to wake up. She just wanted to go back to sleep. To forget.

Her head ached, her chest serving as a constant reminder of the night before each time she took a breath. She was lucky she had healing Fuora; her body was recuperating quicker than average. She tried moving her fingers. They were no longer broken beyond belief, but they were as sore as hell.

William Rogers tried to kill her.

He wasn't who she thought he was. He was a liar. He was evil. A part of her wanted revenge, and another part was terrified. Everything about the night before sent adrenaline and fear through her core. Both of them had survived the Great Battle.

Barely.

Rianne opened her eyes. She had to get ready for school. She was tempted to stay in bed, to reflect on everything that had happened. She didn't even want to try and comprehend how she had gotten back home.

When she sat up, she noticed a boy sitting in a chair next to her bed. He was wearing blue jeans and a black Metallica hoodie. He had been on his phone, but now he was looking at her.

She blanched. "Justin?" All the exhaustion was gone as her brain realized that her Mentor and best friend was in her bedroom. "What are you doing here?"

Justin laughed at her surprised response. "Thanks for the warm welcome to your happy home. How're you feelin'?"

Rianne swung her legs over the side of the bed, so she could look at him properly, her body protesting every move. "What are you doing here?" she repeated. "Are you okay?"

"You're asking me if *I'm* okay?" he asked. "*You* were the one squaring off against your Hunter. You were in terrible shape when I found you, but it looks like you held your own for a while. I'm proud of you."

"It . . . that was . . . you?"

"Yeah. Braedon and I sensed you were in danger. He was promoted to Wise One status a few months ago, so he couldn't get to you. He reached out to me right when I figured out what was happening. He sent me to where he saw you in his vision, and I got to you as quickly as I could. I found the Hunter on top of you. If we'd waited five more minutes, I'm pretty sure you . . ." Rather than finish his sentence, he looked at his phone's darkened screen instead.

Rianne took everything in for a minute. "Justin . . ." She leaned forward. "You came to help me . . . after everything that happened."

He stood. "Why wouldn't I? We could get in a thousand stupid fights, but I would still give my life for my Guardian."

Tears fell from Rianne's eyes. "Justin, I'm so sorry. I should've listened to you." She rushed to him, squeezing him in a hug. "I'm so sorry."

Justin hugged her back. "You're my best friend, Rianne. You don't need to apologize to me for anything. I'm just glad you're alive."

She sniffled. "Thank you, Justin."

"Don't mention it." He chuckled. "You would've done the same for me."

"Rianne! Rianne Sydney Jarrett!" a voice boomed, followed by stomping up the staircase.

Rianne broke their embrace. "Oh, I'm in *so* much trouble."

"Why?"

"I might have snuck out last night."

Justin nodded in approval. "Nice. So, what's your dad gonna say about a boy being in your room this early in the morning? Especially since you're already in trouble?"

"Justin!" Rianne hissed. "You're not helping!" She grabbed his arm and pushed him toward the closet, opening the door. "Stay in here. And don't say anything!"

Justin didn't protest as Rianne shoved him into the closet, his head hitting some of her empty hangers. "Ow!" he shouted before Rianne shushed him. She barely had time to close the closet door when her father burst in. His brown hair was untidy, and his face and eyes were red with fatigue and anger.

"Rianne Sydney Jarrett! Where have you been? I was out all night looking for you! You know what? I don't even want to know. What the hell is wrong with you, sneaking out of this house like that?"

"Dad, relax," Rianne said, holding her hands up. "I'm fine. Calm down."

Matt was speechless for a moment. "Calm? You—you want me to calm down? You *lied* to my face, Rianne, and snuck out of *my house*! I had no clue where you were! You wouldn't pick up your phone. I didn't know if something happened to you or if you were hurt or anything!"

Well, technically, something did *happen to me, and* I *did* get *hurt.*

"Dad, I'm fine! You gotta trust me! I wouldn't do anything stupid."

"I highly doubt that, Rianne."

"How could you say that?" That was like a slap in the face. And it hurt. "You've always trusted me."

"And now I don't. I was worried about you. You're my only daughter, Rianne. How could you do something like that to me? I thought something awful had happened to you."

"Daddy, I—"

"No. No. I don't want to hear any more excuses."

"But, Dad—"

"I said no! Until I can think of a better punishment, you're grounded. And while we're on the subject of *lying*, are there any more secrets you've been keeping from me?"

Rianne sucked in a breath and then realized he wasn't talking about her powers. Her mind was still a blur, but there was one she hadn't told him yet. "I kinda got fired from my job at the restaurant."

Matt looked as if he were about to blow another fuse, but he composed himself. "When?"

"A while ago. Like, six months ago."

"What? Why?"

"I left my shift early without telling Mr. Newman."

"Damn it, Rianne, that is so unlike you. Who knows what you were doing when you told me you were working? I don't even know who you are anymore."

She didn't answer.

"Like I said, I expect you to be home right after school, though I might not be here when you get back." He turned to walk out the door.

"Where will you be?"

"Why should I tell you? You never tell me where *you're* going."

He walked out, slamming the door behind him.

Rianne opened her closet door. Justin was on the floor, his usual joking face replaced by a look of unease. "I'm so sorry," he said as he came out.

She shook her head, blowing it off. "It's not a big deal. He'll get over it."

She looked away from Justin, not wanting him to see the uncertainty in her eyes. Then she saw the time on her clock. "I should get ready. Are you back here in the Standard world for a while?"

"Yeah, I am. It was time for me to come back anyway. I'll be late for school, but I'll find you. Oh, and by the way, you should know that Braedon is pissed. *Royally* pissed." He chuckled at his little pun, and Rianne rolled her eyes.

"What would he be mad at me for?" she asked. "He's the one who cut things off."

"That may be true, but he's still pissed to the extreme. While you were resting, he reached out to me for a status update on you. He's relieved that you're okay, but I did have to debrief him on the fact that you were dating your Hunter."

Rianne would have thrown herself onto her bed and smothered herself with her pillow if she didn't know it would cause her sore body more pain. "Ugh, Justin, why would you tell him that!"

He shrugged. "What would you have wanted me to do?"

"Lie!"

"I'm not gonna face a Wise One's wrath to cover your butt!"

Rianne smiled. "But you faced the Hunter to save it."

He shrugged. "Way easier if you ask me."

Chapter Forty-Nine

Williiam opened his bedroom door and walked into the hallway. His head pounded with each step, and his nose was swollen.

He cursed to himself as he recalled what had happened the night before. His Guardian had gotten away, though not alone. She had help from that damned Sterling Justin Allan. His father had told him about Sterlings—the magical beings with a single magical power, the Affera.

As he walked into the kitchen and grabbed a beer from the refrigerator as he reviewed the previous night's events in his mind. He had Rianne cornered. His hands were on her neck, and she was almost dead.

God, she was almost dead. She couldn't speak or scream. Her body was growing limper with each passing moment, her eyes closing. Her blood ran over his fingertips. Oh, the exhilaration he felt as her breathing slowed beneath him.

William leaned against the counter and then slammed his beer bottle down in frustration. Foaming liquid sloshed out of it and onto the granite surface. "Damn it, damn it, damn it!"

She had almost died. That was the moment when one of the locked side doors flew open, and Justin ran in. He sent him into the seats behind him and then held him there, all with a single hand gesture.

"Allan!" William growled. "I'm gonna kill you!"

Justin said nothing, just hurried over to Rianne and took her in his arms.

He's trying to save her, William realized. He yelled, summoning more of his Motora. His whole body was engulfed in his blue electric energy. A blast went off, and he was freed.

Standing up, he thrust his hands to his sides, covering them in static electricity. "Put her down!"

William expected Justin to refuse, but instead, he set Rianne down on the floor. Then he looked at William and took a deep breath. His eyes were unblinking, his face was stern. "I'm her Mentor, and I'm a lot stronger than I look."

William shot a bolt at the Sterling, but the electricity rebounded with as much force as he had used, maybe more. He staggered backward, stunned. His power had just been thrown right back at him by a royal-blue force field.

Outraged, William threw multiple shots of his electricity, each one more powerful than the last. He put all his frustration and anger into it, ready to kill the being that had stopped him from murdering the Guardian.

This time Justin lifted both hands in front of him, and the blue shield pushed back the blows. With each hit, Justin had to push his feet harder into the floor to keep from being sent backward. William dodged the rebounds this time and heard them hit the wall behind him with shattering crackles.

Then felt himself thrown against the very stage he had hurled Rianne into minutes before. His head rebounded against it. He blinked, feeling dazed and unable to move. Then he felt a hand on his throat.

Unobtrusive

"I told you I'm stronger than I look," Justin said. "Maybe you should learn some strategy."

Without being touched, William's head was slammed into the reinforced wood behind him. It felt as if his skull was splitting open.

Then everything went black.

He awoke in his room, his head throbbing and on fire.

There was no way he should have lost. When it came to powers, he was physically stronger.

It must be because I used too much energy on Rianne. I was tired and reaching my limits when Justin showed up. That's the only—

The front door opened, and in came his mother. It looked like she had been up all night. However, she had an expression on her face that he'd never seen before, at least not directed toward him— anger.

"William Skyler Rogers!" she shouted. She never got mad, either. She had the common sense not to. "Where in the world were you last night?"

William stared her down, an incredulous look on his face. "Who the hell do you think you're talking to?" He was about to take his first swing of beer when she snatched it out of his hand, splattering some of it on his shirt.

Before he could say anything, Jessica was shouting again. "Give me that! You're eighteen, for God's sake! Not even legal!" She went over to the sink and poured the drink into it. William felt his anger rising. Where had she gotten all this audacity? "Now answer the question, William. Where were you all night? Did you know I was out looking for you?"

William said nothing, just pointed toward the sink where his beer had just disappeared. "What the hell is wrong with you? And it's none of your business where I go. You don't tell me what to do."

Jessica exploded. "William, I'm afraid something has been amiss in this household! *I* am the parent, and *you* are the child! I pay the bills, and on top of that, you don't have a job and are still living in *my* house, so I have *every* right to know your business! Do you understand me?"

William rolled his eyes. He did not have the energy for her at that moment. His head was in flames, he was pissed, and he was tired. He turned and walked back toward his room.

"William! Where do you think you're going? Get back here right now! I'm talking to you, young man!"

He continued to ignore her. He had his hand on his doorknob when she grabbed his shoulder and spun him around. He met his mother's furious face as she pushed him into the door.

"Now you listen to me, William. I am *done* with this attitude of yours. I'm over it! If you expect to keep living here, you are going to live by my rules. There is going to be no more drinking, and you *will* have a curfew. If I have to treat you the way your father treated us, then I will do that, but I am not taking your crap anymore. Do you understand?"

William retreated inward. *What would Father have done to me if he were still here, and I told him that I had failed to kill my Guardian last night?* He shook without meaning to.

His father, Henry Rogers, had usually reserved his anger for Jessica, but there were several times when William ended up being on the receiving end. Sometimes it was his fault; majority of the time, it wasn't.

The former Hunter wasn't afraid of damaging his bloodline.

* * *

"Father, just let me kill her. *Please* just let me kill her," William pleaded as he entered the living room. "I promise I'll make it fast, so she won't feel a thing."

Henry looked at his son with dead, drunken eyes. There was a fresh can of beer in his hand, and though the television had a college football game on, he didn't seem to be watching it. He sat in his recliner, one ankle resting on the opposite knee. "Who would you like to kill this time, William?"

"Mother."

He sighed. "And why would you want to do that?"

"Because she won't leave me alone! She keeps wanting me to do something with her. She's driving me crazy, and it's pissing me off. I can't take her anymore!"

"William, don't you think you're being a little dramatic?"

"No."

His father let out a deep sigh. "Just spend time with her, son."

"I don't *want* to spend time with her. *You* don't even want to spend time with her! Why not kill her? You've wanted to ever since you met her, I bet. Grandfather told me that all Hunters want to kill everyone they meet."

Henry didn't answer the accusations, and William saw an opportunity. Maybe he could spin the situation his way.

"Why don't we team up for a few minutes? That's all it would take. This would let me get some extra practice for when I find my Guardian, and it'll be fun. I promise she won't feel a thing."

"No, William. Your mother . . . doesn't deserve that. Not now."

William narrowed his eyes and pouted. "God, killing your Guardian must've made you weak or something," he mumbled as he turned to head back to his room.

His father stood up from the recliner. "What did you say, William?"

"I said you got w—" Henry teleported to William and grabbed him by the neck, slamming him into the wall. His grip was strong and painful, cutting off his air supply.

"So, I got weak, huh? I'll show you how weak I got." Still squeezing, he pulled William off the wall and then slammed him back into it. William struggled for air.

"Father, Father, stop," William begged as he grabbed Henry's forearms, trying to pry him off. William had strength too, but it was no match for his father.

"If I'm so weak, make me let go. Show me how tough our new Hunter is."

"Henry! Henry, let go of him!" William's mother tugged on her husband's arm, to no avail. "Henry, are you drunk again? Let him go! Let him go, Henry!" She slapped him, but he was unfazed.

Henry didn't acknowledge her, just applied more pressure to William's throat. William's brain became foggy, and it was difficult to breathe. *Come on,* he told himself, *come on.* He focused on his electricity. Little sparks came out of his hands and leaped onto his father's arms, but if it did anything to him, he didn't show it. William was struggling, but he couldn't get his powers to work. Not enough energy . . . not enough air . . .

Tears pooled in Jessica's eyes. "Henry, please! Let go of our little boy! Please, Henry, I'm begging you!"

"Get off me!" Henry growled, brushing her away.

Helpless, Jessica fell to her knees and wept.

William's arms fell to his side. His eyes grew heavy, and static filled his mind. His father was killing him.

And then the pressure was gone, and William was on the floor. He took large gulps of air and coughed, holding his bruised throat. His head cleared as precious oxygen moved through his system.

Still crying, his mother crawled over and rubbed his back. "Are you okay, honey?"

He waved her off. "I'm fine," he rasped, coughing.

Henry looked down at them. "Can you speak, son?" His voice held no sincerity. Did he not care that he'd almost strangled William to death?

No, of course he doesn't.

"Yes," William answered. His voice was hoarse, and he didn't look up.

"Yes, what?"

"Yes . . . sir." He growled "sir" through gritted teeth.

"Look at me. Now."

Unobtrusive

William raised his eyes to his father. Henry's eyes were hard and unfeeling, and William longed to look away.

"I never, *ever,* want to hear you call me weak again. My word goes, without question. You are my next in line, and I *deserve* your respect. Do you understand?"

William nodded. "Yes, sir."

"Henry!" Jessica shouted. "You almost *killed* our son over that? How could you?" She took a breath as she fought for words. "You *are* weak, Henry! If you can't take one ridiculous insult from a thirteen-year-old boy, you *are* weak!"

That made Henry angry. The situation wasn't going to end well. It never did. William was only thirteen at the time, but he could name every injury his mother had ever received from his father's hands.

Jessica screamed as Henry grabbed her arm and jerked her off the floor. She tried to wrangle out of his grip, but it was impossible. He was too strong.

William watched his father take his mother into their room and slam the door behind them.

He looked back at the floor, shaking in fear as he listened to his mother's cries for mercy and his father's yelling, telling her to shut the hell up. Three sounds followed—a slap, a body slamming into a wall, and glass breaking.

* * *

William stared at his mother, his mouth hanging open. She didn't sound like the scared, obedient Jessica Rogers anymore.

"William, do you understand me?" Jessica asked in a tone that reminded him of his father.

"Yeah," William whispered.

"That's 'yes, ma'am,' William." She released him. "Now hurry and get ready before you're late again. And you're to come home right after school. You're grounded."

William went into his bedroom to get changed. His pride was damaged, and he wanted to get out of the house as soon as he could. He couldn't even intimidate his mother. His Motora was dormant for the time being. He had used too much energy the night before.

On his way out of his bedroom, he heard the refrigerator open and close. She was probably going to make herself something to eat.

"And William," Jessica said.

Wearing a new outfit, he grabbed his backpack from the spot on the couch where he had thrown it the afternoon before. "Yes, Mother?" He hated this stupid "politeness" thing. She was lucky he was too tired to argue about her newfound authority.

"I likely won't be home when you get back."

"And why is that?" William asked, careful to keep the edge out of his voice.

She didn't. "I'll tell you where I'm going if you tell me where you were last night."

William felt his eye twitch as he remembered what Justin had done. That *damn* Sterling ruined *everything*. His mother would be dead right now if not for him. He could be on a killing spree right now if not for him.

He just growled something unintelligible and went out the front door, slamming it behind him.

Chapter Fifty

Matt watched through the living room window as Rianne drove off to school.

He let out a breath. What was happening to his daughter? Why had they grown so far apart? And why couldn't he do anything about it? They used to be so close, *so close*, but ever since summer, she had changed. They hadn't been getting along as well as they used to. She wasn't around the house often, and when she was, she didn't want to spend time with him anymore. Watching a game together like they had done the previous night had become a rarity.

He shook his head. It probably couldn't be helped. She was seventeen now. She was bound to want her own space sooner or later. But that didn't make it any easier to accept.

He looked at the wall clock in the kitchen. Almost 8:30. He realized he had better get some sleep; his date was at two.

While searching for their kids the night before, Matt and Jessica had reconnected. They got to know the new versions of each other while also reminiscing on the times they had together back when they were in high school. Though he didn't want to admit it at first, he'd had a lot of fun with her.

Matt had been shattered after Chelsea died. He hadn't been interested in dating after that, focusing instead on raising a daughter. He'd had prospects over the years, women who expressed interest, but he didn't want that to make that a priority. He just wanted to make Chelsea proud by giving Rianne the life she deserved.

But Rianne was older now, and so was he. He had to move on with his life and stop being afraid to put himself back out there. Stop being afraid of getting hurt again.

It would take some getting used to. He would have to reteach himself how to act on a date—and around women, for that matter. What were the odds he would meet up with someone from what was a lifetime ago?

As he crawled into bed, he saw Chelsea's photo across the room on his dresser. He closed his eyes, knowing he was making her proud.

Chapter Fifty-One

Jessica looked away from Matt's eyes as he took her hand and interlocked his fingers with hers. They were walking through one of Felix's parks. The path was made of red and tan cobblestones, old and worn out from decades of foot traffic. In different parts of the fresh green grass, among the multicolored flowers, were white benches where some couples were sitting in the early evening sun. Out of all those things, though, she only saw Matt.

The date had been wonderful. Matt picked her up, and they went to an outdoor restaurant downtown to have lunch. That in itself took a couple of hours because of some problems in the kitchen, but she didn't care; the conversations they had made everything pass by comfortably. She had learned so many new things about him and he about her.

Afterward, he took her roller skating—another thing they used to do in their youth. She had always loved roller skating but hadn't gotten to enjoy it after having William so long ago. She was wobbly on the skates—pretty much having to relearn—but Matt held onto her the whole time, laughing and coaching her through it. The whole date had been a dream, a dream that she didn't want to wake up from.

A lot of things had changed. He had grown up a lot. Maybe losing a loved one had forced him to be more mature, or maybe having a daughter and having to raise her on his own had done it. From what she remembered, Matt was always playing childish pranks on everyone in the friend group, and didn't take life very seriously.

Well, he *was* seventeen then. Now they were both in their thirties and had already lived a lot of life, although it had taken an unexpected turn for both of them. Maybe it was fate that had brought them together again. Maybe.

Matt led her to a nearby bench, and they sat down. Not wanting an awkward silence to ensue, Jessica spoke first. "So, um, how long were you with your girlfriend?"

"We met at one of Khalil's parties back in high school. You remember him? Khalil Laudeman?"

Jessica nodded. "Vaguely."

"Well, I was in the living room the first time I saw Chelsea, and I was floored. She . . . she was something else. We dated for about a year, year and a half, and then we had Rianne. So, I think altogether we were together for almost five years. What about you and your husband?"

Jessica didn't know why she had asked that question. Of course, Matt would ask her the same thing, but the last thing she wanted to think about was her dead, abusive husband. "After we graduated, I went to North Carolina for school. I met Henry there, and we had William before I graduated. We got married soon after and then moved to New York. We were together until he passed."

Jessica's hand had been resting between them on the bench, and Matt placed his over hers. "I'm sorry. That must've been hard for you and William. How old was he?"

"He had just turned sixteen, and he took it very hard. He and his father were close—almost as if they were bonded by something I didn't know about. Closer than William and I could ever be. My son and I had been detached before, but after Henry died, we practically became strangers living in the same house. That's why I moved us back down here. I thought maybe something familiar and more low key would be good for us."

"Yeah," Matt said, looking around at the park. "Felix does have a good effect on people. I'm glad you're back down here."

"Me too. You said last night that Rianne's mom died too. I'm sorry to hear that."

"Thank you. It was hard. *Really* hard. There were times when I didn't think I'd make it through, to be honest. But I had to do so for my daughter, you know? Rianne doesn't know that she died. Chelsea wanted me to let Rianne grow up thinking she'd left us. Thought it would be easier for her to take. I guess that's why I'm so protective of her. I think it's also why I take my job so seriously. I want to protect anyone that I can."

Jessica nodded. "I am *so* sorry. I didn't mean to turn this date into something sad like this!"

Matt laughed. "Really, it's fine! Looks like we've both gone through a lot, huh?"

"Yeah. We've both changed—for the better, I think. But on a happier note, this has been one of the best dates of my entire life. Everything has been amazing. Literally amazing."

Matt smiled at her, causing butterflies to erupt in her stomach. "Being with you has been, I don't know, something else. Something I'll remember. Even if you're a blonde now." His brown eyes twinkled.

Jessica pretended to pout. "Don't I look good as a blonde?"

"I think you look beautiful as a blonde or a brunette. Honestly."

She was aware of her cheeks heating up. It felt good to blush, though. She hadn't blushed in what seemed like years.

"And what about my critique for today, Jess?" Matt asked, leaning back on the bench. "How do I score? Has anything changed from when we were younger?"

Jessica smiled, playing with her hair. "On a scale of what to what?"

"One to ten. Just to keep things simple."

"Simple? Okay, then I would say . . . a solid twenty. And yes, you've changed a lot. But in a good way."

"Yes! I can sleep soundly tonight."

Jessica laughed. "You know, Matt, you're really different when you're off duty. It's interesting."

"Do you like my off-duty persona?"

"Yeah. I love it."

They looked into each other's eyes. Jessica felt her heart speed up as he leaned in closer and put his hand in her hair like he used to all those years ago. She closed her eyes and tilted her head up, ready to feel his lips on hers.

The kiss was electrifying, and she wanted to stay in his embrace for eternity.

For the first time in years, she felt good about life.

Chapter Fifty-Two

Rianne dreaded walking up the staircase to her room. About three weeks had passed, and every time she came home, she was scared and hesitant. When was Braedon going to show up?

Things at school hadn't gotten much better. Everyone had figured out that she and William had broken up, since they no longer spoke to each other and kept as much distance as possible. Alex, Chris, and many others asked for details about the breakup, but Rianne created a fake reason. "We had a pretty big fight. One of those that you don't come back from. It was mutual. We're both fine." It was pretty much the truth.

Justin was helping her out the most—emotionally and physically—with her Fuora. She really missed training, and Ellis was relieved that he could fulfill an important part of his new station.

William was taking the "breakup" well. Many girls had already approached him, asking if he wanted to hang out, which he never declined. He wasn't fazed at all. He had gotten into the habit of glaring at Rianne, though, which didn't help the rumors that Rianne had done something that led to the breakup.

She remembered what Justin said about how angry Braedon would be. She had never seen him angry before; he was always in a nonchalant, cheery mood. Then again, she had never seen her father angry either, but he had just gone off.

She opened her bedroom door a crack and peeked inside, something she had done for the past couple of weeks to see if her Protector was there.

Dang it.

Braedon was not happy. He was sitting in her desk chair; he hadn't heard the door open. He was taking huge breaths, trying to calm himself, to no avail. He was also messing with something in his hands—fire. He kept making it grow larger and larger before extinguishing it. Clearly, he was pissed.

Even though he was angry, he was still as handsome as she remembered. She stared at him, trying to memorize his features just in case he left again. His hair was the same, maybe slightly longer, and his facial hair was immaculate, as always. He was wearing a blue denim shirt and tan jeans with brown shoes, and a pair of sunglasses sat on his head. She also spotted a gold ring on his right hand.

She sighed. It was now or never.

She opened the door and walked into the room. Before Braedon could say anything, she spoke. "Braedon, I already know what you're going to say, and to be honest, I don't want to hear it." She set her backpack on the floor.

That comment made Braedon lose what little composure he had. The fire he was playing with vanished, and he stood up and approached her. "Don't want to hear it? *Don't want to hear it?*" She jumped in response to his tone. "Rianne, does it look like I give a bloody damn?" He slammed her door. "You do know how insanely *stupid* you've been?"

Rianne put her hands on her hips. "Stupid? *I've* been stupid?"

"Yes. I would call getting trapped by your Hunter pretty high up there on the idiot list, Rianne."

"It wasn't my fault, Braedon!"

"How was it *not* your fault?"

"He *told* me to go there! I didn't—"

Braedon ran a hand through his hair, then over his face, getting more and more agitated. "You're now trying to defend yourself by saying it *wasn't* your fault that you got trapped by your Hunter, when you *willingly* went to the place he told you to go? Didn't you think that would raise some warning signs?"

"I didn't know my ex was my Hunter, and—" Rianne stopped, pursing her lips.

"Yeah, I already know that bit. Justin told me. Why wouldn't you listen to him? He *told* you something was wrong about William, but you refused to listen! What kind of Guardian are you? Are you that daft?"

"Don't you dare call me that!"

Without meaning to, two amber-colored spheres of energy appeared and swirled around her hands.

"I told you it wasn't my fault! You didn't even train me to be able to tell! None of you did!"

Braedon's tone became mocking. "Oh, *we* didn't train you? When you blatantly *refused* to come to Estona because you were off gallivanting with your Hunter?"

"I didn't want to come to Estona because of *you*! Because of what you said to me! I didn't want to be constantly reminded of *your* rejection!"

Braedon clenched his jaw. "I didn't reject you. I had other things going on. And I'm not your Protector anymore."

Rianne rolled her eyes. "Oh, I know *that* now. But it would have been great to know that seven months ago, Mr. Wise One, sire. Ellis couldn't even tell me what was going on—I'm guessing because you forbade him! You were being selfish!"

Braedon walked up to her until they were almost chest to chest. Both of them refused to back down. "Don't you dare call me selfish. Everything I've ever done and been told to do was for the betterment of Estona and the Guardian line. When I was chosen as an Advancer, I was taken away from my family. Me and Ellis both. We had a younger sister, Rianne. I loved her more than *anything* in the world, and the last time I saw her, we had a fight. We weren't talking when I was taken away. You have no idea how much that ate me up inside. How much it *still* eats me up inside. And *every* day I felt like the same thing was happening with you. Hell, it *did* almost happen!"

Rianne gritted her teeth. "You could've done a lot to change that, but you didn't. Because, apparently, you didn't *want* to!"

He stepped away and turned his back to her, pinching the bridge of his nose between his thumb and forefinger. Then he stomped his foot. "Why are you being so difficult, Rianne?"

"Difficult? *Difficult?* I'm not the one being difficult here. You are! I almost *died*, and you come here screaming at me? I haven't seen you in forever. I . . . I missed you." He looked at her, his hand still to his face. "I was so angry with you, and you wouldn't talk to me. I felt like I couldn't reach out because you had already cut us off. You didn't tell me what was going on with you. You wouldn't see me. You abandoned me. And you didn't even tell me why. And now I know you don't give a damn about me."

"Don't say that!" he shouted, stepping back toward her.

Rianne felt that she should stop, but she couldn't. The words kept coming, flying out of her mouth like a freight train coming off its tracks, about to crash. "You *don't* care, and you *know* you don't! All you see me as is another of your Guardians who you have to protect for the Great Battle. You don't see me as *anything* else. You're blind when it comes to me. When you look at me, all you see is 'the current Guardian.' You don't give a—"

"Stop it, Rianne," he whispered, his voice labored and heavy. "You know that isn't true. When I look at you, I—" He stopped, picking his words. "If I didn't give a damn about you, would I have helped you train when Justin was late? Disobeyed Wise One Alaric and endured the fifteen lashes I received as a result? Defied my fellow Wise Ones—*again*—to make sure you aren't hurt? To see if there was anything you need from me? Anything I can do for you? Hell, Rianne, I'm ready to sleep on the floor again just so you have me there to keep you safe."

Rianne took in everything he had just told her, trying to keep her mind clear. She knew he wouldn't be there with her at that moment if he didn't care about her. Everything he had just said was completely true.

But he could disappear at any moment. He'd already proved that.

"You need to figure out what you want," she said. "You either care about me or you don't. We can pretend that nothing ever happened between us. I don't want to lose you again, but I can't let you hurt me again either."

"But, Rianne," he whispered, "what if history repeats itself, like with Hakim and Elizabeth? What if this doesn't work?"

"Isn't it worth the risk?"

After a moment, he nodded.

He stared into her green eyes, and she stared back into his brown ones. Her heart pounded, but she kept her breathing under control. His hands cupped her face, brushing his thumbs over her cheeks. He pressed himself closer to her, removing the space between them. Then he leaned down, and their lips finally met.

The kiss was gentle at first, soft and hesitant, but it became more passionate the longer they were connected to each other. Months of longing were finally coming together in the culmination of how much they wanted each other.

Rianne placed her hands against Braedon's chest and pushed him onto her bed. Then she got on top of him, kissing him again. He pulled her toward him, refusing to let her go. She started unbuttoning his shirt, her fingers shaking. Was she supposed to be so nervous? Was that normal?

He flipped her onto her back, and now she was looking up at

Braedon instead of down at him. "God, I missed you so much." He caressed her cheek, causing her to blush. She thirsted for his touch.

She smiled. "I missed you too. You're not going to leave again, are you?"

Braedon's eyes searched hers. "Never. Are you sure you're ready? I don't want you to rush into anything. I'll wait for you."

Rianne brushed his lips with her thumb and then unfastened the rest of his shirt, taking it off. She stared at his tan, muscular chest, mesmerized. He was gorgeous in every way. She stroked him with her hand.

"I know you would, Braedon. And that's why I'm in love with you and want to share this with you. Just . . . promise to take care of me, okay?"

He smiled and ran his hand through her hair. "I wouldn't have it any other way. I love you too, darling." He leaned down and kissed her again.

Chapter Fifty-Three

William's mother wasn't home when he returned from school. He relaxed. Though she had made it a habit to be out of the house more often lately, there were still times when she was home and forced him to spend time with her. He wished things could go back to the way they used to be—where she feared him, and he had peace.

He opened the fridge and found no beer or any other alcohol, for that matter. "God damn it!" he shouted, slamming the door. His mother had cleared everything out. *Again.* The club wouldn't open for hours, and he *needed* a drink.

About six months had passed since the night he almost killed his Guardian. He still hated thinking about it. *She was right in my hands,* he thought as he plopped himself onto the couch. He opened his left palm, and a medium-size ball of electricity covered it.

His Motora had three states. The first was neutral, where he used his powers to fix mechanical things or turn a light on and off by releasing or absorbing it. Little things of that nature.

In his second state, he used his powers for killing. His eyes would turn black, indicating he could pull a murder off flawlessly with no clues left in his wake.

The third hadn't made itself known to him yet. His father told him it would make him all-powerful. Maybe that would come when he went on his Great Massacre.

In any case, he still wanted to kill someone. At least fill a portion of the void that was reserved for the Guardian's death and let out some of his pent-up energy.

He smiled as an image of a beautiful girl's face formed in his mind. Courtney from English class. After he and Rianne broke up, she had put herself in the ring of availability. Very fervently too.

He wanted to kill someone.

She was there, untaken.

The perfect candidate.

Chapter Fifty-Four

Courtney Taylor, daughter of the principal of Felix High School, sat at her vanity mirror, running a brush through her long, soft hair. *Thirty-three . . . thirty-four . . . thirty-five . . .* she counted in her head. She made it a habit to brush her straight brunette hair fifty times before she went to bed. It helped calm her nerves.

Forty-one . . . forty-two . . . forty-thr—

Three sharp knocks broke her concentration.

Courtney turned to her window. "William?" Though wondering what he was doing at her window so late, she didn't complain; he was hot. She got up and made sure her pink silk nightgown was fitted properly on her slim body, then put on her brightest, sexiest smile and opened the window.

"Well, well, well," she said, "look who it is."

William smiled. "Well, well, well. Here I am."

"What are you doing here? Need help with something?"

William raised an eyebrow. "You could say that."

She moved out of the way to let him in, closing the window after him. "So, why *are* you here?"

"I haven't been able to stop thinking about you. I've been trying to find the right moment to talk to you about it."

"And you couldn't do that in class or at school?"

William shrugged. "I try to be a good student. We're about to graduate, after all. So, I figured . . ." His eyes traveled up and down her body, and he bit his bottom lip as he put his hands in the pockets of his leather jacket. "why not have some fun before then?"

Courtney smiled even wider. "What I'm wondering is, why go through all those other girls before getting to me?" She twirled a few strands of her perfectly brushed hair.

William moved in closer. "I believe in saving the best for last." Before she could respond, he grabbed her face in his hands and pressed his mouth to hers.

William's kiss became harder, and he stepped into her, causing her to walk backward until they both fell onto her plush bed. Courtney's heart sped up when she felt William's tongue in her mouth and his hands at her hips, slowly but surely sliding her nightgown up.

She pulled away from the kiss. "William, wait."

"I thought you wanted me," he practically growled. "You've been wanting me for months."

"I did. I do! But my parents are in the living room and—"

"Shhh. Relax. It'll be fine as long as you're quiet." He lifted her nightgown until her flat stomach was exposed and placed his hand on it. Then he kissed her neck.

"William . . ." she whispered.

Suddenly, a pang, like a knife, hit her in the stomach. "Ah!" she cried.

"Why are you already making all that noise?" William asked as he continued kissing her neck, chuckling. "I didn't even do anything yet."

That was weird, she thought. "I know. I was—I don't know. It was like a weird—never mind."

Seconds later, it happened again but more intensely. Instead of feeling like a knife, it was more like . . . electrocution. She tried to scream, but William's hand covered her mouth, muffling her.

The pain. The agony. It was like hell.

William's face appeared in her vision. Her eyes widened as she looked into his. They were completely black.

"What's the matter, Courtney? Is something wrong?" He chuckled again.

His other hand was still on her stomach, the pressure increasing with the pain. She tried to fight him off, but he was too strong. He kept her still and silent.

"It's always fun to kill the clueless ones. If I went to someone who wasn't so desperate for attention, it wouldn't be as satisfying, you know? But you, Courtney, you were perfect for what I wanted tonight. You wanted my attention so badly that you didn't even realize you let a killer into your bedroom. Oh, poor, naïve, *stupid* little Courtney." He sighed and somehow increased her pain. "I wonder if you'll make the news when they find your body. Now that's a fun question." He smiled.

Tears rolled down her cheeks. He was a killer? But what had she done to make him want to target her? There was no way he was really going to kill her. There was no way she was about to die. She tried struggling again, but he held her down.

There was no way out.

He grunted and pushed down on her stomach, sending out a huge shock and muting scream. Her eyes stared into nothing, and her head lolled to the side.

William kissed her lips one last time and closed her eyelids.

Chapter Fifty-Five

William got off the bed and stared at Courtney's body, a blissful smile on his face.

God, it felt so *good* to kill. It filled him with a pleasure and exhilaration that he couldn't explain. When he took someone's life, it made him feel in control of everything around him. It made him feel invincible. The best part was, he would never get caught for it. Another benefit of his Motora.

He chuckled. Both girls had been so foolish, so brainless. He had met Maria in a coffee shop in Buffalo. It was during his time out of the school system, and he was bored. Might as well practice, right? He had charmed her, made her fall for him and leave her boyfriend. Made her obey him. It didn't take long. Then he lured her out of her home and took her someplace quiet, isolated, where no one would hear her screams.

When William killed her, it didn't go as smoothly as he had hoped. Maria put up a good fight—she had quite an arm for a girl—but he knocked her out. And then he did his deed—he electrocuted her.

It took around two minutes and thirteen seconds for her to die.

Unobtrusive

Courtney was another on-the-side kill. She was a bystander, and when he was itching for murder, she had been the one to step up. Like a fool.

But his hands were still itching.

He wanted more of it.

More of the exhilaration.

More of the kill.

William opened Courtney's bedroom door, peeking into the hallway. He heard the sound of the TV in the living room. A sitcom rerun. Typical. No lights were on, just the flickering light from the TV. Perfect.

He made his way down the hallway, his hands extended on either side, sliding along the walls. Stealth was definitely on his side.

For a moment.

With his heart pounding in anticipation, William accidentally let off some electricity through his fingers. It crackled as it traveled through the walls, and a small *boom* went off near the television. The screen flickered as it struggled to stay on.

Shit.

Courtney's mother jumped up, clutching her husband. "Jack, what was that?" she asked in a hurried voice. She looked a lot like Courtney. They had the same light brunette hair and small, slender frame. They also had the same seductive voice with a bit of a whine thrown into it.

"I don't know, but it messed with the TV," Jack said. "Did you see anything about bad weather, honey?" With a grunt, he got up and walked over to the television, fiddling with some of the plugs and outlets.

"No, but I can look and see." She grabbed her phone, which had been sitting on the coffee table in front of her, and started searching.

Perfection. There she was, sitting alone on the couch. Unprotected. Vulnerable. An easy kill if she was quiet.

William reached for her, one hand poised over her neck and the other over her mouth. Then he yanked her up and over the couch. She weighed nothing to him.

"Jack!" she screamed.

William cursed under his breath. She had just made things a lot harder for herself.

William knew her husband would turn around and see him, so he aimed his hand at the television. It turned off with a click, as did the lights in the nearby kitchen, shrouding the house in darkness. The electricity rebounded back into his body.

"Gina!" Jack called as everything went dark. He walked around, trying to find a light switch that worked.

William pulled Gina back toward Courtney's bedroom, where the girl's body was lying on her queen-size bed.

"Jack! Jack, help me! Jack!" Gina screamed from behind his hand.

Frustrated, William stopped in the hallway and pulled her close. "Shut. *up.* Unless you want to die quicker, I suggest you keep quiet."

She bit one of his fingers, causing him to yell in pain and let her go. Then she tried to run back down the hallway, but William tackled her and flipped her onto her back.

"Jack!" she hollered again. "Jack! Help me!"

William put his hand on her neck and sent electricity into her. She screamed in pain, but a moment later, she was dead.

"Gina! *Gina!*" Jack yelled.

Now it was his turn.

With his black eyes, William saw Jack stumbling toward him in the dark. William advanced toward him, like a lion about to attack a lost zebra. He could finish him off then and there, but he wanted to have a little fun first.

"Gina? Gina?" Jack asked, now in the hallway, closer to where William stood.

"She's not here, sir." He raised his hands, and two streams of

Unobtrusive

electricity shot out and hit Jack in the chest. He screamed as he was blasted to the floor, wincing in pain as he held onto his heart, electricity coursing through him.

William stood over him, a faux look of concern on his face. "Principal Taylor, is everything okay? You look like you're in pain." He kicked him in his side, and Jack coughed up blood. "Ooh, that one looked like it hurt."

He squatted next to him, his face in the shadows, not wanting to expose himself just yet. "I think you were looking for your wife—and doing a terrible job of it, I must say. But she's dead. Actually, they're both dead. Your wife and your daughter."

Jack tried to reach for William in the dark, but his arm went limp. "I'll . . . I'll kill you . . . you . . ." He coughed more blood, still gripping his chest in pain. He was practically choking on it.

William snorted. "I doubt it. It looks like you're already at death's door." He held up his palm, and electricity shone in the darkness, allowing Jack to see his face. There was more voltage in this one. Even deadlier. It would probably be one of his last kills until he got his second chance at the Guardian, and he wanted to make sure it was a good one.

His poor, poor principal.

Jack managed to strangle out one last word as he looked up at William's face in recognition. "Why?"

William chuckled. "Because killing pathetic Standards like you is way too much fun." Then he put the hand on Jack's head, and with a final shockwave, his principal was dead.

Chapter Fifty-Six

Matt stared at Courtney Taylor's dead body as it was put into a body bag to be taken to forensics. She had been dead for sixteen and a half hours now.

He had been called in by the chief, who told him to assist the murders at this address. Matt knew it was the Taylors' residence, but he hoped that maybe something was wrong with the intel. Maybe one of them would still be alive, but . . .

He shook his head. *How could this have happened?*

Courtney didn't deserve this. None of them did.

A hand squeezed on his shoulder, pulling him from his thoughts. "Hey, man. You okay?" his partner, Benjamin, asked.

Matt shook his head and shrugged. "I just can't believe something like this happened in Felix."

"I know. Our city's pretty quiet, and then we get a call that an entire family's been murdered. Remember that girl from up in New York a year ago? They think it's the same type of thing."

A shiver ran up Matt's spine as he remembered the incident. Maria Garcia. Died of electrocution from the inside. How was any of this stuff even possible?

Unobtrusive

Does this mean he's here in Felix? How do we keep people safe from something like this?

Matt thought of Rianne and sighed. Yeah, Rianne had changed quite a bit, but she was still his little girl. He needed to protect her from whatever this was.

Another person's pretty face flashed through his mind. Jessica. His girlfriend. He loved being able to say that about her. He was so thankful to have her in his life. If she was taken away from him, he wouldn't know what to do.

"Hey, Matt, you okay there?"

Matt didn't answer, afraid of accidentally letting something out if he opened his mouth.

"Hey, maybe you should go to the car. Clear your head for a while."

Matt nodded and then made his way out of the dead girl's bedroom. In the hallway was the body of Gina Taylor. Beyond in the living room, a crime scene officer was taking pictures of Jack Taylor's bloody body before putting him in a bag. The smell of old blood filled the air.

Once outside, Matt took a deep breath, letting the warm air fill his lungs. He looked around the street, where barricades and yellow tape blocked off the perimeter. Some people from the neighborhood were looking on. Why did people find this stuff fascinating to watch? It was anything but. Other officers were keeping the civilians away from the tape, answering questions, and talking with one another.

He leaned against the car with his arms crossed. The school year was almost done, and Rianne and William would be graduating soon. They would both be leaving for school, and both he and Jessica would be empty-nesters.

Then the idea hit him. *Duh, I could kill two birds with one stone,* he thought. Protect those he cared about and live with his girlfriend. He was planning on asking soon, anyway. Why not now?

Chapter Fifty-Seven

A couple of hours later during his lunch break, Matt called Jessica as he sat in his cruiser.

After the phone rang a few times, Jessica picked up. "Hey, babe!"

"Hey, hun. Sorry to call ya at work."

"No, it's fine. I'm on break. How's work and everything?"

"It could be better today. I'll tell you about the details I can share later. There's actually a big reason why I'm calling."

"Mm-hm?"

"Well, I was thinking that it's time to tell the kids about us. I don't know how they'll take it, but I think it's time for them to know. And once they've settled into that, I want you to move in with me. Rianne and William will be leaving for school when the summer's over, and with everything that's going on, I don't want you in that apartment by yourself. Hell, I don't want either of you in that apartment by yourself now."

Jessica was silent for a moment. Matt's stomach did a flip. Silence wasn't a good sign. "Jess?"

Unobtrusive

"Yes!" she shouted into the phone. "Yes, yes, yes to all of that! I think it's a great idea, baby! Of course, we'll move in with you! Oh, I'm sort of relieved, actually. William and I will be so much safer with you around. When do we want to tell the kids?"

"Why not this weekend?"

Chapter Fifty-Eight

"William! William, are you home? I have the best news!" Jessica bounded into the kitchen from the front door.

William sat at the kitchen table with a bowl of cereal in front of him, his spoon in his right hand, his phone in his left. He flicked his eyes up to look at her. "May I help you, Mother?" he asked as he looked back down.

"How was school?" she asked, kissing the top of his head before sitting down across from him. He waved her off, annoyed.

"It was school." The day had been solemn. The death of Principal Taylor and his family had shaken the student body and faculty. Not a lot happened in their classes, and there was an assembly for the last part of the day. Lots of crying. Lots of words. William wasn't mentally present for it. Granted, he was the cause of the sadness that hung in the air, but he was tired. He didn't use too much energy the night before but enough to throw him off for a few days.

"Did your school do anything for the principal and his family who died?"

Unobtrusive

She's trying to do the bonding thing again. "Didn't you say you had news?" he asked, scrolling.

She nodded. "I need you to listen and not get upset, okay?"

He sighed. God, he hated this "playing nice" thing. "Okay."

"So, these past few months, I don't know if you noticed, but I've been out a lot and not just for work. I've been wanting to tell you for a while, but I couldn't figure out the best time—"

"Mother," William said, scooping up another spoonful of cereal, "please get to the point."

She didn't look upset at his tone. Instead, she looked like she was going to burst from excitement. He furrowed his eyebrows. "William, do you remember Officer Jarrett? Matt? Well, we've been dating!"

He dropped his spoon in the bowl. She had a boyfriend? Since when was she even interested in dating? She'd never gone on dates after his father died. He just assumed she didn't want to be with anyone else other than his father. Then again, William hadn't allowed her to have much free time, taking up the mantle of keeping her controlled.

The control that he had lost.

There was a long pause before William could remember how to speak. "What?" he asked. He put his phone down. "You're dating the guy who arrested me?" *And the father of my Guardian?*

That point suddenly hit him. His mother was dating Officer Jarrett, father of Rianne, his Guardian. *What does that mean for us? Will we be forced to see each other more? Well, that wouldn't be a bad thing. She has to die at some point. But if that officer is always around, how will I get close enough to get her alone?*

"I know it might be weird for you," Jessica said, crossing her hands over each other, "but you've been doing really well with your behavior and everything. And, William, it's been a long time since your father died. This might sound blunt, but did you expect me to stay alone forever?"

"Sort of," William answered without thinking. "And you guys have been dating for how long?"

"About six months. Almost seven. We went on our first date after we spent the night looking for you and Rianne."

Six months. Almost seven. He had been oblivious for that long.

Then again, he was more preoccupied with plotting on how to get Rianne to her grave.

William stood up. "I'm not dealing with this."

"William, wait, there's one more thing I need to tell you."

He stopped, eyeing her. He tried not to show that his jaw was tight.

"Matt just asked us to move in with him and his daughter, Rianne. She's your age, and both of you will be heading off to school then, and he's worried about you and me being over here on our own with the murders and everything that just happened."

William fell back into his chair.

"We're going to go over there sometime next week just so you two can meet, and we can all get to know each other. I know it seems fast, but I think it'll be good for us. And you'll only be there for a few months before you head out, and you'll have a room there always ready for you when you want to come back and visit, and . . ."

Jessica's voice trailed off as William retreated into his thoughts. He didn't know how to feel. One part of him was mortified that his mother was dating, and that stupid officer at that. He was also mortified that they would be leaving their apartment to move into Rianne's home.

But another part of him was looking forward to seeing what would happen with this new opportunity. Maybe this was just the thing he needed to get his next shot at the Great Battle. His next shot at killing his Guardian.

Chapter Fifty-Nine

"**R**ianne, come down here, please," Matt called.

It was around 7:00 p.m., and the early evening sun was peeking through her curtains, showering her dark room in red and gold. She didn't notice the beautiful panorama, though. Rianne sighed as she put her pencil down and stood up from her math homework. She was not in the mood for talking with him. Half a year had passed, and she still hadn't forgiven him. What he had said to her was still sore in her heart.

He talked about trust, but how was she supposed to trust him when he could go off on her at any moment? He hadn't even apologized. Neither of them had. The only communication they had had in the past months were little phrases.

"Dinner's ready."

"Can you take out the trash, please?"

"I'm going to work. Love you."

She walked out of her room and went down the stairs. Her father was sitting in his armchair in the living room next to the television, which was currently off. The look on his face was serious and firm—the look he usually got when he was thinking hard about something.

They were about to have a big talk. If he knew better, he would come right out and apologize.

Rianne sat on the couch across from him and folded her arms over her chest and crossed her legs. "Yes, sir?" she asked in a flat voice. She didn't even look at him, instead choosing to gaze at a spot on the carpet.

"Hey, Crayon."

Of course he would open with her nickname. It pulled her at heart in a good way, but she shook it off.

"I know we haven't been talking much lately. I know you're probably still mad from that night. Hell, I'm still mad about it."

She rolled her eyes.

"But there's something I wanted to tell you about me and Jessica."

Rianne sighed heavily. Jessica was his new girlfriend of a few months now. She didn't make an effort to learn much about her, though. It was weird seeing her father in a relationship after he'd been single almost all of her life. When he'd told her, a pit had grown in her stomach, but she tried to be happy for him—even though she was still angry at him.

"What is it?" she asked.

"I know this may seem really sudden and rushed—and it probably is—but I've asked her and her son to move in with us."

Rianne almost choked on her spit. She sat up. "What?" she yelled. "Move in with us? And there's a *son*?"

He sighed. "Rianne, you know what happened with the Taylors."

That had been a blow to her. She'd never liked Courtney, but she didn't want her dead either. When reports came out on how she had died, Rianne had confronted William before class, accusing him. His only response was, "Don't worry. You'll have your time in the spotlight soon."

Unobtrusive

"It's dangerous out there right now, and they're alone out there, and I'm not comfortable with that, so I asked them to move in here."

"And you don't think *I* would be uncomfortable with some random people moving into *our house?*" she shouted. "Dad, this is insane. Can't we talk about this first before—"

The doorbell rang. "That should be them now," Matt said, his mood perking up. He stood and made his way to the front door. "I was just about to tell you, but we wanted everyone to meet now that you and William know."

Her blood froze. *Did he just say—*

She stood up and followed him halfway down the hall. "Dad, wait—"

Her father opened the door, and as he welcomed them in, Rianne locked eyes with the boy with black eyes.

No.

Chapter Sixty

William winked at her as he followed his mother inside. *There is no way that Dad's dating the mother of my Hunter.*

Reality didn't shift. She didn't wake up. Everything was real. Everything was happening. William was back in her life with a vengeance, and he was moving into her home!

She wanted to pass out.

"So, Matt, turns out that Rianne and William already know each other," the woman said after hugging him. She looked to be Rianne's height and had long, curly blonde hair and blue eyes. William had likely inherited them from her. Probably the only thing.

"Really?" Matt said, leading her to the kitchen. "Hey, you two, we're going to be in here real quick."

"Yeah! William told me that they had English together last year."

If only they realized how well they really knew each other.

William approached Rianne, a smirk on his face. "Well, isn't this a lovely coincidence?"

Unobtrusive

She wasn't going to let him sense the fear she felt, even as she unconsciously backed into the couch behind her. "What did you do?" she hissed.

"Whatever do you mean, my dear Guardian?"

"Don't call me that."

"Why? That's what you are. From the way things are going with those two," he nodded toward the kitchen, "we might be stepsiblings one day."

Rianne gagged. "Hopefully you'll be dead before that happens."

His eyes darkened. "I was going to say the same thing."

"What did you do?" she asked again. "How did you set this up?"

William shrugged. "Hey, I did nothing. Apparently, our little rendezvous that night brought them together. I'm just as surprised as you are. I found out about all of this just a few days ago. But, hey, I'm not complaining. If this means I get to get closer to you," he stepped toward her, "and rip the air from your body, I will gladly support whatever our two idiot parents decide to do."

When she saw small sparks jumping around his hands, with a flick of her wrist, her Blade swept around William's ankles and knocked him into the back of the couch. He winced, pulling himself back to his feet.

"Don't start with me, Rianne."

"Or what, you'll kill me in front of our parents?"

"Guardian . . ." he warned, his fists clenched.

"Hunter," she replied, mocking his tone.

He growled in the back of his throat, glowering at her.

Her dad and his girlfriend came into the living room, smiling and laughing. "Rianne, this is Jessica," Matt said. "Jessica, this is my daughter, Rianne."

"Hi!" Jessica said with a smile, offering her hand. "So, you're the artist that Matt has told me all about."

She seemed nice enough. Why couldn't her son have picked up that trait?

Rianne smiled politely. "Hi, Jessica."

William looked at Matt. "And we already know each other," he said, crossing his arms.

"Yep. Good thing you haven't gotten in any more trouble, huh?"

William smirked. "That you know of."

"Dad, can I talk to you, please?" Rianne said. She glanced at Jessica and William, her heart pounding. "It'll be fast."

Matt nodded, then squeezed Jessica's hand before following Rianne into his bedroom. He closed the door behind them. "What's up, Crayon? She and William are nice, right?"

"Dad, they can't move in here."

He sighed, putting his hands on his waist. "I know all of this kind of came out of left field—"

"Kind of?" She crossed her arms.

"I know it's sudden, sweetie, but she's important to me. I want her to be safe. I want all of you to be safe."

Rianne blew air out through her lips. "Are you sure you're vying for all of our safety here? You're letting complete strangers come live with us. After, what, six months? Do you know how insane that sounds?" She looked around, and her eyes fell on the photo of her mother in the green frame. "What do you think Mom would think of all of this?"

Matt's jaw hardened. "Don't bring her into this. She made her decision."

"I know she's dead, Dad."

She heard his breath stop before restarting. "How do you know that?"

She swallowed, thinking back to what Braedon had told her those months ago. "I know she was murdered." The tears she was so focused on keeping inside caught in her throat. "And you didn't think to tell me about it? The truth?"

She sniffled. She didn't realize it had affected her so much.

She'd just pushed it down and tried to forgive her father for lying to her all her life. But now everything was piling up, and she had to get it out or she'd explode.

"You think you know what's best for me. You make big decisions that affect my life, just like you're doing now!" Her voice was rising, but she didn't care. "You never tell me *anything*! You didn't tell me that my mom was killed. You didn't tell me that you wanted to move *strangers* into my house! You can't even tell me you're sorry!"

Matt stared at her, sadness in his eyes. "Rianne, I—"

"And you had the nerve to tell me that you can't trust me after I snuck out. That you didn't know who I was anymore. Well, it turns out I learned from the best. I can never trust you either." Rianne shook her head. "I can't wait until I'm gone and away from you and your damn lies and secrets."

Her eyes on the carpet, Rianne pushed past her father and ran up the staircase to her bedroom, slamming her door as hard as she could, then locking it. She grabbed her headphones from her desk and put them over her ears. She didn't want to hear anything else that night. Her throat tight, she sat on her bed and hugged her pillow to her chest.

Chapter Sixty-One

Rianne opened her eyes, and the bright lights of a carnival filled her vision. Little children ran past her, giggling with happiness as their parents trailed behind them.

"So, where to first, love?" the accented voice she adored asked from beside her.

Turning, she saw Braedon, her heart-stoppingly gorgeous boyfriend. He had to be shirking his Wise One duties again to be with her, something he did often.

"I don't know," she said, eyeing the attractions in front of them. The carnival only offered two choices of entertainment. On her left was the Tunnel of Love, and on her right were the fun house mirrors. She loved the fun house mirrors as a kid. She enjoyed the mazes and wrong turns and learning from her mistakes. But the Tunnel of Love would be the perfect attraction for her and Braedon. The fun they could have in there . . .

It was either a left or a right.

"It's a left or a right, Rianne," Braedon said, repeating her thoughts. "Your choice."

Unobtrusive

Rianne stood there contemplating, her eyes dashing from right to left.

She grabbed his hand and veered him to the right. Braedon didn't protest, so he must've been satisfied with her choice.

Once inside, the two went down a straight aisle lined with mirrors on both sides. The mirrors didn't contort their body images, just reflected exactly what was given to them. Over and over, Rianne and Braedon showed on both sides until they reached a giant mirror branching into two paths. Another left and another right.

Rianne groaned. Making decisions was hard enough, but two in one day?

"Braedon, you choose this time," she said, smiling at him.

He grinned at her and put his finger under her chin, tilting it up. "You're cute when you're indecisive."

All this adoration was overwhelming her, but she loved it. "You're cute when you talk with that accent and use words that make you sound smart."

"Hm." He leaned down and touched his lips with hers, sending shockwaves through her body. "Okay," he said when they broke apart, "how about I go left, and you go right? We'll see who comes up short, and that person will have to find the other in this maze of mirrors. Are you up for the challenge, Guardian?"

"Don't you want to make a bet?" Rianne asked. "You always make a bet."

"It's because you're so competitive, dear."

"You're just as competitive as I am!"

He laughed. "Well, you'll figure out what the prize is when I win. Ready?"

"Definitely. Prepare to lose, Braedon."

Braedon started the countdown. "One . . ." They reluctantly released each other's hands. "Two. . ." They faced their routes, ready to take the challenge full on. "Three!" They went down their paths.

Rianne was full of adrenaline as she ran, determined to win. Her reflected body flashed through the mirrors, and the metal floor clanked beneath her feet. She turned left, right, left, and left again.

A scream echoed throughout the maze.

"Braedon?" she called, worried. Had the scream come from him or someone else? The silence gripped her, sending chills of fear up her spine.

Another scream, louder this time. "Rianne!"

Braedon's voice was full of panic. He was terrified.

"Braedon, I'm coming!" she shouted. She backtracked through the maze until she reached the place where she and Braedon had parted ways.

She followed the path he took. At first it was exactly like hers, filled with numerous turns and mistakes she had to fix as she ran into the mirrors. Each mistake made her jump.

"Braedon, where are you?" called into the big, empty space. "Say something so I can find you!"

A faint whimper replied, echoing over and over again. It was Braedon's voice, and he sounded scared. Something had him petrified out of his mind.

She followed the sound to the center of the maze. It was large and sixteen-sided with a mirror on each side. Each mirror reflected a different side of Braedon, who was against a mirror on the northeast side. His hands were behind him, trapped by invisible bonds, and his head was hanging down. She couldn't tell if he was breathing.

"Braedon?" she asked, stepping toward him.

His head shot up at the sound of her voice, a look of fear etched on his face. Unlike before, his eyes were red and baggy. On his face were various small cuts, but from his temple to his hairline was a gash, as if he had been struck in the head. He opened his mouth, wanting to tell her something, but nothing came out—except a small stream of crimson blood.

Unobtrusive

"Braedon?" she repeated. She continued forward, swallowing her fear and nausea, then stopped when he screamed. He screamed until it sounded like his lungs would burst, and it broke Rianne's heart to hear it. Then his head fell back against the mirror, the blood running down his front.

Was he dead?

No.

And then *he* appeared.

The Hunter.

He was in the middle of the room, his lethal electricity covering his hand. She looked around, desperate. Where had he come from? He didn't say anything. He just looked at her with cold, shining eyes and an evil grin.

"William, what did you do to him?" she whispered as she looked at Braedon's still body against the mirror.

He didn't answer, just stepped toward her. Rianne tried to go back where she had come from, but the entrance was no longer there. She was locked in with him, and she couldn't get away.

There was no way out this time.

She held her hands out in front of her, ready to summon her Blade. "Stop!" she shouted.

He continued toward her, not speaking.

"Please, stop!" she said when he was almost within arm's length. As a last resort she tried to throw her Blade at him, like she had done in training, but nothing came.

She was stuck.

"Please!" she shouted. She wanted to run away so badly, to get to her Braedon and heal him, but the Hunter already had her backed up against the mirror, unable to move.

William leaned down and kissed her cheek.

"Why is this happening to me again?" she cried, closing her eyes as she thought back to that night in the old theater. He was about to kill her. He pressed his body against hers, pushing her against the mirror. He held her arms down by her sides. The mirror crunched in protest, and shards of glass pierced her arms.

He chuckled. "Shhh . . . it's only going to hurt for a while."

His blue eyes turned black, and electricity surged through her, rendering her powerless.

She screamed.

Chapter Sixty-Two

W illiam parked his motorcycle on the curb outside of his new home.

Her home.

The Guardian's home.

He pocketed his keys and headed inside. They were about a month into the new arrangement, but he'd made it work. It didn't take long for him and his mother to move their belongings into the home he had snuck into only a year earlier to gain Rianne's trust. They didn't have a lot to begin with. His mother shared a room with Matt. William tried to ignore them as much as he could, but sometimes conversation was unavoidable. Like always, he kept his answers short, not sparing the edge in his tone at times. He had the upstairs guest room—which was right across from the Guardian's.

His new plan was already in motion. He knew all there was to know about Rianne. Now he just made sure to constantly get under her skin. Pretending to be kind to her was his favorite tactic, especially when they both knew he was anything but. She remained silent and hostile toward him, which created palpable tension, but he thrived off it. He didn't know when a new moment would present itself, but when it did, he planned to take full advantage of it. Until then he had ample time to tear her down. Maybe the time would be soon—their extended spring break had just started.

He went upstairs to his room, passing Rianne's. "Sure it's fine," a male voice said.

William paused. Interesting.

The door wasn't shut all the way, allowing just a sliver of space. William got as close to the door as he could without touching it, leaning against the wall.

"Really weird," Rianne said. "Is Justin already in Estona?"

"Yes. He needs to speak with his father, but he said he would text you soon."

Estona. The magical realm. Who was she talking to? He had learned about the Guardians and their Mentors and Estona through his father and grandfather, mainly the latter. Though he was very young when he received that information, he knew it by heart. Mentors trained the Guardians, helping them get stronger before the Great Battle. Obviously, they weren't doing a great job.

Her voice cut through his thoughts. "I want to talk to you about something. It kind of freaked me out."

"All right. What is it?"

"I had this dream. We were at this carnival, and we went into a fun house of mirrors. We separated—we were playing a game, seeing who could find the other first—and I heard you scream my name. You sounded so scared. When I found you, you had all these cuts all over you, and you had a huge gash across your face. And then you started screaming so loudly. It killed me. You passed out—or worse, I couldn't tell.

"And then . . . and then he came for me. I couldn't summon my Fuora or anything. He grabbed me, and then he . . ." Her voice trailed off.

William smiled. It sounded like he had been in her dreams.

And he'd killed her. Good. He made her anxious. She was still scared.

"Hey, hey. It's all right, Rianne. I'm right here. I'm completely fine. It was just a dream—a nightmare. It wasn't real. That would never happen to me, and your Fuora would never disappear like that, especially if you're scared or upset. And it helps that you've been training again. Understand?"

"That'll never happen to you, Braedon?"

"Never, darling."

Darling? Whoever it was, he was in a relationship with Rianne. That could prove valuable if the opportunity presented itself.

"You promise?"

He chuckled. "Promise."

William rolled his eyes. Those two were morons.

A cell phone went off, and Bradston, or whatever his name was, answered. "What? Yes, I know," he said. "Yes, I know.. . . Leave her out of it. You don't get any say when it comes to me and Rianne, understand? Make sure you're at the palace at noon for the debriefing. Goodbye, Ellis." He sighed. "That imbecile gets on my last nerve."

"Y'all have a meeting about me, I assume?"

"Yes. Being stuck in meetings with those five is infuriating."

"Braedon, you're going to have to forgive them at some point."

He sighed. "Maybe."

"So, what are you going to do with the rest of your day?"

"Well, technically my day is just starting." Rianne sighed in exasperation. "But before my meeting, I have a couple of classes at the high school. I'm *so* relieved I've been given the option to teach when I can."

"I'm happy for you, baby. I know how much you love teaching."

"Thank you, love. I have to get going, but enjoy your evening off. If you need me for anything, let me know. I know you're scared, but you're strong. Be safe."

"I will. I love you, Braedon."

"I love you too, sweetheart." It sounded like they kissed, then the room was silent again.

William pushed off the wall and headed to the bottom of the staircase. *She just keeps making things more and more fun—and way too easy,* he thought.

Chapter Sixty-Three

Rianne smiled to herself, brushing her fingers over her lips. Braedon made her feel like nothing else in the world mattered. She was in love with him, and she was excited to fall deeper as the months passed.

When she opened her bedroom door and turned to head downstairs, her elation immediately.

William was there, leaning against the banister, waiting for her. "Hi, Rianne," he said with a pleasant smile.

Rianne rolled her eyes as she brushed past him and hurried down the stairs. The profound stress between them had deepened since their families came together. They were ready to kill each other, after all.

"Well, that sure was rude," he said as he followed her to the kitchen. "And after I greeted you so nicely."

Rianne pressed her teeth together. He was *anything* but nice, and they both knew it. She wasn't going to fall down the road of naivete again. "Aw, are you going to complain about it some more?"

"I suggest you watch your tone with me, *Guardian*," he snarled.

"You wouldn't want anything to happen to your new boyfriend, would you?"

Rianne stopped dead in her tracks in the foyer. Furious, she spun around and aimed her hand at him. Caught off guard, William was pressed against the wall by her Blade. She pressed her forearm against his throat. "You stay away from Braedon!" she shouted, her voice lethal. "Don't even *think* about going near him!"

But William wasn't fazed. He just smiled, his face smug. "Braedon. So that's his name?" His eyes started to turn black. "I thought I had it wrong." He chuckled. "Looks like I've struck a nerve with you, huh?"

Damn it. She scolded herself as she let him go. She had let her emotions get the best of her again. She had to be careful not to provoke him—their parents were almost home from their weeklong cruise, and having them around provided extra protection for her that was no longer at her disposal.

"How long are we going to keep playing this game?" she asked.

"Whatever do you mean?"

"Why haven't you tried anything?"

William cocked his head to the side. "I could ask the same of you. What, are you scared to make the first move? Afraid of what's going to happen?" He laughed as he headed upstairs to his room. "I can be patient, Rianne. You might not know when it'll be, but I like to wait for the perfect moment."

As soon as his bedroom door closed, Rianne rushed to her room, her heart beating as fast as a hummingbird's wings. She pulled out her phone and sent a frantic text. Several moments later, Ellis appeared.

"What? What's going on?" he asked, looking around the room as though danger was imminent.

"I just really don't want to be alone right now, and I know that Braedon just left to go teach, so I figured that you'd be the next option," Rianne said.

Ellis looked offended. "Oh, so I'm just a backup?"

"Well, technically a third choice, after Justin."

"Oh, that makes it better."

Rianne laughed, pushing his arm. "You know what I mean." Ellis had become a friend to her in the past months, like an older brother. "So, are you and Braedon on speaking terms yet?"

"Nope. He's still upset."

"It's understandable, Ellis. I mean, you did promise not to tell his secret. *And* you told the Wise Ones about me and him. Nothing was even going on!"

"At the time," Ellis said. Rianne used her Blade to reach out and give him a faux burn. "Ow! I said I was sorry!"

"No you didn't."

"Well, not to *you*, but I've said sorry to Braedon. He just doesn't want to hear it."

"You stole his job."

"He got promoted to the most powerful position in the realm!"

Rianne crossed her arms. "Because you wanted his job."

"Details, details." He started to mess with items on her desk, turning on her laptop for no particular reason. Was he that bored? "But seriously, are you okay? I know it's real nerve wracking with everything that's going on."

She nodded. "It is." The old theater flashed through her mind again, but she pushed it away. "I know my training's done for the day, but can't I go back to Estona and just chill?"

"Until your parents come back?" Ellis asked.

"Until my dad comes back, yes."

Ellis rubbed his chin. "I don't know, Rianne. Remember, I can't interfere, and that sounds like I would be if the Wise Ones don't know about it."

Rianne shrugged. "Then don't let them know about it."

"I don't want to be put on probation, either!" Ellis said.

Braedon and Justin had been put on a probation for disobeying

Wise One Alaric during the last Great Battle. They were to be monitored for nine months. If they did anything out of line, they would be sent to trial before the Wise Ones. Their actions actually caused the next battle between Rianne and William to be the first of its kind. Never before had a Guardian and a Hunter fought with both of them coming out alive. Justin didn't receive any physical punishment, but Braedon received fifteen lashes.

Rianne had seen the state of Braedon's back. His body had healed most of the damage, but some scarring still remained, even with healing Affera. She had asked him if he wanted her to take them away—she could do so with her Fuora—but he insisted on keeping them. They reminded him that he would do anything for her and of his love for her.

An idea sparked in Rianne's mind. "Ellis, come here for a sec." She made her way to the floor, sitting cross-legged. She patted the carpet in front of her.

Ellis rolled his eyes and sighed, but he obeyed. "What are we doing?"

She smiled. "We're going to play a game!"

He groaned. "Do we have to? I'm not seven years old."

"I'm the Guardian. You have to do what I say." He opened his mouth as though he was about to contradict her but then closed it. He knew she was right. "Okay, first." She put her hands out in front of her, focused, and her Blade appeared, warm, golden, and swirling through her hands and arms. "Close your eyes. Good. Now make your Blade appear."

He sighed, looking bored. "Why?" She gave him a look. "Fine." He mimicked her stance, closed his eyes, and then his light green energy formed.

"Okay, you can call it back. Keep your eyes closed, though! Now, make your teleportation powers show. Can you make it, like, show up as a visual thing? Like the Blade can?"

"Shhh," he said, concentrating. He inhaled and exhaled slowly, calming his body. Moments later, a silver light, condensed in the shape of a sphere, glowed in his left palm. It was beautiful, with sparkles of white and gold dancing within it.

Pure Affera. Pure, untamed, beautiful magic.

"Wow," she whispered, mesmerized by it.

"Mm-hm," he said, his eyes still shut. "That's just some of my transporting power."

"Some?"

"Uh-huh. Like you said, I just let it show. The actual Affera is still within me. Think of this as a sample."

"Oh, okay. And how do you control it?" She tore her eyes away from it to look at his face before turning back to the Affera.

"The same way you summon your Blade or anything like that. Remaining calm, engaging that happy feeling, visualizing it."

Rianne touched it with one finger, and a shiver ran up her spine. Excitement. There was joy and the unknown in magic, and she felt it in that radiant little ball. She often wondered what having full power would be like. She had little tastes of it with her Fuora and when she came into contact with other people's Affera and could only imagine the feeling of all of the diverse kinds of Affera within her in—hopefully—perfect harmony. She was excited for the moment when she gained ultimate control.

Rianne cupped her hands around the transporting Affera, and it rolled into her hands, as if happy to part with Ellis and be with the Guardian. She held it close to her.

Mission accomplished.

Ellis gasped, noticing the change. He opened his eyes and looked down at his empty hand. "What the . . . How did you—"

"Whoo-hoo! That actually worked!" she cheered, grinning.

"How did you do that?" he asked.

Rianne shrugged, practically bouncing with excitement. "Because I'm the Guardian."

Ellis nodded in approval. "Sneaky." He flicked her forehead before leaning back on his hands.

"Ow!" she yelled, rubbing her forehead with her free hand. "Damn it, Ellis!" She kicked him.

"So, what are you gonna do once you're in Estona?" he asked.

"Find Braedon and spend time with him for a while. Maybe help him teach."

"And how long do you plan on staying?"

Rianne shrugged, and Ellis rolled his eyes again. He looked at the Affera. "Now, to teleport with that, all you gotta do is think of the place you want to go, breathe, and relax. The Affera will take care of the rest."

Rianne looked down at the silvery Affera. It was rolling around in hand like a top. "I'm really excited to try this out! Thanks for letting me borrow it."

"You stole it."

"Details, details." She sighed, glancing around her room. "I just *really* need to get away from here for as long as I possibly can." She paused for a moment, and then said, "I never really asked you about this before, but when Braedon first told me about the Great Battle, he mentioned something about you and the past Hunter." Ellis dropped his gaze. "What exactly did the Hunter do to you?"

"It wasn't good," he mumbled.

"I know. I'm sorry. But I need to know what happened."

"I know you do." He sighed again. "I didn't really know what to do when everything happened. I thought Braedon was dead. I was alone out there, and I just . . . froze. The Hunter came toward me, and I couldn't even summon my Fuora. I can't really explain what happened."

"Justin said the same thing happened to him when he first saw mine," Rianne said.

"It's not a fun feeling. Well, the Hunter kicked my ass, damn near destroyed me. The last time he slammed my head into the ground, I wanted to give up. I wanted him to kill me. It was hard for me to hear at that point; he had burst one of my eardrums. I just remembered him saying something along the lines of joining him. He grabbed my arm and dragged me into the school. He slammed through the door like it was air. God, he was so strong.

"The area was in lockdown, everyone hiding away, and Advancers were there to protect the students. We heard a scream from the secretary, Autumn. She was under her desk in the dark. Before . . ." Ellis put his face in one of his hands, staring at the carpet. "Before he killed her, she had time to press the emergency button. That set off alarms all over the school, warning everyone that the Hunter had breached the grounds.

"And that made him angry. Furious. He went to the first class-room he could find with people inside and killed Stephen, one of my fellow Advancers. Stephen didn't have a chance. God, so much blood.

"The kids . . . they were crowded together in the corner. I could literally feel their fear clouding the atmosphere as they saw how beaten I was, looked at Stephen's body, and saw the Hunter. None of them wanted to die. Not at that age. Not that young. The Hunter let me go, and I fell. I could hardly hold myself up at that point." He swallowed. "After he . . . after he slaughtered them, he made me tell him where others were hiding. The bastard could literally give exact locations of every person in that school. I wouldn't be surprised if he could hear them breathing. He was just toying with me. If I didn't do what he said, he would kill me."

"Why wouldn't you sacrifice yourself?" Rianne whispered. "I thought that was what Advancers were supposed to do."

"You don't know how it feels, Rianne. You don't want to die. Neither did I."

So many emotions flitted through her mind; it was hard to differentiate them all.

Ellis took a deep breath. "Go ahead and get out of here." He nodded to the Affera. "Just don't get me in too much trouble, all right?"

"Are you coming?" Rianne asked.

He nodded again. "I'll follow you there. I just need a sec."

She nodded in understanding. "See you later, Ellis." She closed her eyes and relaxed, her core becoming warm, and imagined the high school's quad.

It happened in a second. She felt light, and her hair swayed. Fresh air filled her nose, and she opened her eyes to see the green grass and trees surrounding the high school. The sun shone over the school with its early morning light, and a cooler breeze drifted through. A jolt of excitement went through her as her body settled. Being in Estona always gave her Fuora a boost. Like a puzzle piece sliding into place.

Rianne opened the main door that led inside to the front office. She had been inside the high school a few times whenever Braedon had to grab something from his classroom but not enough to commit it to memory.

The office was quiet, and the walls were white. A couple of adults were sitting at computers or writing in notepads, and some students were helping out. The halls of the school were empty. The students had probably just begun their first classes.

The office came alive as soon as she walked in. "Oh, my goodness," the secretary whispered. A student in the back of the office dropped a stapler and the stack of papers he had been holding.

None of them said anything for several moments. They just stared at Rianne, and she stared back. She was used to having such a reaction from Sterlings, but it didn't make it any more normal for her.

"Um . . . hi!" Rianne said as she approached the secretary's desk.

She heard a whisper from one of the men at the computers. "It's the Guardian. I can't believe we're seeing the *Guardian* right now."

"My dad met the former Guardian," the woman next to him said. "I can't believe I am too!"

"Oh, my gosh, Ms. Stanton, look!" one of the students shouted. "It's like they've been supercharged!" She waved her hand, and a beautiful young tiger appeared, then laid down on the floor with a massive yawn, mixed with a growl.

"Jesus, Cheyanne, put it away!" The boy who had dropped the stapler screamed, scampering to a corner for safety.

"Oh, don't be a baby," Cheyanne said. "She won't hurt you." She made a kissing noise, and the big cat turned to nuzzle her face.

"Why can't you conjure a cute puppy instead?"

The other adults didn't notice as they manifested their own Affera, marveling at how much Rianne's Fuora affected them. They looked like children receiving a new toy.

Ms. Stanton, the secretary, laughed. "Cheyanne, make sure you put the tiger away once the Guardian leaves." She stood up and shook Rianne's hand. "It is an honor to meet you, Guardian. An honor! God bless you and your mother. May her sacrifice be honored. I know you're going to defeat that wicked Hunter. You will win! We all know you will!"

"Thank you so much." She patted Ms. Stanton's hand, which was still latched onto hers. "That means a lot. I'm going to take care of everything. I promise."

Ms. Stanton sat back down, the smile never leaving her face.

"Oh, and can you not tell Wise One Braedon I'm on my way?" Rianne asked. "I want it to be a surprise."

"Not a problem, Guardian. Anything you ask."

"Thank you. See y'all later." She went out of the office, everyone's eyes following her, and into the deserted hallway.

She should've asked for directions to his room to refresh her memory. It had been months since she had gone to Braedon's classroom. She remembered it was somewhere on the third floor, but it wasn't until she found a plaque on the wall next to the door labeled "Wise One Braedon" that she knew she had found her prize. She opened the door and entered the classroom, finding him in the midst of conversation with a student.

315

"Relax," Braedon said. "You just have to concentrate." He was at the front of the room, a purple vase floating in the air a few feet behind him. He was speaking to a teenage boy who had both hands pressed to his temples, deep in meditation. Everyone was so engaged in the exercise that no one noticed Rianne's arrival.

"Class," Braedon continued, "is Drew making the vase behind me hover?"

"Yes, sir," they answered in varying degrees of unison.

"See, Drew? You're making it levitate. Your power is useful once you can control it. Now, make it fly at me, right at the back of my head. Give it your best shot." He crossed his arms, waiting for the blow. A girl up front gasped. "It's quite all right, Allison. Relax."

Rianne smiled at his calm disposition. He had been teaching for a long time and was used to every aspect of the classroom. He looked so professional and at ease.

The vase trembled, then made its way toward Braedon.

Rianne cleared her throat. The majority of the class—not including Drew—and Braedon turned to look at the person who caused the disruption. His face lit up and he came toward her. She met him halfway. Drew's vase flew back at him and hit his forehead, then clattered to the floor. Drew yelped in pain and rubbed the red mark on his face as his peers laughed and pointed.

"Rianne, what are you doing here?" Braedon asked. They threw their arms around each other in a hug.

"Wise One Braedon knows the Guardian?" a girl with dyed red hair asked.

"Duh, he used to be her Protector, stupid," a boy in the seat next to her said, snickering.

They pushed each other around until Braedon snapped his fingers at them without taking his eyes off of Rianne, signaling for them to stop. "Class, talk amongst yourselves for a moment as I speak with the Guardian," he said, leading her to the back of the room.

"Wise One Braedon, is she your *girlfriend*?" a tall, lean boy in the front asked in a disbelieving tone.

"Actually, yes, Noah. It must come as a shock to you, seeing as you've never had one."

As the class reacted to Braedon's roast, he turned back to her. "How'd you get here?"

Rianne was still chuckling at Noah's offended face. "Do you roast your students like that a lot?"

"Of course," Braedon said. "It's all about building relationships, knowing their language. Now, answer my question."

She smiled. "Ellis."

"Ellis?"

"Ellis."

"How'd you get him to get you here? He knows it's forbidden."

Rianne shrugged. "I tricked him."

Braedon chuckled. "Of course."

"We just played a little game, and he lost."

"So, you stole some of his Affera?"

"Why does everyone keep saying 'stole?' I borrowed it."

"Is he here?"

"No, but he said he would be back soon."

"You probably hurt his massive ego."

"Most likely. And I figured that maybe I could talk to the Wise Ones about me staying until my dad gets back."

Braedon shook his head. "I don't know if they'll let you do that, love."

Rianne lifted one shoulder in a shrug. "They can't go against the Guardian's wishes if they see me in the flesh, right?"

"And she strikes again! We can go after my classes are over for the day." He looked at his watch. "Which will be in a few hours, at around eleven. Want to stay and watch or help out? Today we're doing demonstrations, and I'm sure the kids would love to learn a bit from their Guardian."

"It would be an honor. Now go back to your class before they destroy the room." She looked over his shoulder. "Apparently, my Fuora is already giving them the idea."

Braedon turned around and saw the students playing with their Affera, marveling in excitement as those in the office had. He rolled his eyes, then gave her a quick kiss before heading back to the front of the class, regaining their attention.

Chapter Sixty-Four

"**O**w!"

William, who was sitting at his desk drawing, turned to his bedroom door.

"Damn it, Ellis!"

Everything went quiet again, the only sound being his tablet that was playing a background video.

William cocked an eyebrow, thinking to himself. *Ellis? Who else is Rianne trying to hide from me?*

William got up and went to her bedroom door, putting his ear against it.

"Wow," Rianne whispered.

"Mm-hm. That's just some of my transporting power."

"Some?"

"Uh-huh. Like you said, I just let it show. The actual Affera is still within me. Think of this as a sample."

William's eyebrows furrowed. Transporting power? His interest piqued, he cracked the door open and peeked inside. Rianne and a man with straight brown hair were sitting on the carpet in front of her bed. She was holding something silver and glowing in her hands. Could it be the power they had just been talking about?

The two were talking again, though not about anything important. That silver energy, it had to be the man's Affera.

William's father told him that his Motora came off as a dark blue and white, almost black. When he teleported, there was a flash of dark green. He said something about magic manifesting itself based on the user's personality and energy.

William tuned back in to their conversation. "Bet it's nerve wracking, huh?"

Rianne nodded. "I never really asked you about this before, but when Braedon first told me about the Great Battle, he mentioned something about you and the past Hunter. What exactly did the Hunter do to you?"

William moved in closer as his father was mentioned. Even though it was a long time ago, he remembered his father pulling him into his room and telling him all about his Massacre after he'd returned. How he had decimated both Advancers who had the *audacity* to try to stop him.

As he listened to the story retold by the Advancer, a smile crept onto his face. Rianne's eyes widened as she listened. What a magnificent day for the Hunters' bloodline. His father had done well.

The Advancer finished his story a few minutes later, and after exchanging goodbyes, Rianne disappeared with the borrowed Affera. The Advancer stayed seated on the floor for a moment, then went to the window. Apparently, retelling what had happened during the previous Great Battle had taken a lot out of him.

It was time for William to make his move.

William inched the door open and slipped inside. Raising his hands, his fingers splayed apart, he sent bolts of static toward the Advancer, becoming longer and deadlier. When they struck the Advancer's neck, he screamed and fell to the floor, kicking and screaming. He rolled onto his stomach, attempting to get to his feet, but the pain was too much.

"Well, well, well," William said, crouching near his head, still maintaining his hold on the Advancer. "Looks like I found myself a little plaything. Guess Rianne shouldn't have made so much noise, huh?"

Scratching at the unseen bolts that had a claim on his neck, the Advancer looked up at William. "N-no," he said, gasping for breath.

William chuckled. "Oh, this is just too fun. I get to play with the same Advancer my father toyed with." He stood and kicked the Advancer in the stomach, adding to his pain. Then he grinned. "What? Not going to fight back?" He grabbed him by the neck, adding another shock for good measure, then threw him into Rianne's desk. He hit it hard, then fell to the floor, toppling over a lamp. Another jolt went through him, and he screamed.

William sighed. "Man, you're not going to be any fun." He put his hands on his waist and shook his head. "What choice does that leave me?"

"Pl-pl-please," the Advancer begged, his voice hoarse.

William loved it when they did that. When they asked for pity. Mercy. It made killing them that much more enjoyable.

William looked at the sad soul with mock concern. "Hm? You want me to stop?"

The Advancer nodded, his nose starting to bleed. "L-let me h-help-p you."

It sounded to William like negotiating was in order. He had to get to Estona, and this Advancer was his ticket there.

"Okay, I'll make it stop. But first I need you to do something for me."

The Advancer gave William a pleading look and nodded again. William realized he was willing to do anything to stop the torture. Even sell out the Guardian and his people. He would lead them all to their deaths.

"You see, I have the power of teleportation too." He sat down next to the Advancer as though they were two friends having a conversation, even though the latter was fighting for his life. "All I need is to see the area I need to go, and I'll be there. But I have no idea what Estona looks like, much less where our little Guardian went. Do you catch where I'm going with this?"

The Advancer nodded in response, then closed his eyes. Suddenly, William's vision was filled with hills littered with green grass and multicolored flowers. Off in the distance was a high school.

William's focus was pulled back in the room. The Advancer looked at William with frightened eyes, waiting to be set free. But William just smiled at him. What was the point of taking the fun out of it?

William's eyes went black, the grim smile still on his face. The Advancer screamed, flailing and kicking. His back arching, he clawed at his neck and gripped his chest. Blood dribbled out of his mouth, staining the carpet.

Then he went still, dead, his unseeing eyes staring at the ceiling.

William stood, concentrating on the vision he had received.

Chapter Sixty-Five

William walked through the first door he found. A boring white office. Seven people were working there —adults and students. The office had a light, joyous energy about it. Annoying. Rianne must've been through there.

When he entered, everyone froze and looked at him, their eyes widening in fear. The room seemed to darken, becoming claustrophobic. The lights flickered a few times. A few people began crying.

William approached the desk and leaned on it. "I'm looking for a dark-haired girl, about eighteen years old. Very pretty. She has a pretty big energy about her—probably about the same as mine. She's known as the Guardian. She came through here already, didn't she?"

The woman opened her mouth to answer, but no words came out.

William clenched a fist, and sparks emitted from it. "Answer wisely, ma'am. Don't lie to me. I don't like it when I'm lied to."

"H-H-Hunter. You're the Hunter," she whispered, shaking.

William chuckled. More fear was settling in, filling him with delight. "Yes, I'm the Hunter, and I can feel that she's been in here. So, she must be somewhere in this school. Now, answer my question. Where is the Guardian?"

A movement caught his eye—her arm inching under the desk.

He grabbed her neck in his hand. She screamed as a surge of electricity shot through her. Then she began to sob, but William felt no sympathy for her. How dumb could she be?

"If you even *consider* reaching for that button again, I'll murder you in three seconds flat. Do you understand me?"

Tears running down her face, she nodded.

"Do all of you understand?" William shouted, looking at the others. All nodded but one—a young brunette girl, probably about fourteen. Her eyes darted between him and the door to her left. So simple-minded.

"Don't even think about it, sweetheart," William said.

Undaunted, the girl moved to open the door. A couple of the adults screamed for her to stop, but William shot electricity at her.

She fell to the floor, screaming and shaking in pain, then went limp. Blood trickled from her mouth, and her eyes stared blankly at the ceiling.

There were more screams and crying from everyone in the room. The other teenagers pressed themselves against the wall, sobbing and shaking. The adults were on the floor next to the girl's body, trying to revive her.

The noise in the office was unbearable. William rolled his eyes. Sterlings were dumber than he thought. "Shut up!"

His demand was met.

"Any more stupidity out of any of you, and I will not hesitate to fry all of you into oblivion."

He turned his attention back to the woman in his grip. "I'm going to ask you one more time. Where is the Guardian?"

He saw indecision in her eyes. She didn't want to expose Rianne, but she didn't want to die either. He sent another quick shock through her, and her breathing sped up.

Unobtrusive

"I'm going to give you five seconds to answer me. Five . . . four . . ." As his eyes turned black, she struggled to escape his grip, but he was too strong. She begged for mercy that wouldn't come. "Three . . . two—"

"She's in Wise One Braedon's room!" she shouted. "Room 313."

Chuckling, William's eyes returned to blue, and he let her go. She sat back in her chair, shaking and sniffling.

"See? That wasn't so hard," he said. He went to the door that led to the hallway, but on his way out, he grabbed one of the teenagers by the arm. Everyone else shouted in protest, but William held up his other hand, and they stopped. "Don't try pushing that button or warning anybody about my arrival, or I'll make it my personal mission that you all die first." He looked at his hostage, who was squealing in terror. "Now, why don't you be a good little office worker and take me to Wise One Braedon?"

Chapter Sixty-Six

A new student was in front of the class, ready to test her power. It was an individual check-in day, where Braedon would give the students a facet of their power to perform and then correct them if anything needed fixing. The girl was named Amaline, and she had beautiful long hair, pulled back in a ponytail, and blue eyes. She looked at Rianne, who was standing in the back, with a mixture of nervousness and reverence.

Many of the students would steal glances at her and smile or look away if she caught them staring. Others gazed at her like she was royalty. She didn't know whether to be embarrassed or flattered.

Another thing Rianne felt, though, was their Affera. Their energies. She couldn't place what their specific Affera was until she saw them perform with it, but she could feel the warmth and life radiating from them.

"Hello, Wise One Braedon," Amaline said, bowing her head.

"Hello, Amaline," he replied. "Comment vont tes parents?"

It looked like she wanted to roll her eyes, but she stopped herself. "Bien, Monsieur. Mes parents vous ont dit de faire ça?"

Braedon laughed. "Coupable. They just want you to practice, dear. Now, I want us to practice air elimination today. Same thing as last week. Ready?"

She nodded, placing her hands on the small of her back and glancing at Rianne again. "Are you sure?"

He smiled. "I'll be fine. I always am." He also glanced at Rianne. "Don't worry; she isn't judging you. She's just observing. Stop being so nervous! Go ahead."

Amaline aimed her hands at Braedon, and a light breeze stirred around her, even though all the doors and windows of the spacious room were closed. Her long hair swirled. Then she balled her hands into fists and thrust them to her sides. The breeze turned into a gust, then Braedon grabbed his throat, choking and gagging. A couple of students jumped in response to the sudden change.

The situation persisted for several moments until Braedon waved his hand, telling her it was enough. When he could breathe again, he nodded. "That was definitely a change from before. Excellent job, Amaline. Your speed has improved as well."

She smiled and clasped her hands together in excitement. "That makes me so excited! I've been practicing a lot with my parents—both our language and Affera! So, now you can tell them that I'm doing well in both!"

Rianne smiled. Amaline reminded her of Alex.

"You've been working hard, and I can tell. You've come a long way in your first year. Just make sure you maintain your concentration the longer it goes. An average person can only go three minutes without air, so if you use elimination, you have to match that. The stronger you become, you might be able to short—"

Rianne felt it before she heard it—a massive amount of heat and energy. She turned toward the door. The sound of shattering glass, stone, and metal filled the air, followed by a boom. The students screamed. Rianne was flung to the floor. The desks rammed into one another, trapping some students within them. Others were forced out of their seats. Debris sprayed through the classroom, pelting their bodies. Braedon shouted from the front. Amaline screamed.

Dust danced through the sun's rays as they shone through a hole in the back wall. The students groaned in pain, crying and confused.

Rianne winced and looked down at her side; it was bleeding. She looked up to the front, using a desk to pull herself to her feet.

William.

Her Hunter was there.

No.

Amaline attempted to crawl down from the elevated platform at the front of the room. It looked like her leg had been broken. Braedon was on the floor, his back against his desk. William was next to him, gripping his neck in his deadly hand. Braedon's eyes were wide with fear.

Hostage.

"Amaline, don't move!" Braedon shouted.

"Shut up!" William said, slamming Braedon's head into the desk. Then he turned to the helpless, broken girl and lifted his hand. A small ball of his Motora appeared. He cocked his arm back to throw it.

He's not going to hurt anyone else.

Rianne held out her hands and imagined everything but that moment. A shimmering barrier covered Amaline right before the lethal electricity could hit her. It crackled and dissolved into nothing. Rianne put her hands on the desk in front of her, and the same glowing shield appeared over every student, about twenty in total. Her legs were shaky, but the adrenaline was helping. She was still frazzled, though. She would have to concentrate to keep the shields up for however long the conflict lasted.

William looked at Rianne and smirked. "Wow," he said, increasing his grip on Braedon. "Look at you with your new little tricks. I'm glad I could be here to see it. Speaking of, it's an honor to meet your Wise One boyfriend. I know that killing a Wise One won't give me full power, but it'll be fun."

William's eyes turned black.

"William, no!"

Braedon screamed, thrashing in pain as the electricity entered his body, attacking his heart. His fingers clawed at William's hand on his neck.

"Braedon!" she shouted, running toward them. She slowed, gripping her wound. William held a finger out to her, prompting her to stop. Braedon stopped screaming, and his head relaxed onto his desk behind him, his eyes rolled back. His breathing was shaky, and he looked weak. Sweat glistened on his shivering body.

"Uh-uh," William said, his other hand on top of Braedon's head, eyeing her. His black eyes sent a shiver down her spine. "You know the rules. Another step, and I kill him. I'll make it feel like he's in the electric chair without the sponge."

She remained in place, not daring to move.

"Good girl. So, another funny thing I heard. You had a dream about me, right?" A smug smile stretched across his face. "A dream that I killed your little boyfriend here and that I was killing you."

A few of the kids in the back gasped and looked at her, hoping it wasn't true. She gave them an apologetic look. She hated to see the fear on their faces, but couldn't tell them that the Hunter was lying. That would make her a liar.

"You heard right," William said. "Your precious Guardian had a dream that I was killing her. That she was losing. If she's dreaming about it, doesn't that mean she's afraid of it happening in real life? And I'm pretty sure you all know what happens when the Hunter wins."

A few of them began crying. Their Guardian feared she was going to lose the Great Battle. Their Guardian had dreamed that another Great Massacre would occur, and they and everyone they knew and loved would die. Their one hope believed she would fail. It was already beginning.

A thoughtful look crossed William's face. "Speaking of dreams, let's go ahead and bring mine to life." A pit formed in Rianne's stomach. "I believe there's something beautiful in ending in the place where it started." He glared at her. "And I didn't get to finish what I started with you all those months ago. I intend to. And this time no one better show up to save you, or your precious boyfriend will take your place." He smiled. "See you at the theater, Rianne. Three hours."

He and Braedon disappeared in a flash of green light.

William's last words echoed in Rianne's head as she leaned against a desk, holding her side. She removed the barriers from the students.

Braedon was in William's hands now. If he tried to fight back, he would die. He wasn't strong enough.

A cry of pain broke her out of her thoughts. Releasing her side, she began moving desks, freeing those who had been trapped.

They came first. They would always come first.

Chapter Sixty-Seven

Hitting the floor hard was enough to knock Braedon back into consciousness. He opened his eyes in the darkening room, trying to focus. His body felt weak, like moving one finger would take every ounce of focus he had.

"Get up!" the Hunter snapped.

Braedon had to oblige, even though any movement was excruciating. Braedon tried to rise to his knees. Impatient, the Hunter grabbed his arm and forced him up. The sudden motion made Braedon's world spin as staggered to his feet.

He realized they were in Rianne's bedroom. A pang hit him in the stomach as he thought of her. The look on her face—contorted with regret in the face of his suffering. What if that was the last time he would ever see her face?

A body was lying on the floor. Straight brown hair, white shirt, and black jeans, his eyes staring into space. The carpet was covered in dried blood.

"No. Ellis," Braedon whispered. Shaking off the Hunter's hand, he went to his brother. "Ellis!" He grabbed his arm to shake him,

331

and a shock went through his body. He didn't care, though. He continued to shake his brother but got no response. "Ellis! Ellis! Can you hear me? Ellis, wake up!"

"It's kind of hard to wake someone who's dead, don't you think?" the Hunter said.

Braedon's throat tightened. "Ellis, come on, mate. Get up. Get up!" He took a deep breath. The Hunter had to be lying. Deception was one of their strengths. Ellis wasn't dead. He couldn't be. "Ellis, you have to get up. Wake up." He took Ellis's face in his hands, searching for any sign of life.

"He's the reason I got to Estona in the first place, you know," the Hunter continued. "I can teleport, yes, but I can't teleport to places I've never seen. This Advancer came in handy, though. Showed me what that school looked like. We had a deal: he sells out the Guardian, and I let him go."

But you lied. They always lie.

"No," Braedon whispered, tears running down his face. He stopped shaking Ellis, realizing he was never going to wake up. "No, Ellis. You can't be gone. Ellis, please, no."

Not Ellis. Not his older brother. He . . . he was dead. He was actually dead. Even if Braedon was still angry at him, he would have never in a million years wanted this to happen. The last time he talked to Ellis, he had given him the cold shoulder, ignoring the question Ellis had asked before he went to check on Rianne. He had ignored Ellis out of anger and spite. It was Ada all over again.

The Hunter rolled his eyes. "Oh, suck it up. It was just one of your Advancer buddies. It's no big deal."

"He was my brother," Braedon whispered, staring at Ellis's face. "You killed my brother."

"Ah, that would explain why you two look so alike." The Hunter snapped his fingers, and Ellis's body disappeared in a flash of green light.

"No!" Braedon shouted as the Hunter hauled him to his feet. "Where did you send him?"

The Hunter huffed in annoyance. "I don't know. Probably an ocean somewhere. Now come on. I've wasted too much time on your pity party."

The Hunter didn't care about what he had done. None of them did. They were evil, ruthless beings.

And now Braedon's brother was gone forever.

The Hunter pulled him out of Rianne's bedroom and into a guest bedroom across the hall. "Don't move," he warned before letting Braedon go, but not without giving him an extra-painful shock. The Hunter got on his knees next to his bed, then pulled a clear plastic bin from under it and rifled through it.

Braedon swallowed. What could he be looking for? He cringed as he remembered what those shocks felt like. He had never felt hell like that. It was as if pins were stabbing at his heart, stopping all vital functions. Was that what Ellis had gone through before he died?

I can't die like Ellis did.

Braedon inched back toward the bedroom door, too frightened to teleport. Once he made it out of the room, he crept down the stairs, then made a run for it.

"Hey!" the Hunter shouted.

His heart pounding, Braedon ran toward the front door. Despite his shaking hands, he managed to unlock the deadbolt and wrench the door open. Freedom was so close.

"Hel—" His cry was cut off as the Hunter slapped his rough hand over Braedon's mouth and dragged him back into the house, slamming the door.

The Hunter punched him in the jaw, jolting Braedon's world. Then he wrenched Braedon's arms into an X shape and zip-tied his wrists together. He forced Braedon to his feet.

"God, you Sterlings are so dumb. Try anything else stupid, and you'll regret it." He gave Braedon another jolt through his heart. "Understand?" When Braedon nodded, gasping with pain, the Hunter pulled out his phone. "Almost eight. Good." He closed his eyes and took a deep breath, his eyebrows furrowed in concentration.

Braedon closed his eyes as well, not in concentration but out of fear.

Chapter Sixty-Eight

William and the Wise One appeared in the Felix Theatre Auditorium. It was dark, but William found the fuse box, placed his palm against it, and sent a jolt of electricity into it. The lights that still worked flickered on, cloaking the theater in a dim shroud.

He looked around. There was still blood on the floor from the last time he and Rianne had fought. Chairs had been uprooted and tossed about. He grabbed one and carried it to one of the aisles. Then he looked at the Advancer and cracked a smile. "We have about an hour and a half before our beautiful Guardian shows up to die, so let's make sure our main attraction is ready to go."

He grabbed Braedon's arm and pushed him toward the chair. "Sit." The Wise One glanced at him, breathing heavily, and then obeyed. His wrists were still bound by the zip ties, bleeding as they cut into his skin.

William found a small silver bolt on the floor from one of the displaced chairs. "This'll work," he said. He forced the Wise One's mouth open, inserted the bolt halfway in, then forced his jaw closed again. The Wise One groaned as his teeth hit the metal.

"And now for the finishing touch." William rubbed his hands together to build friction, and sparks leaped around his hands.

The Wise One's breathing became faster and heavier. He shook his head and tried to speak, but he couldn't. It sounded like he was begging.

William chuckled. "Don't worry. I'll do you a favor and make this one fast. It'll just hurt a bit more."

The Wise One leaned back in his chair, trying to push it back with his legs. "No, no, no, no . . ."

William touched the bolt with his thumb and pointer finger, sending a bolt of electricity through it.

The Wise One shook and spasmed, his screams muffled as his jaw involuntarily gripped the bolt. His struggle lasted only about three seconds before his body slumped into the chair, his head resting on his chest. The bolt tumbled out of his mouth and to the floor. That would keep him out for about two hours, William guessed.

He broke the zip ties and then nodded in satisfaction. "Now we wait."

Chapter Sixty-Nine

After William left with Braedon, Rianne helped the trapped and injured students. Even as they cried, broken in more ways than one, she still saw hope in their eyes when they looked at her. One boy hugged her as he sobbed, thanking her for everything she had done and everything she was going to do.

She had to be strong for them; she was their Guardian.

Getting them to sit on the floor, she healed them one by one, starting with Amaline's broken leg. Some students were lucky enough to have escaped with only scrapes, cuts, and bruises. Others were lying on the floor in agony due to fractures, crushed bones, fractured skulls, broken backs, or internal bleeding.

She healed them before she even thought about healing herself. One girl brought over a box of tissues from the toppled bookshelf and pressed wads of them to Rianne's wound, switching them out for clean ones as they got soaked.

She'd just finished helping the most injured students when some Advancers rushed in, taking the kids—whether they'd already been healed or not—to hospitals. Their parents and guardians had already been contacted. An Advancer she didn't know offered to heal her wound, and she let him. She was already tired, and she had to save her Fuora for what was to come.

Justin pulled her into his arms and hugged her. She wanted to cry, but she kept swallowing, keeping it in.

"It's okay," he said. "You're okay. We're going to get him back. You got this. You're going to win. You'll be okay."

Knowing Advancer Marcus would transport her back to the Standard world within two hours, she went back to the office to check on William's victims, but one girl, Cheyanne, had died.

Other classrooms had been affected by William's explosion, but no one else was seriously injured. The Advancers evacuated the school, and details were given to the Wise Ones. She heard that Estona was preparing for a shutdown and lock-in.

Rianne offered comfort and aid in any way she could. The Sterlings were terrified that the Great Battle was upon them, but she continued to be their hope. It was all they had left.

Chapter Seventy

Rianne grabbed the thick chains on the outside of the theater door and threw them to the ground, the sound echoing in the night.

She was alone.

Rianne walked the semi-familiar hallways, knowing her way to the main stage. Not even a full year had passed since the last time she was there.

It felt like time was repeating itself. Just like before, she was alone, heading into a trap.

Braedon was dying or dead.

She touched a hand to her heart, calming herself as she thought of Braedon's smiling face, his chuckle, the way he would roll his eyes at her. Even if she didn't make it out, she would make sure he did.

The main doors to enter the performance area were all locked. A sign to her left indicated the backstage area. Heading in that direction, she walked through the doorway that led her onto the stage. She looked around. The lights were fainter than the last time she was there. The air was still stale, and specks of dust floated in her vision.

She approached the front of the stage, then lowered herself down. She saw the area where she had almost died before. Then she saw Braedon. He was seated in one of the chairs in the middle of the right aisle, his body slumped over. Even from a distance, she could see the bruises on his body and blood on his wrists. He was so still. She couldn't tell if his chest was moving.

"Braedon!" she shouted. She ran over to him, but a flash of dark green light stopped her.

"Uh-uh," William said, shaking his head. "I'm afraid that's not part of the deal, my dear Guardian." He lowered his hands to his sides and shook them. The dark blue sparks of electricity engulfed them. "Oh, killing you is going to be so much fun."

Rianne's reactions came way too slow. He was chest to chest with her in less than a millisecond, and he punched her in the stomach. She screamed in response to the painful shock that followed.

He pushed her again but with his Motora's strength. Rianne sailed through the air, slamming into the edge of the stage and tumbling to the floor.

Rianne got up and created a shield before William could hit her again. Growling, he punched at the barrier a few times before Rianne lost her hold, watching it disintegrate. She threw some of her Blade at him. It hit him in the chest, knocking back over a row of seats.

William pulled himself up, then touched the back of his neck. When he pulled his hand away, he saw blood. "Oh, you're going to pay for that," he said through gritted teeth.

He teleported back to her and punched her in the face. He was about to hit her again, but Rianne grabbed his forearm and twisted it, then kicked him in the stomach. As he went to hit her again, she held her hands up to her face to protect herself and ducked out of the way. Then she straightened up and sent a jab into his chin.

With William off balance, she raised her arms and slammed

them down, using an enormous push from her Blade to drive him into the floor. He struggled to get up, then teleported to another area of the theater to reorient himself.

Rianne looked over at Braedon. How would she get to him without William launching another attack? She rushed over to Braedon and placed a hand on his shoulder, sending a surge of her healing Fuora into him. A moment later, Braedon took deep, gasping breaths, then raised his head, his eyes unfocused.

"Rianne?" he said, his voice weak.

Before Rianne could reply, William grabbed her by the waist and threw her into a concrete wall. She felt her ankle snap.

It was hard to breathe, her chest quaking.

William approached her, his eyes black and a grim smile on his face. Electricity coursed through his hands, ready to strike.

Rianne stood up on shaky legs, her left ankle unable to support her weight. She gripped a crevice on the wall. If she was going to die, she was going to die standing.

"This is your end, Guardian. And after I kill you, all those weak, worthless Sterlings will join you in your death. Including your little boyfriend."

Rianne closed her eyes, ready to take the pain.

She heard William grunt as he thrust his arms toward her, and then—

Braedon screamed.

Rianne opened her eyes open and saw Braedon's arms shielding her, his body taking the blow that was meant for her. His screams filled her ears and echoed around the empty theater. Bolts of electricity crackled as William's fists struck Braedon's chest.

Though it seemed to last forever, it was only a few seconds before William backed away.

Braedon stood there for a moment, his eyes glazed over, then he fell to his knees and keeled over onto his face, blood pouring from his mouth.

Tears flowing down her cheeks, Rianne hobbled to Braedon's

side and dropped to her knees. "No," she whispered. Almost afraid to touch him, when she turned him onto his back, she felt a faint shock. His face was pale, and his body was flaccid, unresponsive.

Rianne pulled Braedon into her lap and placed her hand over his heart. "Come on, Braedon," she whispered, tears flowing on her cheeks and dripping off her chin. "You can't die." The pervasive white glow of her healing Fuora worked its magic again. As he lay on her, some of it also transferred to her, healing her injuries.

As for Braedon, there was no response.

"Braedon, Braedon, come on. Braedon! You can't die! You can't die! You said this would never happen to you! Come on, Braedon, you're a Wise One! Wise Ones can't die! You promised!"

But he didn't open his eyes.

He remained still, not moving.

Dead.

She leaned down to him, touching her forehead to his. "No," she whispered. "No, no, no, no, no, no."

Braedon had died for her when she had no hope of surviving. He had done what he had been chosen as an Advancer to do—protect the Guardian until his final moment.

They had protected each other with everything they had.

Loved each other with everything they had.

"Braedon, wake up," Rianne whispered, her voice hoarse. "Braedon, get up. *Please.* Braedon, don't do this to me. Please."

William chuckled, cracking his wrists and knuckles as his body recharged. "Aw, is our little Guardian upset?"

Rianne wiped her tears on the backs of her hands, then placed Braedon's head on the floor. She kissed his forehead and then glared at William with renewed determination.

Anger like she'd never felt before coursed through her. She hated him. She hated everything about him. He was pure evil, and he had to go.

A new fire burned within her eyes as she stood. Without her prompting, her Blade appeared in her hands, its energy the color of a furious forest fire—red, yellow, and orange—as it coursed in and out of her hands and up and down her arms. Destructive. It flowed through her eyes, extending past her pupils. Her hair floated around her.

Her Blade had finally meshed itself with its master.

William raised his eyebrows in astonishment and stepped back.

"I told you not to hurt him," she said.

Recovering from his shock, raised a hand, palm-up, a ball of his blue electricity sitting in it. He threw it at her, but it dissolved into her shimmering, multicolored screen.

She stepped toward him. William paused, his eyes wide, then he backtracked, trying to maintain the space between them. Rianne smiled and raised an eyebrow. "Come on, William. You must have something better than that," she said, sounding bored.

His eyes narrowed, and he pressed his hands together. When he separated them, in the middle was another bolt of electricity. He reared back and hurled it at her.

Rianne pushed her hands out in front of her, and William's electricity hit the vertical wall of her Blade's defense mechanism and flew back at him, striking him in the face.

As William held his face, groaning and cursing in pain, she closed the distance between them and punched him in his stomach with her Blade—much like he had done to her. He grunted and keeled over. Then she elbowed him in the face, his head snapping back. She hit him in the throat and on the side of the head. Then she held her hands out in front of her and put all of her force into them. The Blade sent him flying back to the opposite wall, headfirst. His body crumpled in on itself, falling to the floor in a heap. Blood was smeared on the wall, dripping down to the floor.

As William remained on the floor, motionless, she made her way toward him. *Is he dead?* she wondered, hoping it was true. *Did I kill him?*

Crouching beside him, her Blade at the ready, she reached

under his jaw to check his pulse. But the moment her fingers grazed his skin, he disappeared.

She gasped, leaping up and turning around. William was standing next to a black box with a lever near the stage. The power box. He was smiling even though blood was running down his face and neck, and he was swaying on his feet.

"Quick science lesson, Guardian," he said. His hand inched closer to the box, sparks flickering around it. "Metal conducts electricity. And if I, in my second stage, touch this, can you guess what will happen?"

The puzzle pieces fell into place. "No!" she yelled, running toward him.

William flattened his hand against the box, and a supernova-like wave exploded at their feet, blasting Rianne back.

William screamed, his hand glued to the metal and his hair flying around his face. His black eyes turned even blacker, as did the skin around them, as he was engulfed by blinding bright blue bolts of power.

With a last devastating spark, everything went dark.

William chuckled in the darkness.

Rianne knew he could see in the dark, but she was as blind as a Standard, forced to rely on sound and touch rather than sight.

Closing her eyes, Rianne concentrated. Then she heard it—a small intake of breath behind her. William was creeping through the darkness. She tensed her body, willing her Blade not to shine. Then she spun around, her fist covered with the Blade, and struck William.

He grunted in pain. "I am so fucking tired of you!" he shouted.

Seeing his fists covered in the higher-powered electricity, she had to be careful. With his new power range, one hit would be fatal.

Every time William threw an attack at her, she dodged it and threw one back at him, but he blocked it as well. They were evenly matched.

Unobtrusive

Electricity ran through his veins as his breathing increased. His electricity was like a fire, and fire needed oxygen to survive, or it would die.

A minute later, Rianne saw an opening as he wavered, looking for another spot to hit her, and she she struck him in the liver, followed by an uppercut. He fell backward, and she jumped on top of him, wrapping her hands around his throat. Her Blade began to squeeze.

William struggled. The two bright orbs around his hands were keeping him alive, but they were blinking like a flashlight whose battery was dying.

He was dying.

"I'm not going out alone," he said. "This was my third . . . and final . . . state. Anything I touch . . . will die."

Then, with the speed he inherited from his father, William's hand was on her stomach, and he sent his last pulse of electricity into her.

Rianne screamed in pain as her Blade shone its bright light.

William's turned blue again, then flickered out for good.

His hands fell.

Suddenly, Rianne felt herself become lighter, as if she were filled with helium. Her body glowed, filling her with warmth.

William was dead.

The Hunter was dead.

But she was still alive. She would go down in history as the first Guardian to beat her Hunter. The first to save Estona from the Great Massacre.

Rianne rolled off William's body, resting on her knees in the darkness.

She thought about how the theater looked when she'd entered. Then she closed her eyes and placed her hands flat on the floor, wondering if her newly acquired powers would listen to their new master.

She felt the warmth she always did when using her Fuora, but more intensely. It made her entire body tingle. Her body glowed, and the light energy left her and rushed through the floors and walls, looking for any wire and place to call their new home. In seconds, the entire theater was bathed in light.

Rianne opened her eyes. It was unlike anything she had ever felt before. It felt like she was whole. Like the world had righted itself.

"This is amazing," she whispered. Then another thought struck her.

Braedon.

She ran back to him and dropped to her knees by his side. Placing her hand on his face, she stroked his cheek with her thumb. "Braedon . . ." she whispered. "Why did you do something so stupid?" He shouldn't have gotten in front of her. He shouldn't be dead.

She sniffled as she moved her hand down to his neck. Then she furrowed her brow. Was that a pulse? She pressed harder.

There it was.

A small, timid heartbeat.

Had her healing worked?

Rianne looked down at her hands. If her healing had brought him back from the brink of death before, now she would be able to save him.

Rianne placed her hand over his heart and closed her eyes, channeling every ounce of her healing power into him.

Then pain shot through her as she remembered William's last words: "Anything I touch . . . will die."

No.

The last of his three stages, he had said, were the deadliest.

Again, Rianne felt as if she had been punched in the gut. She coughed up blood and fell beside Braedon. All of her energy seemed to have been pulled from her. She was so tired. But he looked fine now.

Although she had won, she realized she was going to die too.

Unobtrusive

She didn't think such a thing was even possible. William had found a loophole. Though Rianne had killed him first, he had managed to take her out as well.

She took a deep breath, realizing her last one was only minutes away.

Her arm feeling like lead, she reached over and took Braedon's hand, then closed her eyes.

If she only had minutes to live, she wanted to spend them holding his hand.

Chapter Seventy-One

Braedon opened his eyes, gasping for breath.

He looked down. He was holding Rianne's hand.

Braedon reached over and pulled her into his lap. "Rianne," he whispered, touching her neck. "Rianne, wake up!" He shook her. "Rianne, are you okay? Rianne, please wake up."

When she heard him call his name, Rianne opened her eyes and smiled at him. "You're okay."

He kissed her forehead, then he laughed in delight. "My Guardian won."

She nodded. "I did. I can't believe I did."

"I can," he said. "I had no doubt."

She swallowed, taking in a shaky breath. "Braedon, there's something—" She winced, clutching her chest.

Braedon's eyes widened. "Rianne, what's wrong?"

She waited until she had recovered enough to speak, her eyes watering from pain. "Before I killed him . . . William said he was in his deadliest state. Braedon, I'm going to die, aren't I?"

Braedon felt as if he had just been slapped in the face. "No, no," he said, his heart breaking. "You're going to be fine." He said it as much to console himself as her.

She flinched in pain and screamed, clutching his arms as tears slid down her cheeks. Her body was trembling, and she was struggling for breath.

Braedon could practically feel her agony.

Panicking, Braedon put a hand on her chest. "Hold on, Rianne, hold on." Almost immediately, the familiar dim white light shined. *This has to work. The healing has to work.*

But she kept screaming. The electricity from the deceased Hunter was coursing through her body, straight to her heart, about to end her short life. She wasn't able to concentrate long enough through her screams to heal herself with her new powers. She was too weak. And his healing could do nothing for her.

Rianne looked at him with tortured eyes. "Braedon," she whispered.

He was crying by then too, and when he spoke, his voice was choked up. "Rianne, I'm sorry. I-I-I'm sorry. It's not working. My healing powers won't work. I-I don't know what to do."

Her screaming stopped, then her breathing became slower and slower.

"No. No! Come on, Rianne! You have to pull through. You're the Guardian! You can't die! You can't leave me alone." He took a couple of deep breaths to settle his emotions, but he couldn't. "Rianne, please." One of his tears dripped off his chin and onto her cheek, mingling in her river of tears.

She looked at him, her green eyes heartrending. "Braedon, when I die, take my body back to my dad. Make up a story that William and I were drinking or something, and it went too far. Tell him I'm sorry for what I said, that I didn't mean it, and that I love him. And Braedon . . ." She reached up with a shaky hand and placed it on his wet cheek. "I love you with all my heart, and I'm sorry I couldn't be stronger."

He shook his head, then leaned down and kissed her one last

time. "I love you too, Rianne, with everything that I am." He hugged her, not wanting to let her go. "I love you too."

A few seconds later, she breathed her last breath.

His world stopped.

Silent. Nothing.

Empty.

Braedon began to sob, clutching her body and rocking back and forth like she was his tether. "Please, Rianne, come back. Don't leave me."

Braedon sat there for about an hour or more until he had no more tears to cry. Then he stood with her in his arms and closed his eyes.

They arrived back in Rianne's room. Ellis's blood was still on the floor, a lamp overturned.

Braedon walked over to her bed and set Rianne on it like he had done before. This time, however, her body was lifeless.

As Braedon phoned Matt, he felt his heart break in his chest, unable to take the loss any longer.

Chapter Seventy-Two

Matt rubbed his face, grumbling, "I swear, if this is some sort of joke . . ."

Jessica rubbed his arm, calling William's phone again. "Matt, honey, you need to relax. I'm sure the kids are fine," she said, though she sounded unsure.

They were about twenty minutes or so from Felix. The two of them had just docked back in Galveston from their cruise when Matt received a call from an officer in Houston. He said his name was Thomas Willis and that Matt needed to return to Felix immediately. Something had happened to his daughter.

Matt probed for answers, but Willis refused to give them.

He and Jessica had tried calling and texting the kids, but neither of them responded.

Matt broke into a cold sweat.

When they got to Matt's house, the front door was unlocked.

As soon as they went inside, a man approached them from the living room. Matt was confused. Had Rianne let him in? The man was dressed in a pressed white shirt beneath a gray blazer. He had wavy brown hair and eyeglasses, and he was carrying a pocket Bible.

"Are you Matt Jarrett?" He had an English accent.

"Thomas Willis?" Matt asked.

"No, sir. My name is Chaplain Andrew Morton. I was called here to speak with you."

"Where's my daughter?"

Andrew didn't answer.

"Where is my *daughter?*"

Andrew motioned for him and Jessica to follow him to the living room. When they were all seated, Andrew looked as if he were having trouble finding his words. Finally, with Jessica gripping Matt's arm and his frustration rising, Andrew pulled two photos from inside of the Bible. "Fingerprints were taken to identify them. Are these your children?" he asked, sliding both photos across the table.

Tears started streamed down Jessica's cheeks. "What . . . what happened?" she asked. "What's going on?"

"They were found in Houston," Andrew said, "at one of the rodeo attractions—"

"Where's my daughter?" Matt asked for a third time.

Andrew sighed. "There was an accident at the rodeo. They were injured. Paramedics tried to save them, but their injuries were too severe. They both died."

It seemed as though all sound was sucked from the room. Matt's breath became shallow. "Where are they?" he whispered. He expected Andrew to tell him they were at the medical examiner's office—if any of this was true at all—but instead he gestured with his head.

"They're upstairs."

Matt's heart stopped, then he leaped off the couch, running up the steps two at a time.

Matt thrust Rianne's bedroom door open, and his heart fell out of his chest.

Unobtrusive

She was lying on her bed, her eyes closed and her hands folded across her stomach. Her black hair framed her waxy face like a portrait.

He ran to her side and put his head to her mouth to see if she was breathing. Then his fingers fumbled for her wrist to take her pulse. There was none. Her body was already in rigor mortis.

He fell back on his haunches.

"No, no, no. Rianne, wake up, baby. Rianne. Rianne!"

In the guest room across the hall, he heard Jessica wailing.

Tears poured down his cheeks. He wouldn't be able to live through this.

Matt broke down and screamed until his throat was raw, crying so hard that the entire world could feel his pain.

Epilogue

It had been six weeks to the day since Rianne died.

Braedon teleported to his classroom and sat at his desk, his head in his hands, something he did often now. The room and the parts of the infrastructure that the Hunter had destroyed had been repaired. It looked as though nothing had happened, though the mental scar associated with the attack would remain. All of Estona bore scars of trauma.

In about five minutes, Braeden's students had to be in the classroom, but he didn't care. Even if none of them showed up, he wouldn't have noticed.

He had just come from visiting her grave in the Standard world, something he'd done every day since the funeral. He still didn't want to believe the truth. He didn't want to believe she was under the earth, unable to live, buried in that cold, dark coffin. He would just sit there, staring at her gravestone.

Rianne Sydney Jarrett

Unobtrusive

A beautiful soul and artist who will be truly missed each day that we are left grieving and never forgotten through the days we move on

She had also been given her own memorial in Estona. Though she wasn't with them anymore, she was the Guardian who had saved them all. If only she were alive to see the peace that had finally been restored to the realm after centuries of pain and death.

Braedon cared about almost nothing in his daily life anymore. Even going on his phone broke his heart, seeing the wallpaper of him and Rianne smiling at the camera. His Advancer friends gave him consoling words, supporting pats, and pitying looks. He didn't care about any of it. He felt so empty inside. Without Rianne in his life, nothing seemed real.

Even the other Wise Ones felt the change in Braedon's attitude. After he broke the news of Rianne's death to her father, Braedon returned to the Wise Ones' palace. He didn't look at the others or speak to them. He locked himself in his bedchamber for days. He barely ate or drank. They didn't have to tell him that his brother was dead; he was the one who had found his body.

The mansion was eerily quiet without Ellis there making a ruckus when Braedon went back for the first time. Silence was all that greeted him. Alaric didn't give him orders or commands, as he once did. He had the sense to leave him alone until Braedon came out of . . . whatever it was. And no one knew when that would be.

But most of all, he felt cold inside. The warmth Rianne had given him disappeared with her death. He would listen to voicemails she'd left him and watch videos of her, just to hear her voice. Sometimes it eased the ache, but most times it exacerbated it.

Only when the door to the classroom closed did Braedon finally look up at his students. They were all staring at him, hoping he would speak. Ever since the Guardian's death, he barely said a word to anybody. He hadn't really talked to anyone in the last six weeks. He was like a mime. Today was his first day back.

Sighing, he opened his mouth, then closed it again. What should he say to them? After a couple of moments of thinking, he began in a quiet voice. "Class, I know we haven't had any lessons for a while." He swallowed. "But there is no need for any of you to work on your Affera since . . ."

He couldn't even finish his sentence; it hurt him too much, and he refused to break down in front of his class, especially on his first day back. He hadn't lost it yet in public, and he certainly wasn't going to do so in front of a group of teenagers.

A hand shot up in the air. He nodded for the student to speak. "Yes, Amaline?"

"Wise One Braedon, sire, first off, we all want to say that we're glad to see you back and okay." Her classmates nodded and voiced their assent. "But, um, and I may be out of place for asking this, but everyone has been wondering, um, what happened exactly? In the Standard world, I mean?"

Braedon sighed. He knew that someone would ask the question sooner or later. His students leaned forward in their seats to hear his response. Rumors had sprung up here and there—typical high school behavior—about what had happened during the Great Battle, but no one knew what was fact and what was fiction.

"When I awoke the first time, the Hunter's fists were covered in his electricity, about to kill the Guardian. I couldn't let that happen, so I shielded her, and I took the hit full on. I blacked out again, and my heart stopped over and over again."

The class let out a collective gasp, whispering about the comparison to Wise One Hakim. Braedon closed his eyes as he remembered the intense pain. He would never be able to find the words to describe it.

Amaline shushed the class, waiting for Braedon to continue.

He kept his eyes closed, not wanting to see their anxious faces. He told them the rest of the story, then ended with the horrible conclusion. "After she healed me, she . . . she died in my arms."

The whole room was quiet and tense as they watched him. He

took deep breaths, trying to staunch the tears welling up in his eyes. He couldn't start crying again, not in front of them. But before he knew it, a lone tear fell onto his wooden desk. Then what he had been trying to hold back came flooding out of him, like a dam bursting.

He felt a hand on his left shoulder. Through bloodshot eyes, he looked up and saw Amaline, a sympathetic look on her face. "You were in love with her, weren't you, Wise One Braedon?" she whispered.

Not trying to fight it anymore, he nodded and put his face in his hands, letting the tears flow. The rest of the class crowded around his desk, all of them speaking words of comfort as they let him cry.

Braedon passed the high school's quad, walking across it toward the woods to the west. Alaric had told him that morning that it was time to cross over the barrier and brief the Pale Ones on the Great Battle. They had put it off long enough, and the Pale Ones were probably getting restless.

Braedon could have teleported to the forest barrier, but since he didn't have the spirit to do it, it took him close to forty-five minutes to reach the edge of the elegant evergreen forest.

All Sterlings and Advancers knew of the barrier that was forbidden to cross. Rumors had circulated for centuries of what lay beyond the dark woods, but only the Wise Ones and a select few knew what really awaited there. Forbidden. Against the law to venture over. The Soulless would get anyone who broke the rule if the Wise Ones didn't find out first.

It wasn't Braedon's first time going over to Întunce. He had made a couple of expeditions to the Pale Ones after the first Great Battle between Rianne and William. He hadn't been told about Întunce itself until he became a Wise One. The Soulless preferred to keep their existence a secret.

He looked around, making sure no one was watching. The place was empty. He was in the clear. Then he crossed into the forest, darkness taking over.

Besides it being dark, it was cold. And quiet. He went slightly numb despite his jacket. He still retained his Affera as a Wise One —though they were weakened—which brought him some relief. If he had still been an Advancer, he would have not had protection due to the barrier's cancellation of magical energy.

Being in Întunce made him tremendously uneasy, but he would be out of there and back where he belonged soon. He just had to get to the Pale Ones' castle, debrief them, and answer any question they may have.

As he walked, every now and then, Braedon would lose his nerve and jump at the slightest sounds—the hoot of an owl, the croak of a bullfrog, the scurrying of some nighttime creature. Even the snap of a twig he stepped on himself caused his heart to leap into his throat.

Braedon wandered around in the dark, cold, foreboding forest for two hours before he came upon an opening. It was still as dark as it was in the midst of the forest, but he was relieved to see the sky again through the few trees that were left. The moon and stars were out, glimmering and reassuring.

As he entered a clearing, he saw the town a short ways away. Like Estona, Întunce was densely populated. The only difference was where there were over three thousand Sterlings, there were only a few hundred Soulless. Sterlings could die; Soulless didn't have that luxury.

Hundreds of two- and three-story houses were scattered over the land as well as several blood banks. The banks were where the Soulless stole Standards—and sometimes Sterlings—to be their never-ending food supply until there was no more blood in their fragile bodies to give. He could also see the castle in the distance beyond the town.

Unobtrusive

One thing that unsettled him, though, was that no one was around. None of the Soulless were to be seen or heard.

As Braedon made his way across the clearing, a hiss sounded behind him.

He spun around, looking back toward the trees. Seeing nothing, he continued toward the town, his heart beating faster and faster.

The hiss sounded again, and this time Braedon was thrown onto his back. He screamed, thrashing to escape the grasp of the person who had him pinned.

The person wore all black, including a black hood, so if not for the person's pale skin, Braedon wouldn't have been able to see his attacker's face. The person hissed a third time, then Braedon heard a *shing*, followed by the flash of long white canines. His attacker's eyes were bloodshot and red—terrifyingly red.

"Wait! Wait, wait, wait, wait, wait!" Braedon shouted. "I'm here for the Pale Ones! I'm a Wise One! I'm Wise One Braedon!"

The person cocked their head, and in the next millisecond they were off of him and a couple of feet away.

Gasping for breath, Braedon got up and looked at the Soulless who had almost killed him. Other than the typical black clothes and pale skin, the Soulless had long black hair that went a little below his ears and a thin, circular piercing on his lower lip. His hands were in the pockets of his jacket, and he was supporting his weight on one leg, a cocky smile on his face.

Braedon brushed the dirt off his clothes as he recognized him. "Hello, Nelson. Thank you for not killing me. Couldn't you sense my energy?"

Nelson bowed his head in greeting. "Sorry. I'm thirsty. I wasn't really paying attention."

"And you're still as unobtrusive as usual. How have you been?"

"Thanks for the compliment. It's good to see you too, *Wise One*. Look who's stepping up in the magical realm." He was as sarcastic as ever. "Nothing's changed, really. I'm bored, so I'm thinking about enrolling in college to become a psychologist just for

fun. I'm having a bit of trouble convincing the Pale Ones, though."
He tilted his head. "So, we Soulless hear through the grapevine that
the whole Great Battle business is finished. Is that true?"

Braedon sighed as painful thoughts of Rianne intruded on his
mind once again. "The Hunter and the Guardian have defeated
each other. And neither produced an heir, so yes, it has ended. Your
lot don't have to worry about it anymore."

"*Our lot?* Is that what you Sterlings have been calling us behind
our backs?" He raised an eyebrow. "Even after all we've done for
Estona?"

"Nelson, you only helped out after *one* Great Massacre. It's not
like you've done it a hundred times."

Nelson chuckled. "That may be true, but I still saved plenty of
lives. Including yours."

Braedon said nothing.

"You were close to the Guardian?" Nelson asked.

Braedon closed his eyes and took a deep breath, trying to push
thoughts of her out his mind again. "I don't want to talk about it.
I'm fine." But then her smiling face flashed again, going against the
lie. Nelson was in his head, and he couldn't let himself be read
anymore. Braedon turned away, thinking that if he looked at
Nelson again, he would see the truth. He missed her so much it
made his body ache. He just wanted her back, to hold her in his
arms again. He couldn't survive without her. He didn't want to.

"Why are you so upset?" Nelson asked. "Aren't you going to get
her back?"

Braedon gave him an exasperated look. "What in the world are
you on about? And stay out of my head!"

Nelson ignored his protest. "Isn't there a way to get the
Guardian back? You said you're a Wise One now, right?"

"Yes, but, Nelson, you're still not being very clear."

"I may have only been a Soulless for eighty-four years, but
everyone knows that good can't possibly exist without evil. All the
magic that the Sterlings, Advancers, and Wise Ones have is

supposed to be all good and bring joy and serenity and all that stuff, right? The Affera, or whatever you call it. Well, if that's true, there must be a dark side to it."

Braedon's eyes lit up with understanding. "The Motora."

"Yeah, that's what you guys call it! Affera can't raise the dead, but—"

"The Motora can," Braedon finished, looking down at his hands. Just like the Guardian couldn't exist without the Hunter, good magic couldn't survive without evil. The Wise Ones never explained that concept to their Advancers, but they figured it out sooner or later. It was the dark magic that the Hunter thrived off of. The darkness that everyone had inside of them to some degree.

Staring at his hands, Braedon made a white, snowflake-like energy appear. It danced in his hand as he imagined her face, smiling and adoring. But then he remembered holding her dead body in his arms, his heart breaking, and his hatred at the Hunter for taking her away from him. The energy turned black and swirled like an angry tornado in his palm.

"And that must be the basic foundation. You have to find your true anger, your deepest pain. Tap into your dark side, Braedon, and she'll be back before you know it. You're welcome." Nelson smiled, one of his fangs showing.

She'll be back before you know it. Elation hit him. Rianne . . . he could get her back. And if he got her back, everything would go back to the way it was. Everything they wanted would come true.

He shook his head. "I can't possibly do that, Nelson. I mean, what if . . . how do I even start?"

Nelson laughed. "Braedon, you're a Wise One. You'll figure it out. I'm pretty sure there are books written about all the wonders of magic by the other Wise Ones. And it's not like they can stop you. You were the Protector, and now you're a Wise One. You can do whatever you want."

* * *

Alaric's eyes snapped open. Though his breathing was calm, his heart was pounding.

Something was wrong.

Terribly wrong.

He could feel it.

Braedon was about to do something imprudent, something that could put the entire magical realm in danger.

He thought for a moment, and then reached a decision.

"Hakim," he said, his voice echoing around the room.

He heard Hakim sigh beside him. "Yes, Alaric." His tone indicated he was irritated. He didn't like being forced out of his meditation.

"I need you to contact the Advancers. Tell them to continue their duties. Tell them not to slacken and to work harder than ever before. If they question you, remind them who is in charge." He stood up, throwing his navy-blue suit jacket back on.

Hakim looked at him in disbelief, but before he could respond, Alaric continued. He knew the twins had left their meditations when he spoke to Hakim. "Emil and Piers, we need to enlist two more Advancers." He walked down his steps and headed to the meeting room, gesturing for the others to follow. The guards opened the doors for them as they neared. "One needs to be a Sterling, and the other must come from the Standard world. Make sure you choose the best possible candidates for each."

Alaric had that feeling in his gut again. Braedon had made his final decision. He wasn't going to change his mind, nor would he listen to reason. There was nothing Alaric could do this time.

"Alaric," Hakim said, following him down the hallway as he buttoned his jacket, "the Great Battle is over. The Guardian and the Hunter are dead, and there are no heirs. What are you doing?"

"Really, Alaric," Emil continued. Alaric was walking fast, but they kept up with his long strides. "What are you so worried about? There's no need for new Advancers or for the current ones to continue with their duties. We're finally back at peace."

Unobtrusive

Alaric stopped in front of the meeting room's brown double doors and turned to look at his fellow Wise Ones. The guards waited. He couldn't tell them what was going to happen. Not yet. It was best that they did not know for now.

"Something is about to happen, Wise Ones, and we need as much reinforcement as we can obtain. We need to be ready. I need you all to trust me and do as I say.

"The Battle isn't over."

Acknowledgments

We did it. We did it, fam. After working and praying to get Rianne's story into the world, we did it. This success and realization of a dream isn't just for me. It's for everyone who has worked on this with me, and believed in it as hard as I did.

First thanks will always go to God, my Lord and Savior Jesus Christ. The plot of Unobtrusive actually came to me in a dream when I was in middle school, and I believe so hard that He gave the idea to me. I never gave up on Him in everything I do, and He's never given up on me. Shoutout to the GOAT.

I next want to thank my family. Without them believing and praying that this novel would make it into the world, I would be alone on it, so I'm so thankful that I've always had their support and encouragement. Also, special thanks to Momma and Trace. As a middle school teacher on a way-too-low teacher salary, y'all financing me on the road to self-publishing was invaluable. Momma, Daddy, Derek, Trace, Tristan, Airess, Grandma, Grandpa, aunts, uncles, and cousins, thank you.

Daddy, you came into my life at the time I needed you most. I'm so blessed and lucky that you've never seen me as a stepdaughter. I've always been YOUR daughter. As soon as we met, all we did was roast each other—and we still do that all these years later ('cause, I mean, you're old), but you filled a hole in my heart that had been missing. However, you're not only old :D, you're wise, and you've given me so much advice and guidance about life, God, health, and cars. Even when my eyes glazed over when you go over the intricacies of what goes on under the hood, I appreciate you more than you could know. (I press the pedal, and the car goes vroom). And one day when you are walking me down the aisle, remember that I'm always your girl (and that Cherry loves you more than me for some reason).

Momma, you are my world, and my best friend. I love you more than anything, and without you, I would be literally nothing. You are somehow always right, and though it annoys me sometimes, your wisdom and guidance has always brought me through. Without you, I wouldn't have been able to join band and fall in love with music. Without you, I wouldn't have gotten to college and had the amazing opportunity of studying at and graduating from Texas Tech University with a whole Bachelor's degree. Without you, I wouldn't be the band director I am today, and I always carry you in my heart. You've always worked so hard to give me and my brothers the childhood and life that can only be dreamed of. Your tenacity through everything you've been through is admirable, and I am so so proud of you. If I become half the woman and mother you are, that would be way more than enough. I love you, Mommy.

I also want to thank my Grandma. When my momma was first deployed to the Iraq war, I was old enough to know what was happening and what that meant. My love was always of reading. Something in her told her to go to Walmart and go to the book section. She found a book called *5-Minute Bible Stories*. That's when I learned about God, and how dope Jesus is. Grandma, you've always loved my writing and encouraged me as well. I love you so much, Grandma.

I want to next thank all of my friends who have suffered reading through my book before it got to its final stage. And those who read cringy stories I've written that had no business being around. Yikes, y'all are the real ones. Also thanks to my friends who are reading through the finished product NOW! Whether it was reading a chapter or two back in college, or receiving a rough draft before I even considered self-publishing, thank you for your love and support. The amount of names would take up at least 18 pages, but you all know who you are :)

To Mrs. Black, my 8th grade ELA teacher, and Mrs. Burton, my 12th grade English teacher, thank y'all for always supporting my writing. You two continued to foster my love of reading and writing —especially the classics!—and always read my work, both on Unobtrusive and just random stories I wrote for funsies and for class. Y'all touched students's lives, especially mine. Thank you.

Karin, my editor!!! You were one of the first who contacted me about wanting to edit and work on my book! From our first phone call, I KNEW that you were going to be my partner on this. You are so passionate and knowledgeable, and from the first draft you edited, Unobtrusive was taken to literally a whole new level. Finally having another set of eyes on this thing allowed me to go back in and make changes that made the world of Estona so much more fleshed out and, you know, magical! And I love the finished product! We were truly partners on this throughout the developmental and copyediting stages, and I am honored to call you my friend. I look forward to working with you on the next two novels to continue Estona's story! Thank you for being amazing, and for loving this story as much as I do.

Kevin, my proofreader, thank you! Your constructive criticism was invaluable. Your work combing through Unobtrusive and finding my little, stupid, and random mistakes really helped the flow, and I loved how you would outright say, "This doesn't make sense." Reading through your edits made me enjoy my own story way more, which I know translates to the readers! Thank you, Kevin, and I look forward to working with you again!

Marc, my interior designer, exterior designer, middleman to the artists, creator and manager of my website, guidance counselor, self-publishing world navigator, and most patient and gracious human on earth—your support also means the world to me. I know that I can be annoying and stubborn and picky, but you were there with me through it all! Your kindness and willingness to work and compromise with me through EVERYTHING is amazing. You really had my—and Rianne's!—best interests at heart, and I'm so thankful and blessed that Karin recommended me to you! I'm excited for us to take the fantasy world by storm!

Final thanks goes to you, gentle reader (can you tell that I love Bridgerton?) Without you reading this novel, Rianne's story technically wouldn't be out in the world. I may have written her and these other beautiful characters, but you've aided me in breathing life into them by opening this book and learning about her journey through these pages.

From the bottom of my heart, thank you.

Oh! And thank you to Ronnie and Cherry, also known as Momma's angels, for spending hours laying/sleeping next to me while I worked.

Printed in the USA
CPSIA information can be obtained
at www.ICGtesting.com
LVHW041451091124
796177LV00002B/166